Baron's Prophecy

Book One

The River's Course

Brian Sears

The characters and events portrayed in this book are fictitious. Any similarity to real persons, living or dead, is coincidental and not intended by the author.

ISBN 979-8-9871794-1-3
Ebook ISBN 979-8-9871794-0-6

Cover design by: Brian Sears

"Destiny is not a matter of chance. It is a matter of choice. It is not a thing to be waited for, it is a thing to be achieved."

—William Jennings Bryan

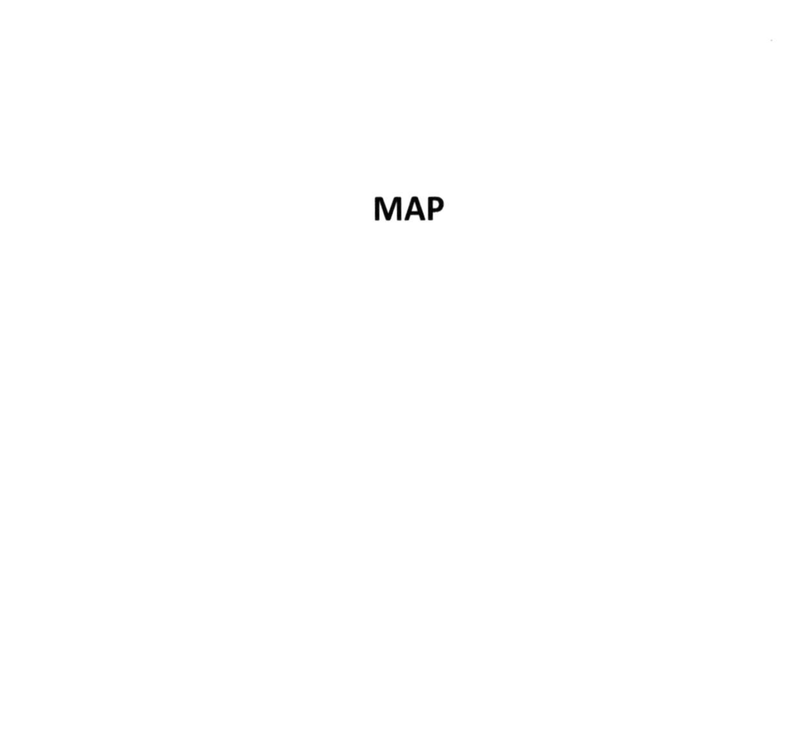
MAP

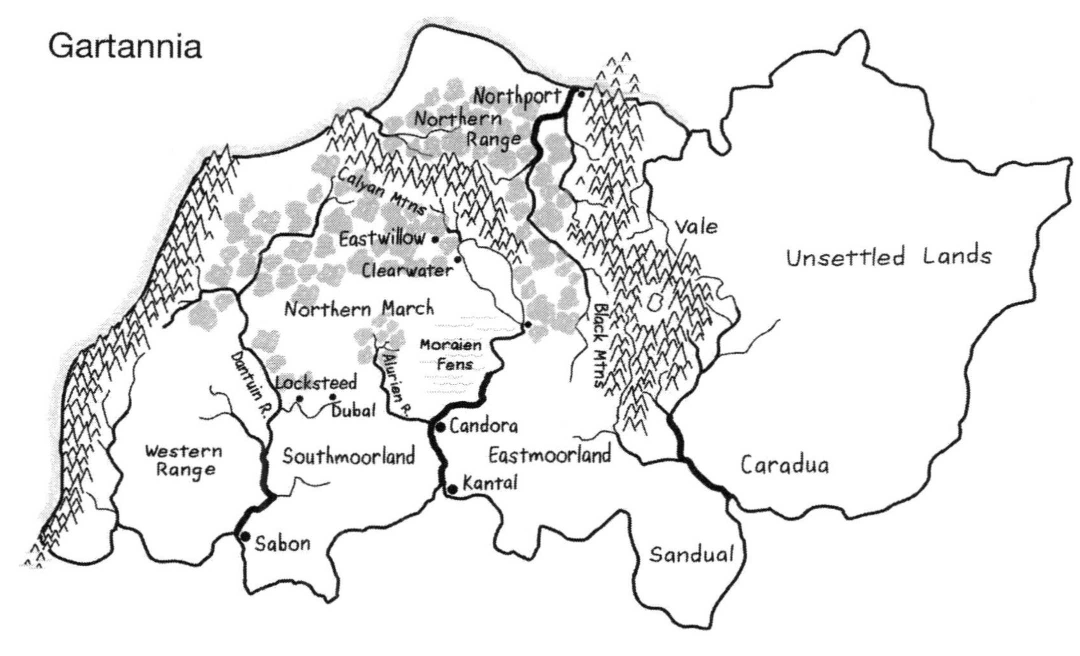
Gartannia
Northport
Northern Range
Calyan Mtns
Eastwillow
Clearwater
Northern March
Moraien Fens
Alurien R.
Dantuin R.
Locksteed
Dubal
Candora
Kantal
Western Range
Southmoorland
Eastmoorland
Sabon
Sandual
Black Mtns
Vale
Unsettled Lands
Caradua

SCHEME

The decaying log cabin had just about reached the end of its usefulness to the group of gray-cloaked transients. It was one of several forgotten buildings scattered across the land used by the roving opportunists in their travels or for occasional meetings, as was the case this day. The fourth one of the group had just arrived on horseback in the sweltering heat and removed the gray riding cloak from his shoulders before entering the cabin's partially shaded interior. He hung it on a rusted nail near the doorway next to three similar cloaks occupying rusty nails of their own.

He looked up at the collapsing roof and commented, "At least there's a breeze through this damned rat's nest. I think it's time you found us a new bunkhouse, Barten."

"I'll see what I can find, Dante."

All were in their upper fifties and sported varying shades of gray-peppering in their hair and facial stubble.

"Any of you heard from Jay or Payne? Have they gotten back from Caradua yet?"

"No word yet, boss," Barten replied, handing their leader a half-full whiskey bottle.

"I don't have time to go back there myself to negotiate with those savages. They'd better have an agreement when they get here." Dante took a long swig. "So, what about that town, Dubal?"

The remaining two men looked sheepishly at one another, then one answered, "The idiots we hired screwed up. The place they picked had no worthwhile loot, but at least they left the people alive this time."

"Yeah, dead men don't talk, do they? Ha-ha-ha, and we need 'em to talk. Well, don't pay those idiots anything this month. And if they try to leave, kill 'em. We're getting too far into this to have a couple of loose-lipped hired thugs mess up the plan."

"Sure thing, boss."

"And what's the matter with you, Gryst? You're sulking every time I see you."

The second sheepish man glared silently back at Dante.

"Lemme guess, you still wanna sail off into the sunset and live happily ever after."

Barten intervened. "Take it easy, Dante. It's been what, thirty-three years now since we came here lookin' for the runaway traitors. It seems like we're just wanderin' from one whorehouse to the next, at least since we tapped out all our leads."

"Yeah? Well, isn't that why we're moving on, to fulfill our new destiny?" Dante took another swig and slammed the bottle down on the table. "So what are you gonna do, just sail right back across that graveyard of an ocean to go home? You wanna be some lackey to the men actually running Arnoria? They don't even remember you exist. We've got a new flock now. The people in this land are nothing but sheep, and they need a shepherd. So you're gonna be a shepherd, and you're gonna be happy. Got it?"

"So we're done lookin' for good then?"

"We're done lookin' for now, unless you got some rock we ain't looked under yet. It's time we start lookin' out for us." He handed the bottle back to Barten and stood up. "Let's get outta this rathole." They took their cloaks and walked outside to where their horses were tied.

"Once we recruit enough mercenaries," Dante said, "we'll start hitting the unprotected villages and horse stables this fall. The supplies should get us through winter, and the loot should be more than enough to keep the mercenaries happy until next summer's little party. Cheer up, boys. Your rewards aren't far away. That's *Dante's* prophecy." He looked back at the dilapidated cabin and asked, "What's it remind you of?"

"What?"

"Ha-ha! It looks like the House of Genwyhn."

And with that, Dante raised his arms above his head and concentrated while a shimmering sphere of bright light grew between his hands. He flung it toward the cabin, and the wall exploded into flames.

THE HUNT

It was hot, really hot. And it wasn't that long after sunrise. The early heat portended a sweltering day. Cameron and his good friend Rylak Callaway had already walked the three miles from Cameron's home to the border of the Sundheim prairie. They had only a short way to go to reach their favorite hunting spot for rabbits. They were both given a reprieve from farm chores for the day, except for the mandatory jobs they had already finished in the darkness of early morning. They walked north, away from the small village of Locksteed, where they had grown up.

"It feels a little odd, doesn't it—not going back to school this fall?" Rylak said.

"Yeah. I never thought the day would come," Cameron agreed. "But you sure cut it close. You barely passed math and history."

"Who needs it? I'm gonna breed horses, not go to some university."

Cameron laughed. "I'm gonna miss it though. We had some good times."

"But now we can go hunting any time we want." Rylak pulled his bow from his shoulder and pretended to aim and shoot. "We probably won't see the girls very much anymore, though."

"It's a small village, Rylak."

"Yeah, but they're not gonna wait forever. Ginny still thinks those weird, blue eyes of yours are *dreamy*." He emphasized the last word with a swoon.

"Ginny? You know I'm not interested in Ginny."

"Why not? You can barely notice that dent in the side of her head anymore."

"It's not the dent, it's her crossed eyes. I'm never sure if she's talking to me or someone next to me."

"She can't help it."

"I know. But who walks behind a spooked horse? Lyla's prettier, anyway."

"Yeah, but she's kinda creeped out by your blue eyes."

"What? Since when? She never told me that!"

"I'm just sayin'."

"What about you?" Cameron asked. "Who are you holding out for?"

"I'm gonna find myself one of those bronze-skinned Sandual girls from down south. I heard they're practically born on the backs of horses."

Cameron laughed. "And their sixteenth birthday gift is a sword. That's a little too savage for my taste."

"Don't be so judgmental."

"Hold up, Rylak. This spot looks good to me."

Cameron wiped the sweat from his brow after dropping his small pack, waterskin, and bow to the ground. He looked around the sun-dappled forest floor and out over the prairie where hot breezes blew the tall, dry grass in swirling waves. This was Cameron's favorite rabbit hole, or so he called it. They sat for a short time, nibbled on snacks from the packs, and drank from the waterskins. Cameron poured water onto his head and rubbed it into his sandy-brown hair to cool off.

"Whose turn is it to flush?" Cameron asked.

"Yours," Rylak replied with an impish smile. Rylak was thinner than Cameron and had jet-black hair, mostly hidden behind a tan bandana wrapped around his head to keep the sweat out of his eyes.

"Are you sure? Every time I flush, you lose more arrows than you hit rabbits. You'll go home with an empty quiver, and we'll barely make one pot of stew with the meat." He laughed and smiled.

"Don't exaggerate. Besides, I have my lucky rabbit's foot today." Rylak pulled a leather cord attached to a large, furry hind foot out of his pack and put it around his neck. "I got this one last spring. See, I worked a hole through it for the strap."

"So now you're superstitious? I'll bet a little practice with that old bow of yours would be more productive than hanging a smelly hare's foot around your neck."

Rylak shook his head and smiled, and after Cameron looked away, lifted the foot to his nose for a quick sniff. He winced, then said, "I'm ready when you are. Go ahead and circle around toward the prairie."

Cameron glanced around at the thick brush near the forest's edge when movement to the left caught his attention. Something much bigger than a rabbit was moving through the prairie. A large deer bounded through the tall, sun-drenched grass and into the trees. His excitement surged. Its eyes would take time to adjust from the bright sunlight to the shade within the forest. He held Rylak with his upraised hand, and with as little movement as possible, picked up his bow and pulled an arrow from the quiver at his feet, never shifting his gaze from the deer.

It stopped and began to survey the surroundings. Rylak had stooped to conceal himself in the undergrowth, and Cameron was already on one knee. He smoothly nocked the arrow over the bowstring and slowly pulled it back. He patiently watched as the deer, not yet sensing their presence, walked further into the forest, coming closer yet to the young hunters. It stood majestically, its reddish-brown coat speckled by sunlight filtering through the branches above. Cameron marveled at its wide, thick body and its spectacular velvet-wrapped antlers.

Cameron felt his heart pounding. He wondered if Rylak, who was only three steps away, could hear it. He had never been presented in all his years of hunting with a more prized quarry at such close range. The deer was now only seventy paces away and upwind. While his adrenaline surged, a warmth filled his chest, and his skin began to tingle. The warmth was familiar. He had felt it before in moments of excitement or anger, but after describing it to Rylak when they were sixteen, he had teased him unmercifully. But today, staring out at the trophy stag, his chest felt like it would sear his innards to well-done.

Cameron knew the deer would soon catch their scent and bolt. His heart pounded harder and faster, and sweat began to roll down his face while the stag still moved toward them. Then, it stopped less than fifty paces away, raised its head and flicked its tail. *It had scented them.* Cameron's senses felt unusually keen. The bow was weightless in his hands, and the breeze over his moist skin felt cool. And as he instinctively let loose the arrow, the bowstring sang a shrill note, unusually loud, piercing the serene landscape. His eyes followed the speeding arrow with exceptional clarity as if guiding its path to the mark. At the same time, his skin was awash with a sensation of icy water. The air he inhaled through a sudden gasp bit his lungs with icy teeth like the first breath of air on a frigid winter day. Simultaneously, a warm sensation had penetrated his body's core and then released with the *twang* of the bowstring.

Cameron was briefly shaken by the unknown and unwanted sensations that had just racked his body. He felt both strength and weakness oscillating through him, and he struggled momentarily to regain control. But his eyes still followed the arrow until it pierced the stag's chest and disappeared. In that instant, a wave of emotions spread through him—sudden fear quickly replaced by agony, then flowing back to fear. He watched the deer startle and then bolt away in a flurry of kicked-up leaves and dirt. The emotions soon faded, and the stag slowed, staggered, and fell to the ground. The emotions weren't his own. They were foreign and disturbing. Somehow, he was inside the animal's head.

Cameron stared out at the fallen deer incredulously. He felt the weight of the bow again in his hand, and he lowered it before turning, wide-eyed, to look at Rylak. His friend had fallen to the ground, his expression fearful and awestruck, and he rubbed his arms to coax back the warmth that had been stripped away.

"What the heck just happened?" Rylak exclaimed.

Cameron stared back with his mouth agape. He had no answer.

Rylak pushed himself up and stood, then scoured Cameron from head to toe with his eyes. He looked the same. "How did you do that? *What* did you do?"

"I . . . I don't know." Cameron dropped the bow and held out his trembling hands to look at them, then at the stag lying motionless near the prairie's edge. Still stunned, he grabbed the bow and nocked another arrow.

"Do you feel alright?" Rylak asked, still stunned himself.

"Yeah . . . I think so."

Whatever it was, it had come and gone. He felt normal again. Cameron walked cautiously toward the fallen deer, and Rylak followed, still watching his friend for some outward sign to explain what he had just witnessed. Experience told Cameron to be careful, but he knew the stag was dead: *he'd felt it.* After verifying it was indeed dead, he pulled out his knife and began the gruesome task of field dressing it. His movements were mechanical and efficient while he tried to make sense of what had just happened.

Rylak helped him in silence, holding open the cavity while Cameron pulled the guts out to form a warm, slimy pile on the ground. With that part done, he found a long branch that would support the stag's weight. Rylak knew they had a long, hot, arduous walk ahead. He bound the stag's legs together around the branch and then the massive, velvet-wrapped antlers to keep them from dragging on the ground.

Cameron went back to where they had left the packs and sat, rinsing the blood from his hands with water from the skin. Rylak did the same.

"Cameron," Rylak finally said, breaking the long silence and drawing him out of his stupor. "I've never seen anything like that before."

"I know . . . I know!"

"Your arrow went clean through that stag, ribs and all, and I found it buried an inch into an ash tree."

"What do you want me to say? I don't know what happened!"

"The hair was burnt around the arrow wound, where it went in. And I swear I saw that arrow glow, or something, when you shot it!"

"Rylak! I know. I was there, remember?" Feeling like he might hyperventilate, Cameron nervously wrung his hands together. He sat still for a time and controlled his breathing, trying to settle his nerves. "I told you about it once before, remember? That warm feeling I get in my chest. It happened this time, too. But then it just got out of control. I was so excited about that deer."

"I don't remember you telling me anything like this before."

"Not like what just happened . . . the warmth in my chest *before* it happened."

Rylak shrugged his shoulders and shook his head. "I don't know. But either way, what do we do about it?"

"Whaddaya mean? We're not gonna do anything about it. And you can't tell anyone! They'll think I'm some kind of freak or something."

"Well . . ."

"Rylak! What's that supposed to mean? You know me better than anyone. I'm not a freak."

"So, what was it then?"

"I don't know. Maybe it was your stupid rabbit's foot."

Rylak looked down at it hanging from his neck. He pulled it off and threw it into the woods.

"I was just kidding," Cameron said.

"Well, whatever it was, I think we should get outta here. Are we still gonna stop at your grandparents' cabin?"

"Yeah. We'll need a break anyway. This thing's gonna be really heavy. And we can use my grandfather's saw to cut those antlers off."

Rylak, still stunned, plopped down on a log with a dumbfounded expression and stared silently at Cameron. What else was there to say? Cameron was clearly as perplexed as he was.

They eventually gathered their packs and bows, then hoisted the branch onto their shoulders, using their folded shirts as padding. The stag was heavy and awkward to carry, swinging to and fro as they walked through the shaded woods. But the new growth in the immature forest to the south soon became too dense to continue with the heavy carcass.

"We need to get out of this stuff," Cameron announced. "Let's cut along the prairie to the road, then we can backtrack to their cabin."

Rylak agreed. So they trudged along, sweating profusely under the morning sun at the prairie's edge. Finally reaching the road, they turned back to cover the short distance to the trail leading to the cabin.

Still reeling from the morning's excitement, Cameron had forgotten what lay along the section of road they now walked. He hadn't passed it in over three years—a large rock formation jutting out of the ground and standing like a monument to painful memories from Cameron's past. He stopped, and Rylak, not expecting it, staggered under the deer's weight.

Rylak was about to say something when he noticed where they were, and he bit his tongue as the irritated expression dissolved from his face. They lowered the deer onto the ground, and Cameron slowly ambled toward the formation. Memories flooded back as he stood there, and Rylak moved to stand beside him.

"This was the spot, wasn't it?" Rylak said.

"Yeah. I can't even remember the last time I was here."

Rylak placed his hand on Cameron's shoulder. "It was six years ago when it happened."

After a long silence, Cameron said, "I don't think I ever told you, but I felt it that day too—that warm feeling in my chest. It was the first time."

"When did it happen?"

"Right after I felt her dying. I was scared, and then really angry. And it was just there."

"Why didn't you tell me then?"

"We were only twelve."

"I always thought it was strange . . . how you knew, I mean. But I remember how close you two were, with your father away at war and all."

"Yeah."

Cameron paused in thought, drawing out suppressed memories while they both stared silently at the rock formation.

After a short time, he confessed, "I knew what she was thinking."

"Huh?" Rylak said, not sure if he had heard his friend correctly.

"When she died, I knew what she was thinking."

"Seriously?"

"Yeah. It was me. She was thinking about *me* when she faded away."

"How could you possibly know that? We were over two miles away when she died, Cameron. Back then, I thought it was some crazy coincidence that you knew, but after today . . ."

"Yeah. Chalk one more up for the freak idea."

"That's not what I meant."

"I know."

"They never caught the horse thieves who killed her, did they?"

"No."

"Why would they shoot her in the back, anyway? And what about all those scorch marks on the ground?"

"None of that story adds up to me either. I'll probably never know the truth of it. My father still blames himself because he was away at war when it happened."

"That's crazy. It wasn't his fault," Rylak said.

"I don't think he retired from the militia just to take care of me. I think he was so racked with guilt he couldn't do his job anymore."

"He was a really good captain, too," Rylak said. "At least that's what Jaeblon and the other men in the village say."

"Well, we're just farmers now. We should get going, Rylak. It's still a pretty good walk."

The young men hoisted the deer back onto their shoulders after a drink of water and continued along the overgrown path to the east, toward Cameron's grandparents' cabin. When it finally came into sight, nestled inconspicuously into the forest's fringe, the idyllic scene captivated them. They had been here many times before, but the beds of colorful wildflowers bordering the cabin and cascading along the fenced pasture were stunning, as if the blooms had orchestrated the showy display for their benefit. They skirted the fence line toward a well-worn path leading to the cabin while a lone horse grazed at the pasture's far end, casually eyeing their approach. And the gentle trickle of a spring-fed stream greeted their ears.

Cameron's grandparents, having spied the young men on the path through open shutters, emerged from the cabin to greet them with broad smiles sweeping across their faces. They were spry and energetic for their age, and both had the same deep blue eyes that Cameron and his mother, Gwen, had shared, a trait quite rare in the native Gartannian population.

Cameron knew them as Gramps and Gram, but their given names were Kenyth and Larimeyre. "Hello, boys," shouted Kenyth. "You've had some good luck today."

"Not too bad for a couple of rabbit hunters, huh?" replied Rylak.

"Bring that over by the woodpile." Kenyth led them behind the cabin. "Prop your end up there, Cameron." Once situated, the deer hung like a grisly trophy.

Their shoulders ached, and their arms were smeared with dried blood. They walked the short distance to the briskly flowing stream where they washed the blood from their arms and knives and refilled the waterskins. Cameron dropped them in the shade by the cabin as he greeted Larimeyre.

"You boys must be hungry," she said, emerging from the cabin with a basket of bread, cheese, and garden vegetables. Cameron sat in the shade with Gram, where the cooling breeze wafted the pleasant odors from the wildflowers under their noses. Rylak surveyed the deer with Kenyth.

"How's Joseph?" Gram asked.

"He's fine." Cameron watched as Gramps cut the tether, releasing the strung antlers. The stag's head dropped, and the massive rack plopped down onto the soil. Gramps started sawing one off.

"I hope that meat doesn't spoil," Gram said, seeing that Cameron's focus was still on the animal.

"Oh, right. We'll get it into the root cellar as soon as we get back home. And I'll take it to Samuel first thing tomorrow." Samuel was the butcher in Locksteed. "You and Gramps should take as much as you want. There'll be more than enough left to split between our families."

"It's a big one alright."

Rylak was sawing the second antler off when Kenyth bent down to look at the singed arrow wound, then curiously prodded it with his finger before glancing toward Cameron.

Cameron looked away and nervously said, "What was that, Gram?" His eyes darted back and forth between his grandparents.

"I just said it's a big deer."

"Oh, yeah. The biggest I've ever taken."

Gramps was questioning Rylak now. But Rylak just stood awkwardly and shrugged his shoulders. Gramps scratched his head. He was the smartest woodsman Cameron had ever known and had been the one who taught Cameron to hunt. And not only that, he had taught Cameron how to make his own bow and arrows. He knew so much about the land, the plants and trees, and the animals that lived in the woods.

Gramps carved out portions of meat to cure while Gram cooked smaller pieces for their dinner, but he seemed distant and distracted during the remainder of the boys' visit, although he said nothing directly to Cameron about the strange ring of singed hair around the arrow wound. After eating, the young men prepared to face the blistering late afternoon sun on the walk home. They would arrive shortly before sunset.

They thanked Kenyth and Larimeyre and lifted the deer back onto their shoulders. It was much lighter after the antlers had been removed. But it was still a long, hot walk ahead. Along the fenced pasture, Cameron suddenly stopped and said, "Hold up, Rylak. We forgot the waterskins."

They put the deer down, and Cameron ran back to where he had dropped the skins by the cabin. Kenyth and Larimeyre were already inside, and as Cameron bent down under the window to pick up the skins, he heard Kenyth talking in a low voice, followed by an unmistakable gasp from Larimeyre.

"Are you sure, Kenyth? It can't be possible. I've never heard of a Gartannian having these abilities. Of course, he does have *some* Arnorian blood. He is our grandson."

"Rylak was definitely holding something back when I asked him about it. Do you remember Baron's Prophecy, Larimeyre?"

"Of course I remember it, but there were so many uncertainties in its meaning. It's been seven generations since those words were uttered. In my mind, the Prophecy faded from hope at least three or four generations ago, and most certainly since Gwen's death." She began to sob.

"I don't know what to think myself, but tomorrow I'll leave to find Errenthal and get his advice."

Cameron stood there briefly while he considered the twists and turns that had marked his day. *What have they been hiding from me? And why?* Perhaps the answers would come soon enough, but now was not the time. He ducked beneath the open window and silently crept away from the cabin, then ran back to Rylak with the waterskins. They hoisted the deer and resumed the trek home. The afternoon was still hot, but a cooling breeze had been building throughout the day, signaling a welcome change in the weather. But Cameron didn't notice. His mind was swirling, and he didn't mention his grandparents' conversation to Rylak.

THE RAID

Cameron slept poorly that night. Early on, he dreamt of happy times in his youth, vivid recollections of his mother, but the dreams eventually wandered to the day of her death. Being at the rock formation the previous day brought to his subconscious a myriad of confrontations that she might have experienced. Several scenarios played out in his dreams, from scruffy horse thieves, to renegade militiamen, to Caraduan nomads, to cloaked phantoms. Each scenario ended in his abrupt awakening as an arrow pierced her back while she fled on horseback.

Later in the night, his dreams wandered to a seemingly more peaceful scene. He was entering a forest through tall grass. The cool, humid air was refreshing. He felt at peace and safe within the cover of the trees and was surrounded by foliage he recognized, though not by name. Then the solitude was broken by an instinctive sense of danger. When he looked around for the source of disquiet, he quickly identified something out of place. His eyes focused, and he stared at an image of *himself*, bow drawn and aimed directly at him. His limbs felt like stone when a sharp, unfamiliar sound broke the silence, and an object hurtled toward him at lightning speed. A wrenching pain seared through his chest, unfreezing his limbs, and he ran instinctively. Shortly, his vision blurred and then turned black. His fear ebbed away into a peaceful blankness, and his limbs became numb.

He awoke at that moment, opened his eyes, and, relieved, found his eyesight to be intact. His heart was pounding, and his skin was moist with perspiration. Gathering his bearings, he found himself in his own bed, at home, and with the morning sky already brightening just before sunrise. The dream had been incredibly vivid and was etched in his memory as if it were reality. This strange connection with the deer was unnerving.

Cameron roused himself from bed and went to the open window. The eastern sky was aglow with the rising sun. Clouds moved overhead from the west with the prospect of much-needed rain. He looked toward the stable to see his father, Joseph, standing and talking with his grandfather, whose horse was nibbling from a small pile of hay next to the stable. Gramps was wearing a long, dark-green riding cape, and the tip of a sword was visible just below the cape's trailing margin. Cameron hurriedly dressed, hoping to catch his grandfather in time to find out about this 'Errenthal.' He had carelessly thrown his pack on the floor the night before and tripped over it in his hurry. But when he finally made his way to the door and ran outside, barefoot, Gramps was already trotting away toward the village. Joseph met Cameron while walking back toward the house.

"Did you lose your boots?" Joseph asked with a smile.

"I was hoping to talk with Gramps before he left. I heard him say something about going to see someone named Errenthal. Do you know who that is?"

"He's just an old friend of your grandparents. But I was talking to your grandfather about these random attacks we've been hearing about in southern Southmoorland. They've been getting closer, and Garth just heard about one near Dubal. He wants to meet with the other villagers at Fenwick's Tavern tonight."

"Will Gramps be there?"

"It doesn't sound like it. He may be gone for quite a few days." He looked back down at Cameron's feet. "Come on. Let's find your boots and get some breakfast. We've got a lot to do before the rain starts."

"I've gotta take that deer to Samuel."

"Already harnessed and hitched."

Cameron glanced behind the small stable, and sure enough, the horse and wagon were ready to go.

"You're not going to make me drag that deer out and load it up by myself, too, are you?" Joseph laughed.

Cameron smiled and ran inside to get his boots.

After breakfast, Cameron headed toward Locksteed, about a mile ride to the south of their farm. But just a short distance down the road, he stopped to see Rylak at his family's farm. The Callaways ran a large horse stable and breeding business, raising workhorses for the local farmers and tradesmen, but also Sanduin war steeds as a hobby. Garth Callaway, Rylak's father, had been breeding them since before Cameron and Rylak were born. Cameron loved to watch the beautiful, sleek animals running in the pastures. They had originally been bred in Sandual, a turbulent region neighboring Caradua and the unsettled lands to the east. Garth had acquired his breeding stock from Eastmoorland, however, a flat region also known for its excellent horse breeding.

Cameron pulled into their farm and found Rylak in the stable. "You wanna come with me to Samuel's?" he asked.

"Can't. My father's delivering a horse today, and I've got a load of work to get done."

"No problem." Cameron looked up. "Looks like it's gonna rain, so you better get at it."

But Rylak was looking at him kind of funny.

"What?" Cameron said.

"Are you feeling alright today?"

"I'm fine. It's not like I'm sick or anything."

"I know," Rylak said. "It was just a weird day, that's all."

Maribeth, Rylak's younger sister, came running out of the house and over to the young men. She gave Cameron a big hug, then went over to see the large deer in the back of the wagon. The three had grown up together, and Cameron considered her like his own sister.

"You should have seen the antlers," Cameron said. She cringed after peeking under the canvas tarp that Cameron had thrown over the animal.

"That's really gross," she said.

"How's the training going?" Cameron asked while looking out into the pasture at the Sanduin horses.

"They're pretty stubborn," she said. "But I've got a couple of the new mares pretty well broken." She stretched the neck of her shirt over her shoulder to show him a fresh, deep bruise. "I got thrown a few times."

"You're the gutsiest girl I've ever known."

She flexed her bicep and giggled.

"I'll see you tonight at Fenwick's," he said to Rylak, then hugged Maribeth again. He jumped in the wagon and snapped the reins, then guided the horse back toward the road. He glanced over to the pasture to watch the Sanduins trotting along, happy for the cooling weather. He was watching them frolic when a dark, shadowy figure caught his attention near the tree line at the far side of the pasture. He squinted, but the wagon lurched over a series of ruts, shifting his gaze away. And when he trained it back across the pasture, the figure was gone, probably just a shadow in the trees.

He focused back on the Sanduins to admire their sleek but powerful forms. They had been bred for speed and endurance but were willful and difficult to train. Then, remembering his conversation with Rylak the day before, he began to picture in his mind a beautiful, bronze-skinned, black-haired girl riding one of the sleek horses across the pasture, a sword jutting upward toward the sky in her outstretched arm. He shook his head, smiled, and rode on.

Cameron returned in time to help his father in the fields before the rain began. Then he cleaned the stable and made a quick dinner before they threw canvas parkas over themselves and walked back to the village. At the tavern, Marty Fenwick, with his prominent mutton chops, and his plump wife served boiled fish and potatoes to the hungry patrons and ale to the thirsty ones.

Joseph and Cameron talked for a long while with Jaeblon, a large, burly man who worked as a blacksmith in the village. He stood taller even than Joseph and took up a good bit more floor space as well. He was holding a pint of ale and spoke through an untamed tangle of facial hair dabbled with bits of boiled fish and potato. Born and raised in a relatively unprosperous area of Southmoorland, he had served in the militia under Joseph and moved to Locksteed under Joseph's wing six years earlier after Gwen's death. He was unable to read or write but was as skilled a blacksmith as there was and as loyal a friend to Joseph as there could be.

"I've heard things from people down south," he said, "comin' up fer wheel bands and such. These brigands have took horses and grain sacks and all sorts a' different things. They've been hittin' farms and stables mostly, they say. And there's talk about a dark, shadowy fella what's been overseein' them attacks. It don't make no sense." He slogged down half of his freshly poured ale as an exclamation.

Another man said he'd heard similar stories and also that the southern district's council, elected officials from the smattering of towns and villages within its boundaries, had activated their volunteer militia to support the small, full-time army. Recent times had been peaceful, being years since mandatory recruitment was invoked during the last Caraduan uprising.

Just then, Garth Callaway and his son, Rylak, walked in and grabbed two already poured pints of ale from the counter and tossed several copper pennies to Marty. They joined the others.

"I just got back from delivering a horse to a farm near Dubal." The village was larger than Locksteed and sat about thirty miles to the east on the Sable River. "I asked about the attack there, and the man said a farmhouse on the outskirts of the village had been ransacked. They wounded two farmhands. But the odd thing is, they left the stable alone and took nothing. The wounded farmhands said the attackers were just dimwitted common ruffians."

Murmuring filled the room before one villager raised his voice and asked, "What do you think about all this, Joseph?" The villagers respected him for his years of service in the Southmoorland militia. He was, in fact, on his way to becoming the captain in command over the entire militia when Gwen was randomly murdered.

Joseph had been standing silently with his arms crossed over his chest. He scratched his chin and took a deep breath, then said, "So many of these attacks seem coordinated, but others seem to be haphazard. It makes me wonder if it's even the same men behind them all. But I remember back in the wars, the nomads would sometimes send out small bands of men to attack and quickly retreat. The raids weren't meant to inflict much damage but to test the defenses of our encampments. They were probing us to find our weaknesses. These attacks might be meant to test us . . . *or*, maybe they're looking for something."

"But what could they possibly want?" Cameron asked, clearly unsettled by the discussion. During his lifetime, Southmoorland had been relatively peaceful. His life had been touched only once by random violence.

"That's the question," Joseph said. "Until they're caught and interrogated, we won't know. And the fact that they've evaded the militia for this long kind of worries me."

"Are you willing to keep up the training, Joseph?" Garth asked.

"Until harvest, but that's not far away. And as long as the men are interested."

The rising murmurs confirmed their interest. He had offered to train the village men to defend themselves with swords and knives. He had, after all, trained plenty of men during his career in the militia. But many of the villagers, and especially the wives and mothers, were increasingly unnerved by the reports of violence against farms and businesses in the south. They wanted to be proactive, so Joseph had been training interested men two or three nights a week for much of the summer. Jaeblon had offered the yard in front of the smithy as a training site and a crate of surreptitiously acquired swords for training weapons. Cameron and Rylak had been particularly enthusiastic about it. But in the end, Joseph hoped they would never come to need it.

It wasn't the first time Cameron had picked up a sword. After Gwen's death, Joseph had returned home to raise Cameron and started farming full-time. He wasn't particularly attuned to parenting and struggled to find common interests with his son. But swordplay was something he knew well, and what twelve-year-old boy didn't fantasize about swashbuckling swordsmen or heroic cavalry pushing back the invading

Caraduan nomads? It wasn't exactly a simple game of catch or four square, but it was what Joseph knew. And Cameron relished the time spent with his father, though their playful diversions eventually turned instructional as Cameron grew.

About ten days later, the harvest began. The routine activity in and around the village changed as it did every fall. Jaeblon was busy repairing and banding wagon wheels and fixing broken farm implements while the farmers were harvesting. The local community members bartered their goods at markets in the village centers, which is what Cameron and Joseph happened to be doing in Locksteed on that fateful day—the day that changed Cameron's life forever.

They were arranging baskets and crates of vegetables they had harvested over the previous two days in the back of their wagon when Cameron heard rising screams and pounding hooves coming from the north road. Maribeth Callaway soon appeared, galloping into the village on a Sanduin mare. She was pale as a ghost and frantic as she pulled the horse to a stop in front of Cameron and Joseph. She tried to catch her breath while muttering hysterically, "They've attacked the house . . . they want horses . . . Father and Rylak are in the stable! They're going to burn our farm." And she began to look faint.

Cameron pulled her down from the horse and supported her while she wavered on her feet. "Who attacked, Maribeth?"

"Bandits, thieves, I don't know! There are at least fifteen of them."

Cameron looked at his father, who was already untying their horse. A small crowd was gathering, and Joseph shouted to mobilize all able men to meet at Jaeblon's workshop. Joseph mounted his horse, and Cameron said to Maribeth, "I need your horse." She didn't argue.

Jaeblon heard the commotion and was standing outside holding a large hammer when they arrived. "Grab the swords," Joseph yelled, "they're attacking the Callaway farm!"

The Iserman brothers sped into the yard, having also been at the village center. The only other men immediately available were a young farmer named Seldon and Samuel, the butcher. Thankfully, all had participated in the arms training. Jaeblon and Joseph gathered swords from Jaeblon's stash and distributed them to the men.

"We're too few," Joseph said, looking at the small posse. "But we might already be too late. Find your courage, we have no choice but to go now." He led the small group to the north road as fast as the horses would fly.

The seven-man posse kicked their heels into the horses' midsections while the dirt road passed beneath them like a blur, but not fast enough for Cameron. He was gravely worried about his friends—*his family*. He held fast to the reins with his left hand and kept a crushing grip on the sword's hilt with his right. The other men held similar poses, none having sheaths for their borrowed weapons.

They rounded a bend in the road and came over a gentle elevation in the prairie as they approached the Callaway farm. Gray-black smoke rose and trailed east of the farm. Seeing it transformed Cameron's worry into anger. The stable's north end was ablaze, and smoke billowed upward. The south doors, which usually stood open during the day, were closed, and a swarm of dark figures, fifteen or twenty by Cameron's estimate, moved in a frenzy around the inferno.

The Sanduin mare surged ahead of the others, and Samuel wasn't far behind. They urged the horses forward and continued to pull ahead. Joseph called in a commanding voice, "Fall back!" His authority was clear. Cameron and Samuel slowed to rejoin the other men while they continued the charge toward the farm. Joseph spoke again in a booming voice, reciting out of habit through emerging memories of his days as field commander, "We're outnumbered, but we'll enter this fray together. That's our only advantage. Put aside your anger and remember what you have learned." And they left the road, heading directly toward the stable. Joseph kicked, accelerating to the front of the group, and led them toward the largest cluster of men near the stable.

Seeing them approach, the band of attackers arranged their formation, readying themselves for the assault. Those on foot looked at one another in consternation, while three moved away behind the larger group and apprehensively fumbled with their bows. All wore similar gray armbands, a sure sign that they were organized mercenaries.

Joseph drove toward the forward horsemen, and Cameron followed. Jaeblon and the Iserman brothers felt no comfort in fighting on horseback. They slowed and clumsily dismounted near five enemies on foot. Seldon and Samuel confronted the first attackers who emerged before them.

Joseph seemed to rise taller in his saddle with the approach. He was an imposing figure and approached with such deliberate intent that many of the enemy faltered. Fear shadowed their faces. Joseph bellowed, "For Southmoorland we fight!" as he plunged toward the leading figure. He brought his sword down with such force that his opponent's defense was futile. Joseph quickly recovered and slashed to his left, blocking a meager blow from the next opponent. Pulling back on the reins, he spun the horse with a leftward jerk and finished the man before he could recover.

The other attackers briefly scattered, then turned and came back upon Joseph and Cameron, who were now side by side. An unsettling warmth filled Cameron's chest, and he felt his strength and focus sharpen. He parried several blows while his nerves began to unwind. His father's words came back to him. He parried another blow and quickly countered, gashing his opponent. The next suffered wounds as well while two others fell to Joseph's experienced hand.

Jaeblon and the Iserman brothers were surrounded by five unmounted mercenaries. They fought with their backs to one another and fended off the attackers' blows. Jaeblon's strength proved too much for his opponents, and he dealt lethal blows to two. When he turned to aid the Isermans, Calob was dealt an injury to his arm. He recovered and blocked another swing aimed at his neck while Jaeblon stepped forward and nearly removed the attacker's head. The other two quickly retreated from his terrifying wrath.

Seldon and Samuel were in a fray with four mounted men. They kept themselves side by side, emulating Joseph and Cameron. Neither had served in the army and had only the limited training Joseph had provided in recent days. They parried lethal blows but were ineffective in striking back. They each suffered wounds on their arms and legs as they unknowingly drifted closer to the archers. Their opponents, on command from the archers, backed away, leaving them open. Seldon was closest and took two arrows while Samuel's left shoulder was deeply scored by a third. Seldon collapsed to the ground with mortal wounds.

The archers pulled arrows from their quivers and nocked them for a second volley. Samuel was helpless watching the swiftest pull back the bowstring to shoot, but an arrow suddenly plunged into the man's chest. The timely impact disturbed the archer's aim, sending his arrow just over Samuel's shoulder. Startled, the remaining archers turned to see Rylak standing next to the burning stable. He was placing another arrow to the string and training his sight for a second shot. Samuel saw his opportunity and spurred his horse to charge. The archers twisted round and fired at Rylak, just missing him in their haste.

Steeled by anger, Rylak held steady and fired, hitting his second mark in the chest. While the third archer pulled another arrow from his quiver, Samuel was upon him and dealt a wicked blow, cutting through the bow and inflicting a vicious wound. Samuel, enraged, finished the archer with a thrust of his sword.

Garth appeared behind Rylak with a pitchfork, the only weapon he could find in the stable. He ran to Seldon, who lay limp on the ground. The four horsemen who had engaged Seldon and Samuel retreated, frantic to rejoin their comrades. Joseph and Cameron bolted forward to block them while Jaeblon and the Isermans extended the barrier.

"Drop your weapons and surrender," Joseph demanded. Rylak approached from behind with his bow raised. The attackers were uncertain as their horses nervously pranced. "You will not get another warning," Joseph bellowed while brandishing his blood-stained sword.

Cameron, startled by an unusual tingling sensation spreading over his skin, glanced around. An ominous, gray-cloaked man approached from behind at a distance of seventy-five paces. The remaining mercenaries were now congregated to each side of the cloaked figure, the footmen having mounted horses left by their fallen comrades.

Cameron watched the gray-cloaked man raise his arms overhead as a shimmering, fiery light emerged and grew between his hands. He rode a tall, strong, jet-black stallion. Its nostrils flared, and Cameron distinctly saw icy vapors come forth when it breathed. Cameron felt suddenly afraid and called out a warning to his friends.

Without hesitation, the cloaked man pulled back his arm and hurled the fiery ball toward Joseph just as Cameron shouted his warning. It flew as if directed by its creator's will. Joseph glanced back and instinctively kicked his horse into motion. The fiery missile struck the horse's midsection, throwing Joseph to the ground. His foot caught in the stirrup, and the horse toppled upon him.

Unwavering, Rylak let loose his arrow and felled one of the four nearby horsemen. The others took advantage of the distraction, spurred their horses and bolted around the stunned blockade toward the gray rider. Garth, seeing Seldon's mortal wounds, rushed over to Joseph to help his friend.

Cameron was transfixed by the strange, cloaked figure. He dismounted and walked forward with Rylak to stand by Jaeblon. The enemy host held their position now forty paces away, the mercenaries still flanking the gray rider who sat motionless with icy breath rhythmically escaping his nostrils.

Jaeblon shouted, "What manner'a evil is that? It's unnatural is what it is. You best be gettin' back to whatever deep hole ya crawled outta afore I lay yer head down in this here pasture." He defiantly planted his sword into the dirt.

Behind them, Cameron could hear the men struggling to move the fallen horse from his father, but he was afraid to release his gaze from the cloaked figure. The stranger raised his arms as another fiery orb began to grow in his hands, and his anger pierced the distance between them through his calculating gaze. Cameron's skin tingled like a thousand needles prodding through his clothes. His heart began to pound, and his consciousness began to focus inward. The images reflected through his eyes seemed to slow down, and his skin became cool. Feelings of hate and anger washed through him, but they were not his own. He briefly closed his eyes and saw himself, Jaeblon, and Rylak as if through the gray devil's eyes. And in an instant, he returned to himself to see the fiery missile released.

Cameron was already moving forward, guided by an eerie understanding of the gray rider's intent, and he quickly stepped in front of Jaeblon. His skin felt frigid, but the warmth deep within his chest escaped through his arms as he instinctively held them out to shield himself from the fiery attack. What drove his reckless act was beyond him, but when the fiery orb was about to strike, a blinding flash dissipated it. It had come from within him. But the remnant of the fireball impacted squarely onto his chest with a powerful force, knocking him back into Jaeblon and instantly burning like he had stepped into the flames that raged in the nearby stable. His chest seethed with heat where the impact wrought its fury, burning a round patch in his shirt and leaving his skin severely burned. After several moments of searing pain, the heat spontaneously drew away, and the pain diminished.

He was stunned from the assault, but when his mind returned, a dry heat filled the air around him before dissipating into the stiff prairie wind. He focused back on their attacker. The gray-cloaked stranger sat tall in his saddle, his gaping eyes focused intently on Cameron. His horse danced apprehensively, and he tugged the reins to settle the animal. The mercenaries were looking to one another, muttering incomprehensible words in the distance. They were turning their horses away as if to leave but hesitated and looked to the dark stranger for a command.

While the seven men battled against the besiegers, word had spread through the village and surrounding farms. Several armed and mounted villagers appeared over the rise and approached the farm. And with a glint of uncertainty in his eyes, the dark stranger glanced at the newcomers, then Cameron, and finally kicked and turned his horse. He galloped across the prairie toward the woods without a word, and his henchmen followed.

Cameron looked down and felt the reddened skin with trembling fingers before remembering his father. He ran to him, past Jaeblon and Rylak, who stood with incredulous and bewildered stares. Garth was frantically drawing a rope around the head and forelimbs of Joseph's fallen horse. He brought the free end to the Sanduin mare and secured it to the saddle horn. He slapped the horse's flank, and she began to pull while the other men lifted and pushed the fallen horse from Joseph's limp body. Cameron fell to his knees at Joseph's side, and to his great relief heard a gasping breath when Joseph began to stir. His right leg was twisted awkwardly above the knee, broken.

Garth and Rylak ran to the far side of the stable and soon emerged through the south doors, flinging them wide open. They freed the remaining horses from what was nearly a fiery death and watched them gallop, still panicked, into the pasture. Garth retrieved two wooden staves and some cord. He ran back to Joseph and lashed the staves to either side of his leg as a splint.

Beth Callaway, Garth's wife, had locked herself in the house during the siege. With the danger apparently passed, she left the house and ran to Seldon. She brought with her several strips of cloth to bind wounds but was horrified to find Seldon had already succumbed to the arrows. She gently closed his eyes while tears streamed down her cheeks. She stayed her grief, rose to her feet, and chased down Samuel to care for him.

Joseph remained on the ground where he had fallen. Every breath brought a wince of pain to his face. Cameron checked him over carefully, but his ribs and leg were the only apparent injuries. The men took him into the house and laid him in Rylak's bed while Beth managed the Iserman brothers' wounds.

Jaeblon took charge of the chaotic aftermath. "You men," talking to the latecomers, "get yourselves back to the village and watch over your homes. Them devils won't be comin' back here any time soon. There ain't nothin' for 'em here, what with them fast horses runnin' loose out there now." There was nothing to be done for the stable. It would burn to the ground. He grabbed another man from the village and sent him east to fetch the healer from Dubal. He was the closest around. And finally, he walked over to Joseph's horse, the one killed by the gray rider's first fiery attack. The charred flesh went deep into the horse's midsection. Almost certainly, it had died quickly.

Jaeblon found Cameron in the house. Beth had corralled him and was gently slathering honey over the burns on his belly and chest. Jaeblon leaned over and looked closely, then jabbed his calloused finger into the tender skin at the burn's center. "Ow!" Cameron winced.

Beth smacked Jaeblon's arm and glowered at him before he expressed a rumbling "Hmmm." He licked the honey from his finger and said, "Ain't that peculiar now? It don't feel like it, but that hide's a darn sight tougher'n it looks." He looked into Cameron's deep blue eyes and added,

"Your mum had them same eyes . . . and some peculiar rumors followin' her too."

Cameron's self-conscious stare erased as he looked questioningly back at Jaeblon.

"Go away, you big oaf," Beth said sternly.

Jaeblon rumbled a half-hearted laugh, then went in to see Joseph.

"Don't you pay any attention, Cameron," Beth said, then went back to applying the honey.

Garth and Rylak were at Joseph's side. He was in misery.

"The stable's near done burnin'," Jaeblon told them. And with a deep sigh, he added, "The men took Seldon's body back to the village. We'll be givin' him a right proper burial in a day or two."

Garth winced and closed his eyes, trying to hold back tears.

"Them weren't normal horse thieves, Garth," Jaeblon said. "It's a right sure fact."

"They've gotta be the same ones we've been hearing about," Rylak said.

"Did they give any clue what they was all about?" Jaeblon asked.

"Not really," Garth said. "They just wanted horses. I was inside the back fence with Maribeth training a young Sanduin when they came. She saw them first, a group of riders coming out of the woods to the southeast. Two were already holding burning torches, and several others had drawn swords. Some were riding two to a horse, and I figured they'd come for horses.

"I feared for my family. I was afraid of what they might do even if I gave them what they wanted. I figured our only hope was to get help and hold them off as long as possible. I told Maribeth to fly to the village as fast as her horse would take her. I knew the Sanduin could outrun them, but the men had a shorter run to the road. I told her to go and don't stop for anything, no matter what happened.

"She lit out across the field, and three men broke away to cut her off. I watched while I ran back to the stable. She shot past them so fast they never had a chance to react. They tried to follow, but I knew they'd never catch her.

"I yelled for Beth to lock herself in the house. Rylak and I closed the stable doors and barred them from the inside. One of the men who I thought was their leader tried to negotiate with us. He said he'd leave us alone if we just gave him all the horses. I could hear the others laughing, and I knew I couldn't trust him. I knew our chances were better waiting for help. Then they set fire to the north end. If you hadn't shown up when you did, I'm sure they would have killed us.

"But I never saw that gray-cloaked one at first. He came after you showed up, after we put up a fight. It was unnatural, what he did." But neither Jaeblon nor Rylak told Garth what Cameron had done. Garth hadn't seen it.

After Beth finished, Cameron ambled back outside. He had heard Garth's comment. He gingerly sat down with his back against the cool stone wall, the sensation contrasting sharply with the burning over his chest and belly. He watched the stable's remnants burn as smoke trailed overhead. The horses stood safely out in the pasture, their nerves finally calmed in the open air.

Rylak came out after him. He absorbed the scene of destruction before sitting next to Cameron. "The captain seems to be doing better. His breathing is easier, but that broken bone in his thigh has him just about in tears. My mother says he'll be laid up for a long time."

They sat in silence, but Cameron could sense the tension behind Rylak's unsettled expression. Finally, Rylak asked the question that Cameron knew was coming. "How'd you stop that fireball, Cameron? You saved Jaeblon's life, but we all saw what the first one did to your father's horse." He leaned forward to look at Cameron's reddened chest and abdomen.

"I wish I knew, Rylak. Somehow, I just felt like I had to do it. I didn't feel like there was any danger in it. I don't know, maybe it was just a stupid impulse. But . . . I could see through that man's eyes. I knew what he was doing. It was just like what happened with that deer."

"There's some connection here, Cameron, with that gray-cloaked man, I mean. I don't know what it is, but there's too many similarities."

Cameron was silent.

"Six years ago, my dad said there were scorch marks on the ground near that place he found your mom."

"I know. It crossed my mind too. And Jaeblon just said something kind of odd—something about peculiar rumors following my mom."

"I don't know," Rylak said. "But maybe you should ask your grandparents. Your grandfather took quite an interest in that burn wound on the deer. He asked me about it, but I didn't say anything. Maybe we should ride out to their cabin and let them know about all this. We should at least let them know about your father's injuries."

"I don't know if Gramps will be there. He left the day after our hunting trip. But you're right, I should at least let Gram know what's happened."

"The captain will stay with us until he's healed," Rylak added. "It's the least we can do. He helped save our farm . . . and our lives."

The young men watched as two village men loaded the bodies of the slain mercenaries onto the back of a wagon and carted them away. They would be buried in some obscure place with no monument to mark their disdainful existence.

IDENTITY

The healer arrived from Dubal late the following morning. Garth and Cameron helped him put together an elaborate sling and traction system for Joseph's leg. He made Joseph drink a tonic made from distilled grain alcohol and herbs that Cameron had never heard of before. Joseph became sleepy, and much of his pain seemed to wash away. The healer set the bone with Jaeblon's help and placed Joseph's leg in the sling and traction. Regardless of the effects of the tonic, Cameron left the house for the gruesome event, not wanting to watch his father go through the ordeal.

"He'll need to stay put for two to three months," the healer said, "depending on the speed of healing. He has several ribs broken as well, but I don't see any other serious injuries. I need to get back to Dubal, but I'll come back in one week to see how he's healing." He provided additional instruction for Joseph's care and also attended to Samuel's wounds before leaving.

Beth had to coax Cameron to show his burns to the healer. Several ugly blisters had formed since the previous day, but the healer thought it would all heal uneventfully, scarred as it might be. He thought the honey was as good as anything he had to offer and gave his blessing to continue it. Garth paid the healer in coins and begged him to be prompt in his future visits, ensuring payment for his time.

Cameron was satisfied with Joseph's care and knew he was in good hands with Beth Callaway. He wanted badly to talk to his father about what had happened, but Joseph was in no condition. And still hoping he might find his grandfather back from his journey, Cameron decided to ride north to his grandparents' cabin. Garth wouldn't allow him to go alone, so Rylak joined him. They rode Sanduin mares, their best chance to escape an unexpected encounter.

The day was overcast but comfortable. They covered the distance quickly and arrived at the cabin by midday to find Larimeyre home by herself. The young men gave a full account of the previous day's battle, and she was measurably shaken, especially when they described Joseph's injuries. But when they described the gray rider, she sank into a nearby chair, visibly trembling. She said nothing for a long time, and Cameron felt like his gut was in a vice. *What did she know?*

She sat while deep in thought, then finally looked up at Cameron and said almost in a whisper, "And *you* survived him." She stood, and Cameron went to her, not sure if she was steady yet. She gently opened his shirt to look at the burns, then held him by the arms and looked deep into his blue eyes. "Your mother did *not* survive one like him six years ago." She sighed. "Perhaps your grandfather was right about you."

She stood back and cast him a purposeful look. A spark shown in her eyes while her expression took on a stern character. "You are the last in my family line, Cameron Brockstede—*and you are in grave danger.*" The words came to him as water comes from a breaching dam, and his gut wrenched.

"I want the two of you to sit down. It's time you learn about our family's past, Cameron." Out of habit, she busied herself preparing food and drink for the young men. Cameron and Rylak made themselves comfortable at the table, waiting respectfully for her to begin. She returned with a variety of food, then coaxed them to eat while she talked.

"You're the seventh generation of our family to live in this part of the world, Cameron. My great-great-grandmother was Althea, daughter of Halgrin of the House of Genwyhn. I know these names don't mean anything to you now, but they hold a tremendous importance to me and our ancestors. Althea was born in Arnoria, a land not so different from Gartannia. She and her father were the only surviving direct heirs in the family that held stewardship over that land for countless generations. But her father foresaw the imminent destruction of his family by the growing power of a rival faction called the Khaalzin.

"The Khaalzin, as I understand through stories passed down within our family, were corrupted supporters of a rebellious new leader. Apparently, some were distant relatives of our own family, and they sought over many generations to replace our direct ancestors in leadership of the Arnorian people. But they were authoritarian, and their power grew while they recruited more and more allies throughout the land.

"Halgrin made a difficult decision to send his wife and only child, Althea, across the ocean, here, to Gartannia. He sent them secretly to keep them hidden from the Khaalzin. He believed if he could keep his bloodline alive, that the House of Genwyhn could be restored one day."

"But Gram," Cameron interrupted, "if Halgrin's family held power for so long, how could they be overthrown so easily?"

"Through the stories, I gathered that our family led and protected the Arnorian people through peaceful means. That they weren't prepared or equipped for a violent power struggle may have led to their eventual downfall. Halgrin hoped for the Arnorian people to flourish under peaceful governance as they had for countless generations, outside the control of the Khaalzin.

Larimeyre reflected silently for a moment, sullenly. Her eyes looked past them. "Or perhaps the strength in our family simply dwindled away. Perhaps Halgrin didn't have the strength to stand against them, as I didn't have the strength to protect Gwen." The spark in her eyes diminished while the painful memories resurfaced. Guilt still gnawed at her resolve.

The young men respectfully waited for the memories to pass.

"You see, Cameron, the people of Arnoria are different. Our family is different . . . different at least from the Gartannian race. Arnorians carry a trait known as channeling. We all have it to some extent, but certain traits can be passed on through families that grant stronger abilities. And those traits ran deeply in our family, once upon a time, anyway."

"So this channeling ability, is that what was happening to me when I shot that deer and when I stepped in front of Jaeblon?"

"I'm certain it was. I would never have believed that you could inherit these abilities with your father being Gartannian. Your blood is only half Arnorian, Cameron." She paused, pondering old thoughts. "I'm ashamed to admit that I had hoped these traits were fading from our family so we might eventually see peace and be able to live outside this shadow of fear. My father and I had very limited abilities, but the traits came back in your mother. She was so young when it started. But by then, rumors were circulating about sightings of the Khaalzin in Gartannia. After five generations, they had followed us across the ocean to destroy us, even here. We were forced to flee the small village where our families had settled in the north and came here with Gwen to hide her. She was so impulsive, and her actions were drawing too much attention, even in the north where our village was mostly of Arnorian descent.

"We thought we'd succeeded in keeping her safe. She grew and learned to control her impulses. She eventually met your father and wed. Your father is a wonderful man, Cameron, and I'll admit that I was most joyful at the time, believing this would end our accursed pure Arnorian bloodline. There wouldn't be any reason for these damned Khaalzin to pursue us anymore.

"Then, on that terrible day six years ago, one of the gray riders caught your mother unawares. Your grandfather and I believe the rider and his henchmen happened upon her by pure accident. As you know, she was returning home after visiting us, and they must have passed her on the road. He probably saw her blue eyes and confronted her. Errenthal found signs of their pursuit along the road. Instead of turning onto the path coming back to our cabin, where your grandfather and I might have helped her, she chose to protect us and kept northward on the road. They overtook her near the forest."

"Why didn't you explain all this before, Gram? Maybe someone could have tracked them and caught them."

Gram reached across the table and put her hands gently around Cameron's clenched fist. "But they did, my dear grandson, *they did.* Your grandfather and Errenthal tracked them. They were able to intercept and kill the gray rider and his men before they could pass word on to the other Khaalzin. If they had failed, I suspect none of us would be alive now. Please understand, we had to keep this quiet for our family's safety. These past six years have been difficult for all of us, Cameron."

Rylak sat attentively, quietly taking in the story. "I've heard the name Errenthal before."

"Yes, but you'd more likely know him by his common name, Erral. He's one of the trackers sent from Arnoria to pursue the Khaalzin. His charge is to protect our family."

"He's the gray-haired trapper who comes to the village to sell animal pelts. We've seen him plenty at Fenwick's Tavern, usually sitting by himself."

"He's taken to spending more and more time near this village but still travels widely across the land watching the Khaalzin. Your grandfather is searching for him now, and I hope he returns soon. I'm afraid it may already be too late to find this gray rider before he reaches the others. When they hear that there's a young man here who can dispel their attacks, they'll come with their full number. That's why I say you're in grave danger. This has put the entire village at risk, I fear."

Cameron looked into her face. There was no mistaking the flame in her eyes. The recent events had rekindled a long-smoldering fire within her. She looked in every respect the heir of a noble line, but he had never seen it before. She stood, and the young men followed her lead, then helped her clean up from the meal.

She began to scurry around the house and clearly became more flustered while her mind raced. She finally stopped, took two deep breaths, and said, "Rylak, I want you to ride home today to warn your family, and feel free to pass on what I've told you today. We have no reason to hide it any longer. Oh my, I have so many things to get ready here. Cameron, I need you to stay and help me pack and prepare the house. Kenyth has taken our horse, so I'll need to ride back with you tomorrow morning."

Cameron spent the remainder of the day tending the livestock and preparing the cabin for what might be an extended absence. He moved two goats into the fenced pasture and returned to the cabin to help Gram. She had already packed the perishable foods into a bag they would take with them, then rummaged through two worn trunks containing what Cameron suspected were family heirlooms.

"Come here, Cameron. It's time that several family possessions pass on to you." She had gathered several items from the chests and laid them aside. The remainder she returned to the chests. The two largest items were wrapped in cloth, which Gram removed. "These would have passed on to your mother in time, but with her death, I was ready to bury them so deep in the ground that no one would ever find them. Your grandfather stopped me. I never imagined circumstances would be what they are."

The first item was a sword. The hilt and guard were intricately crafted in a manner that Cameron had never seen. He removed the blade from its sheath and marveled at the smooth, bright, polished metal. "This looks nothing like the steel on my father's swords."

"It's different, but I'm afraid your grandfather would have to explain that. But I do know the blade was forged over two hundred years ago by some of the most skilled smiths in Arnoria. Althea brought it with her on the ocean crossing. How well she might have been trained to use it, I really don't know. The fact that she even had it is very telling. How fearful they must have been of the Khaalzin. Our family cherished their role as peaceful stewards for so long."

She unwrapped the second parcel and handed Cameron a round shield made of light metal wrapped tightly on its outer surface with stiff leather. The metal was strange, having a bluish tint, and was lighter than expected for its size. "This shield was sent with Althea as well. It bears the crest of our family on the front, but the face was wrapped with leather to hide it. The crest is distinct, so it was covered out of caution. Althea's father was very clear when he sent it with her—it was meant to pass on within our family."

Cameron recognized the third item. "That medallion's familiar. Mother used to wear it. I wondered what happened to it after she died." He took it from Larimeyre and looked closely at the engraved design—a tree in full foliage beneath an open eye. "She always kept it hidden under her clothes. Does the engraving have some meaning?"

"That's our family's crest. Or rather the crest of the family of stewards. It signifies our commitment to oversee and protect the land, including all living things, plant and animal. The same crest is on the shield. I had given it to your mother many years ago. Please forgive me for taking it back, but it just wasn't the right time to pass it on to you. It isn't safe to be shown casually.

"And this final item is purely of sentimental value." She handed him a small, soft leather pouch. He opened it and removed a short, silver chain necklace with a prominent pearlescent stone set in a delicate silver backing. "Should you choose a wife one day, you will offer this to her to wear until she bears you a child. By tradition, it's passed on to the firstborn. Your mother wore it from the day of her marriage until you were born. I know it must seem superstition to you, but I believe it carries some virtue."

"Don't we have any other family in Gartannia? There must be cousins, other lines branching from second- or even third-born siblings since Althea."

"Unfortunately, no. Since Althea, there has been only one surviving offspring each generation, and that sometimes makes me wonder if our family bears a curse. These items pass to you as the rightful heir of the House of Genwyhn. We should sleep now, Cameron, and make an early start in the morning."

Cameron slept poorly that night. The past two days' events had his head swimming. He was angry about being kept ignorant of his ancestry. The feeling was quelled, however, by the reverence he felt for his grandparents. He could sense the ambivalence in his grandmother, although her spirit was undeniably stirred with the awakening of his abilities. His future was now even more uncertain. He was concerned about his father. How would he keep the farm running? Could he even stay if his presence brought danger to his family and friends? Eventually, Gram stirred him from a restless sleep early in the morning. She left a note for Kenyth should he return to the cabin, and they headed to the Callaway farm.

DEFIANCE

Beth Callaway welcomed Larimeyre into their home. With the added responsibility of Joseph's care, she needed the extra hands. Many villagers had come to offer their help and support as well, and the men were already working to rebuild the stable. Garth's livelihood depended on completing it before winter.

But Larimeyre became increasingly concerned as the days passed, and at the end of eight days, she gathered the Callaway family together. "You've been such good friends and like family to Cameron, Joseph, and Gwen when she lived. I beg your forgiveness for what my ancestors and I have brought to your peaceful lives. I know Rylak told you some of our story, and it's your right to know the truth about our situation. Our family has been persecuted for generations, even before they fled to this land. They came here believing, or hoping, that they would finally be left to live their lives in peace. But that wasn't to be. The motivations for these men to continue pursuing us are complicated and irrational, but nevertheless, they are here. The gray-cloaked rider that led the attack on your farm is only one of six whom we believe to still roam this land. Some or all of them will most likely return soon to find Cameron. His identity was, regrettably, unmasked when they attacked the farm ten days ago."

Garth interrupted, "Larimeyre, you don't need to ask for our forgiveness. The attack on our home had nothing to do with you. These men were looking for horses, not for Cameron."

"That's true enough, Garth, but when they return, they'll destroy anyone or anything in their path to sate their desire to destroy our family. I had hoped Kenyth would have returned by now, but we're running out of time. You've already seen what they're capable of, and they'll come with strength and powers that we just can't repel. We have no choice but to leave this farm and warn the village."

Beth gave a concerned look and said, "But how will we move Joseph? He's in no condition to travel."

"She's right, Beth," came Joseph's voice from the next room. "I don't stand a chance if I stay here. None of us do for that matter. Our only hope is to hide for now and somehow create a diversion to draw them away from the village."

The group moved into Joseph's room. He was looking stronger each day. The healer had returned two days before as promised and adjusted the traction on his leg.

"Well, Captain, what do you suggest?" asked Garth.

"My house is small, but it'll do. And the stable's dry enough for extra beds. I'm not sure I could make it any further than that. Splint my leg and take me by cart in the morning. Pack what you'll need for several days. You can't return here for anything. Once they return, they'll surely be watching the farm. As for the diversion, I'll need to think on that a little longer."

The Callaways began making preparations. Joseph asked Cameron and Larimeyre to remain momentarily. "I feared this day might come, Larimeyre. I can't bear the thought of losing another of my family to these damned Khaalzin. And I'm helpless to protect you."

"We'll find a way, Joseph," she replied.

"I don't know if we can do it without Kenyth." He proceeded to give Cameron instructions to prepare their small house for the move.

The next morning, the two families moved necessary supplies to Joseph and Cameron's house. Garth and Cameron applied a splint to Joseph's leg, and they moved him as gently as possible to the cart. The ride was bumpy and painful, and he was exhausted when they finally settled him into the bed and reapplied the traction.

Garth halted work on the stable and instructed the villagers to prepare their homes as best they could against another attack. Jaeblon joined his friends at the Brockstede house. The men found a small hillock to the north of the Callaway farm with prairie grass tall enough to conceal their position, and they took turns watching for any activity at the farm.

At dusk on the third day since leaving the farm, Rylak sat forlornly upon the hillock. He was just nodding off into a light sleep while sitting cross-legged in the grass when he was startled by the sound of galloping horses moving north along the road. He looked above the grass and saw two dark figures guide their horses from the road toward his house. One dismounted and ran directly to the house, checked inside, and quickly returned to his horse while speaking something to the other man. At this distance in the darkening sky, Rylak couldn't clearly identify the men, other than their dark cloaks.

The two men spurred their horses to a gallop and continued north on the road, quickly approaching Rylak's position. The sudden departure took Rylak by surprise, and in a rush of adrenaline, he impulsively ducked and moved toward the road, bow in hand. He muttered to himself, "*Are you kidding me? You couldn't give me just a little time to warn the others?*" The riders advanced, and without thinking, Rylak stood with his bow drawn and an arrow trained on the first. He nearly released it before recognizing Kenyth. His heart was pounding, and his arms began to shake after lowering the bow.

Kenyth and Erral pulled their reins, and the horses slowed, rearing up at the shadowy figure. Seeing him lower the bow, they circled back while trying to steady the excited animals.

"Stay your hand, Rylak. I'm not ready to die just yet."

"I'm sorry, Kenyth, but, boy, am I glad to see you. I thought you were gray riders."

"Where is everyone?" Kenyth asked.

"Joseph's house. Our farm was attacked several days ago—"

"We heard the news just now from Fenwick," Kenyth interrupted, "though you'll have to fill us in on the details. Do you have a horse?"

"Yeah, just down the hill."

"Then mount it and ride with us."

Rylak retrieved his horse from the bottom of the hillock, and the three men rode briskly toward the Brockstede farm in the night's deepening darkness. Rylak yelled ahead as they approached that they were friends. Garth, Cameron, and Jaeblon emerged from the shadows with weapons in hand.

"Kenyth, we've been hoping for your safe return. What news?" asked Garth.

"Let's talk in the house, we may not have much time."

While the others went inside, Kenyth and Erral took Cameron aside. Kenyth spoke directly, "Cameron, is it true, that you stood against the Khaalzin?"

Cameron raised his shirt to expose the healing blisters. "He would have killed Jaeblon. I had no choice."

Kenyth glanced at Erral. "Then there's no question where they're headed. We need to act quickly."

Erral stood in astonishment. "You should be dead, young man. How did you—"

"Later, Erral," Kenyth said, then led them into the house.

Larimeyre hugged Kenyth as he entered. "I've been so worried about you," she said. "And I'm so joyful to see you, Errenthal."

They crammed themselves into the small bedroom where Joseph lay. Kenyth looked down at him, bound in bed to the traction, and said in dismay, "This complicates our situation."

"I'm glad to see you too," Joseph replied, though he plainly read the anxious concern in Kenyth's expression.

Kenyth looked around at the others in the room and continued, "Before I tell you where I've been, I need to introduce Errenthal. He knows the Khaalzin as well as anyone in Gartannia. He followed them across the ocean over thirty years ago and has done his best to keep us safe from them ever since."

Blue eyes marked his Arnorian heritage as Erral lightly bowed to the others in the room. He was lightly bearded and his dark hair heavily grayed. An olive-green cloak partially concealed a worn shirt and patched pants, and his leather boots were weathered and heavily scuffed.

Kenyth continued, "The Khaalzin have been wandering this land all these years searching for Larimeyre's family. But in recent years, they haven't been searching as intently, apparently focused on other tasks. But this attack on your farm has changed that. When Cameron stood against the gray rider, I'm afraid it turned their attention back to our family.

"About three weeks ago, I went to look for Erral and found him tracking the movements of one of the Khaalzin and several mercenaries near the Western Range. While we observed, a messenger arrived bearing news of some importance to him. Their entire band left in a hurry, headed back into Southmoorland.

"The messenger went to the north, so we followed and finally caught him. We had no trouble getting him to talk, and he told us about a skirmish in the western part of Southmoorland. We pressed him further and he divulged his orders—gather the gray riders and meet near Dubal to destroy the last remnants of old Arnorian royalty. We've returned with all the speed our weary horses could muster."

Erral stepped forward. "We don't know how far behind us they may be. The six remaining gray riders have good horses and will most likely come ahead of their small mercenary army. The messenger that we overtook won't complete his errand to one of the six, so we may have only five to deal with. But even so, we can't hope to overpower them."

Joseph propped himself up. "Larimeyre's instinct was right. We need to get all of you away from here and come up with a plan to draw the Khaalzin away from Locksteed."

Larimeyre looked at Erral and Kenyth. They were exhausted. "When's the last time you slept?" she asked.

"Two nights ago," Kenyth said. "We had to get here before the Khaalzin."

"You'll sleep tonight," she commanded. "You can't go on like this. We'll make preparations while you get some rest and leave first thing in the morning."

"I won't argue. I could barely keep my eyes open in the saddle. If we're lucky, they'll be delayed waiting for the sixth." Kenyth and Erral went outside to get their packs from the horses, and Larimeyre followed.

Garth whispered to Rylak, and they left the house as well. Cameron shuffled outside and wandered around the side of the house to collect his thoughts. Everything was moving so fast, and he felt like he had no control over any of it. Then he overheard his grandparents' rising voices near the stable, so he wandered closer in the darkness to listen.

"But we've been hiding our entire lives, Kenyth. Where are we going to go?"

"It's better than the alternative, Larimeyre. If they figure out who you are, you know what will happen."

"I won't hide anymore. Hiding didn't save Gwen."

Erral said, "We can all get away, Larimeyre. We'll go back to one of the northern settlements, or the forest retreat. We'll be—"

"We'll be what? Safe? But what kind of life is that?" Her anger was apparent. "They'll be relentless now that we're exposed. There's no hope for a peaceful life."

The men were silent.

"And now they're after our grandson. What did he do to deserve this? He has no part in this. Where is *he* going to go?"

"We'll watch after him," Erral said.

"They know his face. He can't hide."

"Then what do you propose?" Kenyth asked.

There was a silent pause. "I'm staying here. For too long my family has hidden like cowards. I won't continue on that path."

"What about Cameron?" Kenyth asked.

"You and Erral can take him north. Teach him what you can and try to keep him safe. He's all that's left of my family."

"Larimeyre—"

"You won't sway me from this. My family has lost every shred of honor it ever had. We've hidden for too long, waiting idly for our salvation to come to us, or simply to be quietly forgotten."

"If that's truly your choice, then we stay together," Kenyth said. "You know I would never leave you."

"I think you're both making a grave mistake," Erral said, "but it's not my place to stand in your way."

"Look after him, Errenthal. He's all we have left." They returned inside to sleep.

Cameron could hardly believe what he was hearing. He wandered away from the house toward the well, kicking his feet in the dirt as he walked. Jaeblon's hulking figure stood in the distance, illuminated by the starlight under a clear, cool night sky. It was apparently his turn on watch. Cameron pushed himself up and sat on the stone rim of the well, contemplating his situation.

So what's gonna happen? Am I supposed to just leave everything behind? And who the heck is Erral, anyway? He scraped his heel up and down the rough stones and mortar that formed the well's wall. *I'm eighteen. It's not like I was born yesterday. Why do they get to decide what's gonna happen?*

He thought back to his grandmother's words at the cabin several days earlier. *My mother was killed by these savages. Why? What possible threat could she have posed to them? This doesn't make any sense.* A vision of the deep scorch wound that killed his father's horse popped into his mind. *Geesh! And there's six of them.* He gently felt the healing burn on his front. It was still quite painful, and the sticky honey was a nuisance.

And what about my father? What if these gray riders do end up finding the house? That one will remember him. We don't just have to lead them away from the village; someone has to lead them away from our farms, too. No easy answers came, and his thoughts swirled in a confused jumble. *I guess Gram knows what she's doing, doesn't she?*

He had to move. The air around him felt thick with indecision, and he wanted to escape it. His father would know what to do. He walked back into the house, quietly shut the door, and tiptoed past Erral, who was already asleep on a thin mattress lying on the floor. His grandparents must have been in the other bedroom. Beth and Maribeth were busily sorting and wrapping food rations. Beth put her finger to her lips, warning him to be quiet, and he went in to see his father, shutting the door behind himself.

Joseph watched Cameron glumly saunter over to a stool next to the bed and sit. Cameron, uncertain of his words, stared distantly across the room. Joseph waited patiently for his thoughts.

Cameron said, "How's your leg feeling?"

"My leg, it's well enough. Broken bones are bearable, but seeing you thrown into this mess and not being able to help you is not. Tell me what's on your mind, son."

"I don't know where to go from here."

"I know. It's like we bumped a hornet's nest. No matter what direction you go, you're likely to get stung. Running into that gray rider has undone everything we worked to rebuild after your mother was taken from us. And now, I question the wisdom in keeping your mother's past hidden from you. It was more folly than wisdom."

"How could you have known? I mean, this whole situation may have deeper roots than any of us realize. They weren't looking for me or Gram when they raided the stable. I know they have a quarrel with our family, but what's to stop these Khaalzin from asserting their power over all of Southmoorland, or Gartannia?"

"Hmm." Joseph considered the question briefly. "I wouldn't call it a quarrel, it's *fear*. They see your mother's family as a threat to their power. And as for their ambitions in Gartannia, I think that's a conversation better left for another day. Our concern right now is for your safety."

"Gram and Gramps are staying."

"What?" Joseph asked, stunned.

"I heard them talking outside. She said she doesn't want to run anymore."

Joseph pulled his hand through his hair and sighed. "I wasn't expecting that."

"What's gonna happen to her?"

Joseph looked up. "They'll kill her."

Cameron's eyes gaped. "They want Erral to take me somewhere north, to hide."

Joseph thought for a moment, then said, "That might be the best thing . . . for now."

"But for how long? And is there really anywhere that they can't find me? I just want things the way they were. We were doing fine, you and me. I didn't ask for any of this."

"I'm sorry, son. Your mother didn't want to be part of this either. But we made the best of it. I understand why you might feel hopeless right now. But remember, you didn't bring any of this on yourself. I don't mean to sound like a military captain, but there is something that I used to tell my soldiers, and I truly believe the words. I don't know if it'll help you sort this out, but just indulge me: It is in times like this that many of our ancestors have risen to their greatest honor. Through the courage in their hearts and the strength of their convictions, even the meekest of men and women have changed the course of history. They are remembered for their courage and their valor. Remember this—when you are faced with uncertainty or despair, follow your heart and hold true to your convictions, for that is where your true strength resides."

"I don't have any convictions," Cameron said softly.

"You will."

Cameron left the house feeling no more sure of himself than when he entered. Joseph's words would require some digestion. Jaeblon watched him shuffle toward the dirt path leading to the fields beyond the house. It was a difficult situation for a young man of eighteen years.

It was sometime later in the night when Jaeblon's attention was roused by the sound of rapidly approaching horses. He moved closer to the house but didn't yet sound an alarm to those sleeping inside. Finally, a familiar whistle sounded over the clattering hooves, putting Jaeblon a little more at ease, but he kept his sword drawn. Garth and Rylak emerged from the darkness riding bareback on two Sanduin horses while leading a third.

Garth dismounted near Jaeblon. "We found three in the pasture. The others were hidden in the dark. We would have kept searching, but a light appeared in the window of our house. There were men and horses outside. We got away as quickly and quietly as we could with the three Sanduins, but I can't say for sure we weren't seen or heard."

Jaeblon grunted. "Well, at least we know they've come. We best wake the others and get prepared. Rylak, get them provisions they're packin' and saddle up four o' them fast horses. If there's any chance for 'em to get away, it's with them fast horses."

Kenyth and Erral, awakened by the commotion, came out of the house.

"It's time to go," Jaeblon announced.

"They were just at our farm," Garth added.

Erral glanced around. "Where's Cameron?"

"He's out to the fields. Gone some time ago." Jaeblon pointed.

Erral looked at Kenyth imploringly. "Go talk to her. See if you can change her mind. We'll go together. I'll get the horses ready."

Kenyth disappeared into the house.

Rylak and Garth quickly saddled two of the Sanduins they had just recovered, and Erral saddled a third already in the stable. The fourth

Sanduin, however, wasn't fully broken yet. Garth struggled with the temperamental mare and was just about to give up when Erral took her bridal. She calmed enough for Erral to place his hand on her neck, and he gently stroked up to her head. She snorted and fluttered her upper lip and finally settled down. Garth, amazed at the sudden change, saddled her while Erral spoke softly by her ear.

"You've got a knack," Garth said.

"Something like that," Erral replied before getting the packs secured.

Rylak came from the stable with Cameron's sword, shield, and bow, then lashed them to the packs he had already put on Cameron's horse. Larimeyre and Kenyth emerged from the house. They both wore swords at their sides but carried no packs or supplies of their own. Larimeyre wore a silver chain around her neck bearing a medallion identical to the one she had given Cameron, and her hair was pulled back into a loose braid. She wore aged leather vambraces studded with ornamental bluish-silver metal along the length of each forearm. Recent events had instilled a sense of pride and determination in her that her ancestors had lost generations before, and her appearance gave testament to it.

Erral walked forlornly toward her, knowing she'd made her decision.

"Errenthal, my protector and my friend," she began solemnly, taking his hands. "Your service to our failing house has been steadfast and honorable, though I regret that I haven't lived my life in a manner more deserving of your devotion. I bid you to leave us now and take my grandson to keep him safe. I'll admit, I've held little hope, but the Prophecy may yet live in him despite these many long years. My time grows short, and I choose now to stand and fight for what little honor my family may still have left. Teach Cameron what you can, and may you one day show him the beautiful land of Arnoria. It won't be my destiny to see it."

"Your words leave me with a heavy heart, Larimeyre. But I'll do as you ask." She hugged him, then he turned and walked away to climb into the saddle atop the spirited Sanduin mare.

Garth spoke for the others. "Good luck, Erral. Tell Cameron that he'll be constantly in our thoughts and that we'll see one another again in safer times. These horses should serve you well. They're the fastest in Southmoorland."

Erral thanked him and with a heavy heart directed the mare into the darkness, leading the second Sanduin mare to find Cameron. He followed a path bordering the recently harvested field. Erral knew the land well enough to find his way in the dark, and he guessed that he would find Cameron on a small rock prominence at the field's far side.

Erral announced his approach and found Cameron atop the smooth rock surface.

"The gray riders are close. We have precious little time to slip away. Your grandmother has asked that I guide you and keep you safe for now."

Cameron jumped to his feet and sprang to the ground. "Have they attacked the house?"

"No, but they're dangerously close. We've packed lightly, and your sword and bow are secured to the packs. We'll go north and hope they don't pick up our trail."

Cameron pulled the sword from its bindings and secured it to his belt, then mounted the horse. "What about the others? They won't be safe staying here."

"Your father can't travel, and your grandmother has made her choice to stay. You won't change her mind. Now, we must go!"

Cameron grudgingly followed Erral through fields to the north while keeping a safe distance from the northward road to their left, though they would eventually have to follow the road through the forest near the Sundheim prairie. They had gone less than half a mile when Cameron looked back to see several brief flashes in the direction of his house. Erral had seen them too and quickened the pace to the north.

ESCAPE

The gray riders emerged from the darkness shortly after Erral had parted from Larimeyre. As Garth had feared, they had followed their trail to the house. Two riders came forward from the road, and Larimeyre stepped out before them with Kenyth at her side to block their advance.

"You are not welcome here," she stated defiantly. "The one you seek is long since gone from here."

"We'll see for ourselves," growled the forward rider. "Here or not, we *will* find him eventually." And they moved closer.

Larimeyre saw the shadowy outlines of three more riders near the road. They were hopelessly outnumbered, but she remained steadfast in her resolve. "I will not yield to your aggression."

The forward two riders dismounted, drew their swords, and quickly advanced on Larimeyre and Kenyth, prompting the remaining three riders to break and charge forward.

Larimeyre and Kenyth drew their swords, and the air grew chill around them. They stood with honor and resolve as the Khaalzin advanced.

Then, from the darkness behind the stable, Garth and Jaeblon bravely charged forward on horseback to intercept the three riders. Rylak stood back in the darkness and released a series of arrows at one, but the gray rider, with unnatural quickness and strength, blocked each one in a shower of sparks and splinters. The Khaalzin sheathed his sword and sent a fiery missile at Rylak, barely missing him and forcing him to retreat into the darkness.

Garth and Jaeblon were outmatched and were soon knocked from their saddles. They continued to battle, but even Jaeblon found it difficult to match the strength and skill of the gray rider. Larimeyre and Kenyth stood fast, but Larimeyre's strength and stamina were clearly lacking. Her swordsmanship was rudimentary, and she had never been tested in physical battle before. Despite her resolve, Kenyth was compelled to engage not only his own attacker but the other as well. The fifth rider continued to send fiery missiles into the darkness toward Rylak.

It wasn't long before Garth lay wounded on the ground. Jaeblon was subdued and forced to his knees, bleeding from wounds on his arm and forehead. The Khaalzin placed their swords to the men's necks, and the man engaged with Larimeyre called for her and Kenyth to yield. "We'll finish your friends if you keep up this futile defense."

Larimeyre and Kenyth, seeing their friends defenseless, backed down and dropped their swords. They were forced to their knees. The Khaalzin's leader stood before Larimeyre and pulled the medallion forcefully from her neck. He spat on it and threw it to the ground, saying, "So here you have hidden these many years." Kenyth struggled, but the Khaalzin kept him subdued.

The leader continued, "Is this the best that the House of Genwyhn can offer? The blood of your family runs thin, likely mixed with the blood of common men by now. But then, your family was weak generations ago in the homeland. Why would I expect differently now? But there *is* one more. The boy, where is he?"

Larimeyre remained silent.

"Won't you tell me, perhaps to spare the lives of these common men? Ah, but of course you wouldn't give me your only heir." He strutted around her with a contemptuous sneer. "When I find him—and I assure you, I will find him—I'll spill his blood and put an end to your family forever. That's the prophecy of the Khaalzin."

The leader turned to look at Jaeblon and Garth. "What of you common men? I would barter your lives for the boy. Which of you will tell me where he is and reclaim your worthless life?"

Jaeblon was breathing heavily, and his wounds seeped streams of blood. He looked at the leader and said, "I'd see you devils boiled in yer own blood afore I'd give ya another word!"

"Then we'll start with the queen," the leader bellowed, mocking her attire. He turned toward Larimeyre and trained his sword on her neck. Seeing the Khaalzin's intent, Maribeth let out a bloodcurdling scream from the house where she and Beth helplessly watched through a window. Her scream briefly distracted the leader but was quickly obscured by Cameron's approaching voice.

"Noooo!" he yelled as he sprang from the darkness beyond the house. He hurtled across the yard on the Sanduin mare with his bow trained on the leader. A fire illuminated his eyes as he let loose the arrow. The missile sped in a flash of crimson fire, guided by Cameron's will toward the Khaalzin's leader.

Cameron's sudden appearance startled him, allowing Larimeyre to duck beneath the sword as it whistled through the air. The leader spun and rolled, using his momentum to just avoid the arrow that singed his cloak. Cameron deftly drew his sword and continued his charge toward the leader, who again rolled to avoid Cameron's reach. Kenyth sprang to his feet in the commotion and pushed his captor away and into the path of Cameron's fury. The keen Arnorian sword shallowly scored the neck of the Khaalzin, drawing its first blood in Cameron's hands. Jaeblon knocked the feet from under his subduer with a powerful swing, then ran toward the stable.

Only several paces behind Cameron came Erral, his olive-green cloak trailing as if he flew on wings. His sword gleamed in his drive toward the first two Khaalzin. They dove to the ground to avoid the powerful Sanduin that showed no sign of faltering in her path. Meanwhile, Rylak took advantage of the distraction to bury an arrow in the fifth rider's arm.

Jaeblon whistled for Larimeyre and Kenyth, then released the saddled Sanduins from the stable. Larimeyre agonized while she watched her grandson's reckless charge, then broke free with Kenyth from the stunned Khaalzin. Cameron and Erral drove through a second time, again knocking the villains from their feet. Finally, Larimeyre and Kenyth mounted the horses and kicked them into motion. Jaeblon pulled Garth to his feet and dragged him into the stable, barring the door behind them. The Khaalzin's furious leader barked orders to his men, "The boy! The boy's the one we want. Don't waste your time on the others. We'll run him down like the frightened fox he is."

The victim of Rylak's arrow turned with a cold gaze into the darkness and pulled the arrow from his flesh. Rylak, holding his breath, kept his composure and lay motionless in the tall grass. Fortunately for him, the injured rider followed his leader's command and spurred his horse in pursuit of Cameron and Erral.

Once Erral sighted Kenyth and Larimeyre fleeing, he whistled for Cameron to follow. The four sped through the fields and veered toward the north road. Their only chance was to outrun the Khaalzin. They would lead them away from the farm and the village. Erral muttered to himself, "*I hope Garth was right about these horses*."

They covered the distance along the dry dirt road quickly to the forest's border by the Sundheim prairie. To their dismay, the five gray riders kept pace but lagged behind by some two hundred paces. But they were far enough ahead to avoid the Khaalzin's fiery attacks.

Erral spoke in turn to each of his companions as they sped along. "We'll take the road through the forest. We know this path and forest better than any."

The blackness of the moonless night enveloped them. They entered the forest road in single file with Erral taking the lead, still at a full gallop. But in the darkness, Cameron could feel his horse begin to falter, unsure of the path ahead. He sensed her uncertainty. From behind, Kenyth yelled, "Show the horse the path in your mind. You know it well enough."

"*Are you joking with me?*" Cameron muttered. Then he thought about the connection he had with the deer, but it wasn't something that had come to him voluntarily. He didn't understand, but what did he have to lose? Cameron concentrated on the path with its many turns and narrow places, anticipating each turn in succession. The mental imagery along with gentle guidance using the reins and shifting his weight seemed to put the mare at ease. In turn, Cameron developed trust in the horse, and they galloped through the forest at a quickening speed. They lost all sight and sound of the gray riders after penetrating the dark forest, though it was impossible to know if they were gaining distance from their pursuers. The Sanduin horses sensed the urgency in their riders and held the pace, displaying the impressive stamina for which they were bred.

Still in predawn darkness, they continued toward the forest's northern border. But with growing exhaustion, the horses began to falter and slowed. Kenyth moved forward of Cameron to speak with Erral. "We should separate. I'll turn west with Larimeyre along hidden paths to make our way back to the cabin. As far as I know, it's still undiscovered by the Khaalzin. You're better off alone with Cameron. Follow the creek bed to the east. It's just ahead. If we're lucky, they'll miss our separation in the dark and follow my tracks to the north. It'll give you more time to escape."

Erral agreed to the plan. They came upon the creek, and Erral led Cameron in a sharp turn to the east, hoping to conceal their trail over the creek's dry, stony margin. They continued along the creek until the northern range of the Sundheim prairie opened before them. Erral decided to chance a brief stop at a water pocket. There would be no water for many miles across the prairie, and the horses had already been pushed severely. The men found empty waterskins in their packs and filled them while the horses drank. And with no sign of the Khaalzin behind them, they were quickly on the move again. They followed the creek bed for another half mile before finally entering the arid prairie, again urging the horses to a rapid trot.

A gentle glow began to show over the horizon before them, and they continued east for another twenty miles, pushing the horses to near exhaustion. The rolling hills at the center of the expansive Sundheim prairie now dominated the otherwise featureless land. They climbed and briefly rested at the top of a high hill. In dismay, they looked back to the west to see their path clearly visible through the vast expanse of tall prairie grass. At the very limit of Cameron's sharp vision were three dark figures, nothing more than specks in the distance.

"I only see three riders," Cameron told Erral. "Maybe two stopped to tend their wounds."

"Your vision's remarkable, Cameron. I can't make them out at this distance. But you may be right, or perhaps they separated to follow your grandparents. We can only hope they're safely hidden back in the forest. We have a good lead on these three, but there's no hope of completely evading them in this prairie unless we can hide our path. Come along, we may have one chance yet if our luck holds."

They turned southeast but were forced to dismount and walk the exhausted horses. Despite the urgency in their escape, their bodies enjoyed a reprieve from the saddles. Water was more plentiful in small ponds tucked in the green hills, and the horses slowly regained their vigor. But the hills eventually gave way again to featureless prairie, and urgency forced them to push the horses further. The sky was overcast and the midday cool, helping to preserve the horses' undaunted spirit. Erral slowed the pace, knowing that many miles lay ahead.

Early evening finally came, and hunger gnawed at Cameron's belly. The sky began to darken in twilight, and Erral saw in the distance what he had hoped to find. A large herd of wild horses was grazing in this sparsely populated area of Southmoorland. Erral spurred his horse forward, and Cameron followed.

"We need to make some distance before we lose the light," Erral said. "There are several of these large herds roaming just west of the Alurien River." They slowed as they approached the wary herd. Cameron saw the trampled ground and deduced Erral's plan.

The herds typically meandered aimlessly across the prairie while they grazed, breaking into smaller groups and reforming sporadically. Cameron and Erral entered the maze of trampled prairie grass. They zigzagged through the grazing paths and finally redirected their course to the northeast, toward the northern arm of the Alurien River. They slowed the pace considerably in the moonless night. The horses were sluggish from the brutal pace and relished the opportunity to graze for a time even in the darkness of night.

Cameron and Erral were exhausted as well, but they dared not stop to sleep. They would look for cover under daylight within stands of trees pocketing the river valley. So they trudged through the weary night and into the morning, leading the horses on foot. The tall prairie grass was left behind, and the ground became rockier with scattered scrub plants and tufts of short grasses. The terrain was gradually becoming more defined by the prominent rock. Ages of water and wind had eroded the land, leaving a turbulent array of rocky hills and precipices. The men wound their way through the coarse landscape, still walking the weary horses and staving off the overwhelming urge to sleep. But they saw no further sign of the Khaalzin when they began a gradual descent toward the river.

The valley opened before them, but the river was still far off to the east. Numerous stands of trees and mature wooded areas filled the landscape below them. They continued down into the valley for another mile until they came within one of the larger woods. There they slept the remainder of the day. Thunder and lightning would not have roused them from their deep slumber.

When they finally awoke, the sun was just setting over the valley's western rim. Cameron dug into his packs and found a small parcel with dried meat, nuts, and dried fruit. He looked to Erral and asked, "Why didn't you tell me there was food?"

Erral looked at the parcel and said, "I didn't know it was there. Rylak must have put it in your pack. You're lucky to have such a close and loyal friend."

"I hope I get a chance to thank him someday," he said gloomily.

"Thanks to these sturdy horses, you might just live to see that happen." Erral paused as his expression became stern. "It was foolish, what you did back at the house."

"Maybe."

"There's no maybe about it. But it was also courageous."

Cameron said nothing.

"But we were lucky. It seems to have worked out for the best. They would have killed your grandparents if we hadn't gone back. Of that, I'm sure. And maybe the others."

"Why was she just giving up? I don't understand."

"Shame. I sensed it like the reeking odor from a skunk."

"And you were just going to leave her?"

"I swore an oath to protect your family, Cameron, but not to question their motives or interfere in their decisions."

"If you're supposed to protect her, then why are you with me? I'm sure she's still alive."

"Are you not one of her family? Not part of the House of Genwyhn? She put your life before her own. Pride and honor can be powerful emotions, sometimes more powerful than the will to survive. But to protect our young is probably the most powerful of all instincts. One day, you may understand that."

Cameron willingly shared the small food portions with Erral. They talked together until dark, then left the cover of the trees and headed east toward the river. The autumn rains hadn't arrived yet, it still being early in the season, so they easily crossed the gently flowing waters in the shallows.

Their path continued east and north, gradually climbing the gentle slope to the valley's eastern rim. As the ground leveled off beyond the eastern margin, Erral turned to the north and continued along the valley rim until daybreak. They concealed themselves along a rocky outcropping before the sun climbed into the late morning sky and flooded the valley with light. From this vantage, Cameron was able to see a small group of men on horseback far across the valley's western reach. Erral surmised that they were the Khaalzin's henchmen, now joined in earnest search for their prey.

Erral and Cameron left the valley rim and headed into the barren lands to the east. The terrain was increasingly coarse and rugged. The ground lacked fertile soil and supported only scrub and woody vines. Very few scattered trees existed here, their branches stunted and nearly leafless. The thick, woody roots stretched over rock searching for veins of shallow soil and any crevices that might harbor scarce moisture.

"I've been through this land before," said Erral, "and there is little to sustain either horse or man. If we continue, it would be several days travel across this desolate land to the Moraien Fens, and a dangerous and miserable trek through the fens as well. Though that is the way away from our enemies."

Erral looked to the south. "The southern route is just as barren. The Candora River lies across the path to Eastmoorland and can only be crossed by ferry. Those will be watched, no doubt, by spies working for the Khaalzin.

"I believe we should continue north from here to the wooded Alurien highlands that give birth to this river. From there, we have several days' ride across the Northern March to the vast forest to the north. There's a small cabin deep in the forest where we can stay for the winter. We built it years ago, and it's well-hidden, though I haven't been there in over two years. We'll travel during the day for now, at least until we reach the highlands. This terrain is too dangerous even by moonlight."

So they continued north knowing the Khaalzin still searched for them in earnest. Their trail would be difficult to follow over the bare rock, but their pursuers remained dangerously close nonetheless. For three days they wound through the rocky landscape along the river valley's eastern rim. At nightfall, they were forced to return into the valley to find what food and forage they could to sustain their journey. The valley was becoming narrower and shallower as they approached the highlands. Erral was a skilled tracker and was able to conceal their presence through the barren lands sufficiently to avoid the searching eyes of the Khaalzin and their henchmen.

THE HIGHLANDS

Erral and Cameron finally entered the wooded Alurien highlands as steep hills and valleys came before them. Abundant groundwater flowed to the surface through springs, invigorating the lush landscape. Wild game and edible plants satisfied their hunger for a time while they made the gradual ascent. No villages existed here, but scattered cabins and trails met their path occasionally. The cabins were mostly abandoned, severely weathered, and in disrepair.

"We need to be cautious," said Erral while changing course to avoid a conspicuous log cabin ahead. "Most of the men who inhabit these lands are either deranged loners or hiding from something in their past. Either way, they distrust anyone who passes through. We don't need any trouble with them. Also, the Khaalzin will surely come here searching for us, and the fewer eyes that see us, the better our chances will be."

The wooded landscape was refreshing. The autumn colors were beginning to show in the trees, and a cooling breeze swept gently through the leaves. Cameron fondly recalled walking endlessly through the woods with his mother on many similar days near home. This was her favorite time of year.

Erral knew the highlands well, it being something of a crossroads for his previous explorations and travels through Gartannia. He would have preferred traveling at night, but the terrain was too difficult in the dark. Occasionally, lightly used paths afforded good progress, but their direction of travel mostly forced them through rougher terrain. Numerous ravines cut through the hilly landscape. Some they could cross, but others required lengthy detours to find passable ground for the horses.

After four days in the Alurien highlands, they felt refreshed. The Northern March was no more than two or three days away at the current pace. They had seemingly avoided any contact with the reclusive highlanders, and Erral was increasingly optimistic about their chances of reaching safety in the vast northern forest.

Cameron awoke early the fifth morning and crept quietly away from camp, hoping to bag something for breakfast. He made his way down a steep wooded slope into a ravine. Near its bottom, Cameron followed a smooth stone wash cut into the rocky floor by the intermittent seasonal rains that coursed southward to the Alurien River. This particular wash was mostly dry, and he carefully wound his way through the rocky maze of the deep-cut ravine with his bow in hand, alert for animals using the scattered water pockets in the creek bed. He rounded a vertical rock wall when an unexpected sight struck his heart cold. Before him knelt a gray-cloaked figure, busily packing gear into a small pack, barely twenty steps away.

Both men were aware of one another simultaneously. The gray-cloaked man stood quickly, leaning lightly on a long wooden staff while his right hand moved deftly to the handle of a knife slung from his belt. Cameron gazed briefly at the hooded stranger's shadowed face, dropped his bow, and moved his hand to the hilt of his sword. Both men froze momentarily, and as the stranger turned his face into the early morning light, Cameron clearly saw piercing blue eyes sizing him up. "*Khaalzin!*" Cameron muttered. Terror and hate raged through Cameron while he instinctively drew his sword.

The stranger saw the glint of the blade exposed under Cameron's hand, considered for an instant, and released his grip on the knife. He glided forward and swung the staff toward Cameron's head. Cameron raised his sword to parry the blow but realized too late that it was only a feint. The other end of the staff swung low and took Cameron's feet from under him. He fell to the ground with a dull *thud*, and his breath escaped him. He wrenched open his eyes just in time to see the staff fleetingly before it struck his right temple. First, a flash of light, then pain exploded in his head, followed shortly by blackness, and he knew no more until late morning.

When he regained consciousness, Cameron found his mind wandering through a fog. His senses were dull and direction was uncertain. Then he heard voices in conversation as the fog began to recede. One was familiar—*Erral?* The other was unfamiliar, but they spoke to one another as if long acquaintances. Gradually, light began to penetrate the fog while a splitting pain crept into his head, and the voices became clearer.

Cameron opened his eyes to see the blinding sun rising in the eastern sky. It was painful. He pulled his arm across his eyes to block the light, realizing then that he wasn't bound. He remembered the gray-cloaked man—*Khaalzin?* His head hurt too badly to rouse himself further, so he lay there listening to the conversation.

". . . the horses have impressive stamina." Cameron recognized Erral's voice. "We had a fair lead on them, which gave us an opportunity to hide our path through the wild herds. We made our way across the river valley and turned north to these highlands. We're headed across the Northern March to the northern forest retreat. I was planning to overwinter there with the boy."

He continued after a short pause. "So we've narrowly escaped the Khaalzin for now. I fear we would have been snared without these sturdy horses and the generosity and courage of Cameron's friends. And it's certainly some comfort running into you, Caelder, unlooked for in our flight. I'm deeply concerned for Larimeyre and Kenyth, though the searching eyes of the Khaalzin, I suspect, continue to be bent toward the boy."

The boy! Cameron was incensed at the youthful reference after all he had been through in recent weeks. But he supposed no urgency to quarrel over words with the smoldering agony still filling his head. He was content to listen to the discourse of these men, obviously old friends.

"I only wish I could have been there to help you, Erral." The voice was unfamiliar. "I'm sorry to have delayed your travel this morning, though I'm happy to have the chance to hear your story. To face five of the Khaalzin and escape unharmed is fortunate indeed."

"We were lucky. The boy is impulsive—and reckless."

"So I found out." Caelder chuckled.

"The delay is unfortunate, but I'm thankful you restrained yourself to the walking stick. As long as the Khaalzin weren't able to see us across the valley when we turned north, their pursuit should be slowed considerably. I doubt the delay this morning caused us any disadvantage. Nonetheless, it may be prudent to have you linger here for two or three days. You can draw them away from our trail if necessary."

"I'll stay for three days, and if I see no sign, I'll return to Locksteed to search for Kenyth and Larimeyre. For now, the boy seems to have become your priority. But are you certain the reports of his abilities are accurate? It seems unlikely. You know that my hopes for the resurrection of the Ehrvit-Dinal have waned since we lost Gwen. And the strength in the blood of our people here dwindles with every passing generation."

"I understand your skepticism, Caelder. His mixed blood goes against the Prophecy. The pure Arnorian bloodline of Genwyhn is unfortunately at an end." Erral paused and sighed. "But we made an oath to protect the line of stewards as long as they survive. And as for Cameron's abilities, I didn't witness the incidents that I described to you, but I have no reason to doubt those who did. Nevertheless, the Khaalzin believe he's a threat, and their purpose is clear—to destroy any last vestiges of the House of Genwyhn. To them, the Prophecy remains a warning against their sovereignty."

"They'll learn soon enough through their spies that Cameron doesn't carry pure Arnorian blood," Caelder surmised, "but I doubt they'll relent in their pursuit. Teach him what you can, Erral. His life will be difficult, and I fear he won't be able to hide from them for long."

The words echoed in Cameron's mind, and he acquiesced to a fitful slumber. When he finally aroused just past midday, the pain in his head was considerably reduced. He opened his eyes to sunlight gently filtering through the colorful autumn leaves. He considered feigning unconsciousness awhile longer, not wanting to confront the man who subdued him so easily. *I guess I still have a thing or two to learn.* Slowly he sat up, unsure if the pain in his head would worsen, but found only a mild throb beneath the tender lump on his temple.

Caelder, seeing him rise, came to him and knelt. "Don't try to get up too quickly." He paused. "I hope you'll forgive me, Cameron. When we met I reacted too quickly."

Cameron was finally able to focus on Caelder's tanned, hardened face hidden behind a short, graying beard. His appearance gave testament to a harsh, arduous life. His blue eyes penetrated Cameron's gaze and conveyed sincerity in his apology. "I don't deserve an apology, but I'll take your hand to help me up." Once he was on his feet, the forest began to spin. Caelder supported him until the swirling subsided.

"My name is Caelder. You should come and sit awhile longer. You don't look quite ready to mount a horse yet. Maybe some food will help." He guided Cameron to a log where he could sit and offered a simple meal. After eating, Cameron did feel better. The aching in his head, however, would take time to improve, and he knew the ride would be miserable.

Erral finished packing their meager supplies. "Caelder, like myself, came from Arnoria to pursue the Khaalzin. He keeps mostly to the northern lands to watch over the remnants of our people who settled there. They're descendants of refugees who managed to survive the ocean crossing from Arnoria in their flight from the oppression of the Khaalzin. Though you might think otherwise," he said with a subtle grin, "we were fortunate to run into him. I'll feel better knowing he's looking after your grandparents. We'd best be moving along now, Cameron."

As they rode away, Cameron looked back at Caelder and asked, “Would you please look in on my father and let him know I’m alright?”

A subtle nod was his reply.

HISTORY LESSON

Cameron and Erral continued north through the gradually thinning forest. The early autumn leaves were just beginning to drop while the more level terrain of the upper highlands granted them a faster pace toward the Northern March. On the third day since leaving Caelder, the cool, breezy morning ushered them through a young oak forest with browning leaves and into the opening arms of a flowing prairie dotted sparsely with oaks. The Northern March was a vast oak savanna that marked the northern border of Southmoorland. It was the gateway to the expansive forest wilderness that stretched unendingly along the savanna's northern edge.

Under mostly clouded skies, they spent several unlabored days traveling across the savanna. Erral seemed to know this land well, and they kept a good distance from the sparse roads and trails, still wanting to avoid the searching eyes of the Khaalzin's spies. Feeling more at ease as the days passed, and to help pass the long hours, Erral grasped the opportunity to recount ancient lore regarding the history of Arnoria and Gartannia, though much of the lore he would describe was already lost to the Arnorian population since the Khaalzin's brutal emergence.

"Millennia removed, an ancient race of men was said to have existed on a massive continent under the dominion of an assemblage of gods. It's said through ancient lore that the gods bickered over the nature of their charge to oversee mankind. They became entangled in a war that led to the creation of a fissure across the continent as a means to settle their dispute. The land was slowly separated, creating Arnoria and Gartannia, each under the dominion of different gods. A tempestuous sea opened between them to further isolate the two dominions from one another. Its waters bore the fury of the bickering gods. And to that matter, I can bear witness, though that story can wait for another day."

Cameron listened with interest. It was apparent that Erral relished telling stories to share his vast knowledge. To Cameron, it was a bit surprising, though, knowing Erral lived his life in relative isolation. But it would help to pass the time.

"The gods who ruled the separate dominions imbued their subjects with different traits according to their own motives. On one hand, the gods over the Arnorian race wanted their subjects to hold sway over the natural world—plant, animal, and the soil itself. That men should have authority to manipulate nature pleased them. So, Arnorian men and women were granted special abilities that would help them maintain stewardship over the land they depended on. On the other hand, the gods over the Gartannian race wanted them to have an equal place in nature with all other living things, recognizing that men can be prone to misuse their powers.

"Whether or not one believes the divine provenance of the two races, our histories bear evidence to the narrative. For many thousands of years, the Arnorian people lived in relative harmony with nature and with one another. The underlying thread that held our culture together was a common reverence for the natural world, and our energies were bent on peaceful governance and stewardship over the land. But Gartannia's history, as you know, is marred by repeating cycles of conflict and war over land, power, and culture, followed by short-lived times of relative peace and tolerance."

Cameron thought about his father's career in the military, repeatedly quelling raids and incursions by the Caraduan nomads from the unsettled lands to the east, and understood the last point. He pondered Erral's words and recalled his grandmother's mention of the channeling abilities possessed by the Arnorian people. "So, I don't understand why Arnoria's peaceful existence ended, and what does *channeling* have to do with it?"

"In the ancient language, channeling is referred to as ehrvit-daen, though it's more accurately translated as life-channeling. For better or worse, it's what makes the Arnorian people different from Gartannians."

"Arnorians can make those fireballs," Cameron said.

"Yes. But that's only part of it. Ehrvit-daen is about harnessing the energies of nature that exist around us, and not just for violence, but to understand and commune with nature itself. Nature's energies can be channeled in a variety of ways—to augment strength and agility, to interact with your horse, to sense what we cannot see or touch—but it's a gift to be cherished, not abused. To control nature's energies as you saw the Khaalzin do is unusual, and it underpins the corruption that was Arnoria's demise. There was a time when it was unthinkable to use these abilities as a weapon against others."

"Not everyone in Arnoria can do that?"

"Relatively few, and not all who have the ability choose to use it. Many people think it's magic and are understandably wary. And ever since the Khaalzin corrupted the powers of ehrvit-daen to sate their lust for power, the population has become cautious of anyone capable of that kind of violence. But it wasn't always that way."

"How so?"

"The strongest of the Ehrvit-Dinal often held positions as regional marshals. They were fair-minded men and women who enforced the laws and swore oaths to a code of ethical conduct. They were loyal to the family of stewards, your ancestors, in fact, who oversaw all of Arnoria."

"What are Ehrvit-Dinal?"

"They're the men and women with the strongest channeling abilities."

"Are you one of them, one of the Ehrvit-Dinal?" Cameron asked.

"Some would argue that my strength in ehrvit-daen doesn't quite measure up to the standard, though I am one of the Traekat-Dinal, or a tracker, as the people like to call us. We all have abilities in ehrvit-daen to some degree."

"So," continued Cameron, his curiosity piqued, "when we led the horses through the dark forest that night, was that ehrvit-daen?"

"It was. And it's the most common attribute of ehrvit-daen in the Arnorian population. Most are capable to some extent, if they choose to use it."

"I saw a show once at the traveling carnival where a woman was reading people's minds. She called it telepathy."

Erral laughed. "I've heard of those shows, too. But they're just an act, I'm afraid. Ehrvit-daen allows us to sense strong emotions, needs, or desires of moderately intelligent animals, but the stronger minds of men and women are beyond such intrusions. It's most useful with horses and dogs but won't get you very far with less intelligent animals like rabbits and squirrels. The connection can be felt when you're touching or very close to the animal, like riding a horse or petting a dog. You can imagine how connections like that might foster a closeness to nature, the world around us that we would otherwise take for granted. For thousands of years, it fed our desire to remain as devoted stewards of the land."

Cameron was silent for a long time, and Erral granted him solitude to digest his words. It was a lot to take in and strange relative to Cameron's life experiences.

But Cameron was thinking about the strange events in his own life: the stag, whose death throes he had experienced from a distance, and then sensing, even seeing, the Khaalzin's intent during the Callaway raid. He had unintentionally made connections with both, but the events clearly weren't as simple as Erral described. Self-conscious, Cameron chose to keep the experiences to himself, for the time being, anyway.

Back on the trail the following day, Cameron said, "So, yesterday, you said the gods wanted the Arnorian people to have a connection with plants, animals, and the soil. How can you have a connection with plants and soil? They don't have thoughts."

"That's true, but remember, what I said comes mostly from folklore. I've never witnessed anything like that myself, but the emergence of men and women who could commune with the soil, trees, wind, and fire were commonly fabled in children's stories along with mythical beasts like dragons and sea serpents. Such tales were drawn from times long past and most likely originated in the fanciful minds of storytellers. Though I haven't experienced it myself, those stories most likely bear some truth. To commune directly with the energies of nature would be a rare gift, indeed."

"Gram said our family had strong traits, but they still let the Khaalzin take over control of Arnoria."

"That's true, although the strength in your family, perhaps, isn't as strong as it was many generations past. Their success had more to do with a commitment to respectful stewardship and, I suspect, was tied more firmly to the reverence the population held for them. And to this day, the people still hold fast to the hope that your family will return to stewardship.

"And even if ehrvit-daen remained strong in your family, there are always others within the population who have similar strengths. Other family lines possess strong traits, and random emergences of Ehrvit-Dinal within the general population occasionally occur. And it was within these factions, as well as distant relations of the House of Genwyhn, that greed and lust for power grew. But it wasn't until another leader emerged, one who could unite them, that a real threat to the peaceful stewardship over Arnoria arose.

"It was over three hundred years ago that a charismatic man named Tryst Garavet recruited Ehrvit-Dinal within one of the less prosperous Arnorian regions, where an underlying discontent smoldered. Disease and cycles of famine and drought that were beyond anyone's control had taken a toll on the people there. Tryst was cunning, opportunistic, and power-hungry. He gradually wrested power from the regional leaders by making and fulfilling promises of prosperity for the people. His reach over the land grew, and so the reverence for the House of Genwyhn began to dissolve.

"Tryst gradually injected authoritarian controls over the population through his charismatic deception, always justifying his actions in the best interest of the people. His henchmen, now referred to as the Khaalzin, fell to his beguilement. They became his enforcers and enjoyed status and wealth under his leadership. The previous leaders who looked to the House of Genwyhn for guidance to deal with this deception unfortunately received none, as generations of peaceful existence left them unprepared for such an insidious assault on their leadership. Once Tryst's true motives were openly discovered, it was too late for the people to resist.

"Tryst Garavet eventually passed, but authoritarian rule persisted under a succession of repressive leaders. Schools were closed and replaced with regional academies that forcefully recruited and brainwashed children shown to possess strength in ehrvit-daen. Parents struggled to conceal their children's abilities, but it was a difficult task to control the impulses of the young. Open travel between regions was restricted to thwart organized resistance, and oppressive taxation was imposed to sate the regional governors' greed. So the Arnorian people, once content and prosperous, continued to suffer under the Khaalzin's tyranny.

"Members of the House of Genwyhn were gradually forced into hiding, exiled, or killed if they dared to stand against the Khaalzin. Seeing the danger and futility of their situation, many of the heirs bowed to the new authority for the sake of survival and were allowed to live openly with the people. That leniency was abandoned, however, with the Prophecy's emergence."

At the mention of the Prophecy, Cameron looked up as Erral met his gaze.

"You've heard reference to it before, I gather?" Erral said.

"I overheard my grandfather mention it at the cabin."

"What did your grandparents tell you of it?"

"Nothing. They didn't know I was listening."

"Hmm," Erral muttered, then reflected in silence for a long while.

The pause only fed Cameron's curiosity, and his impatience grew. "So," he finally said, "are you gonna tell me what it's about?"

Clearly wanting to evade the topic, Erral paused again before responding. "You have to understand, Cameron, that superstitions, when inflated by longing and hope, can take on a life of their own. There was a time in Arnoria when prophecies were fashionable, and there was no shortage of them. Some predicted events that would come to pass, though mostly by chance, but most were simply forgotten in time. They were usually invented by attention-seekers."

Why is he evading my question? Cameron stared unblinkingly at Erral.

Erral saw the irritated impatience in Cameron's expression, sighed, and finally recited:

"Hope will come where none is known
A seed will bear on winds of despair
Over raging waters fate unknown
Return to us Genwyhn's heir."

Cameron waited, but Erral offered no more. "Is that all? It doesn't seem like much for people to get worked up over."

"That's the Prophecy in its common form. It sums up the original words that predicted the return of an heir of the House of Genwyhn."

"So, that's why Gram gave up hope when my mother was killed? She figured our family's Arnorian blood line was ended."

"Her faith in the Prophecy had waned long before your mother was murdered, I'm afraid."

"But people still remember it. How long has it been?"

"Over seven generations since the words were uttered," Erral said. "I won't deny, the source of the Prophecy is more credible than most, and that, along with people's longing to return to the days of prosperity, has helped it to persist." Erral sighed. "The people still cling to it as a beacon of hope."

"Where'd it come from?"

"An elderly sage on his deathbed. His name was Baron. He was a loyal advisor to the House of Genwyhn for most of his life. According to the story, he was stricken with illness and entered a delirium for several days. Taking no food or drink, he was thought to be in his final hours when his disjointed ramblings became unexpectedly coherent. His attendant realized he was repeating the same phrases over and over and transcribed the words as he remembered them onto parchment. They were the last coherent words the sage would speak in his mortal life.

"The original parchment was taken to Halgrin, the reigning heir of the House of Genwyhn at the time. Halgrin was in exile in Arnoria with his wife and his only child, Althea. One could surmise that the words had a deep significance to Halgrin based on his decision to separate his family. He sent his wife and only child on a dangerous voyage into remote exile in Gartannia, a land he knew almost nothing about. An unknown number of ships carrying Halgrin's wife and daughter, other exiles, skilled tradesmen, and families looking for relief from oppression were entrusted to the dangerous sea. No ship ever returned to Arnoria to report the refugees' fate.

"To his dying day, Halgrin never lost hope for the return of the House of Genwyhn to stewardship over Arnoria. After separating his family, he focused his energies toward consolidating a scattered resistance against the Khaalzin. A clandestine guild of the Ehrvit-Dinal who remained loyal to him was established. It was the beginning of the Traekat-Dinal, the group to which I have devoted my life. They traveled secretly about the land gathering information and forming a network for communication. In the beginning, the Traekat-Dinal sought to organize the Arnorian people to mount resistance and openly face the Khaalzin. But since the passing of Halgrin, they continued their work without a clear forward path.

"And as word of Baron's Prophecy spread, paranoia began to grow in the minds of the Khaalzin. Superstition has always been one of their weaknesses. They began a campaign to destroy any remaining close relatives of Halgrin's line. They were actively searched out and ruthlessly killed by the unconscionable savages. And to further the people's misfortune, the Khaalzin discovered the secret of Althea's passage out of Arnoria. So, generations later, and without knowing whether she had even survived, the Khaalzin's leadership hatched a plan to pursue her heirs across the sea to destroy them.

"So the situation of the Arnorian people has become dire," Erral concluded as they reached the end of the trail through the Northern March, "and many have lost all hope of a return to the days of peace and prosperity. Discontent grows deep roots, but without a strong leader to solidify the patchwork of resistance, the power wielded by the Khaalzin remains insurmountable."

THE CROSSING

On a cool autumn afternoon, Erral led Cameron into the northern forest along an overgrown, little-used trail. The now leafless aspen trees gleamed grayish-white in the sun against the forest backdrop. The trail guided them through the dense, early growth at the forest edge to the progressively maturing older growth forest within. The forest, its floor now blanketed in striking yellow and red maple leaves, transformed around them into mixed hardwoods including oak, elm, ash, and basswood. Stands of hemlock pocketed the forest with their shadowy green ceilings. Deer and other wildlife warily watched the travelers from safe distances. A peaceful quiet overtook the land as the wind shrank to a gentle breeze, and the forest sounds were dampened in the moist air.

The second day in the forest brought thickening clouds and an early, light rain. Erral sensed worsening conditions and guided the horses into a large hemlock stand. The green branches gave privacy and protection from the strengthening wind. They constructed a shelter from the rain and were able to gather enough dry wood to keep a warming fire as refuge from the cold.

Cameron had been thinking about Erral's discussions and had a lot of questions. "How did you come to Gartannia, and how did you eventually find Gram and Gramps?" he asked while the cold rain drizzled down around them.

"That's a long story," Erral said thoughtfully. "But if you'll indulge me, I'll give you a little background first. You recall the history that I gave about the origin of Arnoria and Gartannia. Well, it follows that rumors abounded in the Arnorian population regarding the existence of another land similar to our own and only three weeks' journey across the sea. The prospect of adventure, as you might imagine, enticed more than a few to attempt the crossing. Rare was the sailor who returned from that land to tell about it, and their stories were usually mocked and discounted as fable. But similarities in their stories described an impassable, rocky, and mountainous shoreline. One storied traveler, Lahret Mahnwel, was said to have traversed the rocky shallows along the coast's southern end only to have his ship damaged beyond repair on a rocky shoal. He and his crew returned to Arnoria in an unfamiliar ship. Several embellished accounts of how he acquired that ship and made the treacherous return journey against the prevailing winds circulated for generations. It was presumed, though, that he was rendered aid after eventually finding a friendly port."

"My father told me about the ports and coastal towns in southern Southmoorland," Cameron said. "He's been there before, back when he was still in the militia."

"And it was most likely one of those ports where your ancestors arrived generations ago. But back in Arnoria, we had no information to verify that Althea and the other refugees successfully made the passage or what their fate might have been even if they made landfall. Regardless, plans were laid to send five trackers across the sea after hearing rumors of the Khaalzin making the passage. We built five ships in secrecy, which was no easy feat, inside of a little-known cove hidden within the rocky shoreline of the northeastern realm. It had been carved out of the cliffs by an ancient waterfall and was all but inaccessible by land. The shipwrights lived in natural caverns eroded out of the rock. Resources were scarce, forcing us to transport timber and other materials by sea, and access in and out of the cove was at the tide's mercy. So for eighteen long months our shipwrights and craftsmen labored in harsh elements to finish building them.

"In summer's waning days, the first tracker was finally sent, accompanied by a heroic crew. Each of the others, in turn, was borne at seven day intervals on a different ship. The sea had a reputation for being treacherous and could quickly build massive swells in the unpredictable winds. Even short travels along the coast were dangerous for all but the most seasoned sailors and traders. Safe ports along the eastern coast were few and far between, but regardless, the ships left in the dark hours of night to avoid the scrutiny of unwanted eyes upon the horizon. I was the last of the five to sail.

"For my experience, the passage was as dangerous as we had envisioned. The voyage lasted twenty-three days before we finally sighted land. For the first eight, we sailed with the strong prevailing winds and felt reasonably secure in the newly built ship. But I'll admit, even in the mild weather, the massive swells that we sailed over were daunting. Then, a storm arose, coming on us with incredible force. The swells became enormous and broke at their crests in a fury. The crew brought down the sails in the rising gale, lest they be torn or the masts broken from their footings. The winds changed and swirled around us like we were caught in the middle of a duel between the gods themselves. The swells came from varied directions and would randomly merge with one another only to break in unpredictable torrents. I lost count how many times we pitched and recovered. But three times the cresting waves caught us broadside and rolled the ship, and the masts plunged beneath the surface. The ship recovered twice, but on the third roll, the main mast splintered and remained in the water's grip when the ship righted herself. The deck hands released their safety lines long enough to cut the lanyards, and if they hadn't, the trailing mast would have taken us down for sure.

"After the gale withdrew, the crew rebuilt the mast using sections of timber stowed in the ship's hold. We limped along for three days before the spare sail was rigged.

"We eventually sighted land and sailed up and down the coast to gain bearings, but we saw no signs of settlement. Mountains rose from the coast for as far as we could see to the north and south. I searched for any sign left by the first four trackers but saw no markers from the ship's vantage. I chose a landing site along a broad stretch of beach and came ashore in a small skiff with limited provisions. The ship sailed south where the seas seemed calmer in search of a safe harbor to perform more permanent repairs, but I never heard from them again.

"I found no safe passage inland from that site, so for fifteen days I drifted south along the coast alone in the skiff. Progress was slow and dangerous, but I finally found Caelder by his marks. He had been the fourth tracker to cross and had explored further south along the coast with no other contact, and his way inland was also blocked by sheer cliffs. He described impassable waters just off the coast to the south due to strong currents and rocky shoals hidden under the waves. We headed back north, and after a month found Turk, the youngest of the five. He was the first to cross and had been let off somewhere along the northern coastline. He worked his way south, but like Caelder and myself, had no contact with the other two trackers or any settlements. He nearly perished trying to scale the cliffs in the rough seas to the north and had all but given up hope by the time we found him."

"What happened to the other two?"

"I presume their ships sank in heavy seas, or perhaps they died somewhere along the coast. We never found any signs."

"What about the cliffs and mountains? How'd you get past them?"

"We came ashore at low tide where we were able, but it was never more than a small beach at the bottom of some sheer cliff wall. We stayed warm using driftwood for fires and ate fish or lobsters when we could catch them, but always the cliffs and mountains were impassable. Then on one calm day, we rowed out far enough from shore to see a gap in the mountains, a low pass, but sheer cliffs along that part of the coastline prevented us from reaching it. The walls were broken only by deep crevices eroded by the waves. In our growing urgency, we began to explore the deeper openings in hopes of finding a path up to the mountain pass. We lost one skiff when we were dashed against the rocks, thankfully able to swim back out to safety. But one day, to our good fortune, the sea relented enough to allow us to enter one of the wider openings in the coastal wall during high tide. We timed our entry between swells and rowed as fast as we could through the opening. A wave came in behind us and tossed our skiff deeper into the passage and around a bend probably one hundred paces back into the fissure. The turbulence was immense, and we truly believed it would be our end. But as we were pushed further around the bend, a large stone arch appeared ahead. The skiff overturned in the turbulence, and we swam for the arched opening, hoping to find a safe haven from the deadly waves. It was a cavern, less turbulent, but even so it was like floating in a sloshing bucket.

"We lost most of our supplies, and the skiff was damaged beyond repair. We floated there, bobbing up and down with the waves while we considered our folly. But as our eyes adjusted to the darkness, we saw a lighted opening above us through a narrow fissure in the rock. A ledge wide enough for a foothold was above us. And as the water rose and fell with the waves, Turk positioned himself next to the wall. After countless attempts, he was finally able to place himself close enough to get a handhold when a large swell raised him up to the ledge. He climbed into the fissure and through the opening onto the bluff above. Caelder had fortunately salvaged a rope, and so we were able to escape the cavern with our lives.

"The journey through the pass was difficult with winter fast approaching. Snow already covered the ground where we climbed through the highest elevations, but we eventually emerged into the arid plains of the Western Range. We were grateful, as you can imagine, to find hospitable lands after such a difficult journey."

Cameron was awestruck by the trackers' perseverance, and he listened intently while Erral continued his tale.

"Being in an unknown land, we decided to explore independently for the sake of gathering as much information as possible. Turk went south, Caelder east, and I to the north. A pact brought us back together exactly one year later.

"Turk was the first to catch the Khaalzin's scent during his travels through Eastmoorland. He spent the latter part of that first year tracking their movements and learning their motives. Caelder and I found several small settlements of Arnorian descendants scattered about the land, although most are located in the more isolated regions to the north. Even after seven generations, we found some still wary of strangers and secretive about their origins. Many have forsaken their heritage altogether and just want to live their lives in peace. It took a long time to gain their trust since rumors of the gray riders and their search were already spreading.

"As planned, we met back at our starting point one year later. We had learned that seven Khaalzin were actively searching for one specific family, and we presumed that family to be the descendants of Althea, although we still didn't know whether she survived or where her descendants might be. So we disbanded again with a clearer purpose and a basic understanding of the lands that we now traveled.

"It took another six months before I found the settlement where your grandparents first raised your mother. One of the villagers whom I entrusted with my own secrets finally confided that Althea's descendants had indeed lived in that village for several generations. But your grandparents had chosen to quietly move away with their daughter some years before. Oddly, nobody in the village knew where they had gone. As it turns out, your grandparents were concerned about the attention that Gwen was attracting when she came into ehrvit-daen at such a young age. She was just too impulsive. They knew the rumors of the gray riders and sought to protect themselves.

"After another two and a half years of searching, I found them near Locksteed. I remember that day vividly. It was a warm summer evening, and the townsmen had gathered at the old tavern, like they still do since Marty Fenwick began running it. I found a quiet corner where I could overhear the conversations around me. One man was retelling a story he'd heard from his daughter. A stray dog had wandered near the school during lunch break, and one of her friends coaxed it over to where they sat eating. She described how the girl was petting the dog and somehow got it to perform tricks—rolling over, sitting, and the like. But the odd thing was, she never spoke any commands. The men laughed it off, joking that it must have been a runaway circus dog. But after that, I frequented the town, selling furs and pelts, but it wasn't until the fall market that I finally found your grandparents. I recognized them by their blue eyes.

"They had quietly assimilated into the community while your mother grew and learned to control her impulses. They were happy, and your grandmother felt a sense of freedom from the burden of her heritage. Consequently, they weren't as welcoming as I had expected when I first approached them. In time, they warmed to my presence, and we became good friends. I took it as my charge to watch and protect them from the Khaalzin while Turk and Caelder watched over the settlements and kept an eye on the Khaalzin's movements.

"Our enemies have proven to be very powerful. They've enlisted countless dishonorable men from across the land as spies and henchmen. Though we've been able to watch them from a safe distance, we find ourselves ill-equipped to rid the land of their presence. On two occasions, their searching eyes came too close to Locksteed. I was able to lead them away by planting misinformation in distant villages. Tavern gossip can be a very useful tool."

Erral paused in reflection as if gauging whether to continue. "We've done our best to keep a watchful eye on the Khaalzin, but there were only three of us to watch seven. Six years ago we lost track of one, who, by sheer coincidence, ran across your mother on the road. Her murder was unconscionable, and the circumstances dealt us all a heartrending blow. We had failed our appointed task." Erral paused to collect himself, and he noticed the sullen expression on Cameron's face through the shadows. "Your grandfather and I found them, you know. We picked up their trail and caught up in two days. One Khaalzin and two of his henchmen were camped for the night. The one on guard duty fell asleep, so we were fortunate to catch the Khaalzin in a midnight stupor. So now there are six remaining."

Erral watched Cameron for some reaction, but he simply sat in reflection, unconsciously fingering Gwen's medallion, which he now wore around his neck. Erral could sense something weighing on Cameron's mind, so he prodded him for his thoughts.

Cameron finally opened up. "That day my mother was murdered I felt her fear. I felt her pain. I felt her . . . *dying*. It was like I was there."

Erral's brow furrowed as he contemplated this.

"And that day the Callaways' farm was raided, I sensed the gray rider's intent." Cameron paused, hesitant to continue. "And I could see Jaeblon and myself like I was looking through his eyes."

The furrows in Erral's brow deepened, and he looked at Cameron as if he might glean some rational explanation for this. None came.

PROVISIONS

The clouds thinned after two rainy days. They were both hungry and becoming gaunt through their focused travels. Erral had been considering getting provisions to carry them through the approaching winter and had steered their course to the northeast through the woods toward a small, secluded settlement. The community was predominantly of Arnorian heritage, Erral had informed Cameron. He had developed strong friendships there many years ago but visited infrequently since finding Kenyth and Larimeyre.

The land began to rise and fall before them as their journey continued into gently rolling wooded hills. They came upon a lightly used road winding through the undulating terrain and continued along it to the north. After reaching the peak of a large hill, the view opened to the northeast and revealed a beautiful distant mountain range highlighted in sun and shadow from the midday sun. Cameron pulled his horse's reins to stop her and stared out at the incredible view. He was awestruck, having never seen such a beautiful sight.

"Those are the Calyan Mountains," Erral said. "They extend northwest all the way to the northern sea and to the southeast to the shores of Clearwater Lake. There are a handful of small settlements in these foothills, some originally settled by Arnorian refugees. Despite the long, harsh winters, people have thrived here in relative seclusion, and the number of settlements has grown."

The sun was approaching the western horizon when the men came over a rise, and a small village revealed itself in the distance through the leafless tree line. A narrow river passed through the shallow valley before them, and the sparse dwellings that comprised the settlement were nestled on a wooded hillside just above the river. The flats on the river's near side were used for cropland and pasture. Grazing sheep speckled the landscape in the distance.

They continued along the road toward the dwellings and turned down a long lane lined with apple trees. At the end of the lane stood a cedar-planked house, a stable, and another small building. Two large dogs emerged from the stable as the men approached and began growling and barking menacingly. Cameron instinctively pulled the reins and halted his horse.

A slightly built young woman wearing oversized dirty trousers and a well-worn sheepskin jacket emerged from the stable behind the dogs. She appeared to be about the same age as Cameron. Without a word, she gave a stern look toward the dogs, and they quieted and trotted away toward the house to lay down. She looked back at the approaching men, and Erral pulled his hood back to reveal his face. A warm, glowing smile lit her face when she recognized him. "Errenthal! It's been a long time since you visited us."

Erral dismounted, and the two old friends embraced, exchanging the pleasantries of reunited friends after a long absence. While she spoke with Erral, her eyes occasionally turned toward Cameron as if studying him. They were a striking deep blue color, unique and mesmerizing. Her light brown hair was shoulder-length, windswept, and slightly tangled. Soft cheekbones and a delicate nose appointed her moderately tanned and lightly freckled face, though partially obscured by streaks of dirt. But his attention was drawn to her eyes. They seemed out of place in her otherwise tomboyish appearance. Notwithstanding the striking color, there was something different about her gaze. It was strangely keen and softly penetrating, as if she could see beneath the superficial layer. They weren't the darting eyes of one who looks but doesn't really see, but were focused and steady. Nor were they the common eyes of one who sees only what light reveals. Her intermittent glances toward Cameron seemed interminable, and he felt almost naked while under her gaze.

She could sense his discomfort and turned to him after a cordial pause in conversation with Erral. She offered her hand in greeting along with a genuine and comforting smile. "My name is Alanna," she said with a self-confident air. "I've never seen you with my good friend Errenthal before."

She glanced back at Erral, who ashamedly stepped forward and said, "My manners have evaded me. Forgive me, Alanna. This is Cameron. He'll be keeping my company," and he glanced at Cameron, "as an apprentice for the time being."

Alanna paused, not quite able to hide a brief look of confusion before returning a pleasant smile back in Cameron's direction. "I'm pleased to meet you, Cameron."

She turned back to Erral and asked excitedly, "Did you bring any interesting pelts with you this time?" She glanced at their horses and saw they traveled lightly, and her expression turned to disappointment.

Erral lied, "No, I sold the whole lot in the last town. We're just here for provisions, I'm afraid. But I promise you'll be the first to know the next time I come to the village."

"I'll hold you to that," she replied with a smirk. "I'm sure I would have been able to name all of them this time. I was just finishing chores and getting ready to make dinner. You'll join us, won't you? You both look famished!"

Erral glanced at Cameron, who looked like he had just been offered the prize-winning pie at the midsummer festival. Erral laughed and said, "How could we ever refuse that offer?"

Alanna's bubbly enthusiasm was transparent in her broadening smile, and she bounced back toward the stable. She turned and added, "You can stable your horses in the open stall, Cameron. Father will insist you stay with us for the night."

Cameron looked to Erral for affirmation, and he nodded amusedly. Then, as if reading Erral's mind, she added, "He's down in the fenced pasture checking on the sheep. And you can wash up behind the house before dinner." She disappeared briefly into the stable before heading to the house.

Erral saw the amused and curious expression on Cameron's face. "You should have known her when she was younger." He laughed and added, "She's a wonderful girl, but very talkative. Be discreet regarding our situation." He headed toward the pasture to find Alanna's father, Jared Forsythe.

Cameron stabled and fed the horses, then made his way to the house. Alanna's voice rang out from inside, "There's clean water near the door, and would you please bring an armful of wood in with you?"

Cameron washed and did as instructed, placing the wood in the bin next to the fireplace. It was warm and cozy in the house. He had forgotten what it felt like to have warm shelter since fleeing Locksteed. Alanna was busy preparing the meal in the kitchen where a pot of bubbling stew simmered on the wood stove. Cameron glanced around the room and noticed a framed drawing above the firewood bin, a portrait of a beautiful woman. He saw a strong resemblance to Alanna, but the woman appeared somewhat older. He was just about to ask Alanna who the woman was when she spoke from around the corner in the kitchen. "That's my mother. I drew the portrait after she died three years ago."

Her voice startled Cameron, but he asked in continuation, "What happened to her?" Cameron paused, hoping the question wasn't too forward.

"She contracted a fever. The doctor tried every remedy he could think of, but nothing seemed to help," she said matter-of-factly. "It was especially hard on Father, but at least we still have each other. My older sister lives nearby, but she's married."

Cameron sat in a chair near the fire and reflected on the loss of his own mother. His thoughts soon turned to his father lying in bed with his broken leg and ribs, and he wished he could be there to help care for and protect him. The same rumination often occupied Cameron's mind during periods of quietude in their forced travels.

He emerged from his thoughts and found himself staring blankly at his feet, suddenly aware of the same feeling he had when Alanna's gaze penetrated him earlier. He looked over to see her standing motionless, dinner plates in hand, looking at him. Just before she turned away to finish setting the table, he glimpsed a reflection from the fire in her moistening eyes. She withheld her gaze as she darted back into the kitchen and discreetly blotted her eyes on her sleeve. It was awkward, so Cameron changed the subject. They talked about raising sheep, recent weather, and old stories about their schoolteachers. Her bubbly personality was refreshing.

Jared and Erral returned to the house, and the four ate dinner together. Jared was equally as welcoming and friendly as Alanna. It was evident that they rarely had visitors from outside the area, and Jared prodded Erral for any information about the more routine goings-on throughout the land. Cameron assumed Erral had given Jared some account of their exploits earlier in private, and throughout the evening conversation they carefully avoided any discussion of the circumstances surrounding their journey.

"So, you raise sheep and run a supply business?" Cameron asked Jared.

"Yep. It's the only way to make ends meet. The small building by the stable is the supply store."

"But there's no sign out front," Cameron said.

"It's a small village. Everybody knows it's there. But, unfortunately for you and Erral, I don't have everything you need. I've been planning a run to stock up a few things, so I'll just move it up a couple of days."

"I'm going with him tomorrow, Cameron," Erral said. "You might as well stay and help Alanna with the chores. We should be back by dinnertime."

"Great!" Alanna chirped. "I can show you the sheep." Her enthusiasm drew a smile over Cameron's face.

Early the next morning, Erral and Jared were on their way. It was a chilly morning, and the ground was covered in frost. Cameron noticed that Erral had shaved and was wearing a different riding cloak. *Sensible*, he thought. He had almost forgotten their delicate situation in the comfort of Jared's home. Cameron and Alanna enjoyed one another's company through the day. Her positive outlook on life was evident in her perpetual smile and frequent laughter. She rarely stopped talking, and Cameron willingly drank in her stories and experiences. Nothing seemed to escape her attention, and her intelligence shined through like the full moon on a clear night.

But the attribute that Cameron was most impressed with, and perplexed by, was her keen intuition. He wanted to ask her about it but decided it would be too intrusive, so he left his curiosity to smolder. He considered Erral's description of ehrvit-daen and quietly wondered if she was descended from Arnorian refugees.

Late that afternoon, after finishing chores, they relaxed in the house. After a lull in conversation, Alanna delicately said, "I don't mean to pry, but I could sense something was bothering you yesterday—it's your family. You haven't said anything about them." Her deep blue eyes held their steady gaze toward Cameron.

He looked up at the portrait of Alanna's mother, trying to avoid her penetrating eyes. He had sensed the day before that she somehow knew what was on his mind. He considered his words before replying, not wanting to give away too much information. "My mother died six years ago, so it's just been my father and me to work the farm." He briefly thought about making up a lie but had a strong sense she'd see through it. "He was thrown off his horse recently, and now he's recovering from some injuries. But our good friends are looking after him while I'm gone."

Alanna looked perplexed. "You must have pressing business with Errenthal to have left him. I'm sorry to hear about your mother. How did she pass?" She studied Cameron's face for several moments and could sense his discomfort. "I'm sorry, please forgive me. I can see it's a difficult subject for you."

"Yeah," Cameron replied quietly. It was, and he felt no need to hide the fact.

She stood abruptly and forced a smile to lighten the mood. "Do you want some hot tea? I'm going to make a pot."

Cameron nodded, thankful for the change in conversation. He had grown to like Alanna and felt that he could trust her. He wanted more than anything at the moment to open up and talk about recent events and subdued feelings, but Erral's caution kept his lips tight.

Alanna went to the stove and lit a fire to make tea. She began softly singing to herself while she prepared the kettle. Cameron recognized the melody from deep memories but couldn't make out the words. He listened intently and realized it was a different language. But he retraced the memory of the melody to his mother, who used to hum the same tune when she tucked him in at night or when she was busy doing house chores. It was soothing and pleasant to his ears.

Erva läen danessa tu-fräenla zien
Hue räesh dinarhlen frie täebu he rhåne lehr
Oën hahlret frales rah zien
Fryhshnäen ervahn hē whäenla daloene
Ryl hysmien vhånet durhanen
Yhnarhen Genwyhn a frohse remyt

Ha shyhl bräese nehren tre froën
Niven phör häeshlen divaēse
Nu präenla deu bren vuåla treis
Nehr vhislen go jällsten trez frohlensåf
Ählenfroën rah shïu ne wyenshȯene fre
Hẽ valios lȯ wielense ohsålie prȯfen
Vēsa len weurquuis a mërzen tu-nuevä

Ńïs ha ruentä finisle ynfrȯelish tra
Übriin her wohnensrä nhaēn
Hẽ phuåne hu dïhnehne hu frie
Rah shïue coviële al täewhele
Hoëlse nehne dalåfre ceste

He waited until she finished the song and asked, "Where did you learn that song, and what language is that?"

"It's just an old folk song my mother used to sing. I'm surprised you don't know it, blue eyes," she said with a smirk.

Cameron was slightly startled by the inference but understood her meaning. He was starting to get used to her intuitive insights. "I've heard the melody before, but never the words."

"It's old Arnorian. Nobody uses that language anymore, at least not around here. My mother told me the translated version once when I was young, but I don't remember the words in common language. I just remember thinking the song is so much prettier in the original language. My grandmother told me once that a lot of the old folk songs were still sung in old Arnorian because it's such a pretty language to hear. But so many of those old songs are forgotten now."

"The one you were just singing, what's it about?" Cameron was curious because he recognized the word 'Genwyhn' in the body of the song and secretly wondered if it referred to his own ancestors.

"It's an old legend, or prophecy, I think. I wish I could remember the translation for you. It has something to do with the return of the old stewards of Arnoria. I don't really know much about that except for stories my grandmother used to tell. She always thought it was important to know whom your ancestors were and where they came from because it's such an important part of our identities."

"So what do *you* know about your ancestors?"

Alanna's face lit up with a humorous smile as she recalled, "Grandmother used to brag about how important her great-great-great-grandmother was in Arnoria. She was an adviser to the family of stewards." Her smile broadened. "But I always thought it was ironic that if she was such a great adviser, why did she end up fleeing the land along with the stewards?" She laughed. "But I never mentioned that to grandmother."

Cameron allowed a wry smile to creep over his face. He was briefly intrigued by her ancestral connection to his family, but then considered that most of the refugees who came to Gartannia probably had some sort of connection.

"What about your family, Cameron? What interesting stories do you have about your origins?"

He fought the urge to spill out the stories that his grandmother had told him and Erral's account of Arnorian history, especially Halgrin's story. It would have made for interesting conversation, but his sense of humility and the need for discretion helped to bind his tongue. He simply offered, "I know my mother's side of the family has Arnorian heritage, but my father's family has lived in Southmoorland for as many generations as they can remember." Steering the conversation away from the topic of his mother, he continued, "My father and the other men in the family were mostly military men. They fought against the Caraduan invasions over the years, and occasional regional uprisings. Otherwise, we're just farmers."

He glanced back at Alanna and saw that she was looking a bit sideways at him, scrutinizing him again with that penetrating look. A strange, uneasy feeling crept over him. It felt as if she was reaching inside his mind with invisible tentacles, trying to pry his thoughts open. The sensation then waned. He felt silly for having such a ridiculous idea, but then the feeling returned and became stronger. She was no longer looking at him, but her mind was focused as she absentmindedly adjusted the kettle over the fire on the stove.

His uneasiness grew when foreign thoughts and visions swept into his mind. Cameron ineffectively resisted what felt like an intrusion into his brain, but his instincts sensed a defensive urgency as a subconscious panic threatened to scatter his thoughts. He felt a warmth suddenly fill his chest, and his mind sharpened, quickly focusing through a blurry glow. He was swimming in a sea of thoughts and memories that weren't his own, and he felt simultaneously exposed. He could feel their minds connected. Instinctively, his own thoughts retreated as into a dense fog, hiding from the scrutiny that he sensed. The warmth in his chest washed through his mind like a cleansing wave. Then, as quickly as it came, the intrusion was gone, the entire episode happening in less than five blinks of an eye.

Cameron shook off the disorientation after the fog receded. He looked over at Alanna. She had fallen back and was sitting on the floor several steps away. Her deep blue eyes were wide with a hint of fright, and her face wore an incredulous expression. Unsure of what had just happened, he stepped toward her, wanting to help her up, but she quickly rose and backed away. She crossed her arms to ward off the coldness in the air surrounding Cameron. He stopped. "Alanna," he said softly with a comforting intent, almost questioningly. She looked back at him, the fear erasing from her eyes while a diffuse blush filled her cheeks. She looked toward the door, for a path to escape, and darted away.

Cameron went to the window to see where she went and watched her disappear into the stable. He wanted to follow but knew better. She needed to process and collect her thoughts, as did he. Feeling awkward and stunned by what had just happened, *and what did just happen?* he mindlessly finished making two cups of tea. He wasn't sure just what she had done, but he knew she had initiated it. *She was prying into my mind.* He'd never experienced anything like it before. And he wasn't sure whether he should be angry or amazed, or both.

After a time, he took two deep breaths to calm his nerves and headed out to the stable with the tea. Stopping outside the open stable door, he cleared his throat and softly said, "Alanna, are you alright?" There was no answer so he bent closer to the doorway. "Alanna?" He heard gentle sniffles coming from inside. He crept into the doorway, peering around the frame, and found her sitting on a bench. Her face was buried in her hands, and she appeared to be crying.

"I'm alright," she finally said in a soft, vulnerable voice. She looked up at Cameron with teary red eyes and motioned for him to sit next to her. He moved to the bench slowly and sat, still clutching the cups of hot tea. "I'm so sorry, Cameron . . . and ashamed," she burst out. "I don't know why I do it. Mother and Father used to get so angry with me. They punished me more times than I can count. And I alienated so many of my friends when I was younger I could hardly find anyone willing to play with me anymore." She ran on, barely taking a breath. "Father told me it would get me in really big trouble someday."

The flood of words finally stopped. Cameron sat staring forward, wide-eyed and motionless, still holding the tea and not quite sure what to say. He stretched his right hand in front of Alanna, like a peace offering, and she quietly took the tea. They both sat there, staring straight ahead, and simultaneously sipped from their cups. It was the most awkward moment either of them had ever experienced. They had just exposed their naked minds to one another, however briefly, a result of youthful impulse and inexperience. They were kindred spirits, in a sense, and they both felt surprisingly unburdened by the incident, despite being equally perplexed.

Cameron was the first to break from their trance. A smile started in the left corner of his mouth and spread gradually across until his face was fully involved in silent laughter. Alanna, also realizing the youthful innocence of what had happened, snuck a peek from the corner of her eye at Cameron. His silent laughter was contagious, and the smile spread to her face. She allowed her embarrassment to ease, and they both laughed aloud.

After the laughter abated, Cameron said, "I've never had that happen to me before . . . well, not exactly like that anyway."

"It's an Arnorian trait. At least that's what my grandmother told me. I started doing it when I was only four or five years old."

"How'd you learn to do it?"

"I didn't learn it. It just started happening. My friends used to get creeped out when I knew things that they thought were secret. I finally figured I was some kind of freak when I was about ten."

"What happened then?"

"My grandmother explained it to me. She said other people from Arnoria could do similar things and not to worry about it. She said I was 'rather special' and that I should just learn to control it and not intrude in people's thoughts."

Cameron looked at her with raised eyebrows.

"I know," she said defensively. "You don't have to say it. I didn't always listen to her."

"I wasn't going to say anything."

"Yes, you were."

Alright, maybe I was.

"Some people's minds are easier to get into than others," she confided, "but, until now, nobody ever knew I was doing it. I knew there was something different about you. I felt something when we met. But I couldn't get at it, and it was making me really frustrated." She paused for a moment while considering her next words. "What exactly happened in there? How did you know? And how did you close it off? The air was so cold! It really scared me."

Cameron considered the breadth of his situation. So many things weighed on his young mind. Although he found comfort in Erral's company and considered him a friend, the generation gap created a natural distance in their relationship. He wanted so badly to confide in Alanna and felt almost obligated to do so after the afternoon's events. The biggest problem he saw in that was the possibility of exposing Alanna to the dangers of being entwined in his situation. Ultimately, his need to confide won out, and he said simply, "Ehrvit-daen."

Alanna looked at him quizzically.

The sun was sinking toward the horizon, and Cameron wanted to explain everything to Alanna without being interrupted by Jared and Erral, who were expected home anytime. They layered on more clothing and walked down to the pastures with the dogs. Cameron started at the beginning and explained his plight as it related to the gray riders, including his mother's death. Alanna had overheard rumors about the gray riders but knew little about them. She was enthralled by his description of ehrvit-daen and the limited Arnorian history that Cameron recounted from Erral. He recited the Prophecy in its common form as Erral had told it to him and mentioned that his family was somehow involved with that. He omitted the complicated details of its origin. What he wasn't able to explain, because he couldn't find the right words, was the manifestation of ehrvit-daen that she had witnessed in him during that incident in her kitchen. In fact, he omitted the details of his previous experiences with the same.

Alanna drank in his account. She felt sadness and pity for all that he and his friends and family had been through. She feared for his safety and well-being. But above all, she promised to keep her knowledge a secret.

Erral and Jared were at the house when they returned from the pastures. Cameron helped to unload the wagon before they ate a hastily prepared evening meal. Erral sensed an imminent change in the weather and made preparations for an early departure in the morning. They had a three- to four-day ride to the cabin, depending on weather conditions. Neither Cameron nor Alanna slept much that night, and Cameron welcomed the early start.

Their horses were heavily loaded with sacks of flour and cornmeal, dried fruits, nuts, salt, and seasonings. Other supplies and implements were already stocked at the cabin, assuming thieves or vandals hadn't happened upon the secluded dwelling. Alanna watched through the window while they packed their supplies and ventured outside only when they had finished. She gave Erral a long hug and wished him well. She handed Cameron a woolen cap and blanket and said, "You'll need these to stay warm this winter. I hope you'll come back again. You're always welcome here." Her eyes displayed a sadness he hadn't seen before.

They mounted their horses and sauntered down the lane. The sky behind them was beginning to glow crimson red and orange over the horizon, but to the west, clouds filled the sky. Cameron was saddened to leave Jared's comfortable home, and he longed to be back home with his father. They had gone only a short distance down the lane when Cameron felt a subtle tug on his mind. He opened it, no longer afraid of the intrusion. It required focus and concentration, but he felt the connection. There were no words, but he sensed her sadness at first. A cloudy image of Erral and himself riding away, like in a dream, entered next. Feelings of friendship and longing washed in like ripples in a pond. But as the distance between them expanded, the connection faded, and he felt the sadness again, unsure if it was Alanna's or his own.

THE CABIN

The clouds advanced from the west, bringing with them a chilly headwind. Misty rain and wet snow tormented them for the latter part of the day, giving the wind a deeper bite while they traveled through the forest west and north. They endured the precipitation off and on for almost four days before finally reaching the cabin. Fortunately, the provisions remained dry enough under waxed canvas, and they eagerly unpacked the supplies into the cabin.

The cabin had been built by the trackers in a remote and rugged region of the forest. Being pocked with rocky hills and ravines, the area was rarely traveled, and it was far enough from any settlements that hunters or day travelers would not likely venture there. The log structure had a planked and shingled roof, was small, and boasted a sleeping loft raised above one end of the single room. A stone-and-mortar fireplace sat at the other end and served their cooking needs in addition to warming the small space.

The dwelling had not been used for close to two years. A fallen branch had broken several shingles from the roof, and small forest critters were nesting inside. So they busied themselves cleaning and repairing for several days, and despite the hard work, their moods improved in the warm shelter, and their saddle sores finally had a chance to heal.

The setting was serene. Leaves, still showing hints of yellow and red, blanketed the ground. Water rose from a nearby spring, forming a small creek that snaked a course into an ever-enlarging ravine. Crumbling sandstone rock faces adorned the coarse, wooded topography. Ephemeral ponds filled small depressions, and a larger woodland pond lay placidly not far from the cabin. It provided a stock of panfish and catfish to supplement the small game that they were able to hunt or trap through the winter, though cold stretches made it difficult to break through the thickening ice.

Erral's purpose in coming to this secluded site was twofold. Firstly, he needed to remove Cameron from the immediate danger posed by the powerful Khaalzin. Even in the company of Caelder and Turk, they would be no match against the gray riders' abilities. The power that comes with a command of ehrvit-daen is formidable, and the trackers, although loyal and skilled in their capacities, simply had no hope of defeating the gray riders in a face-to-face confrontation. Erral understood ehrvit-daen better than most but was not endowed with the same abilities as Cameron's ancestors or the Khaalzin, which advanced his second purpose. He knew well that Cameron could not remain hidden forever, nor did he believe Cameron would tolerate seclusion for long. Erral had seen glimpses of something within Cameron that he did not understand, and by his reckoning, the boy shouldn't have any capacity for ehrvit-daen at all. He needed to assess Cameron's abilities and teach him what he could to help him survive on his own.

Many Arnorians held a strong faith in prophecies, understandable given the superstitious nature of people in general. Erral had become a skeptic in that regard and placed very little, if any, hope in the return of an heir of Genwyhn to authority in Arnoria. But he had not always felt this way, and he had taken an oath to protect the family when he was much younger and more willing to lend his countenance to the Prophecy. And he remained faithful in his mission to protect the descendants of the line of stewards who had served Arnoria with such compassion and virtue for so many generations. Whatever Cameron's fate was to be, Erral was compelled by his loyalty to Kenyth and Larimeyre to protect and instruct him at their bidding. And so he focused his energies to that end.

As far as instruction was concerned, Erral proved to be patient and insightful, understanding the youthful tendencies of independence and stubbornness. He kept his lessons varied and incorporated his teachings into their daily activities. He had a knack for surreptitiously creating complications that would require Cameron to learn new skills or to come up with new solutions. Often, Cameron didn't realize that he was being taught but felt more like he was educating himself. After all, what eighteen-year-old can't figure it all out by himself? Much of what he learned was a deeper understanding of the natural world and simple survival skills. Erral also laid the foundation for understanding the movement of heat and energy through the natural world, knowing it would help to guide Cameron in understanding and controlling his rather unique abilities.

"Energy can be stored and changed from one form to another, transferred from one object to another, used to perform work or heat something," he explained. "The food we eat, whether plant or animal, contains stored energies that can be transformed by our bodies into the energies that allow us to move and work and sustain the vital warmth in our bodies. Wood can be burned to transform its stored energy into light and heat. Also, natural imbalances in the physical world create forces that drive seemingly spontaneous events like wind, rain, and lightning strikes, sometimes with extremely violent consequences."

"It's a little weird that I never learned these things in school," Cameron said.

"But your teachers weren't preparing you to survive the Khaalzin. They expected you to be a farmer or a tradesman."

"I suppose," he replied. The knowledge opened his mind to more detailed observations of the world around him and emboldened his inquisitiveness. What this new knowledge didn't provide, however, was a detailed map to harness and control the abilities associated with ehrvit-daen.

Erral explained, to the best of his ability, the nature of ehrvit-daen. "Imagine a web that fills all of space, invisible and unable to be felt by our tactile senses. It fills the air around you and passes through the ground, the trees, your body—everything. It fills all of space and has no physical barriers."

Cameron looked at Erral skeptically. "I have no idea what you're talking about. I don't feel anything like that around me."

"I'd guess that I had that same expression when my mentor explained this to me as a boy," Erral said. "I'll show you an example that might help convince you that such unseen things really exist."

Erral removed two small pouches from his belongings. From the first he removed two fragments of metal and handed them to Cameron. "Bring them close to one another," he instructed.

Cameron slowly brought them together, and he could feel them pulling toward one another as the distance between them closed, ultimately snapping together. He pulled them back apart with some effort and looked at Erral in amazement. "What are these?" he asked.

"Magnets," Erral replied before taking them back and laying them apart from one another on the table.

"I've heard of them. But it's kind of an odd thing to be carrying around with you, isn't it?"

"They're not just instructive, like I'll show you. They can be useful, too." From the second pouch he poured metal filings into his hand, then sprinkled them between and around the magnets. "Have you ever been given phony silver coins as payment?"

"No. Not that I know of." He watched Erral sprinkle the filings onto the table and guessed at once that it was iron. He knew it from the reddish-orange discoloration on some of the particles. The filings arranged themselves in arcing lines, distinctly connecting between the two magnets, and some were pulled directly onto the magnets' surfaces. Cameron looked in amazement as the particles clearly responded to some invisible force.

"If the phony coin has iron in it, like they usually do, the magnet will stick to it. I travel and sell pelts to make a living, so you can imagine I've had plenty of people try to cheat me. That's why I carry them—and they're an amusement for the children in the villages where I stay." He then moved the magnets to a different place on the table and sprinkled salt granules around them. The salt lay randomly distributed, unaffected by the magnets.

"A web, of sorts, exists around the magnets," he explained. "It affects the iron filings in such a way as to betray its presence and show its form, though you and I otherwise have no ability to sense its existence. The salt, like us, is unaffected by it.

"So by extension, consider that there exists a different kind of web filling the space around and within us. Within this web are fluctuations of energy, or something akin to energy, that we aren't aware of without some way to sense them."

"So, I think I see where you're headed with this. The abilities of ehrvit-daen come from the ability to connect with this web of energy, or whatever it is."

"That's right, Cameron, but it also involves learning to channel and concentrate these energies to some useful end. For some it comes easily, like an instinct, but for others it requires training and time. Some of the Ehrvit-Dinal who practiced deep meditation described an awareness of tiny energy fluctuations, like a thousand needles gently prodding throughout their bodies. They found that they could suppress them or draw upon them from the surroundings, and the fluctuations moved freely in and out of them through the web. Such a keen awareness is unusual and requires a depth of concentration that I certainly could never attain. But suffice it to say, like the iron filings around magnets, the Ehrvit-Dinal possess some trait that allows them to interact with this ever-present energy web. Perhaps the gods themselves are imbued with this trait, if you're inclined to such faith. And to take it one step further, perhaps there is some truth to the legends of mythical beasts and the strange powers they possessed in ancient times.

"Also, the ability to interact with or stimulate energies through this web can be passed on to our children in the same way we pass traits like appearance and behavior. There is, in fact, an organ in our bodies that's thought to function for this purpose. As a hunter, you've surely examined the organs of animals that you've harvested. With some small variations, the organs of different animals are basically the same. But in our people, there's something distinctly different inside the chest."

Cameron winced at the thought. "But how could anyone possibly know that?"

"Before the Khaalzin's oppression, there were regional academies where healers would go to develop their skills, and they studied human bodies. But these, along with other intellectual pursuits, have been abandoned since the Khaalzin corrupted the purpose of the academies. Invitations to study at the academies in Arnoria were highly valued, even more than here in Gartannia, and the intellectuals who ran them were greatly respected. It'll take generations to recover the knowledge lost to their corruption.

"I hesitate to mention it, but after the Khaalzin's emergence, an ugly period in Arnorian history saw people, especially children, murdered for those organs. Deranged cults would actually ingest them thinking they could gain the attributes of ehrvit-daen. It didn't work, of course, but the stories remain as a reminder of the ugliness and corruption that can live inside men and women, especially when moral leadership is abandoned."

One other detail of instruction required attention. It had to do with Cameron's shield, given him by his grandmother. Erral waited for a relatively warm midwinter day and asked Cameron to bring the shield outside to a fire he had started away from the cabin. He cut away the leather covering from the shield's face. Doing so revealed the intricately etched emblem of the House of Genwyhn, the tree in full foliage under a watchful eye. It was a masterful piece of artwork. The otherwise bluish-gray metal had been treated in some way that created a greenish hue over the tree's foliage and a darker gray hue over the tree's trunk and branches. It was subtle but rather beautiful. The eye was made from an untarnished, bright silver metal and was inset into the front surface just above the tree.

"This leather cover won't help you anymore. The Khaalzin know your face," he explained.

Erral told Cameron to hold the shield at arm's length and place its face directly into the now raging fire. He did so hesitantly, not advancing it quite all the way into the flame. Erral chuckled quietly, expecting the tentative approach. Cameron expected the shield to quickly heat up and was ready to loosen his grip as soon as the backs of his knuckles felt hot. But surprisingly, the warmth was tolerable, and he inched forward while glancing back to Erral, wondering if his face would betray a practical joke. The air washing around the shield was hot, and he ducked his head behind it to avoid singeing his hair. The shield was getting warmer, but he could still maintain his grip. He finally pulled away as the air became increasingly uncomfortable to breathe.

Cameron flinchingly touched the shield's face and found it to be warm. "This can't be made of steel," he said. "Steel would be too hot to touch, and heavier." He turned the face toward him to get a better look and noticed the inset that formed the eye in the emblem was faintly glowing white. He gently touched the eye, then reflexively jerked his hand back. It was extremely hot.

Erral took the shield in his hands out of curiosity. "I wish I could show you the subtleties of its use, but I don't possess the abilities to take advantage of it." He weighed it in his hands and absentmindedly felt around its surface. "Larimeyre revealed it to us years ago. But the legends of shields like this are obscure and mostly forgotten. Caelder and Turk were courageous enough to test its capabilities, though." He smiled as he recalled some old memory. "It was a foolish thing, but Turk was still quite young." He laughed but didn't elaborate any further.

"But it isn't just a defensive armament," Erral continued. "The Ehrvit-Dinal who master its use can mount a rapid and powerful counterattack. It somehow enhances the ability to channel energies, both to disperse and to focus. And you're right about the metal, it isn't steel but rather a rare metal alloy. The inset isn't just an adornment but is integral to the shield's function, although I honestly don't understand how it works."

Cameron thought back to the day the Callaway farm was attacked, recalling the burn that he suffered from the gray rider's assault. Perhaps the shield would have protected him.

Erral handed the shield back to Cameron. "The process of forming these metals was commonly thought to be alchemy, but there wasn't anything magical about it. Very talented metal smiths worked with experts who somehow extracted and refined rare metals from the ores mined out of the mountain ranges in Arnoria. Items like this are quite rare, and I fear the knowledge that led to their making has been lost through generations of oppression. Keep this shield close, Cameron, it could very well save your life."

Erral thought long and hard about how he might further instruct Cameron. So far, Cameron had never voluntarily channeled energy. His only experiences were subconscious or instinctive in a moment of excitement or fear. Given that his heredity was atypical, Erral wasn't sure if Cameron would even have the capacity to voluntarily channel energies or safely control them. Normally, the Arnorian people would come into their abilities as children, if so endowed, and would learn to use and control them through intuition and experimentation. He was in unexplored territory and had no map to guide his instruction. He couldn't teach Cameron directly, but perhaps he could help him along the path to discover his own channeling abilities. He devised a strategy and implemented it early in the winter.

"Do you remember the night we fled Locksteed, when we rode through the forest to the north of your home in the dark?" he asked.

"Of course."

"Kenyth told you to guide your horse, and I sensed that you must have felt some connection there."

"I did. She responded to me."

"Good. We'll use that as a starting point. Horses are probably the easiest animals to work with. You'll need to refine and strengthen that talent before we can move on."

They went to Cameron's horse since he had already made some level of connection with her before, and Cameron had no difficulty opening his mind to her. He knew from his short time with Alanna what the connection should feel like, though the mare's mind was far simpler than Alanna's. He commanded the mare, but she made no response.

"I don't think she understands," Cameron said.

"Remember, you can't use words or phrases. Language is beyond her. You have to learn from her mind what she'll respond to. You have to show her your will and urge her toward an action. Provide her with mental images."

"I'll give it a try." He spent a long time with the mare that day and eventually felt her growing weary of the exercises. But he had made progress. His concentration had improved, and his bond with the mare had grown.

"Tomorrow, work on conveying emotion and praise. I think you'll find that she responds even better. They're not so different from humans in some ways."

His mental focus sharpened with more practice over subsequent days, and he enjoyed the exercises so much, he spent more and more time with the horses. Ultimately, adapting that focus to enable Cameron to voluntarily channel energy was Erral's hope. But despite his efforts, conventional and innovative, he was unsuccessful by winter's end. He had, however, been successful in teaching Cameron other skills. Joseph had taught him basic military swordsmanship, and Erral built on that foundation with a more refined approach, focusing on agility, balance, quickness, and even some dirty tricks to use in a pinch. He taught him to use a wooden staff, a knife, a tree branch, or even a rope to defend himself. He passed on what knowledge he could, but the rest would be left to fate.

Erral kept Cameron occupied as best he could, knowing the isolation from his family and friends would be difficult. Regardless, Cameron increasingly longed to be home. Joseph would hopefully be fully healed by the end of winter and relearning to walk. But he knew his father would not be able to plow and plant the crops on his own. He would have help from the Callaways, but it wasn't enough to assuage the guilt stemming from his absence.

The unfairness of his situation nagged at him, and a smoldering anger had been growing in his gut. The insanity of being targeted with such hatred simply because of a remote ancestral connection was difficult to digest. He had been separated from family and friends through no action or fault of his own. How could the Khaalzin consider him to be a threat? Why was he hunted like a rabid dog and living in an isolated corner of the woods away from his family? He was forlorn, and Erral knew it but offered no immediate remedy. Even worse, Cameron could think of no solution other than to face the Khaalzin openly and accept his fate. Then he thought of his grandparents. They were hunted as well. Who would look after them? And then he thought of his mother, and the anger swelled in his heart. It was hidden away in a deep place all those years. After all, he had nowhere to direct it. He had been kept ignorant of those responsible, but now he knew.

It was a warm day in early spring when a spark of hope came to Erral's eyes. The snow was melting, and green and red buds were beginning to appear on trees. Erral was away checking traps while Cameron prepared to straighten a bundle of arrow shafts. He had been collecting shoots and branches through the winter, and one bundle was dry enough to work on. His grandfather had taught him the art, explaining that certain wood types would soften under heat and reharden after bending and shaping. The difficulty was in applying the right amount of heat over a fire without burning or weakening the wood. So in his isolation, Cameron found a useful purpose for his shield. He found that if he laid it in the fire for several minutes, the eye inset would get hot enough to provide a convenient heat source to bend the shafts without charring the wood. The rest of the shield was quite warm but would not burn him while he manipulated the wooden shafts over it. He even wondered if it was invented for this purpose because it worked so well.

But it was one of those mornings where everything seemed to go wrong or be more complicated than it should be. Earlier, he had pulled on wet boots because he had forgotten to put them in front of the fire the night before. A melting snow sheet fell from the roof onto his head when he closed the door coming outside, and the damp firewood required multiple lightings before he had a workable blaze. But the thing that dampened his mood the most was his persistent rumination over his desperate situation and exile from his family. So when he pulled the shield from the fire and laid it faceup over two nearby logs, he was not as careful as he should have been.

He set to work laying an arrow shaft over the hot inset and gently pressed his weight down over the two ends, straightening the slight bend. The logs supporting the shield shifted under his weight, and he toppled forward. He would have regained his balance, but one foot caught on a branch lying on the ground, and he instinctively reached forward to catch himself as he fell. His hand came down on the shield directly over the hot inset. He realized too late, and the searing hot pain in his palm reminded him of the day's ongoing wrath. He reflexively pulled his hand back while momentum carried him forward and onto the ground, coming to rest with his face nearly in the fire. He smelled the foul odor of singed hair as he rolled away, letting loose a litany of expletives he barely remembered he knew. And he broke—the restraint on his temper fractured like a glass barrier under too much strain.

Cameron got to his feet and kicked the branch, but the tantrum had too much fuel to end there. He grabbed the bundle of shafts and launched them into the woods, then the shield headed toward the ravine. The burning firewood, in turn, scattered over the ground when he brought the smaller of the two logs to bear on the fire pit. Then, having run out of objects to throw, he cursed and stomped toward a pine tree in front of the cabin. He snatched a large pinecone from the ground and threw it at the cabin door. Three more followed in rapid succession, but the flood of anger continued to swell inside. And with the final flurry of his tantrum, he grabbed the last pinecone in sight and mustered all the strength he had to obliterate it against the door. He felt the warm sensation in his chest and the burning in his injured palm as he let it fly, and a split second later it exploded in flames against the door.

Cameron stood wide-eyed and mouth agape, staring at the cabin door engulfed in flames. The sight was sobering, and his emotions quickly evolved from anger to amazement to fear. *The cabin was burning!* He gathered snow from the ground and threw it against the flames. It had no effect, so he tried rubbing snow against the burning wood. After three handfuls, he finally extinguished the fire. And he stood there, dumbfounded, staring at a perfectly round charred scar on the cabin door.

Across the open space behind him, the horses stood calmly where they were tied and stared at Cameron while chewing bark they had nibbled from a nearby tree, indifference and amusement in their eyes. Then their heads turned simultaneously, as if choreographed, to see Erral emerging from the woods carrying a dead raccoon in one hand and a trap in the other. Their gaze followed him while he strode around the cabin's front, taking in the unexpected scene. His stride never broke or varied, and he made no comment. He just kept walking past Cameron, who stood facing the charred door, awestruck and still holding handfuls of dripping snow. Had Cameron turned to look, he would have caught the amused smile on Erral's face as he walked past and down to the creek to clean the raccoon.

Erral thought, *That's progress, I suppose.*

DISCOVERED

Spring arrived in full splendor. The snow had finally melted even under the densest shadows darkening the forest floor, and the brilliant white trillium blooms were opening, blanketing patches of the leaf-strewn ground. Both Erral and Cameron were restless from their winter captivity, but Cameron was feeling especially eager to return to Locksteed, no matter the risk.

"I need to go home," he said one morning. "I can't keep hiding here while my family and friends are still exposed to the Khaalzin. I just hope they haven't harmed anyone else since we left."

Erral made no attempt to disagree but held a pensive look before saying, "I won't try to stop you, Cameron. I've been thinking about what our next step will be, and I must admit that I've had no great revelations." He paused again in thought. "We'll need to proceed carefully. Rushing into danger without a plan and without the aid of our allies would be foolish at best. I understand your frustration, but you need to be patient just a little longer. I need to meet with Turk and Caelder, or at least get word to them if we intend to move from here."

Cameron let out an agitated sigh and buried his face in his hands. "I can't wait here any longer! We can look for them on the way to Locksteed!"

"Let me consider our options, Cameron. Finding Turk and Caelder may prove difficult. I had expected one or the other to come here with the arrival of spring, hopefully with some knowledge about the Khaalzin's movements or intentions. We'll be better prepared for a journey if we at least know what they're up to." Erral knew there was little to gain from remaining in hiding. He had taught Cameron what he could, and it appeared that Cameron wasn't likely to gain a useful command of his energy-channeling abilities any time soon, if ever. Even after the burning door incident, he had not been able to make any progress with Cameron's command of ehrvit-daen.

But the arrival of Turk the following afternoon made any further deliberation unnecessary. Cameron returned from hunting to find a third horse tied out front of the cabin, and upon entering, Erral was sitting at the small table talking with a man Cameron had never seen before. He was several years younger than Erral, tall, and sported a thin and wiry build. His facial hair was sparse but matched his nearly shoulder-length, dark-brown hair.

Erral introduced Cameron to Turk, who graciously stood to shake hands. Brilliant blue eyes contrasted sharply with his other features, though his eye contact with Cameron was brief. Cameron pulled up a stool to join the conversation. Turk's attire was similar to Erral's and Caelder's, and the only weapon he carried visibly was a large, plain hunting knife that hung from his belt.

Erral said, "We were just discussing your grandparents, Cameron. Caelder was able to find them last fall after our chance meeting in the Alurien highlands. They were pursued by two Khaalzin and forced to make their way to another woodland retreat north of Locksteed. Caelder spent a good part of the winter with them."

Turk added, "Travel was nearly impossible in that area for most of the winter. They were snowed in early, and the snow just kept coming and coming all winter. They were stuck, but it also kept the Khaalzin from moving freely. From what I could tell, the Khaalzin spent most of the winter further south."

"What about my father and the village? Have you heard anything?"

"I haven't been there myself, but I haven't heard of any disturbances since you fled. I do have contacts who've traveled near there, and I'm sure they would have told me if anything was amiss."

The news was comforting to Cameron, although he had hoped for more direct information. "So, if the Khaalzin are in the south, we should be able to head back and meet up with Gramps and Gram."

"I wish it were that simple, Cameron," Turk said. "They *were* in the south, but with the end of winter, the Khaalzin have renewed their search. Their mercenaries are roaming the north already." Turk was holding a narrow leather strap in his hand and began fidgeting with it while looking down at the table. "But, Caelder plans to bring your grandparents to this cabin. It's more remote and better hidden than the other retreat. I've come to enlist Errenthal's help in drawing the Khaalzin's eyes away while they make the journey here."

Erral's expression grew concerned. "Are you sure it's worth the risk of traveling in the open? They may be better off staying where they are for the time being."

Turk wound the leather strap into a coil in his fingers, and his knee began to bounce up and down. "It may be risky," he said, "but Caelder thinks it's the best option right now. The plan's already in motion, and Caelder's counting on us to follow through. We should leave tomorrow morning. You should be safe here, Cameron, until Caelder and your grandparents arrive."

Cameron was more than eager to be reunited with his grandparents, but Turk's edginess left him with an uneasy feeling. Maybe there was more danger surrounding Caelder's plan than Turk wanted to let on.

Erral sighed and finally conceded, "It sounds risky, but perhaps together we'll stand a better chance against the Khaalzin. If Caelder is counting on us, then we have no choice anyway. So, what's your plan? What does Caelder need us to do?"

Turk laid out the plan. He and Erral would travel back toward the other retreat, stopping to scout the few small settlements along the way and plant misinformation about the family's location. If the Khaalzin or their mercenaries were about, the trackers could do whatever was necessary to ensure the safety of Kenyth and Larimeyre.

Turk remained somewhat aloof into the evening, and Erral packed his gear to prepare for the journey. Both men retired early, anticipating a predawn start.

Cameron remained at the cabin, dreading the isolation. Winter had been difficult enough even with Erral's company. But the prospect of seeing his grandparents lightened his heart tremendously. He tried to keep busy to pass the time. In addition to going about his daily routine, he took some time to pack his traveling gear and the few provisions that remained. He wanted to be ready in the event Turk's plan failed, requiring a rapid exit when Caelder and his grandparents arrived.

His anticipation and hopefulness for their arrival was difficult to contain. The day after Erral and Turk left, he went out to search the surrounding woods for healthy branches and shoots to make arrow shafts as he often did to distract himself from his worries. He didn't really need them since he had gathered plenty before, but walking was therapeutic. He had wandered a good distance to the west of the cabin when a subtle uneasiness crept into his mind. He stopped to scan the woods, listening for any sounds, and then a sudden movement to the west caught his attention. It was a large bird taking flight from a tree in the distance, just over a small sandstone ridge that crossed in front. He recognized it as an owl when it flew overhead. *That's odd, they usually fly away when I spook them.* Perhaps a predator had wandered nearby, and his curiosity got the better of him. The ground was obscured from his sight beyond the ridge, so he crept forward, crouching in his approach to the crumbling sandstone face.

Cameron slowly raised his head above the ridge face until his sightline exposed the ground beyond. He froze, and his heart was paralyzed mid-beat when his gaze fell upon two gray-cloaked figures in the distance. One was on horseback, and the other had dismounted, now crouching down on one knee to examine the ground. He could just make out the soft sound of their voices when they spoke to one another. The man on the ground pointed in Cameron's general direction after looking up—the direction of the cabin!

As the gray-cloaked figure mounted his horse, Cameron roused himself from the shock and ducked his head back down. *They're following Turk's trail.* The revelation struck him like a hammer. He turned to scan the terrain that lay between him and the cabin. He crept away, making as little noise as possible, and headed toward a shallow ravine to avoid their line of sight. He skirted around another elevation, then ran toward the cabin. His thoughts were racing by the time it came into view, and he considered the likelihood that the Khaalzin had picked up Turk's trail and had been tracking him for who knows how long. *And why had Turk been so edgy?*

There was an urgency in his movements, but he kept his wits while he untied the horse and led her to the front of the cabin. He saw the scorch mark on the door and realized he had marked himself. The gray riders would know, and they would pursue him doggedly. He had to fly as fast as he could. He quickly saddled and secured his packs to the horse, thankful he had at least partially packed the bags before. He was halfway mounted when he remembered the shield and Erral's words—*Keep this shield close, Cameron, it could very well save your life.* It was propped against the cabin wall. He had it in hand in a moment, mounted the horse, and trotted away to the east.

The mare sensed his excitement and wanted to speed on, but he initially held her back. If the gray riders heard her pounding hoofbeats, they would be on him immediately. He needed to get some distance between himself and his pursuers before letting her run. Every moment counted.

He needed only to get away from the cabin unseen. They would need to find and follow his trail. It would take time. Though once they found the cabin, it wouldn't take long to see the signs of his hasty retreat. His mind fought against panic, and he struggled to keep his composure. But it was enough to calm the mare. His neck soon ached from repeatedly looking over his shoulder, certain he would see them in pursuit. But his luck held. He saw no sign of his pursuers.

When he felt the distance was enough, he let the Sanduin open her stride, and he guided her to the east through the sun-drenched forest. He knew the nearby terrain, but as they ranged further from the cabin, his progress was slowed by the ridges and ravines punctuating the landscape. He subconsciously headed in a southeasterly direction, the way they had come to the cabin before winter. His mind was focused on escape, not where he would ultimately go. He glanced behind frequently at first, dreading the gray-cloaks' appearance, but they had not come fast enough to catch up with him yet.

Dusk arrived and travel became impossible under a moonless sky. He was forced to stop lest his horse suffer a leg injury on the rough terrain. The only consolation was in knowing the gray riders would not be able to follow his trail in complete darkness, and they would stop for the night as well so as not to lose it. He pulled the wool blanket and cap out of his pack and wrapped himself up, but the familiar sensation against his skin scarcely eased the bitter bite of loneliness.

As soon as dawn arrived, he was on the move, walking and guiding the horse in the dim early light. After a short time, he was back in the saddle and moving quickly through the forest. The land was leveling off, and the ridges and ravines were left behind. His pace quickened, but Cameron's fear and dread remained. And he had never felt so alone.

He knew the trail he left behind in the soft ground would be easy for the gray riders to follow, so he pushed onward with little rest. The time spent over winter building a strong mental connection with his horse was paying off. He knew how far he could push her without risking exhaustion or injury. By the end of the day, he recognized the landscape not far from the tiny village where he had met Alanna. He guessed that the trail leading into the village wasn't far, so he pushed forward despite the passage of dusk into darkening night. The late push paid off, and he turned toward the village on the familiar trail.

Cameron considered the next step in his escape, but he was uneasy and torn with conflict. He still had several miles to travel along the trail before he would reach the village. He struggled the entire time with indecision about stopping at Jared and Alanna's farm to beg for supplies or just passing by to avoid exposing them to his danger. Ultimately, desperation overshadowed caution, and he steeled himself to stop.

The trail descended into the village and followed the swollen river's course. He recognized the lane heading up the hillside to Alanna's home but continued a short distance beyond to the wooden bridge that crossed the narrow river to the pasture. He realized he was probably being overcautious, but fresh hoof marks going straight to Alanna's door was an unnecessary risk. He left the mare in the fenced pasture to graze and jogged back across the bridge to the lane.

Cameron approached the house along the footpath, blending his footprints with Jared and Alanna's, and found the windows dark. A sudden outburst of barking took him by surprise and scared him nearly out of his boots. He stumbled and fell away from the noise as the glowering canines advanced on him. He regained a smidge of composure and reached his mind out to calm them. It seemed to work because they stopped barking, but one continued with a low, insincere growl, letting him know it would take more than that to completely ease its mind. He whispered to the animals, hoping they might recognize his voice, and gently got to his feet, then offered his hand out for them to sniff.

Candlelight glowed through the window of the front room now, and a shadowed figure was looking out. Then came Alanna's muffled voice, "Who's there? I can see you out there!"

"It's me, Cameron," he said, hoping his voice wasn't carrying too far. "I need help, Alanna."

He watched the shadow move from the window, and the front door cracked open. "Cameron? Is that you?"

"Yeah, it's me. Please, can I come in?" His voice was desperate. And then the familiar touch of her mind on his reassured him that she had not forgotten him. The dogs trotted away while Cameron went to the door. Alanna's hand reached out and grabbed his sleeve, then pulled him into the house. In the candlelight, her eyes instinctively went straight to his, as she had a habit of doing, like she would pry every detail from him before he could open his mouth to speak.

"What are you doing here, and at this time of night? What's wrong? Are you in trouble? Where's Erral?" Her voice was increasingly frantic as she unloaded the barrage of questions. "Come in and sit. You look exhausted," she continued, not giving him even a moment to respond. She led him into the next room to sit by the fireplace and tossed in some wood to strengthen the dying flames.

"Is your father here? I should tell him everything too."

"No. He left yesterday with the big wagon to restock supplies from Clearwater. It's two days travel each way."

"I don't know if I should have come here, Alanna. I don't want to put you in any danger. They're after me, the gray riders! They found the cabin early yesterday, and I just got away before they saw me. If it wasn't for that Sanduin mare, they would've already caught me."

Alanna stood and went to the front window to peer into the darkness. "Where's your horse, Cameron? How far behind are they?"

"She's down in the pasture, and I'm not sure how far behind they are. I left in such a hurry. I didn't have time to pack much food, and there are some other things I'm gonna need. I'm sorry for this, Alanna, but I just stopped long enough to see if you could help me. I don't have any coins or anything to trade."

Satisfied that all was quiet outside, she returned to Cameron. She knelt beside him and propped her right arm over his knee, gaining a vantage to gaze into his panicked eyes. "They can't possibly be tracking you in this darkness," she said while studying him. Alanna saw the desperation in his eyes. She peered deeper, and Cameron felt it, but he had neither the strength nor the will to close his mind to her. She saw the fear and loneliness within him, but she also sensed his exhaustion, not that his appearance wasn't enough to give it away.

"You're exhausted, Cameron, and I'm sure the Sanduin is too. You need to sleep." She rose and went into the bedroom to change out of her nightgown and robe.

Cameron slouched into the chair to wait and let his mind settle while soaking in the fire's warmth. Alanna returned with an armful of bedding and propped a pillow behind Cameron's head, then covered him with a blanket. "You rest and I'll put some food and supplies together."

"I should help," Cameron said, then started to get out of the chair. He felt the weariness in his legs. Alanna pushed him back down and froze him with a glare. Her command came to him, but her lips never moved: *Stay there and sleep!* And he wasn't prepared to argue with that.

When Cameron woke, daylight was streaming in through the windows. He shook off the confusion that comes with leaving a deep slumber, and panic immediately filled his mind. "What time is it?" he asked, jumping to his feet.

"It's just shy of midmorning. I tried waking you earlier, but you were sleeping too deeply." Alanna rose and walked to the fireplace, picked up a covered plate, and set it on the table next to a bread loaf and butter. "Go wash up. I made bacon and eggs."

"I don't have time, Alanna! It's so late! I need to get moving!" He ran from window to window and looked outside for any signs of the gray riders.

"You need to eat, Cameron. Just sit down and eat something before you go."

He ran out the front door and into the yard and peered toward the pasture. The Sanduin was nowhere to be seen. He pushed his fingers through his hair, grabbing and pulling at large clumps. "I need to find her!"

Alanna was behind him, clearly growing frustrated. She grabbed his arm and spun him around. "Listen to me!" she yelled, pushing her hands into his chest as an exclamation. "Cameron! You need to take care of yourself. Starving and exhausting yourself won't help you against those gray riders. You might as well just finish yourself off and save them the trouble!" She whirled around behind him and shoved him again, this time toward the open door. "Your horse is in the stable, fed and watered, which is what you're going to do right now." She added a final shove toward the house for emphasis.

Cameron was more than uneasy about the lost time, but he conceded to her demands. He had forgotten his hunger in the rush to escape the gray riders. He washed and quickly ate the breakfast while Alanna saddled the horse and secured his packs. She had filled them with food and other necessities for travel. She led the mare from the stable just as Cameron was coming out of the house.

"I can't say enough to thank you for this, Alanna. Your friendship means more than you know. I'll pay you back someday, but I need to figure this out. Everyone around me's gonna be in danger until then."

"You never told me what happened to Errenthal. Why isn't he helping you?"

"He went to help my grandparents. They were being chased too. I don't know how to find him, other than going back to the cabin and waiting. But I can't risk it now."

"Where will you go?"

"I have no idea, just away for now."

"Be careful, Cameron," she said while giving him a firm hug.

Hoping he still had a lead on the gray riders, Cameron mounted the horse and headed down the lane. But before he made it even halfway to the road, his fears were realized. A gray-cloaked man on horseback, apparently waiting there to make a dramatic appearance, sauntered into the open from behind a hedgerow. Cameron halted his horse next to an apple tree and scanned the area for the second gray rider, but he remained hidden. The rider continued his slow advance toward Cameron until his scruffy bearded face was in plain view. A devious yet arrogant smile crept over his face, distorting his features. He pulled his hand across the front of his neck, stretching the collar of his cloak to expose a recently healed scar on the left side of his neck. Cameron's sword tip had left the gash just a few months earlier.

"Remember me?" the man said as his smile morphed into a scowl.

"No, but I will now that I see your ugly face," Cameron replied with a worried glance back at Alanna. "I only wish it had gone a little deeper." He glanced to the east to see if the way was clear, but the gray rider surmised his plan.

The rider quickly raised his right fist in a signaling gesture. "I wouldn't do that, boy!"

Alanna screamed. Cameron turned in time to see the second gray-cloaked man overtake her from behind. They briefly struggled, and he quickly subdued her with a knife held to her throat.

"Alanna!" Cameron watched in horror but soon realized the man wasn't going to harm her, at least not yet, but she was clearly being held as his bargaining chip. "What do you want?" he said vehemently, turning back to Scar-neck.

"You know what I want, boy. The question is, how badly do you want the girl to live?" The rage in the man's voice was palpable.

"How do I know you'll let her go if I give myself up?"

The gray rider's rage escalated. "You won't know! And you aren't in a position to bargain." He paused while his horse danced in place nervously, and his temper briefly softened. "I don't care about the girl, and killing her won't give me what I want, if that makes you feel any better."

Cameron looked back at Alanna, helpless in the Khaalzin's grasp. Seeing no other option, he dismounted. He couldn't live with himself if any harm came to her.

Alanna watched him, and her expression melted from terror into helpless pity. "Cameron, no!" she cried, her voice trailing off into a whimper.

Cameron stepped away from the horse and bent down to his knees. "Just let her go, if there's any shred of humanity in you."

Scar-neck dismounted and drew his sword. He strutted over and stood before Cameron, then gloated contemptuously over his prize. "As you wish, my lord."

Alanna watched the scene in horror. She couldn't accept this. She *wouldn't* accept this! She forced her emotions to ascend out of pity, to disgust and hatred, and then to rage. She looked over to the Sanduin mare, and with a fury she'd never felt before, she cast her will to the animal. Then her gaze focused on the shield and sword strapped to the saddlebag, blistering an image into her mind.

Cameron knelt before the gray rider with thoughts of his family and friends filling his head, not wanting his time with them to end this way. But he could reconcile his death with the understanding that the world was guided by forces far beyond himself. He wasn't afraid to die, but knowing that his decision to come here had put Alanna in mortal danger was unbearable. Then, with no warning, a painful flash struck his mind, and he knew it was over—*or was it?* The flash split through his thoughts and materialized into an image—his shield and sword—and in that brief moment he felt Alanna's presence in his mind. *It was a message.*

Alanna harnessed what remaining strength she had and focused her mind toward her captor just as the Sanduin charged forward at Scar-neck. The sudden equine assault startled the man holding her, creating just enough distraction for her to find an opening. She pried into his thoughts in her rage and inflicted a searing pain. His head felt as though it would explode. He unknowingly dropped the knife, fell to the ground screaming, and held his hands to his head as if to keep it from coming apart.

Scar-neck, readying himself to execute Cameron, was savoring his victory when the Sanduin charged. She reared back after two strides and brought a flurry of hooves down upon him. Cameron lunged for his sword and shield, now bound to the packs Alanna had secured to the mare, but lost his grip on the sword when the horse sped on. Scar-neck rolled to safety, suffering only bruises from the mare. Cameron saw the second gray rider writhing in agony while Alanna ran toward the shed, and holding only the shield, he stood to face Scar-neck.

Scar-neck glowered and approached with an arrogant stride. They circled one another while Scar-neck prodded at Cameron like it was a game. Then he attacked with a flurry of blows from his sword. Cameron managed to block or dodge them all, but he knew his disadvantage. He looked around for something, anything to use as a weapon. His sword was with the horse over a hundred paces away, and he dared not turn his back on his enemy. He blocked several more blows when an arrow whizzed past. Alanna had taken a bow from the provision shed but obviously had no experience using it. She fumbled another arrow while trying to nock it, finally succeeded, and fired a second wild shot.

Scar-neck was enraged. He assaulted Cameron with increased tenacity. Somehow, and likely owing to Erral's training, Cameron continued to block the barrage. He saw an opportunity and lunged at Scar-neck, knocking him back with the shield. Scar-neck regained his composure, and Cameron could sense the strength of ehrvit-daen in him. A fiery light began to smolder in Scar-neck's left hand. He dropped the sword and cupped both hands around the flame. Cameron instinctively backed away, putting himself between Alanna and their enemy as the cold air bit at his exposed skin.

"Get out of here, Alanna!" he yelled to her just as she released another arrow. It flew toward its mark but splintered and scattered in a shower of sparks when Scar-neck blocked it with the fiery orb. He quickly recovered and threw the orb with a diabolical fierceness, and Cameron braced himself.

He felt the impact and heat after instinctively moving the shield to disperse the blow, then turned around to see if Alanna was alright. She had fallen to the ground and covered her face with one arm but appeared uninjured. He took stock of his own body and found no burns or injury. The shield felt light in his hand. He tilted the face toward himself briefly to see the inset eye glowing with an intense white light, far brighter than he had seen after putting it in the fire. He felt an unusual strength and mental awareness while he held the shield back in front of his body.

Scar-neck was furious. His eyes were demonic, and he strode forward while preparing another fiery attack. Cameron backed up even further, where he could more easily protect Alanna from the next assault. Again it came with a vengeance while Cameron held the shield in defense. This time the heat was more intense, and Cameron felt the energy spilling over from the shield into him. He felt the heat in the air, and his instincts allowed him to draw upon it. His thoughts and senses were intensely sharpened, and when he looked toward Scar-neck, he saw a subtle, shimmering disturbance in the air along the path the fireball had taken. The energy within him was overwhelming, ready to burst out like an overburdened dam. He instinctively focused a path along the disturbance to guide his response to this senseless attack. The stream of energy that unleashed from the shield's inset eye was both blinding and deafening. It followed the path set in Cameron's mind like a lightning bolt, finding its mark in the center of Scar-neck's chest. The look of disbelief was etched into his face even before he fell to the ground, and Scar-neck had seen his last rising sun.

Cameron felt searing pain in the hand holding the shield, and he reflexively threw it to the ground. He looked over to where the second gray rider had fallen. He was gone! Cameron fetched Scar-neck's sword and searched around and in the buildings, but the man had fled. He returned to Alanna to find her standing over Scar-neck's body. She was looking down at the corpse in shock, and a subtle trail of smoke rose from the smoldering wound on the man's chest.

"Why is this happening to you, Cameron?" Her eyes flooded with tears. "This is all so reckless and senseless." She turned to him and tentatively reached out, loosely grabbing his sleeves. For once, she held her gaze away from his eyes and began to sob, then said in a shaky voice, "You were going to let him kill you, for *me.*"

"What other choice did I have?"

She pulled him close and buried her face into his shoulder, still sobbing. "I never could have lived with myself if he had."

The commotion had drawn the attention of Alanna's neighbors, and they began to arrive at the house as word spread through the village. After a time, Alanna's sister came with her husband. She was hysterical at first, then overjoyed to find Alanna was alright. She tended to a small cut on Alanna's neck between a profuse succession of questions and hugs.

The village men gathered around Scar-neck's body and whispered quietly amongst themselves, then began to speak openly. They were questioning who the man was, where he came from, and what his intentions were in this secluded village. They inspected the wound that had killed him. It was clean and penetrating like he'd been impaled with a broad stake, though it bore a thin rim of burned tissue. They turned the body over and found a nearly identical exit wound on his back, but there was no blood. The men began whispering again and occasionally glanced at Cameron, who was now standing alone with the Sanduin and stroking her coarse hair. His discomfort was apparent, and he wanted nothing more than to ride away.

Alanna sensed his discomfort and grew irritated by the whispering. She decided to clear the air. She walked decisively over to Cameron, grabbed him by the arm, and dragged him toward the men. "This is Cameron, my friend. He came to us for help because these savages have been trying to kill him! That man's dead because Cameron was protecting me. And he wasn't alone. There was another who ran away."

Cameron said, "And he'll eventually be back with others like him. They've already killed one man from my village back in Southmoorland. They mean to destroy me and my family." He paused in reflection. "I'm sorry to bring my troubles to your village, but I didn't know who else to turn to." He glanced at Alanna.

The men were silent, and then an older gentleman who had wandered over by Cameron's horse lifted the shield from its bindings. He had noticed the emblem on its face and now carried it toward the group while still staring at it. He turned it toward them and asked, "Does anyone else recognize this?" The group looked around at one another but said nothing.

Then, the old gentleman's wife walked forward to get a closer look, and she ran her hand over the intricately etched surface. "I would guess that very few of us have ever seen this or would remember its significance. It represents the Arnorian stewards, the protectors of our ancestors." She turned and walked over to Cameron and scrutinized his blue eyes. She appeared awestruck, yet still uncertain, and finally said, "Who exactly are you, young man?"

Cameron stared back for a moment and told her the truth, "Althea's heir."

Her eyes widened, and she took his hand in her own. "So the family of stewards still watches over us. Thank you for protecting our Alanna. If you ever find yourself in need, our door will always be open to you."

Her show of support impressed the group of men, as was her intention. Their murmurs escalated into louder deliberate conversation, and two men ran off to fetch a cart and horse. They returned after a short time and loaded Scar-neck's body onto the cart next to several shovels. They asked no questions and rode away to bury the villain's remains.

Alanna took Cameron's hand to lead him into the house and felt the warm, raw, blistered skin on his palm. He winced from the touch, and she gasped. "Cameron! You've been burnt. We need to bandage this."

"It's fine for now, Alanna. We can tend to it later."

"No, it needs attention now." Alanna led Cameron over to where her sister, Maelynn, and her husband, Brandon, stood. They introduced themselves while Maelynn wrapped Cameron's hand with clean cloth. They insisted that Cameron and Alanna stay with them until Jared returned from Clearwater. Cameron was reluctant, but Alanna coaxed him to stay for one night. "That other man's probably far away from here by now. I don't think he'll come back by himself."

"There's four others out there, Alanna."

"But only two followed you here."

"I guess you're right. It'll probably take time for him to find the others."

Alanna and Maelynn went inside to pack her things while Cameron and Brandon went down to the pasture to collect the dogs from their watch over the sheep. They loaded into Brandon's cart and were soon on their way. Maelynn wrapped her arm around Alanna and held her tightly all the way to their home. Cameron, who was deeply absorbed in his swirling thoughts, followed on the Sanduin.

DUO

Cameron was awakened the following morning by a loud argument between Alanna and Maelynn. The early dawn light was already filtering through the window. He heard his name mentioned more than once in their discussion. He dressed and made his way to the kitchen where they were still talking, but the conversation came to an abrupt halt. Maelynn folded her arms across her chest and turned away with an exasperated look. Alanna was seated and looking awkwardly down at her feet. The tension in the room was like molasses.

"Look," he said, "I don't want to be the cause of argument here. I'm really sorry for the trouble I brought with me. I'll be on my way as soon as I pack my things."

"I know that, Cameron," Alanna replied. "And I'm coming with you." She looked defiantly at her older sister, who reeled around and slapped her hands down on the table.

"Alanna! You don't know what you're doing. You don't know what you're getting yourself into. This is dangerous business, and you won't be safe!"

Taken by surprise at her announcement, Cameron added, "She's right, Alanna. I don't even know where I'm going from here. I just know I need to leave this village so the Khaalzin will leave you alone. You've already done more for me than I could ever repay. It'll never be safe for anyone to be near me."

"Fine, I'm tired of arguing," Alanna said, and she stormed into the bedroom, slamming the door behind her. Maelynn wheeled around and stomped outside, past Brandon, who was just coming inside to attempt to mediate the argument.

He let her go and closed the door. "I'm sorry for that," he said to Cameron. "They're two of the most hardheaded women I've ever known, especially when they're together. I don't think Maelynn holds anything against you. She's actually very sympathetic to your situation. She's just worried about Alanna. She's got a history of making impulsive decisions and a real knack for getting into trouble."

Brandon's insight was no surprise to Cameron, but without Alanna's quick actions the day before, he would have parted ways with his head. He truly did owe her everything.

The two men ate breakfast together while the women cooled off. At first, there was a lot of commotion coming from the bedroom, then it was quiet. After cooling off, Maelynn came inside and sat with the men to eat. She asked, "Were you serious when you said you don't know where you're headed?"

"Unfortunately, yeah. But I'll figure it out. I'll probably go east to the mountains and then south to Eastmoorland. I'll find my way back home from there."

"Where's home?" she asked.

"Southmoorland, on the Sable River."

"You're a long way from home already," Brandon said. "That route'll take a long time. You might be able to barter a ride south on one of the barges traveling Clearwater Lake. Otherwise, the path around the lake's pretty rough. And with the snow melt this time of year, the mountain river'll be swollen over its banks. And beyond that, the foothills of the Calyan Mountains come right down to the lake's edge. It's pretty rough terrain. Not to mention, bandits that prey on the lake's merchant traffic use that area to hide."

"He could go south from here, around this side of the lake to avoid all that," Maelynn said, half questioning the idea.

"That's true." Brandon considered the option. "But it would take you through, or at least near, the city of Clearwater. It sits right on the lake's western bank. It's a busy place, and you'd pass a lot of travelers on the road. Getting around the Moraien Fens would be almost impossible unless you stick to the road. It's wet and barren, and you'd be completely exposed on the road. There's nowhere to hide. Then, crossing the Candora River into Eastmoorland would take you through another populated area, and the ferry crossing would certainly be watched."

"The fewer eyes that see me, the better. According to Errenthal, these gray riders could have spies anywhere. So I think my best option is to keep to remote trails."

"Well, whatever path you choose, I wish you good fortune and safety," Maelynn offered. "If you're ever back this way, know that you're always welcome here."

Cameron thanked them again for their hospitality and started making preparations to leave. Alanna still hadn't come out of the bedroom, so he gently knocked on the door and announced that he was leaving. There was no response, and Cameron's heart was heavy. Part of him wished that she could come with him. A bond had formed between them that he couldn't quite fully explain, making his departure this time particularly painful. Her refusal to come out to at least say farewell just added to the pain.

They left the house, and Cameron turned toward the stable to see the Sanduin mare standing outside, packs already secured and Alanna perched in the saddle.

Cameron's eyes widened in astonishment. "Alanna! What are you doing? How did you get out here?"

Maelynn expelled a groaning sigh, "Argh! She climbed out the window. Alanna! When are you going to grow up?"

Alanna glared at her sister from atop the horse and quickly retorted, "When are you finally gonna notice I have grown up? I'm not a child anymore!"

"Maybe not. But have you thought about what Father would have to say about this? He'd skin you alive if he knew what you were doing!"

Alanna hadn't really considered her father's point of view regarding her plan, but Maelynn was right, he would put a quick end to it. She reflected for a moment, and then her demeanor softened. "I know he wouldn't approve, but you know he's been overprotective toward me ever since Mother passed." She paused briefly. "And what do you think Mother would have to say about it?"

The question surprised Cameron, and it seemed to strike a chord with Maelynn. Her expression softened as well, and she replied in a shaky voice, "That's not fair, Alanna." Her eyes were visibly moistening.

"Why isn't it fair? She's still part of us. What would she say, Maelynn?" Alanna's voice was more insistent.

The tears welled up in Maelynn's eyes, and her vivid memories offered up the response to Alanna's question, her voice tremulous as she recited the words that their mother gave them while languishing in her final days of life: "Be true to yourselves. You have to follow your own hearts, my dears, no matter the consequences nor the ones who stand in your way." Maelynn broke down and cried.

Alanna, starting to cry herself, jumped down and ran to her sister to embrace her. They held each other for a long time. When they finally separated, Maelynn caressed the side of Alanna's face, and they exchanged their love and goodbyes without words. Maelynn turned to walk to the house, unable to bear watching her little sister leave, and

Alanna said, "Please tell Father I'm sorry and that I love him. I can't explain why, but I have to do this."

THE PROPHECY

The Sanduin mare barely noticed the added weight of Alanna's slim frame as they traveled northeast along the trail leading out of Eastwillow. The final stretch of cleared path following the narrow river ended within the last small settlement in the region. So they left the river, which veered to the north, and made for the southern margin of the Calyan Mountains.

In the forest's seclusion, they felt no urgency and traveled for several days toward the mountain's foothills. The leaf buds had opened, and spring was entering its full glory, raising their spirits along the way. Progressively broader openings appeared in the forest canopy and exposed the mountain range's expanding beauty.

They alternated riding and walking, talking and laughing all the while as their friendship deepened. Alanna talked incessantly, and her conversation seemed to have no boundaries. Her bubbly nature and propensity to laugh were spellbinding to Cameron, and he never tired of her conversation. After spending the entire winter ruminating over his woes, Alanna's diversion was wholly welcome.

The traveling companions came to a large valley in the foothills. Awash in color, spring wildflowers cascaded down its slopes to the valley floor, spreading all the way to the swollen river's stony margin. The expansive river flowed with a dangerous force despite the relatively shallow grade before them. Across the river, the foothills were steeper in their ascent toward the looming snowcapped mountains.

Despite having plenty of daylight left, it was a perfect place to camp for the night. After a restful sleep, the next day afforded an opportunity to explore the river further upstream into the foothills. They were looking for a place to safely cross the icy waters, but the river was narrower in that direction and flowed violently over rocks and around massive boulders. After spending a second night, they packed and headed downstream, hoping to find a shallow crossing. They followed the river for three days. Cameron attempted to cross twice where the river's depth appeared promising but stumbled into deep channels at the river's center both times. Mountain tributaries entered the river from the opposite side, increasing the river's volume and force the further south they traveled. Crossing it appeared futile, as Brandon had warned.

Cameron's mood turned glum as he built up a fire to cook their dinner. A turkey had wandered too close to camp earlier that morning, and he had struggled to use the bow with the still-tender burn on his hand. He nearly missed the shot. But Alanna was unusually quiet while he labored over the fire. Her normally buoying conversation faltered as she quietly considered their situation.

Cameron was erecting a spit to suspend the bird over the fire when she finally broke the silence. "I've been thinking about the Prophecy that Errenthal told you about." She recited it perfectly from memory:

"Hope will come where none is known
A seed will bear on winds of despair
Over raging waters fate unknown
Return to us Genwyhn's heir.

"I've been trying to understand why these Khaalzin are so obsessed with destroying you and your family. Did he say anything else about it?"

Cameron thought back to the day Erral had mentioned it. "He said it was the common form of the Prophecy. I'm not sure what he meant by that, and I didn't ask. He didn't seem to have much faith in its meaning, though."

"Well, the gray riders must have faith in its meaning, because I can't think of any other reason why they'd be after your family after all these years."

Cameron thought more about it. He had knowingly omitted details of the Prophecy's origin in their previous conversations. "There's more to the story than I told you before," he said, then expounded on the details about the dying sage, his deathbed uttering, and Halgrin's rather extreme response to the prophetic words by sending his wife and daughter on a dangerous ocean crossing into exile.

"So there *is* more to this Prophecy. I wish Errenthal was here. If he truly doesn't believe in its meaning, he might not have told you everything he knows about it."

"Maybe so, but I don't see how an old folk tale is gonna help me here, and now."

"Maybe it won't, but that doesn't make me less curious about it. I know someone in Clearwater who might know more about it. I want to go there," she added, making her position very clear.

Cameron was beginning to understand the stubborn streak in Alanna. Her persistence in pursuing what she wanted was admirable, but he found it to be a bit annoying at times too. And he knew this was going to be an unshakeable pursuit. "I'm not completely against doing that, but I'm worried about going to such a populated place. We've managed to lose those gray riders for now, but I'm afraid their spies might put them right back on my trail again."

"But sometimes hiding in plain sight can be just as effective as trying to hide in the shadows. They might not expect it."

He wasn't sure if her logic made sense, but he wasn't in the mood to argue. "It looks like we're going that way anyway, so maybe it wouldn't hurt to do it. But it still worries me, so let's try to make it a quick side trip."

Alanna's face lit up, and a broad smile appeared, like a child receiving an unexpected gift. Cameron couldn't restrain his own smile. Her enthusiasm was infectious.

She rummaged through her pack and pulled out spare clothing and soap, then proceeded to remove her shirt and britches.

"Alanna! What are you doing?" Cameron said while he spun around to look the other way.

"Taking a bath and washing my clothes in the river. What's it look like?"

"But the river's way down there!"

"Are you serious? What, you've never seen a girl before?"

"No . . . I mean yes . . . I mean no! It's like seeing my sister naked, if I had one, which I *don't*, but I *wouldn't!*"

She smiled and quietly laughed behind his back, then pulled her britches back up and headed toward the river. "You're such a juvenile!"

Cameron groaned and shook his head, then turned his attention back to the naked turkey and rotated it slowly over the fire.

***

A lightly used trail emerged next to the river as they approached the northern end of Clearwater Lake, and Cameron felt increasingly exposed. It afforded easier travel, though Cameron's twitchy nerves revealed the anxiety he still harbored over the encounter with Scar-neck and his cohort just days before. Eventually, the river spilled into the lake at its northern end, and the trail followed the western bank toward the city of Clearwater. It soon joined with the main road leading into Clearwater, a road that Alanna had traveled several times before with her father while accompanying him on his provisions business. Travelers were more common along the main road, and attempting to avoid them was pointless. Being attuned to Cameron's unease, Alanna studied the eyes and faces of everyone they passed, looking for any signs of malintent, but they all seemed to be preoccupied with their own business.

They reached the city's outskirts late in the day, and having no money to stay at an inn, they found a secluded spot well off the road in a stand of pine trees to make camp. The next morning, they rode into the city amidst the throng of city dwellers, travelers, merchants, and day visitors from the city's outskirts. Alanna made inquiries with the clergy at two churches situated near the city entrance in hopes of tracking down her source. At the second church, she found a clergyman who knew the man for whom she was looking. Her source was a retired clergyman himself, having moved to the city after finding himself unable to continue his ministry at Alanna's local church. He had suffered from a progressive neurologic condition and chose to relocate with his wife to be closer to their children and more skilled healers.

The cleric informed her, sadly, that the man had passed away two years earlier, but his wife was still living in the city with one of her children. After getting directions to her home, Alanna persuaded Cameron to join her in a visit to pay their respects at the very least.

They arrived at the home just before dinnertime and received a warm welcome. Layra Fenmohr remembered Alanna and her family well from those many years before. "It's such a wonderful surprise to see you, Alanna. How are your mother and father?"

Alanna informed her of her mother's passing, and Layra was visibly saddened. After reminiscing for several minutes, Layra invited Alanna and Cameron to join the family for dinner. They graciously accepted, and afterward, Alanna approached the subject that had brought them there in the first place. "I was hoping Pastor Fenmohr could help me understand some old folklore. I remember him talking about our settlement's ancestry and history quite a lot. It seemed to be important to him."

Layra replied, "Yes, he was always fascinated with our heritage. He always said that to really understand ourselves, we had to understand our forbearers and their life struggles. Whether or not we're conscious of it, their lives form a part of the fabric of our own existence."

"I was wondering about the translation of an old Arnorian song." And she began to sing the song she had sung while Cameron visited her home the first time.

Layra recognized it immediately and joined in. After finishing, she smiled and said, "I haven't heard that song in a very long time. It's a pretty verse. My mother used to sing it to me when I was young. I'm afraid I don't know the translation in common language, but I'm sure my husband would have known it."

Alanna's face sank.

Layra saw her disappointment and thought for a moment, then offered, "I do know of a man who might be able to help you, though. I don't know what condition he's in, or even if he's still living, but my husband used to visit him while he could still get around. They shared similar interests, including Arnorian history."

Alanna looked at Cameron, and he nodded. It would be silly to come all this way and not try. So Cameron and Alanna stayed with the family, at their unyielding insistence, for the night. The next morning they were off in search of Dannen Yungbred, a retired scholar from the local university in Clearwater.

The scholar proved easy to find. He was well known by the community surrounding the university, which was located on the lakeshore at the city's southeastern corner. He was living under the care of his daughter. When she introduced them to Dannen, he was sitting in his study in a complicated-looking wheelchair, holding a book in his hands.

Dannen was elderly and suffered from a persistent tremor. His limbs were stiff and contracted. His hair was gray and tousled, and his skin showed the lines of a life long-lived. They watched as he struggled to turn the page of his book. Alanna walked directly to him and turned the page, then knelt before him to look into his eyes, all the while keeping a comforting smile on her face.

Cameron watched her with admiration. She was one of the most genuinely open and caring people he'd ever met. He realized in that moment that he had already prejudged the man by his appearance to be senile and unlikely to be able to help them, and he felt more than a little ashamed. She looked at Dannen as a man, like any other, and not as an invalid. When she spoke to him, she spoke as she would to any man with full mental faculties. She was unassuming because she saw inside him, through his eyes, and didn't just focus on his outward appearance.

"Thank you for seeing us," she said when he returned her gaze.

"Oh-ho-ho," he gently laughed in his hoarse, airy voice. "I don't get many visitors anymore," he continued with strained effort. His tremor seemed to wane when he spoke, only to return again after finishing. "I would guess that you are here on some sort of intellectual quest." He smiled back at Alanna.

"We are," and she glanced over to Cameron. "We actually came at first looking for Pastor Fenmohr. I had several questions for him about Arnorian folklore. I was saddened to find out he'd passed away. He was very close to my family and community many years ago. But his wife seemed to think you might be able to help us in his place."

"He was a very dear friend and missed by many. I would be delighted to help if I'm able."

"Thank you," Alanna replied, her face glowing with genuine appreciation. "There's an old folk song with, I believe, Arnorian origins. I was wondering if it relates in some way to an old prophecy that involves the stewards of that land." She began to sing the song, and feeling mildly embarrassed, her cheeks flushed. She watched as the lines on Dannen's face seemingly melted away while a gentle smile appeared, and his tremor gradually lessened until it was barely perceptible. Alanna appreciated the lulling effect the song had on him. The embarrassment left her, and her voice strengthened. She hadn't intended to sing the entire song, but she finished it after sensing her audience wished it so.

Dannen smiled as broad a smile as he could muster, gently laughed a hoarse laugh to convey his pleasure, and unsuccessfully attempted to clap, his stiff muscles not able to comply with his mind's command. "That was beautiful, my dear. It is one of my favorite songs. And you are right about its relationship with the Prophecy. It is, in fact, *the* Prophecy."

"Are you able to translate the words?" Alanna asked him.

"Well, the song is just a loose translation of the true Prophecy. The old Arnorian language is a beautiful, romantic language, and it was used by poets and songwriters for its . . . aesthetic appeal, I suppose. The Prophecy was originally stated and written in the common language, at least to the best of my knowledge." He coughed weakly but then continued his slow, fragmented discourse in an increasingly hoarse voice. "The few writings and artifacts of that time period that we have been able to collect are all written in common language, with the exception of some artistic works."

"I see," Alanna interrupted, recognizing he was heading into a tangent. "Do you know of anyone who can translate the song back into common language? I'm curious about its meaning."

"Oh . . . well, let me think," he said, then closed his eyes in thought, and his tremor became almost violent. "Oh, yes," he finally declared after opening his eyes again. "It should be in the small cedar chest." He struggled to turn his head to look at his daughter.

She took his hint and moved to the far side of the room to rummage through a collection of boxes and chests, finally pulling out an old cedar chest. She opened it and asked, "What are we looking for, Papa?"

"It should be a rolled parchment bound with two red strings." Dannen had a rather large collection of historic documents in his possession. The small cedar chest contained Arnorian artifacts, items which he had collected over the course of his life. The university didn't consider the artifacts pertinent to its educational mission, so he kept them in his personal collection. His daughter found the parchment and proceeded to untie the strings. It was yellowed and appeared fragile from age, so she handled it gently. While she unrolled it, Dannen added, "I am curious about your interest in this. You've presumably come a good distance to satisfy a simple curiosity."

"Yes," Alanna replied. "My mother used to sing that song to me, but I never really concerned myself with the meaning in the words." She paused and briefly considered how much information to divulge, ultimately deciding to be open about her request. "And . . . we were wondering if there might be a reference to Cameron's family line—Genwyhn."

"Ah, so it *is* more than simple academic interest. Well, go ahead and read it aloud. We'll see what this Prophecy has to say!" He ended with another coughing fit.

Dannen's daughter handed the parchment to Alanna, and Cameron moved next to her to read along. The words were smudged in places but still readable:

"Hope may yet come where none is known
The winds of despair may bear a seed and carry forth
Over raging waters fate unknown
Through lives of men dark seasons shall pass
New hope be found in him pure blood
An heir of Genwyhn to return at last
Three are foreseen to return again
To span the hopeless divide
The path of a second is veiled in fog
Pure of heart though world awash in treachery
Allegiance uncertain a choice to be made

And worth unseen by eyes of men
But clearly discerned through those more keen
A gem in the rough shall complete the three
Born anew under astral sign
And in darkness leads them in unity
Uncertainty veils our destiny
Until their souls converge."

"A mystery to be sure!" Dannen punctuated after Alanna finished reading.

As Cameron read along, he wore a puzzled look on his face. "Where did these words come from? I mean, who wrote them originally?" he asked, hoping to verify the connection with Erral's account.

Dannen closed his eyes as if searching the recesses of his mind for the answer, and responded, "As I recall, the story holds that these were the last worldly thoughts of a rather important intellectual man close to the ruling family. What was his name . . ." and he paused in thought for several moments. "Oh, yes, it was Baron, I believe. It was written several generations past, and before the exile of his people into this land. As the script implies, it is a prophetic statement, and one that was apparently taken *very* seriously."

Alanna copied the words onto a parchment that Dannen's daughter kindly provided. While she was busy with her task, Dannen looked at Cameron and said, "So, it appears this Prophecy makes reference to your family after all. I should be interested to learn what you know about your ancestors. As you see by now, I've spent considerable time researching Arnorian history."

Cameron was hesitant, given the nature of his predicament. But Alanna nodded her encouragement, and he knew that he should return the elderly gentleman's generosity. So Cameron sat and discussed much of the history that Erral had provided him during their travels. Cameron made no reference about the Khaalzin coming to Gartannia or his current situation. Dannen listened intently without interruption, at times appearing to fall asleep, but Cameron soon realized his closed eyes were simply an indication of his mental processing.

When Cameron finished, Dannen said thoughtfully, "You have indeed enlightened me, young man. You've tied together so many loose ends in my understanding of this history. I would like to meet this Errenthal one day and pick his brain clean."

Cameron had spoken for quite a long time, and Dannen was clearly becoming fatigued. His daughter discreetly motioned that they should let him rest, so they took the opportunity to thank him for his time. As they were leaving the room, Dannen spoke, "Oh, wait a moment!" His sudden movement sparked another coughing fit, but when he recovered, he asked his daughter to fetch another item from the cedar chest. It was a thick journal bound in leather and wrapped with a protective cover. "I would like you to have this. I have no further use of it, nor do I know anyone else who would. You may find some of the entries to be interesting, I believe."

Alanna took the journal and thanked him again before they said goodbye.

LAKE ESCAPE

It was shortly after midday when they left Dannen's home, the day sunny and warm for early spring. The companions' spirits were lifted, not just by the weather, but also by their encounter with Dannen Yungbred. Alanna wore an irrepressible smile. Regardless of whether the new information they gleaned about the Prophecy would be helpful or not, they still felt a sense of accomplishment, and accomplishments demand celebration. So, they decided to make the short walk through the university to the lakeshore to enjoy the view.

The university grounds were well-kept and provided plenty of open spaces for the young students to study or socialize. The students were particularly plentiful on the grounds, enjoying the picturesque day on the lakeshore. They mingled and frolicked, and professors even joined their groups in lively discussions. Cameron and Alanna meandered across the grounds toward the lakeshore, feeling perhaps a little out of place in their dirty, worn clothing and leading the laden Sanduin mare. They were aware of the curious stares from the students but did not concern themselves. They soon found a quiet spot next to the lake where they tied the horse and sat, leaning their backs against an ancient oak.

The view was stunning to Cameron, who had never seen a body of water this large. The lake, deep blue and shimmering under the midday sun, stretched to the horizon as far as his eyes could see. A gentle, cool breeze wafted in from the lake, and Cameron stood to unpack provisions for lunch. Alanna was unable to contain her curiosity about the journal, so she opened it to the first page and read it aloud.

Herein, the records of Aldenahr Lehrvyst, Captain of the Tryst-Froele, ninth ship to sail from the port of Brysmäen, Arnorian Calendar 9623, 20th day of the 3rd lunar cycle.

9623,24,5 We successfully made port south coast of Gartannia, port city of Sabon, at the mouth of the Dantuin River, date 9623,10,5 - forty days since sailing from Brysmäen. Met by first mate Tyhbahnis from the third Brysmäen ship, Tryst-Gueveyr, the first ship to successfully make port this location. Reported fifth Brysmäen ship, Tryst-Fahren, also arrived with less than half survival of souls on board. No reports from remaining ships.

We encountered severe seas during crossing, losing two mates and three passengers. Successfully navigated rocky shoals off southwestern coast. Ship sold at port with aid of Tyhbahnis, who remains in port employ and in vigilance for future arrivals. He has provided map to first settlement by passengers of Tryst-Gueveyr to the far north. We have begun the journey along the Dantuin River as of this writing in good weather, early summer.

The people of Gartannia have been accommodating, but still wary of our presence. The land is peaceful and regionally self-governed. We are hopeful.

"This must be referring to the original Arnorian refugees," Cameron surmised.

"What do you think happened to the other ships?"

"Well, from Erral's account of his crossing, the seas were really dangerous. His ship was damaged and nearly sank. So, I'm guessing they didn't make it."

"How desperate they must have been to take such a risk." She closed the journal and finished her lunch, quietly imagining the horrors the refugees must have endured. They sat a while longer, talking and laughing, their cares set aside for the time. And as the sun passed well into the western sky, they left the serenity of the university's lakeshore and walked north toward the city's port district. But being unfamiliar with the city, they wandered through random streets and alleys filled with local residents going about their daily business. After passing several streets, they noticed that foot traffic had become sparse and seedy-looking characters lingered in alleys. Though they didn't consider themselves targets for robbery, having not even a copper penny between them, Cameron realized that the beautiful, young Sanduin mare gave the appearance of wealth.

It wasn't long before four young men took notice. Cameron realized that he and Alanna could not have appeared more out of place than they did, and he rightly became concerned for their safety. Alanna, who had been her usual talkative self, became anxiously muted when she noticed the group of young men leering at them. They continued to walk along, trying to appear unconcerned. Alanna finally whispered, "Should we turn around, or just keep going?"

Cameron was considering the same options, and his instincts told him to keep going forward. He understood predatory behavior and didn't want to appear fearful. "We'll keep to our path," he said.

The four men casually moved into the street a short distance behind them and followed. Cameron and Alanna heard their snickering and whispers but did not turn around to look, still hoping to avoid a confrontation. But the four men had no intention of letting them pass through without some compensation, voluntary or not.

"Hey, you," one shouted, "I don't know who's prettier, the girl or the horse." They all laughed.

Alanna whispered, "Just ignore them, Cameron. We'll be out of this neighborhood soon enough." They quickened the pace.

The four men, seeing their targets moving faster, sped forward to intercept them. "There's a toll to be paid for using my street," the same man yelled, obviously the gang's leader. They caught up, and the first two grabbed Cameron's shoulders from behind, pulling him to a stop while Alanna ran forward to grab the mare's bridle.

Cameron stopped at the horse's hindquarter, aware that his sword was hidden under a saddle blanket just within reach. "I'm not looking for trouble, and we have no money," he said, trying to maintain a calm voice while turning around to face the predators. Two already held knives in their hands.

The leader laughed and stepped past Cameron toward Alanna. He was a creepy-looking young man, probably twenty or so, with worn clothing and long, stringy hair. "I didn't say I wanted money," he said, then laughed while unpleasantly studying Alanna.

At the same moment, a vision forced its way into Cameron's mind as it had during the encounter with the Khaalzin. He saw Alanna's intent. One young man was already standing behind the Sanduin, and Cameron suddenly lunged forward and pushed one of the knife-wielders to the same spot just before the mare bucked and kicked. Both men were caught by surprise and landed, stunned and bleeding, nearly ten steps from where they had been standing.

Cameron wheeled around and grasped the sword's hilt from beneath the blanket, pulling it cleanly from its sheath to confront the second knife-wielder, who was still gaping at his two mates on the ground. Alanna deftly stepped to the mare's other side and placed her hand on the mare's shoulder, guiding her to rear back. The mare pummeled the leader with a flurry of kicks. He cowered back and ran for his life, showing no concern for the fate of his mates. The final adversary, now alone, glanced at Cameron's sword and nearly soiled his pants, then sprinted away as fast as he could.

Cameron and Alanna looked at one another, wide-eyed and speechless. They noticed the two men on the ground beginning to stir, so they jumped into the saddle and sped away through the streets. Drunkards staggered from the mare's path, and street urchins marveled at the sleek Sanduin bolting past. But after passing several intersections of streets, the people began to give them irritated looks and stern admonishments for riding within the narrow streets. In fact, they would have found themselves under the scrutiny of constables had they been seen, so they wisely dismounted and led the mare along. After their pounding hearts finally settled, they started to laugh, perhaps naively, but they couldn't resist.

They led the mare back toward the waterfront in the city's heart and spied the long piers that served as the city's main port system just a short distance away. Although evening was approaching, the piers still bustled with activity. Fishermen were arriving after their day's work in a variety of boats, large and small. The fish-cleaning stations were inundated with fishermen under a swirling vortex of seagulls, and a throng of fish vendors and restaurateurs haggled over the day's catch at the base of the piers.

Several shorter piers just north of the main pier system were relegated to ferry services. Sailing ships of various shapes and sizes were docked, but most appeared suited to transporting livestock, grains, and merchandise. Cameron had come to this place hoping to speed his journey home but had never traveled by boat before. So they passed around the stench and carnage of the fish-cleaning stations to get to the ferry piers. Alanna held her nose and tried not to breathe, but nonetheless, dry heaves overcame her, and she nearly tossed her lunch. Cameron chuckled, earning himself a swift kick in the shin when they were finally past.

Cameron spoke with the ferry captains, inquiring about passage down the lake and ultimately the Candora River. He learned that the ferries would go as far as the lake's southern end, where they unloaded cargo onto river ferries for the final leg south to the river cities, or, ultimately, the coastal port. Most had no interest in carrying passengers, but those that did asked an exorbitant price. And the cost to carry his horse was nearly as much as he could get by selling her. Dejected, he rejoined Alanna and headed back toward the city's outskirts to bide the night.

At the campfire that evening, Cameron confided his frustrations to Alanna. He felt aimless and longed to return home. But Alanna understood the conflict in his mind. "You've been put in a difficult situation, Cameron. I don't see a clear path forward for you, but for now, maybe simple survival should be enough. And I'm pretty sure that mindlessly running straight into danger won't end well."

"Maybe so, but running away like a scared rabbit hasn't helped my situation either. My father used to tell me that sometimes we need to fight, and sacrifice, for what we believe in."

"But I'll bet your father never ran into a fight without a plan," she smirked. Cameron knew she was right about that. "Do you believe in destiny, Cameron?"

"I've never thought much about it, but no, not really. I don't think our lives are preplanned, if that's what you mean. I think we guide our lives by the choices we make and the actions we take."

Alanna considered his response for a moment, then rebutted, "Our choices and actions guide us to a place and time, a destination maybe, but I think that might be a nearsighted view of what destiny is. What I'm getting at is, maybe there's a larger purpose for each of us in this world. I don't see it as an endpoint necessarily, but just a part that we're meant to play in some grander scheme."

"That's a really deep thought. Did you step in a puddle of wisdom back at the university today?" Cameron laughed and then dodged a handful of kindling wood. "But seriously, what's with the philosophical talk tonight?"

"I was just thinking about Baron's Prophecy. I know it's a leap of faith to think that prophetic statements can foretell the future, and maybe some come true simply by chance. But it makes me wonder if there really is a grand scheme for the world, and a prophecy is just a small glimpse through a window into the future of that scheme. And our decisions and actions do nothing more than create small ripples, like tossing stones into a river. They have a momentary influence, but the river just keeps flowing, eventually erasing any sign of the stone."

"I get what you're saying, and I guess it makes sense. But why should someone be allowed to look through that window into the future?"

Alanna looked intently at Cameron's eyes, smiled and said, "That's a really deep question, Cameron." And she laughed.

"And what if I dropped a boulder into the river and changed its course?" Cameron said.

"Ha! You couldn't lift a boulder, so it's a stupid question." They both laughed and playfully tossed kindling back and forth until their dinner was cooked.

Later, Alanna pulled the journal out of her pack and removed the loose parchment tucked inside. She turned it to the firelight and read the Prophecy aloud to Cameron. After finishing, she reread three lines:

> *"New hope be found in him pure blood*
> *An heir of Genwyhn to return at last*
> *Three are foreseen to return again.*

"It sounds to me like the heir of Genwyhn that this Prophecy refers to is full-blooded Arnorian, and it says that three heirs will return. But didn't you say you were the last one in your family's bloodline? Are you sure there weren't other children somewhere through the generations, like cousins, that might have started a parallel family line with pure Arnorian blood?"

"I don't know of any other family line. My grandmother was clear about that. The only living direct descendants are Gram and me."

"Well, it doesn't make any sense then, unless I'm misinterpreting something."

"I don't see how you could interpret it any other way. I understand now why Erral didn't seem to take it seriously. It's nothing more than a dying man's dream." With that, Cameron stretched out next to the fire under his blanket to consider his path for the next day while Alanna thumbed through the journal's entries and quietly read.

Cameron woke the next morning having committed to returning home, even if just to see that his family and friends were safe. He would consider his future after that. But without Erral, he didn't know the land well enough to chart a safe path home. They would need a map, at the very least, to get a rough bearing for the journey. They left the camp and headed south on the road, passing into the city's western district. Beyond the city to the south, the road would lead them to the remote lands bordering the Moraien Fens, but first, they would detour further into the city to find a map.

Alanna recalled a large map tacked to the wall in a merchant's shop where her father did business not far from the main road. Her memory was accurate, and the map provided at least a general bearing for their travels. They left the merchant and were leading the horse back toward the main road when Cameron froze in his steps. He was staring ahead, and Alanna followed his gaze to a group of four men not thirty steps away leading horses directly toward them into the city.

Cameron regained his composure and instructed Alanna, "Keep going!" while he quickly walked around the mare to conceal himself. Alanna casually glanced at the men, who wore gray armbands around their upper arms, as they passed by.

Once clear, Cameron nervously rejoined Alanna and said, "Those are the same armbands the gray rider's henchmen wore in the raid on my friends' horse farm. If they're here, it means the gray riders aren't far away!" He anxiously scanned the street for any gray-cloaked figures.

Alanna saw that Cameron was nearing a state of panic. She glanced around and tugged his shirtsleeve, hinting that he should follow, then led the horse down a side street to the left. After a short distance, they came to a livery stable where several horses were tied. She tied the Sanduin next to them, rummaged through her pack, and pulled out the journal. "You stay here and stay out of sight. I'll be back." And she scuttled away back toward the main street.

"Wait! Where are you going?" he asked in vain as she disappeared. He loitered nervously by his horse for a short time before noticing the livery owner repeatedly glancing over while shuffling back and forth doing chores. Trying to appear nonchalant, Cameron unpacked and repacked provisions, then fiddled with the saddle and tack.

Before long, the owner's curiosity apparently reached a threshold, and he wandered over by Cameron. "That's a fine horse, young man," he said to Cameron's relief. "She's a Sanduin if I'm not mistaken."

"Yes, a Sanduin with a good temperament to boot." He continued repacking while trying not to look too fidgety but could sense that the man was a little suspicious of his loitering in the stable yard. "I hope I'm not bothering you," Cameron offered. "I'm just waiting for . . . my sister to come back. The main street's so busy, I felt like we were in the way."

"Ah, that's fine," the man said, then came closer to caress the Sanduin's neck. He moved to her head, habitually checking her eyes and teeth, then stepped back to admire her muscular frame. "I don't see many Sanduin's here. She's quite a handsome mare. You wouldn't be interested in selling her, would you?"

"No, we have a long way to go yet, and we won't get there without her," Cameron replied with a friendly smile.

"Well, good travels then." The man bustled away yelling instructions to a young boy who had just emerged from the stable with a wheelbarrow full of hay.

Meanwhile, Alanna had run back to the main street and followed the four men further into the city. They met two others with similar armbands near a public well. The men allowed their horses to drink from a nearby trough while they talked with the two newcomers. Alanna ducked into a side alley and tousled her hair, knowing from experience that she would attract less attention from most men looking disheveled. Then, she casually walked next to a man and woman toward the well, where she sat down just out of the men's sight but still within earshot of their conversation.

They were crude and uncivilized, and Alanna cringed at the boisterous talk. But still, she sat and endured it, hoping to glean something useful about their intentions. After a short time, one asked, "What are the gray-cloaks waiting for? I thought we were goin' further north."

One of the newcomers replied, "I guess they changed their minds. They're lookin' to hire more men, and I guess we're searchin' the city for that boy on the black horse. You fellas get your provisions and wait back at the main road. One of the gray-cloaks is gonna put you on watch somewhere down the road for now." They descended back into uncivilized conversation, but Alanna had heard what she needed. She waited for a group of people to walk by, stood up, and blended into the crowd, still keeping her head down and pretending to read from the journal. The men didn't seem to pay her any attention.

She returned to Cameron, who was pacing nervously in the stable yard. "Where'd you go?" he impatiently asked.

"Spying," she replied, and then told him what she had overheard.

Cameron felt claustrophobic. He wished they had left the city sooner, but Alanna reminded him that the roads outside the city were not necessarily any safer.

Just then, the livery owner bustled out to fetch a horse back into a stall. Cameron watched him for a moment, then looked at Alanna and asked, "Have you ever been on a boat before?"

The livery owner turned out to be a fair man, but Cameron knew the price he received for the horse was considerably shy of her actual value. And how would he ever pay Garth back the full value of his Sanduin mare? But still, the purse of coins that Cameron put into his pack was more money than he had ever held. He wrestled with remorse while he and Alanna lugged their packs warily through the side streets toward the ferry docks.

He and Alanna still had to escape their pursuers. They were far too close for comfort. And in reality, the strikingly beautiful black horse had become something of a liability, making them far more visible to their pursuers than they would have been otherwise. So, despite the weight and bulk of the packs, they wound their way through the obscure side streets, finally arriving at the waterfront where laborers, absorbed in their work, crisscrossed the open spaces adjacent to the docks. Looking across toward the ferry piers, they saw workers loading crates and sacks onto the ferry boats from wagons in preparation for transport down the lake.

But Cameron had an uneasy feeling about entering the open space. He stopped and scanned the area, and in the distance, two men were standing like sentinels, looking out of place amidst the bustling activity around them. They did not wear the gray armbands, but something about them caused Cameron to think twice about exposing himself.

He grabbed Alanna's arm and ducked behind a building, then pointed out the two men. She agreed with his suspicion, and once again, after dropping her packs at his feet, disappeared before he could stop her. *Why does she have to be so impulsive? One of these days she's gonna get us both into trouble!*

He watched from a safe vantage, not quite sure what to expect next. After a short time, one of two horses that had been tied near the men reared up, stomped its hooves, and sped away down the main street leading back into the city. The men were taken by surprise, and one sprinted after the horse. He yelled incessantly while he scampered down the street. The second man looked bewildered for a moment, then untied the other horse and sped away in pursuit, having figured his cohort would have no chance of catching the runaway. Then Cameron saw Alanna standing there with a broad smile on her face looking back at him.

Cameron lugged the packs to the main ferry dock. After scanning the ragtag fleet, he spied a smaller cargo boat just being untied. The captain was accommodating after Cameron offered twice the usual fare for both him and Alanna. They loaded their gear aboard and ducked out of sight behind stacks of goods while the boat pulled away. Alanna sat with a smug grin on her face, and Cameron just shook his head with compassion for what he imagined her parents must have gone through while raising her.

THIEF IN THE NIGHT

It would take two days to sail the lake's full length to the beginning of the Candora River. At the end of the first day, the captain steered to the eastern shore and entered a small, protected bay. A long pier jutted into the water from shore where several wooden plank buildings sat. The bay served the lake vessels as an overnight mooring and was only accessible by boat. It was nestled into the lakeside where a steep valley emptied out of the southernmost extent of the Calyan Mountain range. The pier was first come, first serve, and they had arrived early enough to find room to tie along it.

The largest building sported a weathered sign that read Captain's Quarters and served as a bunkhouse and saloon. The second largest building sat next door without signage, but the handful of ladies sitting and standing on the covered porch clearly advertised it as a brothel. The remaining buildings were likely used as temporary residences for the workers.

The rooms were inexpensive, so Cameron parted with a trifle of his newfound wealth so they could enjoy sleeping on mattresses for a change. He asked for a quiet room as far from the saloon as possible, assuming it would be rather loud late into the night. He was right about that. The saloon and common room were buzzing with activity as boat after boat moored in for the night.

Cameron purchased dinner and returned to the room to eat with Alanna. Afterward, he returned to the saloon, hoping for news of goings-on around the lake and further down the river. He found no shortage of men willing to pass along news and gossip, and the only price was a willingness to listen to a few tall tales and exaggerations. Of particular interest to Cameron was a brief mention of increasing mandatory recruitment of young men into the Eastmoorland militia but not related to any uptick in Caraduan raids. Cameron fueled the discussion by mentioning he had heard about unprovoked raids in Southmoorland. The men picked up on his interest and offered more about the Eastmoorland situation. The region was apparently seeing well-organized raids on private farms and emboldened attacks on small villages for supplies, weapons, and horses. It sounded to Cameron like an escalation of what he had experienced back home, and the news was disturbing. If the Khaalzin were behind these new attacks, then there was clearly more on their agenda than just destroying Cameron's family.

They were back under sail early the next morning, and a brisk wind sped them over roughening waters toward the end of the lake. The captain eventually approached them. "We'll offload as soon as we reach the port. You two can buy passage on a river barge if you need to go further south."

By late afternoon, the port came into sight, but the captain became concerned when men aboard a small sailboat hailed them. The boat came alongside, and Cameron saw that the two men on board were frantic about something. When they were close enough to talk over the gusting wind, one shouted, "Turn about and go back! There's trouble at the docks!"

"What's the trouble?" the captain shouted.

"The town's been overrun. It's some kind of militia. They came in the night, subdued the sentries and constables, and have already taken control of the port. They're seizing all the cargo. It's not safe. Go back!"

"Is it a Caraduan invasion?" the captain asked.

"No. We don't know who they are."

Alanna looked to Cameron and whispered, "What should we do? We can't go back to Clearwater."

Cameron had been thinking the same thing. He scanned to the east and west and recalled the map back at the merchant's shop in Clearwater. The Moraien Fens covered the region to the west, and forest blanketed the region to the east, though they were south of the mountains now. He shouted to the men in the smaller boat before they were out of earshot, "Can you take us to the eastern shore?" Cameron knew the cargo boat would risk grounding in the shallows if they tried to get too close to shore.

The two men exchanged a few words with each other and agreed, then circled and came back alongside. Before long, Cameron and Alanna were wading out of the lake onto the sandy shore, still a safe distance from the southern port. The men told them they would find a road running north and south about a mile or two into the forest, but the southern direction would take them directly into the port town.

They soon found the road and began walking north, away from the besieged port. After a short time, they heard approaching hoofbeats, then the familiar rattle of wagon wheels. They ducked into thick shrubs and peered out to see a young family in the wagon moving hastily away from the port town. Alanna ran into the road to hail them, and Cameron followed.

The man looked at them suspiciously at first while his wife clutched their small children, but soon relaxed when he recognized they weren't a threat. "Are you fleeing town too?" he asked.

"No, but we heard there was trouble there," Alanna said. "We were going south on a lake ferry and got the warning. What did you see there?"

"A large militia came into town in the middle of the night and overran the military barracks. They took over the port and executed the town's constables!"

"What did they look like? What were they wearing?" Cameron asked.

"I didn't see them. I only know what my neighbor told me when he stopped to warn us. He said to get out and go north. We have room if you're headed north, but we have to go now."

Without hesitation, they grabbed their packs and jumped into the wagon.

"Where's this road go?" Cameron asked.

"It just goes north. There aren't any towns if that's what you're asking. Marla's family has a small farm about fifteen miles from here. That's where we're headed. I don't think there's anything those marauders would want up this way. There's a road that branches off to the east about ten miles up. It goes into the foothills of the Black Mountains, then south into Eastmoorland."

"That sounds like our best bet," Cameron replied. "Have you heard anything else about these attacks?"

"I've heard some crazy stories from the river barge hands. I honestly thought they were just tall tales. I swear those guys just make up stories trying to outdo each other, but after this attack, I think they were telling the truth."

"What stories?"

"Raids and skirmishes in the south, which aren't unusual when the nomads push in. But the nomads aren't behind the raids, and they started near the Southmoorland border. But the outlandish part is some new weapon they're using, picking out the militia's captains and lieutenants to burn them alive. The enlisted men are just scattering without leadership."

Cameron knew what the weapon was, and he was sickeningly impressed with the cunning Khaalzin. They were thwarting an otherwise strong and well-disciplined militia. The Eastmoorland militia's commanders would have no defense against those attacks. *The Khaalzin are wresting control of Gartannia by force! How far would they go?*

Dusk was approaching when the wagon reached the fork in the road. Cameron and Alanna thanked the family and started hiking along the eastern road. It was little used, overgrown with grass and young seedling trees, but it suited their needs traveling on foot. Six days passed while the road led them east through sparsely populated and forested land toward the looming Black Mountains. Cameron's spirits were severely tested, though Alanna's unwavering positive outlook and incessant conversation buoyed him through the passing days. Her mind was continuously churning, and the breadth of her conversation seemed limitless.

They were just entering the foothills when the road veered south. They slogged up and down the increasingly hilly terrain over the improving road. Eventually, they met a young couple traveling in a small wagon who directed them toward the village of Tandor not far off the main road. Cameron and Alanna needed supplies, so they ventured into the village to the local mercantile where they found food and other necessities.

The villagers weren't overly friendly, which wasn't a problem for Cameron, who preferred to keep a low profile anyway. Being travelers, they were eyed suspiciously. One young man, tall and lanky with black hair, watched them rather intently coming and going from the mercantile, only to disappear around the corner of a run-down shack when Alanna looked back in his direction. His attentive stare had made her uneasy. He wore dirty, worn, and tattered clothing but didn't appear terribly menacing, so she passed it off as further evidence of the general unfriendliness of the folk. They were back on the road after a short time, not caring to linger in the village any longer than necessary.

"I didn't get a very warm feeling there," Alanna said.

"Neither did I. But we got what we needed anyway."

They trudged along the road to the south. The days were getting warmer, so they welcomed the appearance of a mountain river flowing along the east side of the road. The water was clean and clear, having melted and run down from the snow-covered peaks of the Black Mountains to the east. It was frigid but refreshing.

After bathing in the cold water, they found a suitable place to make camp away from the river and to the west of the road. They felt relatively safe in this remote area, having seen no sign of the Khaalzin or their henchmen for days, so Cameron built a fire under the clear, star-filled sky.

Alanna was reading from the journal in the firelight when Cameron said, "How can you spend so much time reading those boring entries? There's nothing interesting in there."

"How can you say that? These were our ancestors."

"Maybe so, but it's still boring."

"Maybe you just need to put it into perspective. Think about what they were going through." She flipped back a few pages and said, "Look, here's one that mentions Althea. Wasn't she the one you were talking about? Your ancestor?"

"Really? It actually mentions her?"

He crawled over, and she held the book to the firelight so they could both read.

9624,14,7 Our difficulties continue. The meager food rations have strained our resolve. The gardens are planted and the harvest anxiously awaited. Additional fields are being cleared for planting next season. We are foraging further into the forests for food. The Gartannian people are kind enough, but we have precious little to barter for supplies.

Lahria and Althea have done much to keep our people optimistic in these hard times, but even so, personal conflicts have led some to consider leaving to establish a separate settlement to the east. I have urged them to stay until we are more firmly established.

Word has come that additional refugees will arrive this summer from the eleventh Brysmäen ship, the Tryst-Scaethyn, having made port in Sabon.

"It's the first time she's mentioned in the entries. And Lahria must be her mother. It must have been so difficult for them to start a new life in a strange land," Alanna repeated.

"I suppose," Cameron replied.

Alanna read several more entries aloud, knowing she had caught Cameron's interest at the mention of Althea. He moved back to where he had been sitting and stretched out under his blanket, but when he began snoring, she rolled her eyes and sighed.

Later in the night, Alanna was awakened to a soft clinking sound followed by light rustling. She half-opened her eyes to see Cameron rummaging through one of his packs, his arms gently illuminated by the dying fire. She closed her eyes again, then in the fog of light slumber realized something was out of place in what she saw. *The shirtsleeves covering those arms weren't Cameron's!* She opened her eyes and lifted herself to get a better look, and Cameron was lying under his blanket sleeping soundly. She looked across the fire to see a shadowy figure silently leaving the circle of firelight into the darkness beyond.

"Cameron!" she yelled. "Wake up, someone's in our camp!" She jumped to her feet and went to shake him out of his slumber.

Cameron awoke in confusion, having been in deep, dream-filled sleep. After several moments, he realized what Alanna was saying, and he jumped to his feet, holding the hunting knife that he kept within reach when he slept. He looked around, but there was no movement or sound in the distance. Whoever had been in the camp moved quietly through the darkness.

"Did they take anything?" Alanna asked frantically.

"I don't know," Cameron replied, then went to his packs to get his sword before going into the darkness to search. He fumbled around, then swore, and finally said, "It's gone! My sword's gone."

Alanna gasped.

Unnerved, he walked two small circles in the darkness around the camp, but neither saw nor heard anything. They built-up the fire and went through their packs to see what else was gone, and the only other missing item was Cameron's coin bag. His heart sank. He had hoped to save as many coins as possible to at least partially repay Garth for the horse. But now they were without resources for their journey, and it would take years to make enough money to pay back Garth.

Alanna, feeling ashamed, began to cry. "I'm sorry, Cameron. I should have known it wasn't you. I saw him there." She replayed the vision of the thief in the firelight over and over in her mind. She had never been victimized like this before. "He was so close. I feel so violated. And so angry! What kind of person would do that?"

Cameron alternated between pacing angrily around the newly kindled fire and sitting in self-pity. "It's not your fault, Alanna. It's not like I did anything to stop it either."

His words didn't make her feel any better, but as she sat replaying the picture back in her mind, something about what she had seen nagged at her. *There was something familiar.* But she couldn't quite put her finger on it. Then it struck her. "The boy! The boy back in Tandor." It was the tear in his left shirtsleeve—she had seen it back in the village. "He was watching us."

"Are you sure?"

"Positive!" She jumped up. "He must have followed us. I'm sure we looked like easy marks. I'm so stupid." She paced for a while, then sat back down. She was silent for a change, ruminating over their misfortune at first, then sulking.

But Cameron's anger was building and finally reached a threshold. He stood to secure the hunting knife to his belt. "I can't just sit here while that worthless thief gets away with this. We've gotten by just fine without coins before, but I can't let him get away with my sword. It belongs in my family."

Alanna, usually having the more rational mind, offered no opposition to his plan to go after the thief. She was equally incensed. "I'm coming with you," she said while wiping tears from her cheeks.

"I think you'd better stay here, Alanna. If I catch him, it's gonna get kind of rough."

"We're in this together, in case you've forgotten." She tightened the laces on her boots and scattered the burning branches from the fire. He didn't argue. They grabbed their packs and walked through the darkness back to the road. After hiding the packs in a nearby thicket, Cameron scored the ground at the road's center to mark the location before they headed back toward the village.

It wasn't long past midnight, and the last quarter moon was rising in the eastern sky. They moved as quietly as possible along the road, remaining vigilant for any movement or sound. They had traveled over a mile when Alanna's eye caught a fleeting glint ahead and to the left of the road. She scanned the shadowy silhouettes at the road's edge as they passed, and the subtle glint appeared again. She veered over to the spot and was stunned to find a sheathed sword propped against a tree. The moonlight had reflected from the hilt's polished surface.

"Cameron," she whispered, "I think it's your sword."

Cameron darted over and picked it up, and sure enough, it *was* his sword. He peered around, realizing the thief had to be nearby, and put his finger to his lips to hush Alanna when she started to whisper something again. They scanned the forest's deep shadows, and roughly a hundred paces in, a small campfire barely flickered.

GARRETT

Garrett Braennen was eighteen years old and well-acquainted with life's harsh realities in remote, northern Eastmoorland. He was born to a free-spirited single mother in a northern woodland settlement where the highly conservative values of the townsfolk created an unwelcoming and judgmental backdrop to her life. His father was not equipped for the responsibilities that came with family life and quietly disappeared shortly after the pregnancy was announced. So, when Garrett was three years old, his mother moved them to the city of Clearwater, where anonymity offered less judgment, to eke out a meager living.

Her job skills were scant, so she descended into cycles of non-virtuous employ in the city's seedier areas. Garrett grew up and spent his days in the rough streets of the local neighborhoods, becoming self-reliant and wise to the realities of the forgotten poverty-ridden alleys. He had no formal education, although his mother did teach him to read and write during intermittent periods of sobriety. She had taken to alcohol to cope with life's bitter realities. And in those bad times, hunger became his only reliable companion.

He had learned to support himself through petty theft in Clearwater's unpredictable streets. Early on, he learned to endure the beatings inflicted by his victims or the city's constables when he was caught stealing. But once he grew into adolescence, forgiveness became scarce and the beatings more severe. By necessity, Garrett became very adept at thievery, and getting caught became a thing of the past. He grew into a quiet self-confidence and plied his trade in relative isolation, interacting only with trustworthy and tight-lipped fences. Street savvy and cunning kept him from being forced under the wing of professional criminals running organized theft rings. And so he was able to help support both his and his mother's most basic needs.

When Garrett was fifteen, his mother's condition became so desperate that he knew he had to move her away from the city. She was the only family he knew, and he did not want to lose her to the obvious end that her life of depravity was leading. He hatched a scheme to steal from a wealthy businessman, and being so accomplished at his trade, he succeeded. He sold the jewels and trinkets that he had taken from the businessman's home, and within two days loaded his mother and their meager possessions into a wagon and left the city. The businessman was well-connected and would have paid off whomever he needed to track down the thief who had taken and sold his property, so Garrett knew he could never return to Clearwater again.

They ended up in the small port town at the south end of Clearwater Lake, where Garrett paid a healer to get his mother safely through alcohol withdrawal. He actually held down a legitimate job as a dock hand until his mother was fully recovered. But he knew the businessman's reach was long, so he and his mother moved again to the small village of Tandor, where he hoped they could make a fresh start in the foothills of the Black Mountains.

Garrett wasn't proud of his past, but neither did he feel guilt for stealing from others to support himself and his mother through those difficult years. Under the circumstances of his childhood, other options simply were not available to him. He worked when he could as a laborer in Tandor, but the remote location and its poverty meant work was infrequent and underpaid. His mother's health was generally poor, and her harsh life left her without motivation, so Garrett took care of her the best he could.

When Garrett was seventeen, his mother caught the attention of a quiet, middle-aged man in Tandor. The two spent more and more time together and seemed to be happy in one another's company. The man was good to her, and although he suspected the truth of her past, he never asked her about it. Garrett saw that they were happy and learned to trust that the man was gentle, having no harmful intent toward his mother. So Garrett started spending more time by himself, venturing out to explore the surrounding lands. Having grown up in the city, the remote lands around Tandor were intriguing and full of new adventure. So he kept no remorse for having left the city's filthy streets.

His mother eventually married the man, and they moved into his small home. It was comfortable enough for Garrett living there during the times that he found work around the village. If work was unavailable and weather conditions tolerable, however, he was gone for days at a time. He was drawn to the mountains and ventured further and further into the remote valleys. Just like in the city, he learned to take care of himself in the expansive wilderness.

Garrett knew better than to steal from the local villagers. To be caught would be disastrous in a small community where such offenses were dealt with harshly. Not to mention, he and his mother would be shunned, and employment opportunities would all but disappear. Besides, he was content working intermittent jobs, and they lived comfortably enough by his standards. That isn't to say, though, that his opportunistic tendencies were completely forgotten.

It is, then, without surprise that his eye would occasionally catch an unwary traveler in the village or on the road. He wasn't above taking from those whom he felt to be more fortunate than himself. After all, they had the means to replace what was taken from them given their privileged existences. At least, that was how he rationalized it. So it was, on a spring day, two young, unsuspecting travelers arrived to visit the mercantile. Garrett followed them discreetly and watched the young man pull coins from a rather swollen purse to pay for supplies, then retreated down the street to casually watch them leave the mercantile. He noticed the sword and shield the young man carried, making him think twice about targeting them. But he decided to follow them anyway, keeping well behind and out of sight.

Near dusk, the two travelers left the road and camped a short distance into the woods. Garrett retreated back down the road and found a comfortable place in the grass to sleep until nightfall. Then, in the darkness of the early night, he crept quietly along the road until he could make out the flickering fire in the distance. He made his way through the trees and tucked himself quietly behind a thicket of grass and shrubs about fifty paces from the campsite. He sat and waited until there were no sounds or movements for some time and the fire had died down. He crept forward and entered the camp near the packs and quietly rummaged through them until he found the coin purse. He pulled it out, and it made a soft clinking sound when the coins shifted. Looking at the two sleeping travelers, he saw no movement but felt an urgency to leave before they woke. He turned on his haunches and noticed the sword propped against another pack. It was intriguing, and he had never held one before. He was reaching for it just as the girl's head rose, so he snatched it and quickly snuck into the darkness.

Garrett was a safe distance from the camp when he heard the girl's exclamations, so he moved more swiftly toward the road and started running back to the village. Before long, he tired and slowed his pace to a walk, knowing he could duck into the woods to hide if he heard them following. He smiled smugly and started humming in quiet celebration.

The coin purse held more coins than he had hoped, and the sword was an unexpected bonus.

His euphoria was soon interrupted when he noticed another flickering fire through the undergrowth in the woods. *Could I be so lucky?* he thought, feeling overzealously confident. He decided it wouldn't hurt to take a look and crept into the edge of the woods, propping the sword against a tree where he could easily recover it. He covered the distance through the woods quietly, listening for any signs of stirring while he inched ever closer to the fire, but all was quiet. He scanned the camp's perimeter, then the area around the flickering fire, and he saw four sleeping figures. Then he heard snorting and gentle shuffling of hooves a short distance away—horses tied just outside the camp.

Garrett stopped and stood motionless, scanning every detail in the shadows. He saw no sentry and no indication that the travelers were awake. Once satisfied, he crept the remaining distance toward a pile of gear, grabbed a medium-sized pack, and carried it back into the shadows. He undid the buckles and rummaged through the contents but was startled by a sudden flurry of sound and movement from behind. He lunged to the side, anticipating the oncoming assault, and the sentry he had not seen in the darkness glanced off his leg. He felt a hand grapple for his ankle but was just able to pull free, and he surged toward the road, unaware of the tree in the darkness. His head impacted squarely, and he crumpled to the ground, stunned and unable to regain his bearings before the man was on him.

The man was strong and held him firmly until his companions were awakened. They tightly bound his hands and feet, then dragged him closer to the fire. Garrett squirmed into a sitting position and sat with his back against a small tree, blood trickling down his face from the gash in his forehead. The men scampered around the surrounding woods searching for any accomplices and seemed to be satisfied that he was alone. They built up the fire and turned their attention to Garrett, who sat forlornly, wishing he had embraced self-restraint instead of giving in to his greed.

The men were well-armed and appeared to be part of an organized militia. They wore the same gray armbands, but one man was clearly in charge. "So, what do we have here?" the man asked as he squatted in front of Garrett.

Garrett sat with his head drooped forward, stubbornly ignoring the man's question. Another man came from behind and grabbed Garrett's hair, pulling his head back while pushing the blade of a knife against his throat. The man said in a coarse voice, “Don’t be shy, boy. He asked you a question. Why are ya sneakin’ around here?”

Garrett’s stubborn defiance quickly transformed into fear. The leader raised his hand to calm the second man’s temper, and the knife relaxed away from Garrett’s neck. “Tell me what you’re doing here,” the leader said insistently.

Garrett’s defiance returned, and he replied, “Isn’t it obvious?”

“Is there anyone else with you?”

“No. I sneak alone,” Garrett curtly added.

The leader stood, obviously irritated, and walked away. “Get rid of him!” he ordered.

Two men grabbed Garrett by the arms, lifted him to his feet, and began to drag him deeper into the forest while the man with the knife followed.

Garrett briefly struggled to no avail, then yelled back to the leader, “Wait! My father’s rich. He’ll pay ransom if you don’t kill me.”

The mention of ransom clearly piqued the interest of the two men carrying him. They stopped in their tracks and looked back to the leader. The leader glanced over and scanned him head to toe in the flickering light, then laughed. “You take me for a fool. Rich boys don’t wear rags. Get rid of him.”

“No, wait! I can prove it. I have more coins in my pocket than you’ve probably ever held. And there’s more where they came from.” Garrett was buying time. He needed to come up with a plan to get himself out of this pickle.

They searched his pockets and found the stolen coin bag. The leader emptied it into his hand and sifted through the coins, surprised and impressed at the boy’s wealth. “Where do you live? And what’s your father’s trade?” he asked, emphasizing his lack of patience by gripping Garrett’s neck and forcing his head back.

“He owns the mercantile in Tandor. His name’s Jayce Carson. He’ll pay you if you let me go, I swear.” Garrett instilled some truth into his story just in case the men were familiar with the mercantile. Jayce was the actual owner, though he was an older man with much older children.

The leader considered the situation and was unable to see any downside to holding the boy for ransom. Being under the employ of the Khaalzin, he was used to acting with a degree of impunity. He was charged with searching this area for a young man and a girl traveling together, and he would not be questioned for taking a day or two to make a little profit on the side. And he doubted that the constable in Tandor would be bold enough to provide any resistance. After all, the boy had tried to steal from them, and demanding a ransom was more merciful than the other option. "Come morning, we'll get payment from your father for our inconvenience," he said.

Being the middle of the night, and showing no regard for his comfort, the men tied Garrett securely to a tree. Four of the five returned to their blankets and slept, and the fifth took over sentry duty. "Keep quiet, boy, or I'll slit your worthless throat," the sentry said.

TRIO

"Alanna, where are you?" Cameron whispered after returning to the road.

Alanna had positioned her thin frame behind a tree on the opposite side of the road after Cameron crept into the forest toward the distant campfire. He had moved in with extreme caution, hoping against the odds that he might still find a way to recover the coin purse. They had briefly argued over the necessity; after all, they had already recovered the sword. But Cameron's anger over the predicament won out over Alanna's pleas for caution. Hearing Cameron's voice, she emerged from her hiding place relieved to see him safe.

"What did you see?"

"They caught him, but I could only hear bits and pieces."

"Who caught him?"

"I'm guessing they're militia, or maybe the Khaalzin's henchmen. I didn't want to get too close. I bet he was trying to steal from them, too. It sounds like they're gonna hold him for ransom."

"Ransom? Who's gonna pay ransom for him?"

"They think his family's rich. They found the coin purse."

"How many are there?"

"Five. There's no way I'm gonna get the coins back. You were right, Alanna, we should cut our losses and get away from here."

She hesitated. "What's going to happen to him?"

"Who cares? He got himself into it. But I think they were gonna kill him before they found the coins."

"Cameron! You aren't thinking of just leaving him with killers, are you? I saw that boy back in Tandor, and he definitely isn't from a wealthy family. What will they do once they figure that out?"

"I'm not gonna risk your life or mine for someone like him. He's not worth it!"

"What do you mean by 'someone like him'? You don't know anything about him! He's a petty thief, not a murderer. How can you condemn him to death over a few coins?"

"What do you want me to do? I can't just start a fight with five armed men." But Cameron knew she was right. Of course she was right. She was being irritatingly rational, a quality he had admired in her before this moment. But in his acquiescence, he came to a compromise. "Fine. I'll give him a chance to save himself, but I'm not putting us at any more risk. Do you still have that small knife in your pocket?"

Alanna handed the knife to Cameron, and he crept back into the woods toward the fire. As he cautiously approached the camp, he saw four men sleeping by the fire, but the sentry escaped his vision. He waited in the still darkness before someone stirred just a short distance from the boy. The man shook his head as if to ward off sleep and tossed aside the blanket that had been wrapped around him. Then he stood and walked over to the boy, checking the ropes that bound him before wandering away to check on the horses.

Cameron seized the opportunity to sneak over to the boy. He approached from behind and hissed a quiet "Shhh" to avoid startling him. He put the knife into his bound hands and whispered, "You're on your own, thief." Cameron crept away into the darkness to rejoin Alanna.

They returned along the road to their packs as morning light crept into the eastern sky. Cameron contemplated their continued southerly path along the road but knew the men back at the camp were likewise traveling in the same direction and would eventually overtake them.

"I think we should go back to our camp and wait for those goons to get past us. I don't want to run into them again." He obliterated the mark he had made on the road to locate the packs. Alanna agreed, and they returned to the camp, just far enough from the road to be hidden but close enough to watch for the group to pass.

All was quiet until the morning sun began to filter through the trees. Alanna napped while Cameron fidgeted on the uncomfortable ground, his hand firmly gripped around his sword's hilt. He was startled by a snapping twig, and he sprang to his feet in a defensive pose, peering into the woods. To his amazement, the boy emerged from the shadows into the open with his hands upraised in a submissive gesture, waiting for Cameron's reaction.

Cameron scanned the surroundings, fearful the boy might have led his captors to their camp. He looked back at the boy and stepped toward him. "You have a lot of nerve showing your face here."

Alanna was awakened by Cameron's voice. Unsure of his intent, she darted behind him and grabbed his jacket. "Don't do anything crazy, Cameron." She peered around him and asked the boy, "What do you want here?"

"I'm honestly not sure," came the hesitant reply. He moved into the clearing. After a brief silence, he carefully reached into his pocket and removed the small knife. He offered it back to Cameron. "I guess I came to return this."

Alanna stepped forward and took it. "That would be mine, thanks."

They stood silently for a time, scrutinizing the tall, wiry boy. Dirty and tattered garb betrayed his poverty, and his boyish features suggested he was perhaps a year or two younger than Cameron and Alanna. He was, however, about a year older. His hair was jet-black with a long, narrow braid centered in the back and secured at the end with a green tie. His face was gaunt, highlighting high cheekbones and a narrow nose and chin, and his expression was pitiful and submissive. Strikingly green eyes portrayed an eerie and mysterious, perhaps even freakish, persona. They were, in fact, quite unusual in color, like emerald illuminated in daylight, and figured prominently in his self-conscious tendencies. Dried blood still streaked down his face from the gash in his forehead, eliciting concern from Alanna.

"Sit down. That cut needs to be cleaned," Alanna commanded. She went to work with a wet rag while Cameron stood over them, still holding his sword at the ready.

"You don't need to stand watch like that," the young man said. "I didn't come back here to cause any trouble. I've had enough for one night."

"And how do we know they won't follow you here?" Cameron retorted.

"After I cut myself loose, I ran the other way. I circled back here after I was sure I lost them." He paused briefly, then said in a concessionary tone, "You probably saved my life, so I owe you my caution at least."

They sat silently while Alanna finished cleaning his wound. Cameron relaxed but remained wary of any movement or sound in the gradually brightening forest.

"Why'd you come back to help me?"

"She made me."

"Don't be a jerk, Cameron! You know it was the right thing to do."

"Whatever! Don't forget we have no coins now. And how am I ever gonna repay Garth for the horse?"

The young man fidgeted and dropped his gaze to the ground as a pink flush spread over his cheeks. He offered in a regretful tone, "I'm sorry about stealing the coins . . . and the sword. At least you found it."

"Sorry you stole them, or sorry you didn't get away with it?" Cameron said.

"To be honest, both."

"Seriously? Do you even have a shred of conscience?"

Alanna stood and stepped in front of Cameron, pushing him away from the young man as tensions escalated. "Take it easy, Cameron. You don't know anything about him or what his life's like. Maybe you should give him a chance to explain himself. And keep your voice down. Those men could be coming along the road any time now."

Cameron turned, stepped away, and propped his back against a nearby tree while still ruminating over the lost coins.

Alanna sat on the ground in front of the young man and tried to entice his gaze. But he was clearly uncomfortable with eye contact and continued to stare at the ground.

"What's your name?"

"Garrett."

"So, Garrett, I assume you live in Tandor. I saw you there yesterday."

"Yeah."

"And you saw us and thought we were an easy mark?"

"Yep."

"And you saw the group of militia and thought . . . what exactly?"

He sat quietly in reflection, shifted uncomfortably, and replied, "I guess I got a little overly enthusiastic."

"Oh sheesh!" Cameron couldn't help verbalizing his annoyance.

Alanna gave Cameron an irritated glance. "It sounds like a rough way to make a living."

"I don't generally get caught," Garrett replied in a soft voice, as if admonishing himself.

"I can't listen to any more of this," Cameron said in exasperation.

"Be quiet, Cameron! If those men hear you, they'll be right back on your trail again."

Garrett perked up and actually made eye contact with Alanna, and she knew she had said too much.

"What do you mean? Why would they be chasing *you*?"

"That's none of your business," Cameron said.

"Did you steal those coins from someone else?" Garrett asked, hoping to level the ethical playing field.

"You would assume that, wouldn't you?" Cameron snipped. "I work to make my way in this world, but I guess you wouldn't know anything about how that works."

"Whatever. You know, I'm really not such a bad person."

Alanna stared directly into his eyes and firmly replied, "Well, I guess that depends on your point of view."

Garrett reflected in shameful silence. After a time, he looked back at Alanna. "Where are you going? I know this area pretty well if you need some help."

"We don't need your help," Cameron said. "We'll be on our way after those men pass through."

Alanna sighed in frustration and walked away to sit by herself. She was growing tired of male stupidity.

They sat in awkward silence for some time. Cameron was beginning to wonder why Garrett was still hanging around and was about to suggest that he be on his way when Garrett spoke.

"Look, I am actually sorry about stealing from you. I'm not so good at being around other people. You saved my life, and I wanna make it up to you. I don't really care why you're avoiding those men. It doesn't matter. I can get you a good ways away from here and avoid the road if you let me."

Alanna kept quiet and let them work it out. Cameron thought for a short time, and despite his anger and pride, knew Garrett offered them the best chance of making some unobstructed progress in their journey. Besides, other than the sword, they had nothing of value left to steal.

"We need to go south into Eastmoorland," he finally conceded.

"I know a safe path or two closer to the mountains. It's remote and hard to travel if you don't know the way. I can get you at least several miles toward—"

"Shhh! Get down!" Alanna interrupted. She saw movement along the road to the north.

Cameron and Garrett quickly ducked behind cover and watched as five horsemen sauntered along the road. They watched until the men passed and waited for the sound of receding voices and hoofbeats to disappear.

"Well," Cameron announced, "if we're gonna do this, let's get going. We'll take your help for now."

Garrett clumsily offered to carry Alanna's pack. She looked at him through suspicious, squinted eyes and declined the offer. He had no difficulty picking up on her silent message and led them toward the road.

Intending to cross, Garrett inched forward to peer in both directions. It was clear, so they started across toward the river. He planned to cross it and make for the mountains beyond. But unexpectedly, a man stumbled out of the forest and onto the road not far away. At first, he didn't notice them while tying the belt to his trousers. But when he turned to lead his horse back onto the road, he spotted the trio, frozen in their tracks from surprise.

“Hey,” the man yelled, triggering the trio’s hasty dash into the forest. This was followed by several loud whistles and more yelling as the man tried to get his comrades’ attention, but they had already disappeared from his sight. Receding hoofbeats followed, and Cameron knew the man would soon return with the full posse. He cursed his bad luck and sped behind Garrett and Alanna, who were already running toward the river.

SEEKING SANCTUARY

After plunging through the river, the three companions ran as fast as they could manage to the east. Alanna quickly fatigued from running with her pack and lagged behind. Garrett insisted she let him carry it, and this time she let him. Cameron stopped to look and listen, but there was no sign of the pursuers yet. Winded, he struggled to ask Garrett where they were headed.

"We need to make it another two miles, and we should be able to lose them. We can't slow down yet."

"I hope you know what you're doing," Cameron replied.

"I get why you don't trust me, but just keep up and I'll get you away from them."

So they ran and ran. After another mile, Cameron stopped to listen and heard the distinct sounds of pursuit but surmised they had not been spotted yet. Despite fatigue, they ran for their lives.

Still ahead of the posse, they reached a steep ravine cut through the loose sandstone layers near the junction of two low, exposed ridges. Alanna looked into the ravine and saw what looked like an inescapable trap. The ravine's walls were nearly vertical and appeared impassable even on foot. Loose rock and sand at the edge hinted at sketchy footing.

Garrett urged them down the near side into the ravine, but after seeing their hesitation, slid down himself. With bolstered courage, they followed by sliding on their backsides to the bottom. Garrett crossed the narrow creek and struggled partway up the loose bank on the opposite side, finally grasping an exposed tree root. He climbed the rest of the way with remarkable agility and disappeared briefly while Alanna tried and failed to scale the loose wall. Garrett returned with a long vine and fed it down. Alanna ascended with Garrett's help while the sound of horses crashing through the understory grew louder. Cameron grabbed the vine and started to hoist himself up, but a pack slipped from his shoulder and tangled his arms. He dropped back down, gripped the pack and tossed it up, then pulled himself up the vine. The horsemen crashed through the woody scrub and up to the ravine's edge while Cameron, panicked from their proximity, scrambled over the top. His foot struck the small pack that he had thrown up, knocking it backward. He reached for it in his panic and missed, then watched it fall into the ravine.

Two horsemen dismounted and jumped into the ravine while the fugitives expended what felt like the last of their energy running away. Cameron turned to see the remaining horsemen frustrated by their quarry's proximity. The two who had jumped into the ravine never emerged, and the leader growled and cussed above them.

Garrett slowed the pace once they were beyond a ridge and out of the horsemen's sight. The land ahead was striped with ridges and valleys leading upward toward the ever-expanding Black Mountains. The massive, intimidating peaks appeared so much closer from this vantage than they had from the road. Garrett offered encouraging words, "They'll have to travel a long way to get around that ravine. Unless they leave the horses behind, we should be able to put some distance between us and them."

Despite their exhaustion, Garrett led them at a brisk walking pace over two more ridges and across the intervening valley. After coming to a narrow, cascading river, they followed it for a time to higher elevations. In all, they covered several miles over the rugged terrain before nightfall and reached the very limit of their endurance.

The air at dusk was already cold, and Alanna shivered uncontrollably not long after they stopped for rest. Cameron gathered firewood, knowing the night would be unbearably cold for their exhausted bodies, and started a fire by a rocky alcove. The pack that had fallen into the ravine held the majority of food rations they had purchased back in Tandor. The few remaining rations that they scrounged from the other packs were scant, though they shared what they could with Garrett. What remained would be exhausted the next morning. The fire flickered in low flames that failed to hold back the cold in the thin air. They suffered a fitful, shivering sleep, and with no blanket, Garrett curled up as close to the fire as possible.

The next morning revealed a light frost painted over the landscape, and at the first hint of light, they continued an eastward march, eventually cresting the peak of a ridge into a beautiful pink and orange horizon highlighting the mountain silhouettes in the distance. Garrett scanned the shadowed range and pointed to a nondescript mountain peak far away. "That's where we're headed. It's about a day and a half walk from here."

Cameron felt more secure with a tangible destination, even though it was an unfamiliar place. Being led blindly by a thief was discomforting at best. For the remainder of the day they trekked along the rugged terrain, up and down the remnants of the foothills and then into the Black Mountains themselves. Tree and shrub cover was sparse at higher elevations, especially at the peaks of hills and ridges. They were potentially exposed to their pursuers from time to time, but somehow they managed to stay ahead of the horsemen. Cameron was thankful that the ruthless Khaalzin were not among them.

Twilight brought the three companions to a secluded canyon recess. Remnants of previous campfires littered the ground, and Garrett confided that he had spent many nights here as a base for his explorations. He recovered a bag of supplies he had stashed in a hole in the nearby canyon wall. In it he found dry tinder and flint for making fires and, more importantly, a thick blanket. Once they were settled for the night, Garrett wrapped himself in the blanket and curled up by the fire.

Garrett talked very little in their time together. He was a loner and had difficulty opening up in conversation with anybody. Even though he had longed for friendships throughout his difficult life, he never had the opportunity to develop any meaningful relationships apart from his mother. And she certainly did not provide him a good role model in that regard.

Frankly, Cameron struggled to find any topic to bring up in conversation with Garrett. Even Alanna, who was normally very boisterous and talkative, felt self-conscious talking to Cameron in Garrett's presence. There was, of course, a complete absence of trust, and she felt insecure speaking her mind in front of him. But she found the prolonged silence unbearable. For her, talking was a compulsion, and she thought she would burst or suffer some sort of catastrophic internal derangement if the silence continued. Alanna knew nothing about this young man, except that he had stolen from Cameron. But she knew that prejudgment was wrong, and she finally submitted to her compulsion and curiosity.

"So, Garrett, do you have family back in Tandor?"

After an awkward silence, Garrett sat up and rewrapped the blanket around himself. "My mother and stepfather live there. It's a really small house, so I don't spend much time there."

Alright, there's a start. Her natural inclination was to follow up with a barrage of additional questions, but she suppressed the urge. "My father raises sheep and runs a small supply business in the little village where I grew up. It's about two days' ride north of Clearwater."

"I grew up in Clearwater. We moved to Tandor about three years ago."

"You must be bored there, especially after living in Clearwater. It sounds like you spend a lot of time out here."

"Yeah, I guess. But it's not so bad in Tandor. My mother's happy there."

"Cameron grew up on a farm in Southmoorland," Alanna baited. But Cameron remained silent.

Garrett read her intent and played along. "You're a long way from home, then."

"And I just keep getting further and further away," Cameron said glumly.

"So, why exactly are these men looking for you?"

"Let's just say it's an old family feud."

Garrett was clearly dissatisfied with the response, and Alanna, not wanting to lose momentum, elaborated, "They seem to think his family poses a threat to their power, so they decided that killing him would be the best solution."

"That doesn't sound very rational. So, you didn't actually do anything to deserve it? I've had people want to kill me, but I mostly deserved it."

Cameron recognized his lighthearted humor and allowed himself a small chuckle.

Garrett asked, "So, why are you going to Eastmoorland?"

"It just seemed like the safest route to get Cameron back home."

"Well, tomorrow morning we'll come to a river in the valley that flows to the south and eventually drains into the Eastmoorland plains. But the plains are a really long way from here, and I've never actually followed the river past this valley. So I can't guarantee it's passable. The way that I wanted to show you was back on the other side of the ravine where we lost those horsemen. But they would have caught us for sure."

They fell back into silence under sheer exhaustion from the day's travel and endured the pangs of hunger until sleep took them. The next morning was clear and cool when they exited the canyon. Upon cresting a high ridge, they paused to view the surroundings. Garrett had been leading them east, and as Cameron gazed into the distance, he saw towering peaks to the north, east, and south. Despite the vast openness around him, he couldn't shake the claustrophobic feeling the surrounding mountains elicited. Cameron looked behind them to the west where the sky was transforming into a dark blue canvas over the lowlands. His eyes adjusted, and he saw a wispy smoke trail rising above the sparsely treed ridges perhaps two miles behind.

"Well, Garrett, whatever your plan is, we'd better get started. They're still behind us."

Garrett led them up a steep slope covered in loose rock and gravel toward the crest of another ridge. It was fully exposed to anyone looking from the west. "This is the last ridge before the river valley. We should hurry."

Footing was difficult, and they slipped backward often. But the slope was even steeper to the left and right. Their lungs burned from the effort in the thin air. Almost at the top, Cameron stopped to peer behind. His keen vision revealed unmistakable movement along the top of a ridge about one and a half miles back. The horsemen were headed straight for them.

The threesome finally crested the peak, revealing a splendorous panorama. Under any other circumstances, they would have stopped to take in the breathtaking view, but urgency drove them forward. Below was an expansive but more gently sloping path. It was covered in loose, eroded stone and led down to an increasingly lush plain covered in the layered sediments from ages of mountain erosion. The snake-like carvings of a meandering river and oxbow ponds adorned the flat landscape, which now filled what used to be an ancient valley between the mountain peaks. The expansive river flat stretched out before them and ushered an approach to a forest of whitebark pine ascending in the distance like a blanket draped upon the lap of the Black Mountains' core. The river meandered to the south through the flats to the limit of their sight. The valley was lush with tufted grass and scattered small shrubs, but there was no cover to hide them along that path.

So they scrambled down the treacherous rock-littered slope and eventually reached the flats. The river was still a considerable distance away, but Cameron and Alanna veered to the south as planned. Garrett slowed and yelled after them, "Good luck!"

Cameron and Alanna stopped, not anticipating Garrett's sudden separation. "What do you mean, *Good luck?*" Cameron snapped. "Where are *you* going?"

"A place to hide for a while," he replied, sensing Cameron's ire. "It's not somewhere you wanna go. It's probably not safe."

"*Safe?* And running in the open from men on horses *is* safe?"

"Look, I can't help you anymore. When I offered to help you find the way, I wasn't expecting to be chased!"

Alanna stared at Garrett incredulously. Her bright blue eyes in the morning sun reflected disbelief, and her expression transformed into one of disappointment, then hopelessness, then defeat.

He matched her gaze and willed himself to look away, but he was transfixed. At that moment, something stirred in his conscience and in his heart, and they were altogether unfamiliar feelings. The cloak of self-interest and self-reliance he labored under for so many years suffered a sizable rent in that moment. He pried his eyes away, but the unexpected feelings were still there. Pity and guilt had already taken root, and he grudgingly gave in to his conscience.

"Fine, but consider yourselves warned. Follow me."

They started directly across the flats toward the river, knowing their footprints would be easy to see in the moist soil. The riverbed was cast in small stones and pebbles, and the water was shallow, providing no impediment to crossing. The grassy expanse was narrower on the far side, but they were severely winded when they reached the first sentries of the pine forest, scraggly half-dead trees that offered little cover for the pursued. But even while they raced further into the ascending forest, the improving cover did not assuage their nagging fears.

With gasping breaths in the thin mountain air, they ascended through the scattered trees and into increasingly sparse cover. Burning lungs forced them to stop intermittently to catch their breath, each time peering behind to the open plain. And with a shudder of panic, they spotted four horsemen galloping toward them across the open expanse.

"Hurry!" Garrett yelled. "We're almost there."

Between gasps, Cameron said to Alanna, "Only four followed us. The fifth must have gone to find the Khaalzin."

The gasping trio continued the ascent through the trees over loose, dry soil until the ground terminated at a rocky shelf. They clambered up the short wall onto a rocky plateau that extended approximately fifty paces from the granite wall's sheer face. To the left of the plateau, shallowly rooted trees continued right up to the rock face. Straight ahead and to the right, the walls seemed impenetrable. The massive, vertical, granite sheets appeared to have been heaved up by the mountains that loomed behind. Standing silent and immovable, the massive peaks projected skyward, thrust upward from the depths of the world by some unimaginable force of nature. And the granite walls set before them guarded the towering mountains in the distance like a fortress.

From the plateau's edge, they ran toward the sheer rock walls. Garrett called for his companions to halt before the towering wall, and taking

Cameron by surprise, knocked him to the ground and brazenly tugged at his left shoe.

"What are you doing, you lunatic?" Cameron objected.

"Just shut up and give me your shoes!"

"Why?"

Garrett wrestled the second shoe off Cameron's other foot and raced away toward the rock wall to the right, where they could now see a gap between the rock face in front and the one to the right.

"Start climbing that tree—the tall one closest to the rock face." He pointed and emphasized, "Both of you, and I'll be right back. I'll lure them into the maze." They stared in bewilderment at Garrett, who turned back again, and seeing the confusion in their faces, shouted, "Just trust me!"

Alanna and Cameron ran to the left and jumped down from the plateau onto the loose soil. Cameron climbed into the lower branches and reached down to help Alanna up, while Garrett passed through the gap and emerged into an open space. He ran across a span of loose accumulated sand and soil, then onto another rocky surface that looked every bit like the entrance to a maze. Boulders and rock spires stretched haphazardly into the distance. The rocky surfaces of this high ground were washed clean of soil and sand by rain and wind and would effectively conceal their faux escape. He knew the area well, and it wasn't the first time he had played this sort of game.

Garrett changed into Cameron's shoes and walked backward across the long patch of sandy soil. Two sets of tracks would have to suffice since time was preciously short. He sprinted back over the rocky plateau and leapt toward the climbing tree. "Break off a branch and toss it down. And keep climbing!"

Cameron did as he was told. He and Alanna continued upward through the branches. He glanced down with a sickening feeling in his gut and said, "There's no cover up here. They'll be able to see right up to the top from down there. I knew I shouldn't have trusted him!"

While Cameron seethed, Garrett swept the ground to cover their footprints, then hoisted himself up to the lowest branch. He inverted his body and dangled by his legs while sweeping away the last evidence of his lingering beneath the tree. Garrett sprang upward through the branches toward Cameron, offering the shoes back to his wide-eyed companion, then inconspicuously stashed the broken branch high up in the tree. After a guileful wink, he climbed into the uppermost branches—and disappeared.

THE SECRET

Cameron climbed the remaining branches that would support his weight and pushed aside the clusters of green needled twigs to reveal Garrett's legs and feet swinging freely in front of the rock wall. He was clutching a rope hanging from the ledge above, and he quickly pulled himself up.

"Unbelievable," Cameron muttered to himself while he helped Alanna into the upper branches. By holding her wrist, she was able to stretch her other arm out to grasp the rope, and she hoisted herself onto the dangling line. She climbed as high as she could, and Garrett pulled her the rest of the way up to the ledge. Cameron heard the sound of approaching horses after beginning his own ascent on the rope. He scrambled up in a panic and swung his leg onto the ledge. He felt his belt loosen after the buckle scraped over the rock ledge and released. His sword slipped away and began to plunge downward. Making a frantic grab for the hilt, he just snagged it with his finger, but the scabbard slipped off. Alanna peered over with wide, panicked eyes to see it fall into the tree's branches. It cascaded down from branch to branch for what seemed an eternity, and then it was quiet—except for the hoofbeats.

Garrett pulled Cameron up, then coiled the rope upon the ledge. They flattened themselves against the rocky shelf and listened to the approaching horses. The sharp *clickety-clack* of horseshoes against rock sounded like a drum chorus while the riders busily searched for footprints. One horseman galloped away over the rocky plateau toward the maze, while the hoofbeats of another softened after dropping down to the loose pebbly soil under the trees. The trio collectively held their breath and waited.

Before long, the man under the trees called the others over. "This ground looks disturbed, but I don't see any tracks."

"Check up in the trees. I'll look further down the hill," said the group's leader, whose voice Garrett recognized.

From the ledge, they heard soft footsteps below. The man had dismounted and now wandered from tree to tree looking up into the branches. Cameron silently cursed himself for dropping the scabbard. They were trapped and already starving, and he knew they had no chance to win a waiting game if they were discovered on the ledge.

Then their luck changed. The man who had ridden to the maze called back, “This way! The tracks are over here!” And the remaining men hurried to the opening in the rock wall before the clicking of hooves receded into the distance.

Alanna whispered, “How did they *not* see your scabbard?”

“I don’t know, but we need to get it.”

“Wait here. I’ll get it.” And before Cameron could argue, Garrett tossed down the rope and was descending into the tree. He found the scabbard about halfway down, lodged along the length of a branch. He quickly ascended back to the ledge and handed it to Cameron.

“Thanks,” Cameron humbly offered.

“Let’s go before they come back.” Garrett walked to the far end of the ledge, climbed up to a shadowy recess, and disappeared inside. A vertical fissure in the rock face extended skyward, widening at the bottom where Garrett had entered it. Garrett slid sideways into the dark space and motioned for them to follow. They removed their packs to fit through the narrow opening, though the passage widened further in. They fought claustrophobia while stumbling over the rocky debris filling the crevice below and finally emerged into a damp, cavernous space.

“How did you ever find this hiding place?” Alanna asked.

“Bats. I saw them fly out of that opening when I was exploring. I figured there was a cave, or something worth crawling into.”

“It’s well-hidden,” Cameron admitted. “But how long can we stay in here? Those men could be hanging around for days when they figure out the maze is a dead end. We’re already starving.”

Garrett sat on a large, flat rock and contemplated the situation. “Yeah, you’re right about them finding a dead end. This whole situation isn’t what I had in mind. I just need to think for a while.” And he found himself at a crossroads.

Cameron and Alanna welcomed the time to rest in the cool space, so they sat quietly to honor Garrett’s private thoughts. Garrett had spent his lifetime carefully constructing a barrier around himself, and that stronghold was currently under siege. The day he burglarized the prominent businessman in Clearwater was the day he effectively locked the door of his personal fortress. Self-reliance was his only ally, and he chose to shut the world out, letting nobody into his private dominion, and certainly not into his confidence. He built his life inside that fortress and protected it as a sanctum. To unlock that door was to forsake that which was his and his alone. The outside world had given him nothing of worth except life itself, and to relinquish his secrets was to give away all that defined him, or so he thought.

His thoughts swirled, and in the dimly lit cavern, he glanced discreetly at Alanna. She sat not far from him, and he admired her profile while she mindlessly pulled knots from her long, tangled hair. Her face was gaunt, and she appeared exhausted. After several moments, her eyelids began to flutter closed, and her head repeatedly nodded. The journey was taking its toll on her, and Garrett began to feel another unfamiliar emotion—compassion. He tried to shake it off and looked away, but it was still there. *How is this happening?* By his reckoning, he had already repaid the debt he owed them for saving his life. He grabbed clumps of his hair and pulled, letting out a low groan, but still the unfamiliar feeling was there. He reclined onto the rock and closed his eyes, contemplating the strange emotion.

Garrett's soft groan had startled Alanna back to wakefulness. His inner struggle was becoming evident to her. She harbored a genuine concern for him, knowing his life must have been difficult, but there was so much she still didn't know about him. Her curiosity was irrepressible, and with cautionary reticence, she allowed her mind to wander into Garrett's peripheral thoughts. She detected no resistance, and he seemed unaware that she was exploring the surface of his mind. She was able to sense his inner conflict and hesitation, though her connection was brief and provided only a vague sense of his struggles. Exhaustion had taken its toll, and her mental exertion tapped the last of her reserves.

"We have to find some food," she said.

"Yeah," Cameron echoed. "But I'm not eating bats . . . not yet, anyway."

Garrett looked back at Alanna's dimly lit profile, and something breached his defenses again, further chipping away at the barrier. Ultimately, Garrett's conscience overruled his self-interest, and he inserted the key, opening the fortress door that concealed his carefully protected life for the first time. "Do you trust me?"

Alanna nodded.

Garrett led them into the deep shadows at the back of the tiny cavern and ducked into a low, pitch-black passage. They spent the remainder of the day moving in and out of passages and open spaces, squeezing through crevices, climbing rock faces, crawling over open rock-strewn passes and massive boulders. He had fastened ropes here and there to scale or descend vertical spans punctuating the hidden mountain pass. Some gaps and crevices were tight for Cameron, whose broader shoulders and thicker chest became a liability. But at day's end, they emerged from a dark, narrow crevice into a wide, enclosed space—another of Garrett's stopping points.

A small woodpile sat near the opposite opening, and a thick layer of dried grass lay on the smooth rock floor next to a heavy rolled-up blanket. There was no breeze in the space, but the air felt cold. Garrett arranged firewood over a pile of old ashes and before long had a small blaze going. The smoke rose and disappeared into the endless narrow gap above them.

"We have to stop here for the night. It's too dark to go any further today. Feel free to finish the water in your skins. I can get plenty of fresh water tomorrow morning."

Their hunger had actually receded during the day's activity as their stomachs grew accustomed to emptiness, but the exhaustion afflicting both body and mind remained. They slept soundly, and Cameron and Alanna woke the next morning to a subtle filtered light from the crevice above. Garrett was already gone but had rekindled the fire. They huddled over the flickering flames to ward off the chill air and waited impatiently for his return.

"I'm so hungry I could eat a rat . . . *raw!*" Cameron said.

"Me too. Where do you think he's taking us?"

"I'm not sure. But I'm getting tired of waiting here. I'm gonna see where that passage leads." Cameron tightened his belt and grabbed his knife, preparing to explore the passage ahead.

Just then, Garrett appeared out of the passage and excitedly asked Cameron for his knife before turning to leave again. Cameron started to follow, but Garrett stopped him and said, "No, just wait here for me. I can't explain now, but I will later." To keep Cameron occupied, he retrieved several sticks from behind the firewood and showed him how to assemble them for cooking over the fire. "Spread out the coals, we're eating this morning!"

Garrett returned a short time later with a skinned and field-dressed animal. It was definitely a fresh kill but was strangely missing its head and one forelimb. The tail had also been cut off, but the shape reminded Alanna of a Caraduan tree monkey she had once seen.

"How'd you catch it?" Cameron inquired.

"It wasn't that hard," he replied, plainly evading the question. He handed it to Cameron to put over the fire.

Being naturally curious, Cameron examined the animal before he skewered it onto the spit. It definitely looked like a small primate. The feet and remaining hand gave it away. He noticed a strange layer of tissue covering the spinal column inside the chest and abdominal cavities. The tissue was firm and resilient and not easily peeled away. He recalled Erral's description of something like this just as Garrett prodded him, "Stop poking it and cook it. I'm starving."

Barely able to wait for it to fully cook, they devoured most of the meat. Once their bellies were satisfied, Alanna asked, "What was that thing?"

"They call them *skrip-patalaen*, but I just call 'em *skrippals*.

"Wait," said Cameron, "*who* calls them skrip-patalaen?"

Garrett, for the first time, actually made eye contact with Cameron and matter-of-factly replied, "The Valenese people."

Surprised, Cameron and Alanna looked at one another, and Cameron said, "Alright . . . *the Valenese people* . . . and can we assume they're friendly?"

"You can assume whatever you want," Garrett said with his usual asocial and condescending flare. But Alanna's disapproving glance forced a thoughtful recasting of the reply. "I mean, the time I've spent with them has been . . . sort of complicated. They're kind of standoffish, but they've never been threatening to me. I've interacted with some of them, you know, trading trinkets and food, things like that. But I honestly don't know how the leaders would react to *your* being here.

"They stay down on the valley floor for the most part. They don't venture up very high into the mountains because of . . . well, like I said, it's complicated."

Cameron was irritated by Garrett's evasiveness, but Alanna was more understanding and inclined to indulge his need for privacy. She had felt his inner struggle.

"Listen, I honestly don't know if it's safe for you to come into the Vale with me, for a lot of reasons. It's not just because of the Valenese people. There are other things . . ." He hesitated, not sure of his next words. His self-protective instincts were roused again.

Alanna sensed his conflict and felt compelled to get her foot in the doorway before it closed. "We've seen our share of danger lately, especially Cameron," she offered.

"Alanna!" Cameron admonished.

"It's alright, Cameron. Garrett has a right to know what he's involved with."

Sensing Cameron's acquiescence, she continued, "Like I mentioned two days ago, some really dangerous men have been after him for almost a year now. And they've actually been looking for his family for generations. One killed his mother a few years ago, and then we had a brush with two others before we ended up here. Cameron had to kill one, in self-defense, of course."

Her story had the desired effect. Garrett was enthralled by the idea of dangerous exploits and better appreciated their predicament. He had never been directly involved in anyone's death, but his curiosity was roused. "How did you . . . I mean, how did the man die?"

"These men are extremely powerful," Alanna continued. "You may not believe me, but I'm telling the truth. They have an ability I never even imagined possible. They can create and project fire, or energy, or something, against other people. Cameron was able to somehow turn it back on him, and it killed the man."

Garrett looked at Cameron's shield, somehow deducing that it was involved, and quietly studied it from a distance. His intuitive interest didn't escape Cameron's notice.

It did escape Alanna, however, as she looked blankly into her lap to reflect for a moment. Then she looked up at Cameron with tears welling in her eyes and said, "I thought we were both going to die that day."

Forgetting Garrett for the moment, Cameron reached over and clutched her hand. "We would have if it weren't for you."

She wiped the tears from her eyes and sniffled. "So I guess my point is, whatever is out there in the Vale can't be any worse than what we've already seen."

"But it's not just me that they're interested in," Cameron said, talking to Alanna as much as he was to Garrett. "They're collecting an army of mercenaries across Southmoorland and Eastmoorland. They've been plundering farms and villages, killing leaders in the local militias, and basically just taking control over Gartannia. It's the same thing they did in Arnoria, where our families came from generations ago. They just want power."

Garrett shifted onto his hands and knees and crawled over to Cameron's shield. He reached for it but hesitated, looking back at Cameron. "Sorry, do you mind?"

"Go ahead," Cameron said.

Garrett studied the shield carefully, polishing parts of the metal with his shirtsleeve and holding it up to the firelight. "Where'd you get it?"

"It was passed down through my family. My grandmother gave it to me. It was made in Arnoria a long time ago, and it's apparently rare. But don't get any ideas."

Garrett grinned, not seeming to be offended. "I guess I deserve that. So, you used this against the man that died, didn't you?"

"Yes, but why would you assume that?"

"Just a guess. Anyway, maybe you *should* come with me to meet them. But if you don't wanna come, I can get food and water for you out in the Vale, and you can go back to the river and make your way down the valley to Eastmoorland. It's up to you."

"I'm coming with you," Alanna blurted.

Cameron was hesitant but agreed. Knowing they might still be lurking around, he wasn't ready to risk running into the horsemen again. So they gathered their packs and followed Garrett into the passage, traveling approximately two hundred paces before coming to a narrow opening illuminated by the late morning sun. Cameron struggled to squeeze through and stepped cautiously onto a narrow ledge. Loose gravel covered a steep downslope in front of him, terminating at the rocky margin of a deep canyon. It appeared likely that a slip on the steep gravel surface would surely end in a tumble over the edge followed by a lengthy free fall down the precipice. But safer ground sat to the right where Garrett had wisely tied a safety rope around a tree. The other end was knotted and pulled into a thin crevice near the tunnel opening. Using the rope, they took turns shimmying along the narrow path before stopping to admire the scenic view.

They stood on the western flank of a massive mountain vale. From this vantage, the vast valley floor spread many miles across, green and lush with a large, pristine lake at its center. Several streams and rivers flowed down from the surrounding mountains, connecting into the lake like the legs of a spider. Waterfalls cascaded from steep mountain faces rimming the valley floor, and snowcaps adorned the larger mountains to the north and east.

A sparse collection of shrubs and scraggly trees surrounded them on the small, level area. The elevation was about one and a half miles above the valley floor, yet the mountains still rose far above them. On the nearby slopes, scattered pockets of trees and other vegetation grew where the mountains yielded a foothold to root, but the higher elevations were increasingly barren. A group of mountain goats stood majestically on a distant rocky slope to their left, and an eagle soared nearby, lofted by the mountain breeze.

The way down was extremely difficult even for the agile youngsters. They walked along narrow ledges and descended abrupt rock faces unprotected from potentially deadly falls. But as they worked downward, the vertical cliffs gave way to steep slopes that guided them into descending valleys. Garrett led them over winding switchbacks and into increasingly vegetated valleys. And it was in these mid-elevations that he became noticeably more vigilant and edgy.

Cameron and Alanna both felt an uneasiness, like they were being stalked. Twice, Cameron's keen eyes glimpsed shadowy movement above them. Alanna sensed a presence but was unable to pinpoint its origin. She reached out with her mind but found every attempt willfully obscured by a shifting veil. Whatever it was, it was intelligent and kept a safe distance from the trio.

They descended ever closer to the valley floor into warmer, humid air. The abundant vegetation took on characteristics of a more tropical climate with thick, broad leaves. Chittering and strange calls belonging to unfamiliar animals filled the air.

In the early afternoon, they had their first encounter with one of the many strange animals inhabiting the Vale. Garrett led them around a blind turn, and they found themselves just a few steps from a small, bear-like creature. Garrett backed away and motioned for Cameron and Alanna to do the same. But the creature seemed not to be alarmed at their presence. Garrett nervously scanned the area before proceeding and maintained a wide berth while they passed around it.

"I don't see any young ones," Garrett said. "The males are normally harmless, but the females can be really dangerous when they're protecting their young. As a rule, keep your distance from anything that doesn't get spooked and run away from you. Some of the animals here can be really unpredictable—and deadly."

Not long after the encounter, Garrett slowed to listen to chittering and clicking coming from a dense pocket of trees. He motioned for Cameron and Alanna to follow while he cautiously crept through the understory. The clicking sounds escalated with their approach and then suddenly stopped, as if on cue. Garrett pointed into the trees ahead, and perched high up in the branches were several gray-haired primates with long tails peering back at the three trespassers. Two others leapt from the ground where they were foraging and climbed effortlessly into the high branches to join the troop of curious observers.

"Those are skrippals," Garrett announced.

Cameron and Alanna watched in amusement. Soon, the creatures lost interest in them, having sensed no immediate danger, and began to move about like acrobats in the trees. After a time, Cameron concluded that catching one would be quite difficult, contrary to what Garrett had said, but he kept his thoughts to himself.

Rabbits, squirrels, and other common animals abounded in the lush environment as well. They were more or less similar to their cousins outside the mountains. The vegetation was a mix of identifiable plants and trees but also strange varieties that they had never seen before. Garrett explained that the climate was always warm or hot in the Vale's low areas, but seasonal climates were more common in the mountain valleys at mid-elevations. He usually found familiar berries like raspberries, blackberries, and blueberries in those areas. The types of berries and fruits in the open lowland were strange to him, so he avoided eating them to be safe. Garrett was beginning to open up as he explained what he had learned about the Vale's plants and animals, but he remained continually vigilant and edgy during the descent. Cameron and Alanna were acutely aware but said nothing.

Darkness came early when the sun dropped below the mountain behind them, and for the night's camp Garrett led them to a shallow cave undercutting a limestone deposit. Despite it being spring, they had gathered a few nuts and berries from the warmer valleys, and combined with the leftover meat from breakfast, they made a decent meal for supper.

The safe and uneventful journey down the steep expanse seemed to buoy Garrett's spirits. Alanna's chatty personality also helped to loosen Garrett's tongue, and he finally opened up about his childhood tribulations and the general background of his life. Alanna listened intently with a hundred questions swimming in her head, but she hesitated to interrupt him. She found herself wanting to read between the lines of his stories and unconsciously allowed her mind to reach out as she had done, mostly harmlessly, as a child. She easily connected into his freely flowing thoughts since Garrett had no reason to suspect such an innocent invasion.

Alanna sensed the emotions and images attached to Garrett's stories. It was a unique ability she had discovered as a child that afforded her another dimension of insight when people told her stories, though her temptation to use it was infrequent. But shortly after connecting with Garrett, she sensed the nebulous presence from earlier in the day. And it wasn't long before Garrett's mind was obscured from her own as if a smothering cloud of smoke came billowing in, rapidly choking even her own thoughts. Then a low, rumbling growl echoed into her mind and quickly escalated to a penetrating howl.

Cameron was startled by Alanna's sudden panic. She spun her head from left to right as if looking for some unseen danger.

"Where's that sound coming from?" she frantically asked.

"I don't hear anything," replied Cameron, now on his feet. Then he was aware of something in the distance, the sound that a predator makes as it darts through foliage, and it was soon accompanied by the footfalls of a four-legged animal moving quickly in their direction.

The screeching howl in Alanna's head became unbearable, prompting her to cover her ears without effect, and she dropped to her knees in agony.

Cameron rushed over to his belongings and fumbled for his sword and shield just before a long, slender creature, clinging low to the ground with stealth-like agility, crashed into the clearing. Its fearsome white teeth were highlighted in the firelight, and its iridescent, bluish-black scaled skin extended from its narrow head to the tip of a long, sinuous tail. Its body twisted like a snake as it came forward on four legs, while great folds of skin draped from the backs of its forelimbs to its torso unfolded in an aggressive display. It was clearly focused on Alanna, who remained paralyzed on her knees, still clutching her head.

Fearing he would be too late, Cameron seized the shield and sword and turned to head the beast off before it reached her. But Garrett was already in front of her holding his hand out as if to ward off the creature. Alanna screamed and still clutched her ears when Cameron moved to join Garrett, but the beast had already stopped, its powerful tail flicking irritably in a serpent's motion from side-to-side. Soon, Alanna's screams subsided, and her hands dropped to the ground in submission.

Cameron froze, not wanting to agitate the creature. It repeatedly snorted through flared nostrils and opened its mouth to reveal a multitude of sharp canine teeth while slowly folding the sheets of skin back against its body. *They were wings*. Alanna recovered and straightened herself to sit back on her heels. As she shifted, the serpent craned its neck to peer around Garrett. It continued to snort with every exhaled breath in an aggressive display, but it did not advance beyond Garrett.

Cameron watched with unbelieving eyes while Garrett slowly lowered himself onto one knee and reached out to place his outstretched hand onto the serpent's neck. It seemed to calm the beast, and its snorting gradually quieted. Then it curled its neck to gaze at Cameron, revealing bright green reflective eyes, and released a soft, growling hiss.

"Cameron, put down the sword," Garrett directed. "She won't hurt you."

Cameron couldn't believe what he was seeing. And though hesitant, he slowly bent over and placed the sword at his feet.

"I told you to stay away," Garrett said softly to the serpent while he caressed her neck. "What's gotten into you?"

Cameron cautiously walked over to Alanna and helped her to her feet. The serpent's glowering eyes followed his hesitant movements, and she released a final, long hissing sound before fully submitting her aggression to Garrett's gentle caresses.

Garrett stood and coaxed the wary creature to the periphery of the camp where he sat with her, speaking gently and softly to calm her. Cameron's eyes were wide with amazement watching Garrett with the strange beast, and he sat next to Alanna, who was still shaking from fright.

"What just happened?" Cameron asked her.

She took two, deep, shaky breaths before looking ashamedly into her lap. "I don't really know. I mean, I think she was protecting him."

"From what?"

"From *me*."

"Oh, no. You didn't!"

"I'm sorry! It's really hard to break old habits. But he didn't even know I was doing it," she added defensively.

"But that doesn't make it right."

"I know! I know. Just stop lecturing me. The point is, *she* knew I was doing it, and *she* stopped me. You remember what I did to that gray rider that was holding me? She did pretty much the same thing to me just now."

"But how—"

"Don't you see? They have a connection. And did you see how intelligent her eyes are?"

Cameron wrapped a blanket around her shoulders, and they watched the creature in silence until Garrett returned from calming her.

"I'm really sorry, Alanna. I didn't think she'd ever do something like that. But she knows I'm angry about it, and I don't think it'll ever happen again."

"It won't, trust me on that," Alanna replied apologetically. "And don't be angry with her. It wasn't her fault. She was only trying to protect you."

Garrett was clearly distracted and didn't fully process her words. He couldn't peel his mind away from mental images of the averted carnage. He knew exactly what this young wyvern was capable of doing to flesh.

If she hadn't responded to him, well, he could never have lived with his decision to bring them into the Vale.

"What is she?" Cameron asked.

"The Valenese call them wyverna. They live in these mountains."

Cameron said, "My mother used to tell me stories about wyverns. But they're mythological, made up in fantasies and children's stories."

"All I know is what the Valenese people told me. I'd never heard of them before. They said they're the oldest surviving intelligent creatures to inhabit this world, and they existed even before the gods that ruled the earliest men. Honestly, it's just a lot of superstition to me, but the Valenese are serious about their traditions and lore."

"Well, she's definitely real," added Alanna. "How old is she?"

"I don't know. She's twice as big as when she found me almost two years ago. Her wings aren't fully grown yet, so she's still just a baby in my mind."

"Well, this explains where our breakfast came from," Cameron said, forcing a smile to his face.

"I was still hoping to take credit for that. But you're right; she takes care of me when I come here. I don't know why she chose me, but she's formed a really strong attachment. When I first found the entrance to the Vale, I didn't go very far from the tunnel, especially after a couple close calls with other animals. Then one day she was there, just watching me. She followed me around but kept her distance. She kinda scared me at first, even though she was smaller, but then I realized she was just curious.

"She used to hang around, kind of in the distance, and I finally figured it out—she was keeping the dangerous animals away from me. So I explored further into the Vale. Eventually, she started to come closer and even slept not too far away. Then, one day, she came right up to me and let me put my hand on her neck." Garrett hesitated for a moment. "And you're gonna think I'm crazy, but we knew each other's thoughts when I touched her. It was like our minds were connected."

"It's called ehrvit-daen," Cameron said. "Or at least, it's one part of ehrvit-daen. She must be endowed with it. Which makes me wonder, what else can she do?"

"So, you actually understand all this? And neither of you even seem surprised by the weirdness of it all."

"I wouldn't go that far," Cameron said. "I wish I understood it better. But, you're right, it all fits in with our experiences lately."

"What's her name?" Alanna asked.

"Aiya."

Alanna looked over at the creature. She was coiled up like a snake with her head lying on top of her slender, curled body, and her green eyes dimly reflected the dwindling light as she untrustingly stared back. *It's going to take some time to earn your trust, isn't it?*

THE VALENESE

The next morning, moisture-laden air pushed over the mountains to create spectacular cloud formations. The billowing masses formed and dispersed, but eventually persisted and pushed over the Vale. Garrett warned Cameron and Alanna of the impending rain and suggested they start the day's hike down to the Vale's floor. They had descended just over halfway the previous day and still had a lengthy but easier way ahead.

Aiya had crept away from the camp sometime in the night and was nowhere to be seen when they started. A short time later, the rain began in a sudden downpour, and lightning sporadically streaked out of the billowing clouds into the surrounding mountains. The rocks and slopes became slippery and forced a slower pace, at least until the grade lessened nearer the valley floor. Their path was filled with loose stones and large boulders that had tumbled from eroding perches over the ages. And they trudged along, weaving through the rock-strewn lower slopes while the rain came down. They were drenched, but at least the gradually warming air in the Vale's basin eased the chill.

Garrett grew increasingly anxious after midday. They were approaching a region inhabited by one of several local populations of Valenese people. This was the group that he had interacted with before, though his edginess betrayed a less than warm reception ahead.

"You seem a little uneasy about this visit, Garrett," Cameron said. "Are you sure this is gonna be safe?"

Garrett hesitated. "They've always been nice enough to me. I think it'll be fine."

"You *think* it'll be fine?" Cameron was just starting to develop a small measure of trust in Garrett, but his defenses reawakened. They were walking into a village of long-isolated people. Their existence was completely unknown, likely for uncountable generations, to the main populations of Gartannia.

"Stop worrying so much," Alanna said. "They're people just like anyone else. How's it any different than walking into Clearwater for the first time? You should be excited."

"You can be as excited as you want," Cameron said, "but as long as Garrett stays edgy like this, I'm gonna keep worrying."

Alanna's curiosity remained irrepressible as they approached the village in the relentless rain. From a distance, they saw crudely planked buildings with thatched roofs interspersed amongst the trees, and children played in the rain outside the village. Before long, the children stopped to watch them approach. They strained to see the strangely dressed newcomers and finally recognized Garrett. They ran back into the village yelling, "Allydracone! Allydracone!"

Every last person in the village capable of walking came out of the dwellings and gathered at the edge of the village in the rain. They were, perhaps, slightly smaller than average in stature. Their clothing was light and made of animal skins or crudely woven fabrics, but in every other way they appeared no different from the main populations of Gartannia.

Garrett proceeded awkwardly, walking with hesitant strides and a submissive posture, clearly not fully comfortable amidst the local people. Two older villagers stepped forward from the larger group, then stopped. They looked past Garrett and scrutinized Cameron and Alanna across the distance. Several latecomers ran from the village carrying strange metallic objects that looked like oblong shields affixed to vertical poles. They ran past the other villagers and shuffled forward in unison, stopping several paces in front of the two elders. They planted the poles onto the ground before themselves to create a crude barrier. Their movements gave the impression of a loosely rehearsed ritual rarely employed.

The three interlopers stopped in their tracks, and nobody moved while the two elders whispered back and forth, sporadically pointing toward Cameron and Alanna. Garrett remained suspiciously silent. Then, the elders walked forward, pushing their way between the shield bearers. They confronted Garrett but remained wary of the two newcomers.

"What is this, Allydracone?" the male elder demanded. And he continued into a tirade of nearly unintelligible words and phrases, never giving Garrett an opportunity to respond. He spoke the common language but used a dialect nearly impossible for Cameron and Alanna to interpret. Garrett struggled to follow the man's angry outflowing and intermittently tried to interrupt, sounding like a stuttering toddler.

While the male elder was busy tongue-lashing Garrett, the female elder continued to scrutinize Cameron and Alanna. Cameron stood with an uncomfortable countenance, watching and trying to understand the elder male. She quickly disregarded him and moved her gaze to Alanna, who returned the gaze with a respectful and confident expression, never allowing her eye contact to break. Alanna saw the face of a long-lived, respected woman of remarkable intelligence, wisdom, and intuition. The elder, likewise, studied Alanna's eyes, and something in them bespoke curiosity, sincerity, and hopefulness. The other elder's tirade was reduced to background noise in those moments, and the woman stepped around Garrett to study Alanna's filthy clothing and tangled hair before returning her gaze to the brilliant blue eyes that had first stolen her attention. She studied them deeply and found no ill intent, then gently smiled while offering her hand forward to Alanna as invitation. Alanna took it, then briefly looked back to Cameron with a smile suffused with excited anticipation. She walked hand in hand with the elder through the parting shield bearers toward the village.

The male elder's tirade was interrupted while he watched the unexpected departure of his companion with the young girl, perhaps feeling abandoned in his task. He shrugged his shoulders and threw his hands up in frustrated surrender, then offered a few strong, last words to Garrett before walking around him to stand face-to-face with Cameron. He looked him up and down before circling to examine his belongings. He touched Cameron's sword, bow, and quiver of arrows, then said in a cleaner dialect, "Weapons, no need here." And he circled to the other side to look at the shield. He tapped it saying, "No need," but stopped short and looked again. He tapped it several times in different places, then licked his thumb and rubbed the metal, paying particular attention to the bright silver inset eye.

The elder called to another villager, "Guyet," and motioned for the man to join him. Guyet was an older man who walked with a prominent limp. He approached, and the elder pointed to the shield hanging from Cameron's pack.

Guyet started to reach for it, then turned to Cameron and asked, "I look?" Cameron nodded, removed his pack, and handed the shield to the man.

Meanwhile, the elder motioned for two other villagers to come over, and he tapped the weapons again. He said to Cameron in a heavy dialect, "They keep safe for you." Cameron looked around at the villagers and saw that none carried weapons. He understood, and being sympathetic to their fears, agreed to let them take the weapons.

Guyet escorted Cameron into the village while Garrett endured a second round of tongue-lashing. They were brought under the thatched roof of a large open pavilion. Here, they were finally protected from the rain while the thunderstorm continued its unrelenting assault on the mountain fortress. The elders shouted orders to the other villagers, who scurried away before returning with food, drink, and woven mats on which to sit. The newcomers were directed to the center while the villagers arranged themselves in concentric circles around them. They offered food to their guests before serving themselves, and they gawked and chattered in their strange dialect until the food was eaten.

Truth be known, the Vale was so impenetrable that the Valenese people had never seen outsiders in their midst, at least before Garrett arrived. They interacted with the other villages for social gatherings, bartering, and governance, but hosting visitors from outside their known world was like welcoming aliens from another planet. The villagers kept a respectful distance and generally deferred any conversation with the newcomers to the elders, who spent most of the mealtime bickering back and forth with one another.

Alanna asked Garrett, "Why was he scolding you?"

"They weren't very happy with me bringing strangers right to their village. It's not that they don't want you here, but I guess I should've warned them first."

"That's understandable."

"*And*, I was here a few weeks ago, and when I left, I didn't really thank them very well. I just sort of slipped out quietly and didn't say goodbye. They're sticklers for their rituals."

"It's not a ritual, Garrett. It's just common courtesy."

Alanna was unsurprised at his behavior, and she suspected that his social skills could use some polishing. "Why do they call you Allydracone?"

"It literally means friend of dragon. They saw me with Aiya once, so they just started calling me that."

"Where do you think she is today?"

"Probably hunting. She eats a lot. Or maybe just trying to stay dry. Either way, she won't normally come down this far into the valley. She's mostly scared of people."

Guyet had positioned himself near Cameron and carefully inspected every detail of the shield while the others ate. He excitedly pointed out details of its design to a younger man sitting beside him and then sat impatiently until Cameron finished eating. Smiling, he reached over and tapped Cameron's arm and asked, "You come with me?"

They walked across the village to a partially walled building with a large stone fireplace at one end. Being somewhat familiar with Jaeblon's blacksmith shop, Cameron recognized it as a crude metal-working facility. The village men had propped the shields with poles along one wall, and strips of unshaped metal and a handful of additional poles were strewn about the work area. Cameron noticed a basket of bluish-gray metallic arrowheads and picked one out to study. It was lightweight and precisely detailed, and it was quite sharp. The metal was similar, if not identical, to the metal comprising his own shield, excepting the inset eye. Cameron complimented him on the workmanship, and he smiled broadly.

Guyet placed Cameron's shield on a tabletop and asked him questions about the metalwork, the color treatments of the emblem, and especially the silver-colored inset. He was disappointed when Cameron had no answers regarding the workmanship but was fascinated to learn its age and also that the art of its making was likely lost to time and circumstance. He nodded his head several times in thought, then scratched it and vocalized a grunt-like, "Hmm." He pointed to the inset and asked, "Dragon-shine?" He anticipated Cameron's quizzical look. Guyet then picked up the shield along with one of the metal poles and held the shield against the pole as he placed the end of it on the ground. He motioned with his free hand a path along the shield, down the pole, and to the ground. Then he grabbed one of the Valenese shields and demonstrated the same motion. "Your shield, no path to put out?"

Cameron was confused. "What do you mean by *put out?*"

Guyet thought for a moment, then reworded the question. "Where does attack-shock go to?"

Cameron remained confused and shrugged his shoulders. "I still don't know what you mean."

Just then, a bright flash of lightning lit the sky, and Guyet excitedly pointed up. "Aha, sky-shock, sky-shock!"

Cameron understood. Sky-shock was lightning. It was a natural occurrence that he had never really thought much about.

"Come! I show you." Guyet led him to a large pen just outside the village and called for two young men to help. Garrett wandered over to join them as well since Alanna had been pulled away by two village women. Inside the cage were three skrippals clinging to the far wall. Guyet's instructions to the young men were unintelligible, but they each laughed and grabbed a pole-shield. They went inside the cage, closing the door behind themselves, and with coordinated movements cornered one of the frightened animals. Its hair stood on end, making it look rather intimidating. The men then yelled to startle it as they lunged forward and planted the poles onto the ground. The skrippal jumped and struck out toward one of the men with a noticeable flash of blue light that appeared to dissipate over the pole-shield's metal windings, then passed through the pole into the ground with a small burst of sand and soil. The men laughed again and left the cage while Guyet smiled.

Cameron watched in amazement at the demonstration of the animal's defense, and he now understood what Guyet meant by attack-shock. And he understood the comparison to the lightning strike. The two phenomena must be similar. The Valenese were using the pole-shields to protect themselves from being harmed by the animals they hunted or unexpectedly encountered.

Cameron asked, "Do other animals here have the same defense?"

"Many do," Guyet responded. "No hunting or travel without take these." He pointed to the pole-shields.

"And these protect you from all the animals?"

"Most, but not wyverna."

They returned to the workshop where Guyet retrieved a stone container holding a small quantity of liquid. He made a small scratch on the inset at the center of Cameron's shield with a pointed tool, then dabbed a single liquid drop onto the scratched surface using a narrow stick. The liquid bubbled slightly over the scratch and turned black.

"Aha! Dragon-shine!" he exclaimed. He cleaned and polished away the scratch while Cameron and Garrett inspected the pole-shields. When he was done, he held the shield in a defensive pose and repeated his previous question, "Where does attack-shock go to?"

Cameron considered his situation and saw no harm in discussing it with Guyet. It was a reminder of the realities and dangers that awaited his return to the world outside the Vale. Cameron lifted his hand and tapped it against the front of his chest.

Guyet observed the response and said with a puzzled expression, "It go inside? For all people beyond our mountains?"

"Not for all people, at least not in Gartannia." Cameron expounded his experience with Scar-neck, and he showed Guyet the still reddened burn scar on his left palm where he held the shield. "There are five others like him, but they came from another land across the ocean, the same place where this shield was made, the same place where my mother's family came from. The people of Gartannia aren't like them—*or like me*."

Guyet saw the sadness that Cameron's realization evoked. He studied the burn scar, and he studied the shield's grip. He was enthralled, and he pondered for some time before finally saying, "I have only little knowledge of ancient lore with this. I must speak to elders. For now, you take with you. It is important for you." He handed the shield to Cameron and led both him and Garrett back to the pavilion where they rejoined Alanna. A short time later, Guyet left the village, walking briskly despite his limp, with a small pack on his back.

Earlier, just after Cameron left the pavilion with Guyet, Alanna was still sitting with Garrett. Her arms were crossed in front, and she was lightly shivering. The female elder motioned to two young women and gave them brief instructions before nodding and winking at Alanna. The two women collected her and led her to one of the many small buildings. There, they provided her an opportunity to bathe and change into dry clothing. They washed her hair while laughing at the tangled mess, and despite strained conversation due to differences in dialect, entertained her with small talk. Combing the knots out was a formidable task, but between them, they were able to manage and surprisingly left most of her hair still rooted in the scalp. The young ladies returned her to Jaletta, the elder, when they had finished.

The rain had subsided, so Jaletta led Alanna around the small village while the people went about their chores. Jaletta was extremely curious about the world outside the Vale. Alanna described her world in generalities, both the good and the bad, and she talked about her immediate family. She alluded to their chance meeting with Garrett, excepting the part about stealing from them, and how he had helped them escape from the horsemen. Her story wandered to the recent uprisings in towns and villages and the Khaalzin, who seemed to be bent on seizing power and control over the land. She related her fears that a full-scale war was in the offing, not to mention the personal safety of Cameron and herself. Jaletta seemed to be sincerely concerned.

"Are the two of you . . . *uhh* . . . bond? You know what I mean?" Jaletta curiously asked.

"Oh, gosh no! We're close friends, like brother and sister almost."

"Ah! I understand. I thought maybe I sense something in acumma, but maybe not him."

"*Acumma?*" Alanna said. "What does that mean?"

"You know . . . *uhh* . . . you commune with, how do I say . . . *natura*."

"I don't understand, I'm sorry."

"You don't know word, or you don't do?" Jaletta asked with surprise.

Alanna wasn't sure, but she thought Jaletta must be referring to connecting one's mind to another's. Maybe the Valenese had similar traits to the Arnorians, and herself of course. "Oh, I think I know what you mean!" Alanna said, excited at the thought of having a kindred spirit or maybe even a community of kindred spirits. With a playful smile, she took Jaletta's hands in her own and asked her to close her eyes. Then she focused her sight on a beautiful flower growing not far from where they stood, and she pushed the image into Jaletta's mind.

Jaletta wasn't quite sure what to expect when she first closed her eyes, but she trusted the sweet girl from over the mountains. Then her awareness of Alanna changed. When the image of the flower suddenly developed in her mind, despite her closed eyes, she let out a startled screech. She reflexively pulled her hands away from Alanna, then opened her eyes, and the image was gone. Her startled expression faded as she watched Alanna's face transform from a playful smile into a visage of sincere regret.

"Oh, Jaletta, I'm so sorry! I didn't mean to frighten you. I thought this is what you meant by acumma."

Jaletta took a moment to gather herself, then sympathetically reached for Alanna's hand and said, "I know you mean no harm. It scare me, but *not* acumma! I have learned of such abilities—*to share thoughts*—from our ancient legends, but this not acumma. Acumma is when connect with natura to learn her subtle ways."

"Oh, you mean *nature*," Alanna said. "The world around us."

"Yes. Tree, stone, soil—everything." She led Alanna back to the now-empty pavilion where they sat together.

Jaletta explained, "I see something in your eyes when first we meet. The spirits of our common ancestors, long past, live in your eyes. But I do not expect *this*. Such things reveal in our ancient lore. But this strange to me and our people now. Acumma different . . . but maybe not complete different to this ability that you share with me?" She moved to kneel behind Alanna and continued, "I believe you can summon acumma, and if not, I be very surprise. It is something must be learned and practice." She stroked Alanna's hair, then gently placed her hands on her shoulders. "Will you try for me?"

"I will," Alanna agreed, still feeling very foolish.

"First, know I am *not* angry with you," and she gently squeezed Alanna's shoulders. "You must close eyes, relax body, and clear mind of everything that trouble it."

"That will be difficult," Alanna admitted. "I have *so* many worries. And my thoughts don't ever stop."

"I know. I sense this. But you still try do it. It require you learn peace in your mind, and much practice. Try!"

Alanna drew in a deep breath, closed her eyes, and tried to clear her mind. Jaletta's comforting grip helped her to let go of many of the thoughts clinging within her conscious mind. And after a time, Jaletta sensed her calmness.

"Now, move hands onto soil. Feel the sand within." Jaletta slowly firmed her grip over Alanna's shoulders and added in a hypnotic voice, "Now sense grains under fingertips. Each and every grain different from others, and yet all connected, as you may eventually see. But for now, concentrate feeling each grain, it size, it place under your fingers. This is focus of mind you must learn."

As Alanna concentrated, she began to approach a meditative state, and Jaletta leaned forward to gently touch her own forehead to the back of Alanna's head. Alanna gently moved her fingers in the soil and was able to appreciate the coarse grains as they stimulated her nerve endings. She endeavored to find ever smaller grains while her concentration deepened and her focus sharpened. She experienced a relaxation of both body and mind like she had never felt before.

Jaletta pulled away slowly and removed her hands from Alanna's shoulders, bringing her out of the trance. She knelt in front of Alanna and smiled. "It is within you, acumma within your reach. I can sense it. But still, much more within your mind that I do not understand."

"Jaletta, I still don't understand acumma, I mean, how it helps you, or your people."

"I will try explain, but is hard to find words describe something not material. But first, allow me to retrieve something."

She walked briskly away and returned shortly with a large basket. She sorted through the contents and removed a roll of cloth, inside of which were several bands of bright silver wire braids fashioned into loops or various straight lengths. Some were simple and others were more intricate, being formed with more than one braid or attached to ornamental pieces of metal. The metal was untarnished bright silver, and the pieces varied in craftsmanship from simple to highly ornamental. Jaletta sifted through the items and removed one of the longer pieces, two lengths of braided wire crimped onto the upper and lower edges of a simple, oval-shaped, flat metal disk. Jaletta held it up and placed the oval disk against her own forehead, wrapping the two braided lengths around her head.

Jaletta explained, "These are ceremonial bands and bracelets, most for marriage or funeral. Some nearly as old as mountains. I sometime use to teach acumma to children. It help them to concentrate. We tell them it have magical powers," she added with a wink.

Alanna admired the piece and said, "It's very pretty on you."

"It will be pretty on *you*." Jaletta took the piece and placed it around Alanna's head, temporarily securing the braided ends in the back. "It not *make* you pretty, it make *more* pretty."

Alanna gently flushed while she admired the other pieces laid out between them.

"This one suit you, Alanna. It my gift to you."

"Oh, I couldn't possibly accept this. It's been with your people for far too long."

Jaletta looked quizzically at Alanna. "You should not refuse gift freely given. It is insult in our custom to do this."

Alanna flushed again and apologetically said, "I didn't mean to offend, you've been so kind to me. I do accept your gift, and I'll be happy to wear it. But, it's our custom to give a gift in return, and I'm embarrassed that I have nothing to offer."

"Your acceptance is only gift I desire. Now, I wish you will wear this at most times, not just for ceremony, and I will explain to you why I wish this. But we make it more comfortable first!" She reached into the basket to remove a roll of dark suede leather and a heavy needle and thread.

Cameron and Garrett appeared with Guyet and two other villagers, talking and laughing as they passed by the pavilion. They glanced over and smiled in Alanna's direction. Cameron turned back to Guyet and continued along, but Garrett's attention was briefly arrested on Alanna, and his pace slowed noticeably. Alanna had no mirror but recognized her changed appearance—combed hair and clean face, not to mention the shining circlet around her head. She reflexively pulled it off and tousled her hair while looking away from Garrett's stare, immediately realizing the self-consciousness of her movements. Garrett looked uncomfortable, turned back to his group, then stumbled as he rushed to catch up.

The awkward, wordless interaction did not escape Jaletta's notice, and her amused smile was soon accompanied by a silent belly laugh. Alanna's face flushed bright red, and her eyes widened at realizing her own reaction. She groaned and buried her face in her hands, and Jaletta's belly laugh erupted into a full-blown peal of laughter. After recovering, Jaletta said, "I know I sense something in acumma." And she laughed again.

Alanna rolled onto her back and lay there until the warm flush in her face subsided, then sat back up to reveal the newly tangled mess of hair. Jaletta called to one of the village women in her strong, unintelligible dialect and started to work on attaching the metal circlet to a strip of suede leather. Soon, the two young women who had helped Alanna clean up arrived with a piece of tan, woven fabric and handed it to Jaletta. She gave them instructions, and they went back to work on Alanna's ruffled hair. Alanna silently relented while Jaletta talked and worked on the headband.

"When Allydracone first come here, we are surprise to learn such large civilization outside our Vale. We thought that he is very different from us. He always inside himself, and he have no connection to natura through acumma—lost soul we thought. We, of course, assume all outsiders same, but now I see is wrong. Then, we see connection to young wyverna. 'What is this?' we ask ourselves. It is very strange. I do not know why this wyverna is attach to him, but natura guides all things to its order. There some purpose between them."

Jaletta worked silently for a short time, then changed the subject. "This metal is rare. What you see here in basket is most of what our people have collect over many lifetimes. We desire it because of beauty and rarity and because of importance in legend. We call it dragon-shine. It come from skin of wyverna. Ha! This leather from wyverna too, but no scales."

"How do you get it from wyverna? Aren't they dangerous?"

Jaletta laughed. "Yes, they are dangerous! But we only take from wyverna that dead, if we can be lucky to find it. They live high up in mountains where our people rarely go. We respect ancient creatures and would never try harm them, but they do not see us same way. They would eat us as soon as they would eat goat!" She laughed again. "It is way of natura. Very few wyverna live at one time. The young are killed by adults if they find them. *Very* territorial. And it rare, but great battles in sky and on mountainsides are fought to death between them. The sounds of their roaring and screeching terrible to hear, but lightning . . . well, I shake in my skin to think of their power. As long as they keep themselves in mountains, it suit me just fine."

"Lightning?"

"Allydracone has not share this with you? Well, wyverna summon lightning through dragon-shine. It is strange in your world, yes?"

"Not as strange as I would have thought a year ago," Alanna quietly replied after reflecting on her recent experiences. "How does it get into their skin?"

"They scratch and dig into mountains to find it and eat it. Or they eat skin of other wyverna that have dead. This why is so rare to us."

"You said it was important in legends?"

"Ah! That is long, long ago," she said as she continued to sew the dragon-shine circlet to the suede leather band. "Before the age of the gods' ire, when earth shook and mountains rose, our common ancestors live as ally with natura, the forces of our world. The energies of natura flow through them and they have closeness with plant, animal, water, and stone. They connect with all. In time, they lose their way and live *over* natura instead of *with* natura. It is said that gods strip them of dominion, but they resist, and in their corrupt choices find ways to regain some power and control. Dragon-shine was one such path. They steal it from wyverna and other now-gone ancient creatures to enable self to wield such powers, because the dragon-shine enable connection to energies that ebb and flow through everything in natura. The dragon-shine used as weapon for power instead of peaceful tool for prosperity.

"That was many ages ago, and our people learn the bad result of such corruptions. As plant and animal evolve and adapt within natura, so have our people. We do not need such power, and we are content to exist as harmony with all that is around us. Those ancient corruptions have abandoned Valenese people over ages, but for acumma only. And that help us understand and respect natura because we are part. We keep dragon-shine as reminder to those corruptions, *and* to trick our children to learn acumma when they are young. Ha-ha! But do not tell them this secret. It really have no benefit for acumma."

"If there's no benefit, then why do you wish me to wear it?"

"No benefit for acumma in Valenese people, but something else within you. The gods favor you, for what purpose I have no reason to know. But I sense no corruption in you, and I have no fear to give it you. And maybe you find some usefulness to wearing it."

The young women finished combing the newest tangles out of Alanna's hair and began braiding it tightly along both sides. Jaletta interrupted them to size the headband around Alanna's head before continuing. "I tell you I will explain acumma, and I try now. It is to sense the many imbalance in natura. It is to understand natura's path, for natura always strive to make balance. When balance achieve, natura rest, and to understand where balance lies is greatest wisdom one can possess.

"As example, to sense certain stress in our blueberry bush help us to know what nutrient is lack or when to water. Vitality in trees can guide us to harvest weakest, even when appearance is same. To sense decay or growth, storm or fair weather, grants us advantage to live in this world. Without this ability, we cannot have respect for all that is around us, and without respect, corruptions more likely to root."

Jaletta had seen Alanna's aversion to feminine display, so she wrapped the soft, tan cloth around the shiny, leather-bound circlet to conceal it, giving it the appearance of a simple cloth headband. After several stitches to secure it, the band was complete, and Jaletta placed it around Alanna's head, tying it beneath the braids in the back.

Jaletta left to attend to her own personal duties, and shortly after, Cameron and Garrett returned to the pavilion. The young men were surprised at the transformation in her appearance. Cameron helped himself to fruit from a basket the villagers had left for them and sat across from her.

"I almost didn't recognize you sitting there. I've never seen you this clean before," he said while preparing to dodge a handful of dirt and sand.

"Very funny! You could stand a good scrubbing yourself," she replied with a laugh. "Where'd Guyet go?"

"I'm not sure. He said he was going to talk to the elders, but then he left the village."

"He probably went to another village to speak with their elders," Garrett said.

"Jaletta was telling me about dragon-shine," Alanna said. "Is Aiya old enough to have that yet?"

"I think so. She has silver streaks running from her belly up to her neck. They're more noticeable than they used to be. I don't know what it's supposed to look like though. Her wings are developing too, but I think she's a long way from being able to even glide on them."

Cameron wondered, "If the wyverna can fly, why don't they fly over the mountains and out of the Vale?"

"Apparently, they don't fly very far when they do, just short distances when they hunt mostly. And I think the air's too thin up that high to support their weight. Besides, wyverns are territorial. I can sense that in Aiya, and I'm not sure she'd ever want to wander that far from where she was born."

"Can you communicate with her from a distance? And can you tell how intelligent she really is?" Cameron asked, hoping to understand these strange creatures better.

Garrett stood and paced around restlessly. "I don't really know. It's hard to explain I guess." He paused and then announced, "I need to go for a walk. I need to see if she's wandering around near the village." And he walked away.

Cameron waited for Garrett to get out of earshot. "I don't understand him. I thought we were finally trusting each other. How can you form any kind of friendship when you just close yourself off like that?"

"I think you should be more patient with him, Cameron. He's not all bad. I'm sure that opening up to people on the streets where he grew up only led to disappointment. And think about how difficult it must have been to take care of his mother and to move her away from the city at his age. He did what he did to survive."

"I know he helped us, but he was also the one that got us into the mess with those horsemen, not to mention the coins. Mostly he just cares about himself. I just don't trust him."

"Well, I think you're wrong about him. I don't think Aiya would've chosen him if he was irredeemable, and she's more intelligent than us." Alanna was clearly unhappy with Cameron, almost defensive in a way, and she moved across the pavilion to read from the journal. Eventually a villager came to offer them places to sleep indoors, away from the insects. Garrett never returned that evening.

Alanna woke up early the next morning and wandered out to the pavilion. The basket of dragon-shine jewelry was still sitting there. She pulled the items out to look at each one, admiring the craftsmanship of the nicer pieces. At the same time, her mind was churning with uncountable worries. So, in the early morning solitude, she set the jewelry aside and decided to try acumma, hoping to settle her mind.

She sat cross-legged and pushed her hands onto the soil. But her mind continued to reel, and she was unable to focus the way she had done with Jaletta the day before. Out of curiosity, she picked up two pieces of jewelry and coiled them in her palms before placing her hands back onto the soil. Though her mind was still churning, something felt different, and she closed her eyes. Odd sensations, like nothing she had felt before, crept into her hands and arms. Her curiosity swelled. She focused on them, effectively pushing the myriad other thoughts and worries back into deeper recesses.

She eventually approached a meditative state as she concentrated more deeply, and the odd sensations began to take on different characteristics, similar to how the individual sand grains felt subtly different under her fingertips the day before. But these sensations were very different, and she struggled to identify their origins. They came from everywhere around her now, and within her. She sank deeper into a trance as her mind focused on them, trying to understand what they were, and then something changed. Her nagging conscious thoughts freed themselves from their tethers, one after another, and steered her mind to places both familiar and unfamiliar. She struggled at times to follow them, and she felt chilled in the efforts. Her trance deepened further, and then images like unfamiliar memories and emotions began to reveal themselves. The cold became intolerable, but her mind was lost amidst the images, reminiscent of a panicked child desperately trying to navigate a maze. She tried desperately to pull herself out of the trance, but her mind sank deeper and deeper into the unknown, into images and memories that weren't her own. There was nothing to grab, nothing to hold onto, and no one to help her.

***

The day before, Garrett had left the village after a sense of claustrophobia overtook him during his conversation with Cameron and Alanna. He found Aiya in a secluded place half a mile from the village and spent the evening talking to her while she rested. Although she never actually responded to him, he felt some comfort in opening up to her, often venting his many frustrations. He knew she had some level of understanding of what was in his mind, but it wasn't in her constitution to react or advise. Regardless, Garrett felt comfortable in her presence and slept through the night curled up under his blanket.

When Aiya roused in the early morning and wandered away to hunt, Garrett returned to the village. It was early, well before the villagers typically emerged from their homes, so he went to the pavilion to wait. He was surprised to see Alanna sitting alone and went to sit with her. She was cross-legged with both hands firmly clenched in the soil, and her head was slumped forward. He quickened his steps, sensing something out of place, and found her violently shivering. He grabbed her shoulders and called to her, "Alanna! Alanna!" But she didn't respond. Her body was rigid and shaking violently, and she was cold to the touch. Panicked, he wrapped his blanket around her, then ran to Jaletta's nearby home for help.

Jaletta pulled Alanna's hands from the soil, and seeing the dragon-shine jewelry coiled under her palms, removed them. She pressed her forehead to Alanna's and fought to keep from recoiling against the onslaught of thought and imagery spilling out of Alanna's mind. She held Alanna's head firmly while speaking in a calming voice to coax her from the deep trance, and still she struggled to fend off the onslaught. To Garrett, the ordeal lasted an eternity before Alanna finally responded. She expressed a low tremulous wail, then her arms began flailing and grasping at Jaletta. Garrett knelt behind her and pulled her arms back, forcing them to her belly while clutching her thrashing body against himself. She was so cold. In time, Jaletta's calming words and embrace seemed to settle Alanna out of her terror. Her body relaxed, and Jaletta released her. She slumped unconscious into Garrett's hold, but the shivering only worsened.

Cameron was awakened by the commotion and ran straight to the pavilion. Alanna was still slumped and shivered violently in Garrett's arms. "What happened? What did you do to her?" he asked, kneeling and lifting her limp head. "She's freezing! Lay her down!"

With Cameron's help, Garrett placed her on her side and then pulled the blanket over her. Cameron ran to retrieve his own blanket, then threw it over her while Garrett knelt beside her with anxious concern.

"I found her like this, Cameron. She was just sitting there. I couldn't wake her up."

Cameron said nothing, and Jaletta moved over to place her hand on Alanna's forehead. "This, she brought to herself, but she is returned to us now. Her mind was not in good place." Jaletta collected the dragon-shine pieces from the ground beside Alanna and placed them in the basket. "Bring her to my bed," she said as she struggled to get to her feet. Jaletta stumbled forward, and a villager took her arm for support while she hobbled toward her home.

Cameron moved to lift Alanna, but Garrett brushed in front and hoisted her light, shivering frame. He stood and briefly glowered at Cameron before following Jaletta. While restraining his anger, he tucked her into the bed and piled more blankets over her before leaving the village. It was a long time before Alanna's shivering subsided, and she remained unconscious well into the afternoon while Cameron sat impatiently at her side.

Guyet returned to the village midmorning with two elders from another village. He had gone to seek advice, but they insisted on coming to meet the visitors from outside. They were, of course, surprised to hear about the commotion earlier in the morning and presumed a not-so-flattering opinion of the newcomers. There was a lot of discussion, arguing, and raising of voices throughout the late morning and early afternoon between Jaletta, her companion elder, and the visiting elders, until Alanna finally woke.

The visiting elders demanded to see her immediately, but Jaletta refused to allow it until she had a chance to speak with Alanna in private. So they spoke with Cameron while Jaletta was with her. They inspected the shield, and they inspected Cameron, especially the burn scar on his palm. He answered questions about the world outside the mountains and about the Khaalzin who hunted him. All the while, Guyet stood quietly nearby.

Jaletta allowed the visiting elders to visit Alanna briefly. She was still in a fragile condition. Afterward, Guyet and the four elders met together again for an equally lively discussion. Ultimately, Jaletta raised her voice in a commanding tone, and when she was done, the discussion was over.

Despite her weakness, Alanna insisted on walking outside. Cameron helped her out of Jaletta's home, and they walked to the pavilion. Garrett had not returned to the village yet, so they sat by themselves in the warm fresh air. Knowing she wouldn't want to discuss the morning's events yet, Cameron sat quietly, contemplating how much he had grown to need her friendship and companionship. Such attachments are oft taken for granted and only consciously realized under threat of loss, as the morning's misadventure had illuminated. And in his mind's idleness, he began to ruminate again about his family and friends and the tribulations he had caused them. And here he sat, in this secluded mountain range, detached and hiding from the specters that wrought these misfortunes. He considered Garrett as well and felt regret for his accusation and distrust of him. So many things felt outside his control, or was it simply his failure to step into manhood and assert himself responsibly? His frustrations, guilt, and sense of failure to family and friends had reached a tipping point.

Alanna sat silently, huddled under a blanket while bits and pieces of Cameron's thoughts and all of his emotions spilled over to her mind. It took no effort on her part, they were just there, amplified no doubt by the dragon-shine circlet around her head. She could feel its influence on her mind. And she felt compassion for him, for his sacrifices in friendship, for his loyalty, for his pain. She had broken a barrier that morning, and she felt it. But if not for Garrett and Jaletta's intervention, it would have irreparably broken her, and she knew it.

"This isn't fair," she said, and then removed the headband, pulling it over her braids. She set it on the ground, looked at Cameron with moistened eyes, and said, "Say what you need to say."

After a long silence, he said what she already knew. "It's been nagging at me for a long time now, ever since my time at the winter cabin. I'm tired of running, Alanna. I don't know what my fate is to be, but I know I can't keep doing this."

In truth, the only reason why he was still running was Alanna. He selfishly wanted and needed her companionship but felt an overwhelming duty to protect her from the dangers that confronted him. She had come into his company willingly and remained because of a bond she couldn't explain, but he still felt an overwhelming responsibility to her.

"You're right," she replied. "You need to face them, and you need to find your family, but you also need to accept that you're not alone in this. This isn't just about you, Cameron Brockstede . . . *not anymore*."

In the intensity of her stare, he could tell that she knew something, had seen something. Her demeanor was changed, and her eyes held a knowledge and understanding that wasn't there before. "What did you see, Alanna?" he asked.

The tears welled in her eyes, but she didn't answer him. She pulled her hands from under the blanket and mindlessly caressed her palms with her thumbs, first one, then the other.

Cameron moved to sit beside her and pulled her right arm over, rotating her palm so he could see it. Emblazoned there was a perfect six-pointed star surrounded by two concentric circles traced out by diagonal hatch marks. "These look like burns," he said.

She reached into the basket containing the dragon-shine jewelry and pulled out the necklace she had curled into her hand earlier that morning. It was a braided strand on which a six-pointed star was hung. "I was holding this," she admitted.

Cameron opened her other hand, and it had similar hatch marks coiled into several interlaced loops, obviously from another braided strand. "Do they hurt?"

"They're fine."

"Maybe you should put that back in the basket."

"It's not dangerous." She dragged her fingers slowly across the soil. "But there's something about this place . . ."

"I think we should leave as soon as possible—tomorrow morning, if you're up to it."

Alanna didn't argue, and before long, she began to nod off under the pavilion. Jaletta arrived to scold her and returned her to bed, then returned shortly to speak with Cameron.

"I do not pretend, Cameron, to fully understand all that happens with her, or with you. I will not speak of her visions, for that is her place to offer you. But I see some of this when I pulled her back to us this morning. Her connection is strong with natura. And I only hope that I do not make mistake in what I give her. She has much to learn control this, but I know in her heart is good.

"Guyet wishes us to offer *you* something. His interest just curiosity, but this choice not so easy. Our people fear corruptions in one who wield powers belonging natura. Our lore teach us be wary and resist corruption and not aid it. But Alanna's mind reveal to me strong corruptions already living in hearts of ones seeking you and who wish destroy your peaceful world. Our world much isolated from you, but we cannot ignore common ancestral connection, so we no want abandon you to corruption. You will face demons, it has been foreseen. But you not face them without be prepared.

"Guyet is making help for you. And I hope for you be safe and keep good in your heart. The gods place you with us, and I sense we are meant help you."

Cameron didn't know how to respond, so he simply said, "Thank you for helping Alanna, but we should leave in the morning."

Jaletta shook her head. "No. You stay two more night for Guyet finish, and for Alanna recover. She no travel tomorrow, not into mountains!"

Cameron hadn't considered the climb. It would be strenuous, so he agreed to wait two nights for Alanna's sake.

The following morning, Cameron visited Guyet in his workshop. Two villagers were bent over a table busily working on a project while an elder from the other village looked over their shoulders and guided their work. Guyet was happy to see Cameron. "I was come get you soon," he said.

He cleared off the top of his main workbench except for a thin strip of silver metal that he had been shaping. He reached behind the bench and lifted a bow, Cameron's bow, and laid it on the bench. Then he picked up the metal strip to show it to Cameron and said, "Dragon-shine." He stretched it over the length of the bow's front surface and proceeded to give Cameron a detailed explanation of his plan to modify the bow. The plan also included wrapping the grip with an unusual-looking leather, scaled with glistening silver and black coloration. It was the same material that the other two men were working with. Guyet explained that it was tanned wyverna hide, quite old but still supple enough to work with.

Cameron agreed to the plan, unsure how exactly the changes would be helpful, but the added weight would be negligible once they had carved a shallow notch in the wood to accommodate the metal strip. If nothing else, it would provide some added strength to the wood. He helped to attach the pieces, making sure the bow's integrity wasn't affected. When they finished, the other men had completed their task as well. They offered the product of their labors, a pair of fingerless gloves made from wyverna leather, to Cameron. The material had diffuse streaks of silver embedment running the length of the otherwise black, scaled outer surface, and each glove was fashioned in a way that placed the most prominent streaks onto the palm. The gloves were long, extending up to the midpoint of his forearms. Cameron pulled them on and found the fit to be good. He offered a genuine smile and sincere thanks to the two men and the elder, all of whom deeply appreciated his approval and gratitude.

The elder took Cameron aside to describe the gifts he had just received so that he might have a better understanding of their usefulness. He described the scaled wyvern skin's toughness and demonstrated by slicing a sharp knife across the glove—while it was still on Cameron's arm—but cautioned that it wasn't completely impervious. Valenese lore suggested the gloves would protect him the same as their hide protected the wyverns from one another's attacks. That piqued Cameron's curiosity. *Are wyvern attacks anything like the Skrippal's, or the Khaalzin's? And since the attack-shock went through the shield and into my body through my arm, would it protect my hand?* He hoped he wouldn't have to find out.

The dragon-shine strip on the bow was ornamental, the elder had said. But more obscure lore hinted that ancient hunters were far more effective in killing prey when they could command its virtues, if nature so allowed. The elder had helped Guyet to duplicate the metal strip from his knowledge of ancient artifacts, but he knew nothing about the manner of its use.

The elder struck down twice with his walking stick onto the planked floor. The loud *cracks* startled the others and were meant to emphasize the words that followed. "I speak against give these gifts, but offer make by elders in council. Jaletta say 'the visions speak truth, and no corruptions within him' and others agree. *I say* the gods favor one deserving but curse to those who seek corruption!" And he emphasized with another *crack* from his walking stick.

Cameron nodded his understanding. Despite his difficult dialect, the elder's caution was quite clear—he wished a curse on anyone who abused the gifts' virtues.

The elder's walking stick had startled the two men, who continued to toil over a second pair of gloves intended for Alanna. Jaletta requested them, but she had a different purpose in mind. The task proved more difficult as Alanna's delicate hands required a more precise fit, but they completed them before dinnertime, giving Jaletta time to present the finished gloves to Alanna and provide her with guidance and caution. The villagers eventually gathered together in the pavilion for a farewell dinner to honor their guests, including Garrett, whose presence was scarce since the previous morning.

Cameron certainly couldn't blame Garrett for avoiding him. He had acted with prejudice when he accused Garrett of having something to do with Alanna's grave condition the day before. When he finally cornered

Garrett, he floundered in making an apology for his behavior. But when he thanked Garrett for helping Alanna, it made a much stronger impression, and they at least began the process of building a more civil relationship. They agreed to meet early the next morning, and Garrett would guide them through the two-day trek out of the Vale.

OUT OF THE MOUNTAINS

The next morning came on the tail of fitful sleep for both Alanna and Cameron. The gateway to the mountain oasis was still distant, but the sense of foreboding weighed heavily on their minds. Cameron looked at his flight from the Khaalzin with self-reproach, and he resigned himself to an inevitable confrontation with mortal stakes, an encounter that he almost relished as an opportunity to dispel the demons of guilt that tortured his mind. But Alanna's apprehension had its roots in visions that she struggled to understand. The only certainty that resolved from them was that she belonged at Cameron's side, to whatever end. Something had changed inside of her, though it was beyond her to identify its cause.

So they trekked back into the mountains. Alanna's physical strength had returned, but her stamina waned as the day wore on. Garrett took her pack at the first opportunity and slung it over his shoulders. Aiya joined them shortly after they left the valley floor and did not attempt to hide herself any longer. Her body was well-adapted to the rugged terrain, and she flitted around like a curious child investigating the world. Alanna was fascinated and watched her movements and behaviors with both interest and amusement. The hike was tiring but not as difficult as the next day's more vertical ascent would be. They stopped at twilight to make camp and built a fire to break the chill in the night air.

Alanna was physically spent, and Cameron remarked that he was happy they hadn't tried to make the climb the day before. She sat leaning against the rock and pulled the journal from her pack while Cameron and Garrett collected firewood. She read several entries aloud to the young men while they worked, and Garrett's curiosity grew regarding the plight of Cameron's family and the other Arnorian refugees.

"So, how long has your family been running away from these bad guys—the Khaalzin?"

"They weren't running away," Cameron defensively replied. "They fled Arnoria because of a Prophecy, not because they were afraid. It was probably the most courageous and dangerous thing they could have done."

Garrett glanced at Alanna, who shrugged her shoulders at Cameron's defensive reply. "I didn't mean anything by it," Garrett said deferentially.

Alanna said, "It's been about seven generations since they came here. My family actually descended from the same refugees, and so did most of my village."

"So what was this prophecy that you mentioned?"

"It's right here," she said, and pulled the loose parchment from the journal. "The first part refers to Cameron's family. Their surname was Genwyhn. I'll read it to you.

"Hope may yet come where none is known
The winds of despair may bear a seed and carry forth
Over raging waters fate unknown
Through lives of men dark seasons shall pass
New hope be found in him pure blood
An heir of Genwyhn to return at last."

Garrett chuckled. "What does that mean, 'impure blood'?"

"No, it says *in him pure blood* . . . but I guess I can see how it might . . . sound like that." She paused and looked back at the words she had copied onto the parchment earlier that spring in Dannen Yungbred's study. Just then, Aiya appeared with her gleaming green eyes at the clearing's edge, her head held low, and she carried a large rabbit in her jaws. Garrett moved away to greet her and retrieve the rabbit. After a moment, Alanna raised her head to look at Cameron, who was nearby busily breaking branches for firewood, and called to him. "Cameron, tell me the story about how the Prophecy was first written again."

"You mean the story about the dying sage?"

"Yes."

"Well, Erral said he came out of a delirium and kept muttering these words over and over. It wasn't much longer before he died."

Alanna pondered for a moment. "But who wrote them down?"

"I think he said it was an attendant. He must have had someone taking care of him."

"So it's possible that it could have been transcribed incorrectly?"

Cameron paused and looked at Alanna with a confused expression. "What are you getting at?"

She stared at the page to read the first few lines again, then looked back at him with wide eyes and said, "Now it makes sense."

"What makes sense?"

"Cameron . . . *the Prophecy* . . . it has to be *you!*"

"What?" He walked over to sit next to her. Together, they reread the words on the page with that one alteration.

Hope may yet come where none is known
The winds of despair may bear a seed and carry forth
Over raging waters fate unknown
Through lives of men dark seasons shall pass
New hope be found 'in impure blood'
An heir of Genwyhn to return at last
Three are foreseen to return again
To span the hopeless divide
The path of a second is veiled in fog
Pure of heart though world awash in treachery
Allegiance uncertain a choice to be made
And worth unseen by eyes of men
But clearly discerned through those more keen
A gem in the rough shall complete the three
Born anew under astral sign
And in darkness leads them in unity
Uncertainty veils our destiny
Until their souls converge

After finishing, he read it again, this time really thinking about the meaning in the phrases. And when he finished, he looked up from the page, and his gaze landed upon the wyvern. She lay just at the clearing's edge. Her tail swept across the ground behind her while Garrett stroked her long neck. Alanna had recognized the intelligence in her eyes, and her devotion to Garrett was glaringly evident. The bond between them was no mere accident or coincidence—she had chosen him for a reason. He whispered under his breath, "Clearly discerned through those more keen."

His gaze moved inconspicuously to Alanna while she focused on the writing. Despite her temporary physical transformation back at the village, she already had ash smeared over her cheeks and nose, and she was back in her filthy hand-me-down clothing. But he had never really considered the beauty in her features before the village, having always looked at her under the light of a platonic friendship. But no—it wasn't that—her true virtues weren't apparent to the naked eye. Her kind nature and devotion in friendship, her intuition and fortitude, and her grounded sense of right and wrong shone brilliantly within.

She finished reading and looked up to see him staring at her. He shifted his gaze to her penetrating, brilliant blue eyes, and with a hint of sudden revelation, he asked, "Alanna, what does the word *astral* mean to you?"

"Well, it usually refers to a constellation or . . ." and she paused, looked knowingly at Cameron, and subconsciously retracted her clenched right fist.

". . . or a star," he finished for her. Cameron reached for her hand and coaxed her fingers open, revealing the branded star on her palm. He gently traced his finger around the still-tender mark and added, "You already knew, didn't you . . . it's not me, it's *us*."

Alanna's eyes confirmed his assumption, and they both looked over at Garrett and Aiya, watching their unexplainable interactions. Cameron thought about their previous conversation in Clearwater concerning destiny and tried to piece it all together, but it wasn't so simple. Recent events further challenged his opinion that people's lives and the marks they would leave on the world were guided entirely by choices and decisions.

Garrett, who was smiling and softly humming to himself, soon left Aiya and returned to the fire with the rabbit. Both Cameron and Alanna noticed how his demeanor changed when he and Aiya were together. Her companionship brought him happiness, and her loyalty to him seemed unconditional. As Cameron considered Garrett's childhood mired in uncertainty and distrust, he began to understand the comfort that this relationship provided without the emotional risks inherent to human companionship. As usual, Alanna had been right.

"What's wrong?" he asked suspiciously. They were staring at him.

Cameron began to speak, but Alanna quickly cut him off. "I'm just really hungry. I'll help you clean it while Cameron finishes the firewood." She looked at Cameron, and they shared an uncomfortable glance before she picked up the book and he returned to the firewood. She marked the page and laid the book on her pack, then went with Garrett to prepare their dinner.

The following day fortuitously brought fair weather for the difficult vertical ascent. Garrett knew the path well and guided their steps. The ropes he had placed were invaluable for climbing slippery slopes and broken rock stairs. They covered less distance this day than the day before, but by early evening they were approaching the rock crevice and tunnels that would lead them into the rugged mountain pass and out of the Vale.

One by one, they climbed the final vertical face to a wide, level area strewn with scraggly and misshapen trees and shrubs. Cameron recognized the place from their arrival into the Vale out of the rock tunnels. Just a short distance away to the right was the treacherous stony slope that lay in front of the tunnel entrance and the safety rope they had used to get past it. He scanned the surrounding rocky slopes while Alanna and Garrett climbed up behind. Movement on the coarse, steep mountain face above caught his attention. A group of mountain goats was moving across the face. He watched them move gracefully along in single file while Alanna was puffing her way up to the level surface. He pointed to the goats, and they both marveled at the agile, sure-footed animals traversing the rugged face. They were moving faster now.

When Garrett reached the top just ahead of Aiya, he caught sight of the goats turning to descend toward them. There was something rushed in their movements, and he became uneasy. He scanned the slopes above them and the sky around them before commenting, “Something isn’t right here.” He saw nothing, but the goats’ descent suddenly turned into a panicked free-for-all amidst a chorus of bleating.

Aiya became agitated, looking and hissing, and ran disjointedly around the rocks and trees. Garrett yelled, “Hurry! Get to the tunnel!” They ran toward the tunnel entrance as goats raced past, across the stony slope, and beyond their sight along a narrow ledge at the edge of the steep precipice. Garrett lifted the safety rope and urged Alanna to take it and hurry to the tunnel. She was halfway across when a panicked goat bolted through, just missing Garrett, and struck her, knocking her hand from the rope. Her feet slipped on the loose rocks, and she began to slide down the slope toward the precipice. She clawed her fingers over the slippery surface, but there was nothing to grip. Garrett watched in horror while she slid slowly down and away from him. “Alanna!” he screamed and reflexively reached for his knife. But it wasn’t there. The horsemen had taken it days earlier.

Cameron raced up behind Garrett while watching Alanna helplessly slide further down the slope, like a slow-motion nightmare, then realized what Garrett was trying to do. He pulled his own knife and slashed the thin rope away from the tree to which it was tied. “Go!” he yelled to Garrett, who immediately lunged forward, running down the slope with his left hand gripping the rope. In a split second his mind judged the distance to the bottom, and he wrapped the rope’s free end around his right wrist and hand. Like an acrobat, he spun his body in a half circle just as the rope became taught, then slid to the ground. His body swung across the ledge, and he stretched his left hand out toward Alanna's groping arm. She raised it as high as she could and closed her eyes just before her lower legs slid over the edge. Garrett stretched further and clamped his hand around her outstretched wrist, arresting her slide with the full length of her legs dangling precariously down the precipice.

Alanna opened her eyes and shakily inhaled to fill her depleted lungs. She refused to look down and instead looked up, first to Garrett, and then to Cameron, only to have her breath stolen again by an involuntary scream. Above Cameron was a massive adult wyvern descending rapidly with outstretched wings. Its head dipped down to snatch a stray goat from the rock face over which it glided. The goat just escaped the beast's massive jaws when its panicked legs missed their holds and slid down the sheer face. The wyvern descended with it and prepared to land in the scraggly trees and shrubs, not far behind Cameron. It remained focused on the goat while landing amidst cracking tree branches and swirls of dust stirred up by its massive wings.

The goat was stunned and struggled to stand after tumbling down the rocks. The wyvern secured its footing and folded in its wings before lunging toward the prey. Unable to recover its footing, the goat's fate was sealed, and the wyvern quickly took it. The massive wyvern lifted the full-grown goat like a rag doll. Uncountable sharp white teeth and blazing emerald green eyes accentuated the serpent's fearsome head, while prominent silver streaking along its body contrasted eerily with the bluish-black scales shingling its hide.

Cameron reflexively crouched and watched the ghastly scene unfold. His eyes gaped while he took it in, and then the realization of their peril struck. He turned back to Garrett and Alanna to see her struggling to pull her legs atop the ledge while Garrett clung to the rope. The wyvern finished dispatching its prey and only then noticed them. It dropped the goat and turned, assessing them through intelligent eyes. It snorted repeatedly and spread its jaws to reveal the deadly arches of teeth and a crimson red tongue. After a threatening roar, it advanced toward Cameron.

By then, Garrett had hoisted Alanna up to the slope, and they pulled themselves along the rope toward the tunnel entrance. Alanna's terror-filled eyes were fixed on Cameron, who was urging them up the rope while standing his ground against the approaching beast. His shield was raised and his sword drawn, but he kept little hope they would be of any use against the massive creature. But as he poised himself against the fearsome monster, Aiya scurried out of the shrubs and crossed directly in front of it, hissing and winding her sinuous body over the rocks.

The adult roared in territorial rage at the sight of the young one and momentarily lost interest in Cameron. But Aiya was fast and maneuvered her lithe body through tight gaps and up and down rock steps to avoid the adult's deadly jaws. While she distracted it, Alanna slid into the tunnel opening, and Garrett backed a few steps down the slope while holding the rope taught. "Cameron, run!" he yelled.

Cameron turned to see Garrett holding the rope and steeled himself to make the dash. He looked back to the wyvern just in time to see the streak of light, like a lightning bolt, emerge from its mouth. The flash was immediately followed by a sharp, thunderous crack, and smoking char blackened the rock where Aiya had stood. Garrett screamed Aiya's name, and Cameron made a run for the rope after sheathing his sword. His momentum was just enough to carry him over the upper slope, his feet slipping on the loose stone, and he grabbed the rope where Garrett held it taught.

"Get in the tunnel," Cameron yelled.

But Garrett hesitated. "I'm not going without her!"

"Trust me, or we're both gonna die!"

Just then, Aiya appeared out of a gap in the rocks and looked at Garrett. Something connected between them, and Garrett pulled himself past Cameron and disappeared into the tunnel. Aiya dashed across the slope toward the tunnel entrance. Her claws scraped through the loose stones and found enough purchase on the slippery rock to cross the distance. Cameron's skin began to tingle, and his hair stood on end. He could sense the imminent attack. He held the rope with one hand while instinctively crouching behind the outstretched shield, then closed his eyes and cringed in anticipation. Aiya scratched and clawed past him on the slope just before the blast came, a deafening force that impacted the shield and spilled around it. But the shield had absorbed much of the blast, and he felt the surge enter him. His thoughts blurred, and he teetered on the verge of unconsciousness. In a terrified burst, Aiya scrambled into the passage, leaping and scraping her way over Garrett and Alanna, who both crouched beneath her assault, and she disappeared into the darkness behind them.

Cameron's stunned body went limp, and he collapsed before the tunnel. His unfocused eyes watched the surroundings dance in a foggy haze, and he heard faint voices as if echoing from a vast distance. His mind wallowed in confusion. Something tugged and pulled on his arms. The still-muffled voices of his companions sounded closer now, and he sensed the urgency in them. He tried to clear the mist from his vision, but it was beyond his control.

Garrett had pulled the shield from Cameron's grip and tossed it into the tunnel, then grappled to pull him into the narrow opening. But Cameron's pack, bow, and quiver made it impossible to maneuver his limp body inside, and the wyvern advanced onto the slope, its great wings unfolded from forelimbs frantically clawing at the ground to keep from slipping down. It moved ever closer to Cameron, slipping on the surface while its wings flailed, and a rumbling growl echoed from its throat. Garrett struggled to remove Cameron's pack, but it was impossible in the confining entrance to the tunnel. Alanna watched helplessly from behind while the wyvern struggled along the slope toward Cameron. Its terrifying mouth couldn't have been more than five steps from his legs when their fortunes changed. The slope was steeper below them, and the beast's legs began to slip downward in its frenzied attempt to reach him. Its claws found no hold, and with an enraged roar, it slipped over the edge and into a free fall along the vertical cliff.

The wyvern twisted its body and fully unfolded its wings, recovering into gliding flight below them and into the open spaces above the Vale. It circled until it found an updraft in the mountain air, then slowly lofted upward on massive wings, mercifully giving the struggling travelers badly needed time.

Cameron emerged from the stupor enough to help his companions remove the gear from his back. Garrett grabbed his arms and pulled him through the opening into the tight space. Garrett and Alanna lifted and supported him through the narrow passage until they entered the small cavern. Cameron collapsed onto the floor while his body continued to shake off the assault. Garrett returned to the opening and gathered their packs and weapons, then went back once more to retrieve the shield. He dropped it on the cavern's floor, where the central inset shone bright white, illuminating the cavernous space, and radiated intense heat.

Alanna stood, still holding a small pack. Her arms and hands began to shake as she dropped it to the ground. Her dumbfounded expression changed to shock. The near-death experience coupled with the wyvern's attack on Cameron had expelled every last drop of adrenaline into her bloodstream, and her muscles began to recoil as her body expended the last of it. Garrett noticed her shaking and hurried over just as her knees buckled. He grabbed her arms to hold her up and remembered how close he was to losing her over the ledge. He wanted to embrace her more deeply but withheld. But when Alanna threw her arms around him, he pulled her in tight and felt her knees weaken. They stood in each other's grip until Alanna recovered her strength. But when she realized the moment's awkwardness, she gently pulled away, and her soft gaze briefly met Garrett's.

It was clear that Cameron was in no condition to go any further that day, for the wyvern's attack had left his mind foggy and confused. The filtered light coming from above was waning, so they camped there for the night. Alanna made Cameron as comfortable as she could next to a warming fire. His head throbbed and his shield hand had suffered another burn from the wyvern's attack. He hadn't been wearing the gifted gloves. After all, who could have predicted the chance encounter?

Aiya explored the recesses and passages in the cavern's vicinity, but she made no pretense of going back into the Vale after her terrifying encounter.

Alanna asked Garrett, "What will happen to Aiya?"

"I don't know. But I can sense she's terrified to go back there."

"I don't blame her. I'm terrified too."

"But it's not just that; something's changed in her since we left the village yesterday. I can't put my finger on it, but she seems more attached . . . if that makes any sense."

"*Maybe more than you know*," she mumbled under her breath.

"What was that?"

"Nothing. It was nothing." She changed the subject and said with a smile, "Back on the ledge, you looked like an acrobat from one of those traveling shows."

Garrett smiled and softly laughed.

"I owe you a big one," she added, referring to saving her life.

He didn't reply at first, but she saw a gentle flush fill his cheeks in the firelight. Then he said, "I think we all owe Aiya a big one too. Did you see her distract that monster so we could get off that slope?"

"She's very courageous."

Garrett's claustrophobic feelings swept over him again, as they often did with any intimation of human emotional connection, and he abruptly stood. He hesitated briefly, then said, "I need to check on Aiya."

Alanna smiled and saw him hesitate again before walking toward the passageway, and she thought, *baby steps*.

It was still early, so Alanna pulled out the journal to read more entries in the firelight while Cameron slept. If nothing else, it helped her to push the constant flood of thoughts to the background, if only temporarily. When Garrett returned, she was lying on her side under her blanket with the journal sitting on the ground behind her. He casually wandered around to place more wood on the fire and saw her eyes closed, then lay down behind her. When she didn't move, he quietly lifted the journal, held it up to the firelight, and curiously read several entries. He lacked formal education, so his reading skills were elementary. Just making out the words in the handwritten passages was difficult, but he gleaned at least something through the exercise. While turning a page, the loose parchment that had been marking Alanna's place fell out onto his chest. He held it up to the light and read the words of the Prophecy before slipping it back between the journal's pages. The arrangement of words in those lines was confusing, much like trying to read poetry, he thought. He stretched out on his back, pulled his blanket up, drew a deep breath and sighed. And it was some time before his churning mind gave in to sleep.

Meanwhile, Alanna's mind raced with repeating visions and unsettling thoughts behind closed eyes. She was fully awake and aware of Garrett, but his secretive curiosity about the Arnorian journal and his new knowledge of the Prophecy only exacerbated the burdens that inundated her brain. How would he interpret the words, and would he even suspect that he might play some part in their providence? Had she, herself, misinterpreted the prophetic words? And what were Garrett's intentions once she and Cameron began the trek south to Eastmoorland? She knew to ask him outwardly would risk the fragile relationship they had begun to construct. She so badly wanted to search his thoughts for the answers to her questions, but propriety and fear of Aiya's reprisal shuttered that window. She reminded herself that fate ultimately draws its own path, and resignation to that, perhaps, helped a little.

Alanna was the first to wake in the morning, and she lay quietly under her blanket. Aiya had curled up close to Garrett sometime in the night, and her rhythmic breathing was comforting to Alanna. After a time, Cameron stirred, then startled fully awake. He sprang up to his knees and frenetically scanned the dark cavern. Alanna sensed his concerned confusion and said, "We're right here, we're all fine." She pulled her blanket off and crawled over to him, embracing him in a firm hug. "I'm so glad you're alright. I can't believe you survived that." Her embrace and soft voice helped to calm and partially reorient his muddled mind.

"I can't remember . . . what happened . . . where are we?" Cameron recognized Alanna, but he was disoriented.

"We're in the passage to the Vale. You don't remember the wyvern?"

"I remember climbing up the rocks . . . we were leaving the Vale. I don't . . . I don't remember how we got here."

"It's alright, Cameron. I guess I shouldn't be surprised. That was a wicked blast you took."

"Wow! My hand really hurts," he said before taking inventory of his limbs.

"I'll fill you in later. I'm not sure it'll stick right now," she added with a look at his wandering eyes.

Garrett watched their interactions and said, "Looks like we'll need to take it slow through the mountain pass today."

They waited for the sun to rise high enough to cast light down through the crevice above. Garrett used the time to coax Aiya back to the opening into the Vale. He stepped out to the narrow ledge and got her to squeeze through after him. She coiled her body around in a circle to look inquisitively back. He pointed and told her to go back into the Vale, but she stood fast and gently pushed her head into the underside of his outstretched arm. He repeated the command, and this time she replied with flared nostrils and a long snort, followed by a soft hiss. She looked directly at his eyes and then slithered back into the opening. Garrett followed her to the cavern and announced, "Well, she won't go back into the Vale. I don't think she's afraid of it anymore. She just refuses to go."

Aiya passed between them and stopped at Cameron. She sniffed up and down his clothing, his pack, and finally the shield before moving toward the opposite passageway. Garrett shrugged his shoulders and finished packing the gear.

They kept a close eye on Cameron while he traversed the more technical parts of the rugged mountain pass. Though his memories remained scrambled, he unquestioningly followed Garrett's lead, much like a toddler dutifully follows his parents. His balance and coordination were impaired at first, but he gradually recovered his physical aptitudes through the day.

When early evening came, the gaps and passages became progressively darker, and they felt along through blackness for a time before finally exiting onto the ledge outside the pass. The twilight afforded an opportunity to climb down from the cold, windy ledge. Garrett tossed the rope over and climbed down, pushing off the wall like a trapeze artist to grab and pull himself into the tree. Then he helped his companions safely down. They chose a sheltered spot in the nearby rock maze to camp while Aiya remained somewhere back in the passage through the night.

PARTING WAYS

Alanna was the first to wake in the morning. She immediately checked on Cameron, who had collapsed into a deep slumber shortly after arriving at the rock maze the night before. He was lying flat on his back with his eyes partially open. He didn't move, so she knelt down and waved her hand in front of his face. No response. She was beginning to worry, so she gently shook him by the shoulders, but still no response. She shook harder and yelled his name, then checked to see if he was breathing when he suddenly startled awake and jolted up to sit. Alanna nearly jumped out of her skin. She shrieked and tumbled backward.

Cameron shook off confusion and sat in consternation, believing he had just woken from a very realistic and terrifying dream. "Wow! That was the scariest dream I've ever had," he said with a wide-eyed stare.

Alanna replied with a mocking flare, "Let me guess, you were being attacked by a massive wyvern."

"How'd you know that?" he asked with sincere amazement that she had guessed right.

Garrett, roused by the noise, laughed aloud.

"I've never had such a vivid dream before."

Alanna stood and brushed the sand off her pants. "It wasn't a dream, dragon slayer. It really happened."

Her comment only fed Garrett's laughter while Cameron's confused expression stirred a giggle out of Alanna. But finally, after Cameron's bemusement turned to irritation, Alanna said, "Relax, we'll explain everything."

Alanna and Garrett replayed the entire scene of the wyvern attack, filling in gaps in Cameron's recovering memories. He sat, taking in every word and shaking his head in disbelief that they had survived it.

"You saved Aiya," Garrett said. "She was right behind you, still in that lightning bolt's path when you blocked it with that shield."

"I guess I owed her that much. I sort of remember how she ran between me and that adult. She definitely bought us some time. But I know I don't want to go through that again. I still don't feel right."

"You weren't the only hero out there, Cameron," Alanna said. "Do you remember how Garrett pulled me up from the cliff?"

"Just a fuzzy memory. It was some crazy acrobatics, I think. I thought for sure you were a goner."

"Just lucky is how I remember it," Garrett interjected, clearly uncomfortable having the incident relived. He stood and left them again to 'check on Aiya' before the conversation went any further.

"He was so brave the way he saved me from falling," Alanna said after Garrett had walked away. "I just wish he could be a little braver in trusting us. I know how he makes you angry, but I think he's making progress."

"After saving you like that, I don't think I could ever be angry at him again."

"Something tells me he might eventually test you on that."

Cameron laughed. "Yeah, you're probably right."

Garrett returned to the camp around midmorning in a sullen mood. Cameron had unpacked his supplies and was sorting through a bag of arrowheads that Guyet had offered him before they left the village.

"What's the matter?" Cameron asked.

"Aiya just keeps wandering around in the passages and outside on the ledge. She seems confused. I don't know what to do."

"Is she afraid to jump into the tree to get down, or afraid to leave the Vale?"

"I'm not sure. But she climbs around on the rocks all the time, so she's probably not afraid to come down."

"She seems really smart," Cameron said. "I think she'll figure it out on her own."

"Yeah."

"But it'll be dangerous for her in Gartannia. She'll scare the heck out of people. And what about when she's fully grown? Will Gartannians be safe from *her?*" He thought about the adult that attacked them. "Maybe she's better off staying in the Vale."

"I don't know. She's got such strong instincts, and she just ignores me when I try to get her to go back." Garrett reclined against the rocks to mull it over.

Cameron worked on attaching the metal arrowheads to shafts, then walked out to the open plateau to try them out. He made a target from an old sack stuffed tightly with grass and pine needles and began shooting the new arrows with his modified bow. He liked the feel of it and was satisfied that Guyet hadn't created any problems with the changes. The wyvern-skin gloves were comfortable enough, but he didn't find any real benefit to wearing them while practicing.

Garrett wandered over to watch out of curiosity. He never had occasion to learn to use a bow, but he was impressed with how accurately Cameron could shoot at fifty paces. When Cameron offered to teach him, he agreed. In no time at all, Garrett was hitting the target's center at thirty paces. Cameron was not surprised, having seen Garrett's physical dexterity on display several times already. He left Garrett to practice while he went to see what Alanna was doing back in the rock maze.

She was sitting cross-legged in the camp, hands on the ground beside her, apparently meditating. Recalling her episode back at the village, he called, "Alanna? Are you alright?"

She opened her eyes. "Yeah, I'm fine. Don't worry, I learned my lesson."

Cameron tried to make conversation, but Alanna was distracted. She wasn't her usual bubbly self since the episode in the Vale. She still avoided talking about it, so Cameron left her to continue meditating.

When he returned to see how Garrett was progressing, he was amazed to see his shooting accuracy even at fifty paces. His competitive nature got the better of him, and he challenged his pupil to a shooting contest. Garrett shrugged his shoulders and agreed, after all, what did he have to lose?

After shooting five arrows each, Garrett proved to be just slightly more accurate. Cameron tried to act indifferent, figuring it was beginner's luck, but losing to a newbie really irked him. After a second round with the same result, Cameron was noticeably irritated, and Garrett couldn't help but be amused. Cameron feigned symptoms in his hand from the recurrent burn suffered in the wyvern attack, although it really wasn't bothering him that much, and he put the wyvern-skin gloves back on. The third round was dead even after the fourth arrow, and Garrett's fifth shot was nearly dead center. Cameron struggled to hide it, but he was becoming downright angry about being bested in archery by someone who had never pulled back a bowstring before in his life. Sweat began to bead on his forehead like the anger and embarrassment that seethed out of his ego.

Garrett stood quietly behind him with a smirk, obviously enjoying himself. Cameron glimpsed the expression just before turning to nock his last arrow, and it pushed his anger to the brink. He restrained his desire to lash out against Garrett's smugness and instead focused the anger into his concentration. The sensation that arose was familiar, and a warmth blossomed within his chest. His focus on the target sharpened, and the bowstring pulled back effortlessly. He felt no compulsion to hold back against the surge of energy and released the arrow. It streaked to the target and flared through with a flash, just off center, leaving a smoldering orifice.

The episode was entirely reminiscent of his experience with the stag the previous summer, except the warmth in his chest was not dissipating, and he could now see the shimmering disturbance in the air along the arrow's tight and narrow path, though rapidly dispersing. He knew from his experience with Scar-neck that it would guide an attack straight to the target while it was sustained. His instinct to release the energy swell was nearly uncontrollable, and in that fractional moment he struggled against an irrepressible rage. The feeling was unsettling—the near absence of self-control—and he struggled to rein it in. He had only experienced this once before, with Scar-neck, and the rage had empowered him. Only this time it came to him spontaneously. The dragon-shine strip glowed intensely, and the urge to destroy the target felt insurmountable, but still, something restrained him. To give in to the urge was to wield an unnatural power and to forsake humility. The words of the Valenese elder echoed in his mind—the gods favor one deserving, but curse to those who seek corruption! If he couldn't control this, he knew he would be no better than the Khaalzin. His conflict lasted but the blink of an eye, though the consequences of his choice would be enduring. Ultimately, he refused to relinquish his self-control, and the energies that had drawn into him gradually dissipated.

From Garrett's perspective standing behind Cameron during this explosive event, what he witnessed terrified him. Initially, he watched the arrow miss the target's center, and his mind prepared for an elated celebration. Then the smoldering hole that was left in the target after the arrow passed cleanly through was unmistakable. The sight erased the smirk from his face, and he felt a sudden chill as the heat was drawn from his body and the surrounding air. A bright glow flashed along the bow's curve, reaching an intensity that prompted him to raise his arm to shield his face, then faded as quickly as it had emerged. He stumbled backward, away from Cameron, and stared through astonished eyes.

Cameron dropped the bow and peeled the wyvern-skin gloves from his hands, casting them to the ground. "How did that happen?" he muttered to himself in bewilderment while looking at his hands. Then he remembered Garrett and turned to see his reaction, but Garrett simply stared blankly back before turning and walking away.

Cameron's mind swirled in his rush to rejoin Alanna, and he described to her what had just happened. "I don't understand it," he said. "I didn't do anything different. I mean . . . maybe I was angry. But, it just happened."

"I don't know, Cameron. All of this is so strange."

With some reticence, he admitted, "I felt almost completely out of control, like I wanted to give in to my anger and destroy something. And I know I could have."

"But you didn't."

"No . . . I didn't."

After a silent pause, Alanna asked, "I wonder, is it possible that the blast you took from the wyvern might have something to do with this? I mean, maybe the way it scrambled your thinking wasn't the only way it affected you."

"I don't know. I guess it's possible. But it just worries me that something could happen, and I won't be able to control it." The power he had felt was intoxicating, and he imagined how any person could be beguiled to use it for their personal benefit or for control over others. The violent consequences of it, like in the hands of the Khaalzin, repulsed him. The image of Scar-neck lying dead on the ground produced a wave of nausea, and he turned pale.

She could sense his concern and stood up to give him a comforting hug, saying, "You're strong enough to handle this. I know what's in your heart, and you need to trust yourself."

Garrett was just returning to the rock maze when Alanna hugged Cameron, and the sight further depressed his mood, even though he knew it was irrational. He stepped quickly out of sight and waited a short time to make his appearance. His reclusive instincts were aroused again. *What am I doing here? Life was just fine before I ran into these two. Now it's all turned upside down. Why did I ever let them into the Vale?*

When he finally rejoined them, an awkward silence enveloped the camp. Garrett shuffled around before breaking the silence. "So, what the heck was that about? I know I've seen some strange things since I found the Vale, but that was *really* out there."

Cameron found no words to reply.

Garrett sat down to settle his thoughts. He could see from Cameron's expression that he didn't have an explanation, so he said, "You know I won three out of three, right?"

Cameron closed his eyes, gently shook his head, and smiled. "Yeah, I guess you did."

"And burning up the target doesn't change anything."

Cameron smiled more broadly. "I know. Maybe I need to make you a bow. I wouldn't mind having somebody who shoots like you watching my back."

"Yeah, maybe someday."

Alanna chimed in, "You mean he outshot you, Cameron?"

"Yeah, at fifty paces too."

She giggled and winked at Garrett.

Although the lighthearted exchange broke the tension, Garrett remained sullen and continued to shuffle around. "I need to get Aiya back into the Vale," he said. "I've thought about it, and I don't think it's a good idea to let her stay outside the mountains."

"I think you're probably right," Cameron said. "I'm not so sure Gartannia is ready for a wyvern roaming around. Anyway, I need to clean up the archery gear. I'll be right back."

After Cameron walked away, Alanna said to Garrett, "We're leaving in the morning. We'll follow the river to Eastmoorland."

"Alright, I figured you would."

"You can come with us, you know . . . if you want."

Garrett laughed awkwardly. "Why would I do that?"

"Well, I think we make a pretty good team when we're together."

"Yeah, but I think most teams have a common goal, don't they? There's nothing for me in that part of Eastmoorland."

"But Eastmoorland isn't the goal. It's bigger than that."

"Whatever. I have no idea what you're talking about."

She paused and looked him in the eye. "I think maybe you do. I know you read the Prophecy."

"What, that? It's just a bunch of poetic nonsense."

"I don't think that's true. And, like it or not, your destiny's tangled up with ours."

"Whoa! Don't try to drag me into this superstitious nonsense. I'm just a simple guy trying to survive in this crappy world. And I'm not exactly having a lot of success at that."

Alanna looked derisively back. "You're kidding, right? Just a simple guy trying to survive . . . who just *happens* to have a pet wyvern? Give me a break!"

"Whatever! Look, I'm not interested in saving the world, alright? You just go along with the great heir of Genwyhn and see how that freak show turns out."

He grabbed his blanket and possessions and stormed away.

Alanna watched him. After twenty or so steps, he stopped, then briefly paced back and forth, but ultimately continued away. And sadness enveloped her.

Garrett spent the night with Aiya in the small cavern within the passage to the Vale. He was up earlier than usual the next morning and sat upon the ledge watching the sunrise. The pine branches yielded but a glimpse of Cameron and Alanna as they left the rock maze and headed down the slope toward the meandering river. Aiya crept out of the passage and lay next to him, then exhaled a lengthy sigh as she laid her head on his lap.

ANGUISH

After leaving the maze, Alanna compulsively glanced back several times, hoping at least for a glimpse of Garrett, but he made no appearance that morning. Cameron sensed her frustration but was not surprised at Garrett. She hadn't told Cameron about her final conversation with him the day before, but Cameron surmised they had an unpleasant exchange from her sullen mood.

She was uncharacteristically silent while they trudged along the valley floor. Clouds thickened, and a foggy mist dampened their clothes and their spirits for most of the day. The soil turned to sticky mud, but the valley remained relatively level for another two days, then narrowed where the silt-laden basin emptied into the descending mountains. The way became increasingly difficult thereafter, but the river at least provided a predictable route toward their destination.

Alanna's mood slowly improved, and she eventually accepted Garrett's abandonment. She couldn't blame him in whole. His selfish tendencies didn't necessarily arise by choice but were in many ways imposed by his circumstances. The Prophecy was, by its nature, open to many different interpretations, though her intuition strongly supported Garrett's entanglement with their own paths forward. But this was not her only disappointment, and the other, she coldly tucked away.

Her sleep was increasingly disturbed by recurring visions. They were more vivid than her usual dreams and replayed over and over since they first appeared at the Valenese village. She was so disturbed by them and by her inability to fully understand their meaning that she tempted danger in the nights by trying to summon them back through acumma, hoping to achieve some resolution. But there was something about the Vale, the inner mountains, or perhaps what lay under the Vale that fostered her transcendent connection, perhaps also explaining the persistent Valenese adherence to acumma. She was unable to achieve it again outside the Vale, maybe fortuitously.

Cameron's thoughts cycled from concern for his father, grandparents, and friends to how he would deal with the Khaalzin when he eventually encountered them, and finally to his ability to safely control ehrvit-daen. He longed to rejoin his family, and that provided all the motivation he needed to forge ahead each day. But he also worried about Alanna. Her eyes appeared sunken, her clothes hung more loosely on her frame, and her stamina faltered from persistent insomnia and a vanishing appetite.

It was close to twenty days of difficult travel through the descending river valley before more gentle terrain aided their progress through an ever-widening valley. They could see the plains of Eastmoorland far off in the distance, and the sight invigorated them. The journey along the remote river pass had offered no contact with or evidence of other people, though they counted over twenty sightings or close encounters with black bears. But the animals were simply curious about the two interlopers and kept a comfortable distance. Three more days finally put their feet on the fringes of a grassy plain speckled with colorful early summer wildflowers. They found a secluded spot near the river's western bank to camp for the night.

Cameron slept soundly while Alanna sat by the fire, unable to sleep, and looked out over the landscape illuminated under the full moon. She was accustomed to listening to the nocturnal critters move about while they foraged in the darkness. On occasion, she reached her mind out to glean what she could from their rather simple minds, one of many diversions that she found to pass time during the lonely nights. She experimented with wearing the wyvern-skin gloves and appreciated a stronger connection to the animals with her gloved hands firmly placed on the ground. On this particular night, she was doing just that when she heard the movements of something much larger around the camp. She recalled the numerous bear sightings over the previous three weeks and was understandably concerned. Against the moonlit backdrop, she caught glimpses of shadowy movements through the trees and shrubs surrounding the camp. Sniffing sounds occasionally met her ears, but when she reached out with her mind, she found nothing but an impenetrable veil. Alarmed, she crawled over to Cameron and shook him awake. "Something's out there, and it isn't going away!"

Cameron sat up, and they peered into the shadows where Alanna had sensed the animal. Cameron grabbed his knife and started to stand just before two bright green eyes appeared, moving slowly out of the shadows where the moonlight now reflected in them. They stopped, and the animal sniffed more aggressively before softly hissing.

Alanna gasped, "Aiya!"

Her exclamation startled Cameron, but he had also recognized Aiya's eyes and the sound of her hiss. The young wyvern crept slowly forward until she reached them, then sniffed Cameron up and down. Cameron put the knife down and gently reached out to stroke her neck, but she skittered away in her usual flighty way, disappearing into the darkness.

"What's she doing here?" Alanna asked.

"I don't know, but I don't think she'd stray far from Garrett. I wonder if he followed us."

Alanna didn't reply, but even in the darkness Cameron saw a glint of elation in her eyes before she turned away.

He grinned and said lightheartedly, "You're so obvious."

She ignored the comment and sat staring out over the moonlit landscape. "What if something happened to him? Maybe she's here alone."

"We'll see. We can search in the morning after the sun comes up." Then he noticed her blanket still rolled up next to her pack and asked, "Still having trouble sleeping?"

"Yes."

After a silent moment, he prodded her, "When are you gonna talk to me about it? You can't keep this locked up forever."

"I know. But I can hardly tolerate having these visions in my head, let alone try to talk about them." The sleepless nights had certainly affected her emotional vulnerability, and for whatever reason, on this night, the feelings began to spill over.

The fatigue that accompanied her insomnia was affecting her daily life. Both her physical and mental well-being were challenged increasingly. Cameron sensed the vulnerability and knew she needed to get it out in the open. "What did you see, Alanna?"

She closed her eyes and began to sob. Cameron sat and wrapped his arm around her, repeating, "What did you see?"

She finally relented and opened up. "So many things . . . so many horrible things. They were digging . . . men in the same tan-colored clothes . . . they were all digging . . . and there were naked bodies covered in blood. And there were fences, or walls, like it was a prison. And they were just throwing them into the graves. There were so many bodies." She paused briefly, crying. "And the people were watching, forced to watch. And they were crying and wailing for their dead loved ones. I was seeing it all through their eyes. I felt their anguish, all at once. I couldn't bear it . . ." She collapsed, sobbing, into Cameron's arms. Their minds had not connected in a long time, but she let him in, and he felt the intensity of her anguish directly.

After a time, she recovered and offered more. "It wasn't just that. There were so many different visions. But that was the worst of them. And I can't make them stop, especially at night. They aren't dreams, Cameron. They're like memories, like I was there. Like I was holding children, just skin and bone, and dirty, trying to console them while they starved. And I was helpless, like there was no escape from some pointless persecution. I don't know where they are or how to help them. And I don't even know if they're real!" She balled up her fists and pushed them to her eyes, trying to contain the anger that welled up inside. "What if they *are* real? How can anyone stay sane after seeing things like that?"

Cameron reached over and took her hand, interlacing his fingers with hers, and listened.

Her demeanor softened as she recalled another recurring vision, emerging like a recent memory. Her tears flowed freely as she described it. "I saw Errenthal. He had a horrible wound on his chest, and he was lying in a bed. And the house was on fire, Cameron! I was trying to save him, and the roof was burning. It fell in, and it was burning in front of me and behind me. I screamed because my back was burning, and I could feel it. It hurt *so bad*. And I screamed for Errenthal . . . but it wasn't my voice . . ."

Cameron leaned in. "Whose voice, Alanna?"

"My father's," she stammered. And she wept uncontrollably.

He sat with her for a long time, willfully keeping his thoughts in check. Compassion for her emotional suffering held back the storm of anger that swelled inside him against the Khaalzin, the perpetrators of their hardships. Somehow, in the depths of his heart, he knew they were at the root of her torment as well. Eventually, Alanna fell fast asleep against his shoulder. He lifted her to place her on the ground, then covered her with the blanket. Exhausted, she slept well into the morning light.

Aiya returned briefly in the darkness while Cameron watched over Alanna. She deposited a dead possum near the fire, looked at Cameron, and lay down to sleep for a short time before disappearing again into the early morning darkness. Cameron was both amused and perplexed by the strange creature, and he was beginning to feel more comfortable around her.

For the first time in weeks, Alanna slept without torment. She dreamed normal dreams about strange adventures, past memories, friends and family. She felt a soothing calm in her restful state under the spell of familiar voices, and she resisted wakefulness while she dreamed of her father and Errenthal conversing outside of Jared's supply shed, like she'd seen them do so many times before. But as she drifted out of her sleep and the dream's imagery faded, the voices persisted. She felt an uneasiness and forced herself fully awake, fearing the emergence of another disturbing vision.

She sat up and turned her bleary eyes toward the sound of approaching footsteps, then tried to focus on the face of the man who stooped down and gripped her arms in his strong hands, pulling her up to kneel in front of him. She didn't immediately recognize his bearded face, but when her father finally spoke to her, she knew it was no longer a dream.

Alanna simply melted into her father's embrace, and for a time she felt the same security she had known as a child. There were no words to express her elation while she clutched him—he was unquestionably real. And in his firm grip, she felt the remnants of his grief and then his newfound joy.

"I thought I'd lost you forever," he whispered.

"I know. I'm sorry, Daddy." But she had thought the same thing about him. His unexpected arrival, in apparent good health, lifted her spirits immeasurably and gave her at least some hope against the recurring visions. *Maybe they weren't real after all.*

Erral and Jared had arrived at the camp earlier that morning, guided by Aiya and Garrett. At Cameron's insistence, they had allowed her to sleep. He knew well the depth of her exhaustion. Jared could barely restrain himself from waking her. Cameron, Erral, and Garrett watched the emotional reunion, then walked into the prairie to give them privacy and to continue their conversation. Cameron and Garrett were just finishing their tale about the Valenese people and their isolated evolution from ancient times. Erral was, to say the least, fascinated by their existence.

When Garrett left them to find Aiya and collect firewood, Cameron took the opportunity to talk privately with Erral. A lot had happened since they were separated at the cabin, and Cameron longed to have Erral's insights into his recent experiences. They meandered along the riverbank while Cameron told him about their encounter with Scar-neck and his accomplice.

". . . I kept blocking his sword attacks, and then he got angrier when Alanna started shooting arrows at him. When he was finally frustrated enough, he attacked with two of those fireballs. The shield blocked them, or absorbed them, somehow, and I could feel the energy come inside me. After the second one, I thought I was gonna burst from it, and then it just released back out. It was like a stream of lightning from the center of the shield, and it followed the line in the air from his last attack, right back to him. I don't know how to explain it, but the air was disturbed somehow where his last fireball flew. I could see it, like the air was shimmering, for a short time anyway." The two stopped and faced one another as Erral processed his words.

"There are very few who can muster an attack that powerful," Erral said. "But you gathered the energy from both of his attacks, through the shield?"

"I think so . . . at least it felt like it."

"Well, like I told you before, my understanding of that shield is limited, but its capacities are beyond what I had imagined." Erral paused while thinking it through and resumed his walk along the river. "Or maybe its capacity is limited only by the abilities of the one who holds it. It would be useless to anyone not endowed with ehrvit-daen, except against a sword, of course."

"But what about that disturbance in the air? It reminded me of the smoke trail a burning ember leaves when you throw it through the air, but it wasn't smoke. It's like it guided my counterattack right back at him."

"I *am* familiar with that. The energies moving through the air cause it, but while it remains it can also guide a new flow of energy, as a creek bed guides the flow of water. The disturbance won't be there for long, and the wind can quickly disperse it like a smoke trail."

Erral thought about the incident more deeply, then explained, "These attacks that the Khaalzin have used against you, well, they require a powerful command of ehrvit-daen. To voluntarily draw in the energies can be difficult enough, but to concentrate and focus that energy even more so. Then, aiming it accurately at a target requires a tremendous amount of practice and time before it can be used effectively. The disturbance in the air that you were able to sense can help to guide another attack, but the opportunity is fleeting and would only be helpful for an immediate counterattack like you described. Without that disturbance, I'm not sure how helpful the shield will be as an offensive weapon, at least not until you have a better command of ehrvit-daen."

"You're right about that. We were attacked by an adult wyvern back in the Vale, and it knocked me senseless. The shield kept it from completely frying me, but there was no way to counterattack."

Erral's eyes widened. "How did it attack?"

"It looked and sounded like a lightning bolt, right out of its mouth."

Erral's eyes widened further, and he glanced at Aiya lying in the sun near Garrett. "So much for fairy tales," he muttered.

"And nightmares," Cameron added.

Erral moved in front of Cameron, seeking his full attention. "The powers of ehrvit-daen are unquestionably within you. Your instincts to use it defensively have served you well, but it won't take the Khaalzin long to recognize your limitations. Without a strong offense, you'll be no match against them. They won't allow you another opportunity like what happened with Scar-neck."

"I need to show you something else." Cameron led Erral back to the camp and pulled his bow from the pile of gear.

Erral took it and examined the dragon-shine strip and wyvern-skin grip. "This is interesting, though it's not familiar to me. Did you modify this yourself?"

"No. A Valenese metalsmith came up with this, based on some old artifacts I guess."

"What's this metal, and what's its purpose?"

"They call it dragon-shine. It comes from wyvern skin. If you look closely at Aiya, you can see the silver streaks in her hide. It's the same metal that the shield's inset is made of."

Erral looked skeptical. "The metals in your shield were mined, and there certainly aren't wyvern in Arnoria."

"But that's apparently how the wyvern get it. They scratch it out of the mountains in the Vale."

"Interesting," Erral said while running his fingers up and down the dragon-shine strip.

Cameron hesitated to continue, the bruise to his ego still tender. But he swallowed his pride and said, "I challenged Garrett to an archery duel back at the Vale. He was beating me, and I got a little bit angry about it. Well, anyway, it was like that day at the cabin when I threw the pinecone at the door, but the energy I felt inside me was a lot stronger. I shot the arrow, and I saw that same disturbance in the air following the arrow's path. I wanted to let the energy go, to follow that path, but I held it in. I know I could have destroyed the target . . . I could feel it, and I felt out of control. I feel like it's in me, to control ehrvit-daen I mean, but I can't summon it myself like the Khaalzin do unless I'm angry or scared."

Erral thought for a moment, took a deep breath and sighed. "Well, in time you may be able to control it better, but for now it will at least serve as a defense." He studied the bow again. "But this bow is strange to me. I've never heard of this metal being used this way. But then, so much has been lost to time under the Khaalzin's oppression. And as for feeling out of control, only experience and practice will help you to overcome it."

The group eventually gathered back together in the camp to talk. Erral, who had been using a walking stick, set it down and unwrapped several layers of leather bindings from his ankle. He sighed in relief to have it off, but his ankle was severely swollen.

"What happened?" Alanna asked curiously.

"That? Well . . ." and he looked at Garrett before continuing. "That's what happens when you stick your nose where it isn't wanted." He laughed, then explained, "Your father and I found a curious tree when I was tracking you and a group of horsemen into these mountains. I think you know the one I'm talking about. After scouting the area, we found your camp and two sets of tracks leading away toward the river valley, but my curiosity got the better of me. When I looked into the tree, I could see it had been repeatedly climbed, and I happened to notice the rope dangling off the rock above it. I had to be sure we weren't overlooking you, so I climbed up. When I got on the ledge, Garrett's wyvern was there. And she apparently didn't want me there. She lunged, and we both tumbled over the edge. The tree branches broke most of the fall, but I ended up with a badly sprained ankle and her jaws attached to my neck." He pulled his shirt collar down to expose several scabs where her teeth had broken the skin.

Garrett said, "It was the day after you two left, and I was sleeping in the cavern in the passage. I forgot to pull the rope up. Aiya woke me, and I followed her to the opening. All I saw was Aiya's tail going over the edge, so I hurried down after her. I think she was just about to do something really bad when I stopped her."

"I've never seen anything like her," Jared said. "I was scared out of my wits. I pulled my knife out, but I don't think it would've been much use."

Erral continued, "But thanks to Garrett, here, I'm still alive to complain about my sore ankle. The first few days walking on it were tough. I never wished so badly to have a horse. But this generous young man offered to guide us and carry my pack." Garrett sheepishly glanced at Alanna, while Cameron discreetly rolled his eyes.

"I can't believe you tracked us all the way here," Cameron said. "How'd you find us?"

"Now that's a long story, Cameron, and one that needs to be told from the beginning. As you recall, I left the cabin with Turk to help ensure your grandparents' safe travel. But I had an uneasy feeling the day after leaving you there. So, I confided in Turk my reservations about leaving you unprotected. He was rather insistent that we stick to the plan though. After all, Caelder and your grandparents were counting on us to follow through. Turk is normally a rather sympathetic soul, and this change in him struck me as unusual. I rethought his plan to divert the Khaalzin away from your grandparents, but something about it bothered me again. The plan was well-thought and reasonable, but I've known Turk for a long time, and something just didn't connect with his usual style. I finally suggested that he continue alone, and I would return to the cabin. Turk's normally coolheaded, but I could sense a subtle agitation in his voice when he suggested we sleep on it for the night.

"I had already made up my mind, but I never told him of my final decision to return to the cabin the next day. He must have sensed my mistrust. He came at me in the night, but thankfully my sleep was light and broken. I was able to react well enough to save my life." Erral carefully pulled up his shirt to expose a partially healed wound located over his breastbone and extending over his left chest under a large bandage.

Alanna gasped at the sight and covered her mouth with her hands. Her face displayed horror, then she looked like she was going to be sick. She stumbled away from the men, still holding her hands to her mouth, and fell to her knees. She vomited, then coughed and choked.

Erral was surprised at her reaction and quickly covered the wound. Jared stood to follow her, but Cameron held him back, saying, "It's not what you think. Let me talk to her." Jared conceded.

The others sat and waited for Cameron while he consoled her. They exchanged several words before Alanna stood and raised her voice, at first toward Cameron, then toward no one in particular. "No, it's not alright. Don't tell me it's alright, Cameron. It's all true. Don't you see it? Every part of it's true! Everything I saw is true! I was there . . . and I saw it . . . and I felt it! And every day I see them and hear them! And I can't bear it anymore!!" She was screaming and teetered on the verge of a nervous breakdown.

She stormed away from Cameron to the other men, who stood, not sure of her intentions. She made a beeline for her father while screaming to the others, "Do you know what it feels like to get burned, to have your back burned in a house fire? Do you know what it feels like?" Jared tried to restrain her as she approached, but she was too fast. She spun him around and pulled his shirt up to expose the deep, healing burn on his back. The sight reinforced the truth in her visions even further, and nausea swept her again. She suppressed it and continued screaming, now directing the words at her father, "Well I do! I felt it just like you!" She was shaking, and her eyes were filled with dread.

Jared turned around and latched on to her arms, hoping to quell her madness. She broke free from his grip and began pounding against his chest, hysterical, while he forced her into a tight hug. And her rant gradually deescalated into sobs. "I felt it just like you! I can't do it anymore. I can't bear all their anguish. I can't watch them suffer over and over and over. And I can't find them . . . I can't find them . . ."

Cameron truly had no notion of the burden she was carrying all those days, but his understanding was becoming clearer. His empathy was real, but he had no idea how to console her. Maybe there was no consolation; maybe there was just acceptance—her pain was beyond his reach.

Jared led her away from camp, and they talked together through the early afternoon. Something had drastically changed in his daughter, and he longed to understand her.

Meanwhile, Cameron described to Erral and Garrett the events leading up to her outburst and her description of the visions from the night before. Erral reflected on this new information for some time. Alanna's clairvoyance seemed more than coincidence, but he simply didn't understand it. It was beyond his experience or knowledge. He finally tucked it away, then offered the balance of his story to the young men.

"Turk came at me with his knife, and I impeded the blow enough to keep it from penetrating through the bone. I was suspicious enough to keep my knife at hand when I lay down to sleep, and I was able to strike a lucky blow under his arm. It severed an artery, and he bled in torrents. I tried to contain it but couldn't, and he knew it was the end for him."

Erral's voice was shaky, and he paused to collect himself. Cameron and Garrett sat with incredulous expressions, mouths agape, waiting for Erral to continue.

"Turk begged for my forgiveness and confessed his complicity with the Khaalzin. He'd left an easily followed trail to the cabin and fully intended to expose your grandparents, Caelder, and myself to the same end."

"But he took an oath to protect us!" Cameron exclaimed.

"And he was human, Cameron. I suspect he became consumed by the perception of futility in our directive. I won't deny that this has been a burden for each of us as Traekat-Dinal. Turk was much younger than Caelder and me, and that may have played some part in his struggle. I have no idea what the Khaalzin might have promised him in return for his betrayal.

"I don't mean to make excuses for him. The oath is sacred. Every man and woman has both good and evil in their heart, but it is their choices in life that determine which they will leave as a legacy in their wake. For Turk, his lack of moral conviction to our oath has left a legacy of selfishness and dishonor. And now, with his loss, we're at an even greater disadvantage against the Khaalzin."

Garrett listened intently, and something in Erral's words connected deeply with him. He stared blankly ahead while his knee bounced up and down nervously. Cameron had seen it before and expected him to get up and walk away to deal with his inner thoughts in privacy, but he stayed.

"What happened next?" Garrett asked, interrupting his own blank stare.

"Well, my wound turned out to be quite debilitating, and I still regret being unable to provide Turk a proper burial. I was unable do it. But, regardless, I made my way back to the cabin not knowing what I'd find.

"When I arrived, it was still smoldering. They had burned it to the ground, but I found no evidence that they'd taken you. I hoped to recover bandages and our store of healing herbs, but they were obviously gone."

Cameron briefly interrupted to offer his account of the close encounter with the two Khaalzin at the cabin, including his hasty escape.

Then Erral continued, "I followed your trail toward the village and guessed that you'd look for aid in your escape. I traveled as quickly as I could, but without clean bandages the wound festered and my mind began to leave me. When I finally arrived at Jared's home, I was in pretty bad shape. He took me in and tended to me, with Maelynn's help, of course, but I lost several days.

"As you probably already gathered, the Khaalzin or their agents came in the night and set the house on fire, and the stable and supply shed. Jared lost everything, but he was able to pull me out of the flames. I finished my recovery with Brandon and Maelynn.

"They gave me an indication of your plans, so I made for Clearwater with Jared when I was able. We arrived to find military recruits gathering at the city's outskirts, and not just volunteers. They've begun mandatory recruitment, which means something big is in the offing. We finally traced you to the supply ferry. The captain wasn't eager to talk, but the distraught father of a missing eighteen-year-old girl can be very persuasive.

"He provided us passage down the lake, to the site where you left him for shore, and my instincts led us from there along the road toward Tandor. There was quite a ruckus in the town with a group of gray-band mercenaries when we arrived, and they were clearly looking for you as well. They separated, and we followed two who took the south road out of Tandor. We subdued them in the night. One had been with the group that chased you into the mountains, and his tongue wagged like a puppy's tail when I pressed him. He was our guide until I was able to pick up your trail again. And that's when we met our new friend and his protector."

Hunger put a halt to further conversation, and Cameron retrieved the dead possum, tossing it at Garrett's feet with a laugh. "This was Aiya's contribution to breakfast, but maybe we can find something a bit more appetizing and fresher." Garrett didn't recognize the invitation to hunt at first, but a second glance from Cameron did the trick. He jumped up, and Cameron handed him the bow.

Two hours later, they returned with two large rabbits. Erral praised Garrett for his success, but Garrett confessed, "They were Cameron's. I missed the first three shots. They're hard to hit when they move."

"I'm sure he would've hit the next one," Cameron said, "but we were both getting really hungry."

They had little else to eat besides dandelions and other greens, but it sufficed. Garrett returned the possum to Aiya, and she happily devoured it.

Jared and Alanna returned to eat in the late afternoon, but Alanna kept to herself and ate in silence. When she finished, she stood to look at the group and said impassively, "I'm sorry for my outburst earlier. I was out of line to put that on you." She walked away before anyone could offer a reply or consolation, stopping only to address Garrett with the same emotionless calm. "Thank you for coming back to us." She left the camp to sit alone in the prairie grass and wildflowers, thinking and meditating until sunset.

The men sat together after Alanna wandered into the prairie. Jared had an uneasy look about him and was the first to speak. "Cameron, I feel compelled to say this, if only to clear the air between us. You probably have no notion of what's been in my mind for the past several weeks, and I wouldn't expect you to. Erral explained your predicament, and I'm doing my best to understand it all. But when Alanna disappeared, I was worried beyond words, and I was angry that you were responsible for it. But after talking to her today, I know this was her decision. I'm still trying to wrap my head around her part in all this, but after the things she revealed today, I can't deny that her heart has led her here."

Jared briefly broke down but continued, "Please understand, none of this makes it any easier. But she made it clear to me today that she's going to see it through to the end, whatever it is that's tormenting her, with or without her friends. So I beg you to promise me that you'll look after her and protect her. She's stubborn and prone to trouble, but I guess you may know that already. She has her mother's spirit, and I know if she were here right now, what she would say . . ."

Jared's voice trembled, and he struggled to complete the thought, so Cameron softly interjected, "You have to follow your own heart, no matter the consequences nor the ones who stand in your way."

Jared, his lower lip quivering, looked up and nodded.

Cameron wanted to assuage Jared's fears, but he knew he couldn't guarantee even his own safety, let alone Alanna's. And he knew equally well that her mind was immovable in her quest against the tyranny of the Khaalzin. He kept quiet about the Prophecy, knowing that she would not have spoken of it to her father. It was unlikely that he would truly understand. But Cameron finally offered his true sentiment, "We'll be looking after each other . . . to whatever end. I don't know if that's what you want to hear, but that's what I can offer."

It was, of course, not what Jared wanted to hear, but then nothing that Cameron could have said would have appeased a fretful father bereft of his youngest daughter, further widening the void already in his life. His willingness to let her live her own life, however difficult for him, was as admirable as it was courageous. Cameron understood this.

After a quiet interlude, they began to discuss plans for the next day. Cameron made it clear that his destination was home. He would head west across the Eastmoorland plains to Candora, where he would find a way to cross the river into Southmoorland and eventually travel to Locksteed.

As much as Jared wanted to stay with and protect Alanna, he knew her path in life was her own, so he planned to accompany the group to Candora, then return home along the northern trade road, past the Moraien Fens, to Clearwater.

Garrett remained silent during the discussion, uncertain of his own future, but certain of his unwillingness to commit to anything. His subconscious impulses, however, would ultimately lead him along the same path as his new friends. A part of him had felt empty and alone after they left him back at the Vale.

And Erral, as expected, planned to accompany Cameron for the time being.

Alanna returned to camp in the twilight. She packed her belongings and readied herself for travel the next morning. Without a word, she curled up under her blanket for the night. The visions returned, and what little sleep she found was encumbered by distress and sadness. Yet she lay quietly through the night so as not to disturb the others or further worry her father.

When she rose early in the morning, she grabbed her things and washed up at the river's edge. She went through her morning chores with a new resolve, pushing the simple tasks to a place of unimportance. The frivolity of her normal thoughts was gone, replaced by focus and determination. She had relegated the dragon-shine headband to her pack even before leaving the Vale, but this day she placed it around her forehead as a private testimony to her conviction.

The entire group soon recognized the change in her. Cameron missed the playfulness in her personality, and Jared grieved for her hidden suffering. Garrett saw it too, although he never really knew her well before her visions began their insidious torment. She walked with them in self-imposed silence toward the heart of Eastmoorland.

PROPHETIC PARANOIA

Dante dismounted and pulled the gray riding cloak from his shoulders, then draped it over the saddle. He joined two other Khaalzin who waited impatiently for their leader to arrive. They gathered between two large encampments, a boisterous throng of Caraduan nomads to the east and a more subdued collection of mercenary soldiers to the west. The armies were purposefully kept separated owing to generally uncivilized intolerance of one another.

"The party's about to begin, boys. They've got the nomads advancing for the diversion out east. It'll keep the Eastmoorland defense from concentrating around Candora. If Southmoorland hasn't sent any more reinforcements, then we'll push right through and retake the damn city. The trade routes'll be under our control, and it'll be over." A devious smile crept over Dante's face. "The shepherds have finally risen."

"What if Southmoorland sends more militia?"

"Even if they did, they'd be completely untrained. They haven't had time to organize. And that's why we're pushing in now." Dante paused and stared at Gryst, who remained silent and apprehensive. "You got somethin' to say?"

"The boy's still out there, Dante. He could be anywhere since they lost him in the Black Mountains. And that girl . . . I know you don't believe me, but she's gonna be trouble too."

"He's just one boy, Gryst. And the girl? Are you seriously scared of a little girl? You're gettin' to be paranoid. Besides, I've got a little plan in case they show up in Candora."

FRAY

Cameron and his companions continued west for several days across Eastmoorland's open prairie, an expansive grassland broken only occasionally by farms and horse pastures. Except for Aiya, the waist-high prairie grass provided no cover in the vast openness, so they followed a main road to speed the journey. Around midmorning one sunny day, they encountered small groups of Eastmoorland militia swarming ahead toward the south side of the road, near a small wood draping the northern slope of an undulation in the prairie. Erral was uneasy about the scene, but curiosity drove them into the wood's cover where they climbed the slope to a better vantage. The wood came to an end at the hill's crest, and they peered out over the expansive prairie to the south.

In the distance, a small Caraduan army was marching in formation toward them. The Eastmoorland militia was in the process of forming ranks half a mile from their vantage point, blocking the advance. The small militia groups they had seen were hustling forward to join the defensive line, which appeared to slightly outnumber the Caraduan forces. Erral scanned the developing scene and remarked, "I've never heard of nomads marching in formation like that. They normally invade in smaller disorganized groups."

The army continued to advance while they watched from the trees. Alanna became anxious. She knew the realities of war, but the senselessness of the impending violence knotted her stomach. And as the Caraduan force moved closer, Cameron identified two dark figures on horseback, one at either end of the advancing line. His anger seethed, and he subconsciously moved his hand to the hilt of his sword.

"We heard a rumor that the Khaalzin target the militia's leaders," Cameron informed the group. "The soldiers are left with no direction." He scanned the Eastmoorland line and saw the red headgear worn by the officers to identify themselves to their men. It was a useful strategy in conventional battle but a predictable folly against the Khaalzin. He pointed. "Look, they're as obvious as can be!" He took several steps out of the wood's cover, then hesitated. He looked back to Erral, then turned and ran for the far end of the Eastmoorland line. After several strides, he dropped his cumbersome pack, bow, and quiver.

Erral yelled after him, "Cameron, it's too dangerous. We don't have time!" When Cameron ignored his plea, he muttered, "That impulsive fool," and began to run after him despite being hindered by his painful ankle. Cameron had bolted ahead and was widening the gap between himself and Erral when Erral realized the futility in trying to stop him. Cameron was almost to the right flank when Erral veered toward the center of the formation where the field captain stood amidst a handful of junior officers.

Jared, Alanna, and Garrett watched the Caraduan army advance, then without pause, charge headlong into the Eastmoorland line under a cacophony of violent battle cries. Alanna gasped, and her thoughts escaped aloud, "Get out of there!"

Garrett stepped forward to watch the battle unfold. His mind soaked in the activity like a game of chess, anticipating and calculating moves by the individual pieces. He watched Cameron push through the throng of soldiers toward the right flank lieutenant, while Erral was being restrained from reaching the captain. His eyes darted from left to right and back again as he took in every detail of the chaotic scene. Then fireworks erupted simultaneously within both flanks.

Cameron had reached the line ahead of Erral and pushed through to the lieutenant leading the right flank. The man was barking orders atop a muscular stallion and ignored Cameron's initial pleas. Suddenly, a fireball streaked into the front line, setting the sergeant ablaze. The lieutenant was flummoxed while the soldiers around the burning sergeant backed away in terror. Cameron was reaching for the lieutenant's leg when he felt his hair stand on end, and he knew the next attack was coming. He lunged at the lieutenant and knocked him to the ground just before a fireball impacted the saddle, sending the frightened horse in flight.

Cameron reached out and pulled both the red plume and the red band from the lieutenant's helmet, then shoved them in front of his face, saying, "You've got a target on your head! Get rid of them or every officer in this command is going to be dead!"

The man was still stunned when Cameron jumped to his feet and scanned the helmets in front. He spied another red band belonging to the second sergeant and forced his way forward through the tense soldiers toward the active melee. From the corner of his eye he watched the gray rider scanning the field for his next target, and he was nearly to the sergeant when the fireball appeared in the gray rider's hands.

Out of the chaos, a snarling nomad suddenly appeared in his path, and Cameron smashed the shield into the man's chest, knocking him to the ground. Cameron lunged forward, holding the shield defensively before himself and the sergeant just before the fireball reached them. The shield deflected the attack, but the force knocked Cameron and the sergeant to the ground. Cameron recovered and tore the red band from the man's helmet before snaking his way back to the rear.

Meanwhile, the guards stationed around the captain intercepted Erral and restrained him. While they argued, the sizzling sound of fire plummeting through the air and impacting flesh began. The sound, along with flashes of light, startled the guards, giving Erral an opportunity. He knocked one guard to the ground and immobilized the second with a quick punch to the throat before forcing his way to the captain. But his lieutenants had seen the commotion and stepped forward to stop Erral as a fireball struck one in the neck. The gruesome injury stunned them, but Erral didn't miss a step. He quickly knocked the helmets from each of their heads before reaching the captain. Regaining a dignified manner, Erral breathlessly addressed the stupefied officer, "I respectfully suggest that you consider removing the bullseye from atop your head." Erral glanced toward the gray rider and waited for the next fireball to be released, for dramatic effect, before grappling the captain from its path.

The captain grabbed his helmet and tossed it far behind. They remained low to the ground, out of the Khaalzin's sight, while Erral explained to the captain whom they were up against and what tactics the Khaalzin were employing. The captain regained his composure, gathered his lieutenants, and began barking orders.

Meanwhile, one sergeant and the lieutenant commanding the left flank succumbed to the fiery assaults. The second sergeant panicked when a third fireball just missed him, impacting the unfortunate soldier beside him. It burned deep into the man's flesh and ignited his uniform. Every soldier within ten paces scattered, leaving the sergeant to retreat, screaming, through the rear ranks.

From his vantage on the hill, Garrett watched the battle unfold, absorbing every detail from orchestrated troop movements to individual swordsmanship. His attention was drawn to the left flank. Three fireballs appeared to hit their marks, and the surrounding soldiers scattered like ants running from a hot brand. Garrett's intensity grew, and he began barking cautions and orders across the distance to unhearing ears.

Following a handful of other deserters, the retreating sergeant broke through the rear rank and continued running up the hill toward the wood. Garrett's frustration swelled, and he started running down the hill toward the left flank. But upon realizing the absurdity of what he was doing, he stopped after several steps.

Alanna's voice broke through the din, begging him to come back. "What are you doing? You don't even have a weapon," she emphasized.

Garrett watched the left flank falter. Soldiers were breaking ranks in increasing numbers. Nomads had broken through and were chasing down the retreating soldiers. The gray rider was mobilizing warriors from his center ranks to take advantage of the breech, and Garrett intuited the smaller force would then have the advantage. He paced back and forth while the retreating combatants closed the distance between the battle and himself. He sped back toward the trees before remembering Cameron's bow, and without a second thought, turned and raced to where it was dropped.

The retreating militia closed the gap faster than Garrett had expected, and he was suddenly in the path of an Eastmoorland soldier being chased by a Caraduan nomad. The soldier looked ahead to see Garrett, and further up the hill, a young woman. Garrett would later surmise the young soldier's embarrassment was so profound that he stopped and turned to face the nomad. They fought one another ferociously, inflicting blow after blow while Garrett ducked and spun to avoid the fury of their weapons. Eventually, the nomad inflicted a final, deadly blow to the young soldier and turned toward Garrett. But thankfully, after two steps, the nomad dropped to his knees and succumbed to his own wounds.

Garrett was terrified, and Alanna screamed through the entire encounter. Jared pulled her back to the trees and into cover while Garrett recovered his focus and grabbed the bow from the ground. He felt Aiya's presence nearby, which comforted him, so he forced himself up and rushed headlong toward the tree line. But he was disoriented and instead found himself running straight toward a pair of oncoming nomads. His eyes widened in disbelief. He barely had time to react, and anticipating the side-to-side slash he had observed the nomads to prefer, dropped and slid under the first nomad's swing, using the bow to help deflect it. He came to rest directly under the nomad, defenseless, while the man raised his saber for a second swing. But a streaking shadow suddenly leapt from the deep grass, stealing the nomad's attention. In an instant, his sword arm was shredded down to bone by ferocious jaws, pulling the man to the ground in the process. Aiya swiftly crushed his neck before dispatching the second nomad in a blur of bluish-black and silver scales.

She made brief eye contact with Garrett before slithering back into the tall prairie grass.

Garrett craned his neck and peered over the grass to recover his bearings. He saw no immediate threat and looked at the bow in his hand, realizing he had forgotten to pick up the quiver of arrows. He recovered it after a quick dash back and then ran toward the trees. To his right, an Eastmoorland soldier was retreating toward him with three nomads close behind. The soldier wore a red band around his helmet, identifying him as the sergeant whom Garrett had watched in retreat, but he was terrified and running for his life. In the moment, Garrett felt both understanding for his fear and disgust at the example he set for the men under his command. They were scattering in his wake, and the sergeant was leading the nomads straight toward himself—*and Alanna.*

Garrett knelt and fumbled an arrow from the quiver. He subdued the urge to look up and focused instead on nocking the arrow over the bowstring. The soldier stumbled in his terror and fell face-first to the ground, opening a clear shot at the leading nomad. Garrett released the arrow, and the nomad dropped in a heap. Terror again gripped Garrett while he fumbled for a second arrow, knowing he wouldn't have it nocked in time to fire before the second nomad would be on him. Just then, the grass to his right fiercely rustled and separated, and Aiya streaked past, taking the nomad by surprise. The third slowed just enough to allow Garrett to release the second arrow, killing the nomad instantly. Garrett gasped, filling his depleted lungs, while Aiya dispatched her latest victim. Forcing his breathing under control, Garrett ran to the Eastmoorland soldier.

The man was frozen on the ground and trembling. Garrett lifted his shoulder and forced him onto his back. "Get up. Your men are scattering. They need you!"

"They're burning us alive! We don't have a chance!"

"The gray-cloaks only attack the officers," Garrett scolded. He took the man's helmet from his head and held it out, then tore away the red band.

The man took the helmet back, and the realization began to sink in. He placed it on his head and looked back toward the fray. Garrett sensed the sergeant's indecision and adapted something Erral had recently said, something that made a strong impression on him at the time. "Every man has both courage and cowardice in his heart, but it is his decisions that determine which he will leave in his wake." It came out awkwardly, he realized, so he added, "They're flanking your countrymen! You need to get your men back and close that gap!"

The soldier stood up, and after briefly looking past Garrett, took the red band and ran back toward the battle. He waved the red band over his head and called to his men as he ran, then steeled himself for the fight. Whether it was Garrett's inspirational words or Aiya's menacing glare from where she stood behind Garrett, that Eastmoorland sergeant helped turn the battle's momentum to Eastmoorland's favor.

Cameron lingered behind the militia while the soldiers rotated in and out of battle, as was the Eastmoorland militia's historic strategy. They were disciplined and fiercely loyal to their homeland. Cameron felt out of place and slowly backed away. He peered over the fray hoping to see the gray rider, but the villain had drifted behind the throng of wild nomads. The Khaalzin couldn't sustain the fiery attacks, as Cameron knew. Each blast would sap energy and stamina, lowering their body temperatures profoundly. He resigned himself to the small victory he'd already achieved, knowing their paths would cross again.

Erral turned back as well, found Cameron, and urged him back under cover in the wood. They looked up the hill to see a small skirmish not far from the trees, then recognized Garrett in the midst of it, appearing and disappearing in the prairie grass. Cameron's heart sank, and he sprinted forward with every effort his legs could muster. Erral lagged behind in his agonizing strides. When Cameron finally reached Garrett, the skirmish was over, and he looked around in wide-eyed amazement. Garrett stood, bow in hand, looking over six slain Caraduan nomads. And not far away, Aiya popped her head above the grass to scrutinize Erral gimping past.

Alanna ran from the trees with her father trailing close behind. She had the same wide-eyed expression as Cameron and was mortified by the sights she had witnessed in such close proximity. Garrett seemed unmoved by the carnage around him, and his gaze fixed back down the hill to the battle. Troops had filled in the gap in the left flank, and the remaining Eastmoorland line held fast.

Erral collected the companions and ushered them back into the wood to form an exit plan, except for Garrett, who remained watching the battle. The tide had definitely turned in favor of the Eastmoorland militia, with their superior numbers and their leadership preserved. The Khaalzin would eventually be forced to retreat with the remnants of their vagabond army, knowing this battle was only a minor skirmish in a much larger design.

REUNION

The travelers returned to the road and continued west. They walked at a brisk pace until they felt safely distanced from the battle. They passed wagons carrying reinforcements, general supplies, healers and medical supplies. One supply wagon stopped, the wagoner eager for information about the battle, and Erral took the opportunity to find out what dangers might lie ahead.

The wagoner passed along rumors about mercenary armies and nomads amassing to the south of Candora. A smaller mercenary force had recently been pushed out of the city, where they wreaked havoc and occupied the trade center for several days. They ransacked homes and pillaged many of the city's stores and warehouses to supply their army.

Candora was a sprawling city located at the confluence of the Alurien and Candora rivers, just south of the Moraien Fens. River barges carrying goods from Clearwater Lake would typically drift south along the Candora River and either stop in Candora to unload or continue further south to the port city of Kantal or smaller towns in between. But Candora was the primary trade center in Gartannia, being on the north-south river route and centrally located on the border between Eastmoorland and Southmoorland.

The Eastmoorland militia had been stymied by the city's occupation because many of their soldiers were engaged to meet the Caraduan forces reportedly moving up from the southeast. But the Southmoorland militia arrived, unlooked for, to aid their neighbors in reclaiming the city.

Cameron, finally feeling that his journey was approaching a meaningful culmination, was exhilarated at the mention of Southmoorland. Although still a long way, the distance between him and his home seemed insignificant compared to his recent travels, and he almost forgot about the war that was closing in around him.

The road that they traveled led directly into Candora, though they were still several days away on foot. But their fortunes turned for the better. The supply wagoner they talked with the day before overtook them on his return trip and offered them a ride in the wagon. He was taking a wounded lieutenant back to Candora to brief the regional captain on the battle. The lieutenant initially protested, but after recognizing Erral from the battle, relented. And after Alanna and Cameron tended to his wound, he was grateful to have them.

"How'd you know the gray-cloaks' tactics?" the lieutenant asked.

"That's a long story," said Cameron. "We had some problems with them back home, and then I heard the stories about their attacks while we were traveling near Clearwater Lake."

"I've never seen anything like it. I don't think they're even human."

Cameron and Alanna traded uncomfortable glances.

"They are *definitely* human," offered Erral. "But they're not from this part of the world. I would see them banished back to where they came from, or dead, if I have anything to say about it."

The lieutenant said, "Well, until that happens, I think we're in for a tough fight. The nomads are trouble enough, but when they're organized like this, well, it'll be hard to push 'em back. We need to report these gray-cloaks' tactics to the other captains. I'll be meeting with our western regiment when we get to Candora."

At first, Garrett was a bit edgy in the wagon, but he sensed Aiya following nearby. He hoped she would be sensible enough to remain out of sight and yet not fall behind. She had suffered a slice through one of her wings from a sword strike, unnoticed until Garrett saw her licking it after the fray. It didn't seem to slow her down, but he worried nonetheless. Every now and then, he caught a glimpse of a shadow moving across an opening or her dark head peering over the grass some distance from the road. She seemed to be keeping up just fine.

The wagoner changed horses three times each day at temporary outposts, so they were able to make continuous progress toward Candora. Late into the second day, Garrett became increasingly concerned about Aiya when they approached the more populated territory around Candora. He asked, "What's the plan once we reach Candora?"

Cameron spoke first, unhesitatingly. "I'm continuing on to Southmoorland. My family doesn't know if I'm still alive."

Alanna grasped his arm and said, "I'll come with you."

"Cameron," Erral began, "your grandparents are safely hidden, and we don't know where your father is. He'd be healed from his injuries by now, certainly well enough to return to duty."

"But he's been retired for years, and after those injuries, I just don't think—"

"If you search your heart, Cameron, and put yourself in his shoes, I think you'll come to the conclusion that it's the only choice he would make."

Jared added, "Erral's right. Take it from another father, he's not gonna sit around waiting and hoping that you'll just walk back through the door one day. Besides, from what Erral's told me about Joseph Brockstede's service to the Southmoorland militia, they wouldn't hesitate to take him back."

The lieutenant perked up. "Captain Brockstede?"

"Do you know him?" Cameron asked.

"Of course. He led the Southmoorland army in retaking Candora. Is he really your father?"

"Is he still here?" Cameron blurted.

"Well, I can't say for sure, but he was in Candora just a few days ago."

"I need to find him!"

Erral endorsed Cameron's statement. "Yes, *we* need to find him, if he's still here. We need to find the Southmoorland encampment."

Garrett nudged the wagoner. "How far?"

"About three miles to the Southmoorland camp," the man replied.

The sun was just setting when Garrett prepared his pack and jumped out of the wagon, saying, "I'll meet up with you at the camp later tonight or tomorrow morning." He scanned the fields and jogged into the prairie.

The military encampments stretched along the city's southern fringe and west to the river's edge. Campfires dotted the landscape, and the flickering firelight reflected from countless tents. The city was tucked along the eastern bank of the massive Candora River and sprawled over a wide area to their north. They arrived at the Eastmoorland officers' field quarters well after sunset under a moonless sky. They helped the lieutenant out of the wagon and into the officers' tent before getting directions to their destination. It was a short quarter-mile walk, so they thanked the wagoner and went on foot.

They wound through several clusters of tents and finally spotted the large circular arrangement of officers' tents. Cameron's eyes were focused on it, and his pace was quickening when they passed a small group of enlisted men sitting outside their tents. One watched Cameron pass in the darkness, and in a low, rumbling voice said, "Well, I'll be boiled in lard." The massive figure of a man stood and stepped forward.

Cameron recognized the voice and stopped in his tracks. It was Jaeblon.

The bearded figure stepped closer to confirm his own suspicion and bellowed, "Well ain't you a sight fer sore eyes!" He grabbed Cameron by the shoulders with his large hands. "And ya ain't no apparition at that. Ha-ha-ha!"

"Jaeblon! I worried about you, my friend," Cameron said.

"Wha'? Well, I ain't worth worryin' bout." He laughed again, then his demeanor turned serious. "Does Joseph know yer here?"

"No. So he's really here?"

"Would I be here if he weren't? Now, git yerself amovin', we gotta reunion to git at! Ha-ha-ha!"

Jaeblon led the group to the circle of tents, laughing and talking. "I won't lie to ya, Cameron, but I didn't know fer sure what if we'd ever see ya again, the way them gray fellas lit out after ya that night."

"I didn't either, Jaeblon, but it's sure good to see you now."

They approached a circle of tents surrounding a blazing fire and a canopied field office. Several guards were stationed around the circle, and a group of officers was seated around a large table under the canopy in the midst of a heated discussion. A guard stopped them outside the circle.

"What's your business?" he asked curtly, though he obviously knew Jaeblon.

"We're here to see my captain," Jaeblon said.

"He's busy right now."

Cameron's heart was pounding. *He's actually here*. He wanted to rush past the guard to find his father.

Alanna sensed Cameron's urgency and held the back of his shirt, not wanting him to tarnish the long-awaited reunion.

Jaeblon stepped forward with a fiery glare and said, "If ya don't git him, I'll be doin' it myself."

"What's so damned urgent?" the guard replied, clearly irritated at the interruption.

"You just tell him Cameron's here to see him. He'll understand."

Another guard, who was notably uncomfortable to be confronted by Jaeblon's hulking figure, came over to block them while the first went to give the captain the message. After a brief exchange of words under the canopy, Cameron heard an exclamation, "What? Where?" The guard pointed in Cameron's direction, then a chair tipped over backward. A man turned in the shadows and kicked the upset chair out of his way, then limped into the firelight, straining to see into the shadows beyond the circle of tents.

Cameron stepped out of the shadows and into the light of the blazing fire. Joseph looked at Cameron in disbelief, then briskly walked over to him, stopping to take in the moment before they embraced. Jaeblon stood by, laughing and smiling. Joseph was not a particularly sentimental man, but tears welled in his eyes to be able to embrace his son again. He said in a soft voice, as if to himself, "I *knew* you were alive." And after a moment, he stepped back from the embrace to scrutinize Cameron, smiled, and looked toward his companions. He took Erral's hand and said, "Thank you for keeping my son safe."

"It's good to see you, my friend, but I'm afraid your thanks are undeserved. We have a great deal to discuss."

"How are Gram and Gramps?" Cameron asked his father.

"They're fine. They've been in hiding, and I haven't seen them since the night you left. Caelder can tell you more."

Joseph looked at Cameron's other companions, and Cameron introduced them before Joseph led them all into a large, lamp-lit tent. Before sitting down with his guests, Joseph said something in a low voice to a guard, who quickly ran off. "I guess we have a lot to catch up on," Joseph said. They talked together for a long while before Joseph recognized Alanna's exhaustion, and he offered her and Jared a private tent in the officers' circle. They kindly accepted and left to get some sleep.

"How did you end up here?" Cameron asked.

"I reenlisted when I was healthy enough. And when this war started, how many of the Southmoorland field commanders do you think volunteered to lead our militia into Eastmoorland against these gray-cloaks?"

Cameron smiled. "Probably just one."

Joseph laughed. "Caelder told me about your chance meeting in the Alurien highlands, so I at least had some hope that you were still alive. But I never dreamed I'd see you wander in like this, right into the middle of a war."

"I was on my way back to Locksteed to find you."

"Well, it looks like you took the long way. But I'm glad you're here."

A short time later, a guard peeked into the tent and announced, "Captain, he's here."

Joseph stood and walked over to open the tent flap. "Well, what have we here?"

Cameron immediately recognized the voice that replied, "Sir, I can explain . . . I mean, it was just a prank, sir."

"Explain what, exactly?" Joseph said, obviously not expecting the response.

"Sir? Why did you call me here?"

Cameron started to laugh, and Joseph stepped aside with a smile. Rylak was stunned and jubilant, and he ran inside to greet Cameron. He wore a militia uniform, having obviously enlisted to fight against the coming invasion.

Joseph laughed again and led Erral out to talk privately while the young men caught up, but on his way out of the tent, he said with a stern face, "We'll talk about this prank situation later."

Rylak's eyes widened, and his smile briefly disappeared after Joseph's comment. Cameron slugged him on the arm and said, "I'm glad to see you haven't changed." They both laughed.

The young men talked into the early morning hours, catching up on recent events and reminiscing. They eventually fell asleep and were woken by guards who shooed them out of the tent at dawn to prepare it for the officers' morning briefing. Being no stranger to discipline, Rylak hurried back to his company before being missed.

Cameron wandered the nearby encampment and soon spotted Garrett sleeping behind a supply tent. "How's Aiya handling all this?" he asked.

"Better than me, if you want the truth. She wants to be close, but I think she understands it's too dangerous here. She's got plenty of cover where she is, about half a mile from here. But I'm still worried she might do something unpredictable."

"I can talk to my father. He could warn the soldiers to leave her alone if you think it would help."

"I'm not sure it would. She's pretty scary to run into, and I still wouldn't trust how they might react. I think I just worry too much. She can handle herself."

Later that morning, Joseph summoned Cameron, Jaeblon, Erral, and Caelder after the officers' morning briefing. "We need to discuss the Khaalzin," he began. "I've stressed to the Eastmoorland leadership how dangerous they are, but their stubborn adherence to convention has been frustrating. They haven't been bitten hard enough yet to actually pay attention to the Khaalzin's threat.

"But the Khaalzin's focus, as I see it, seems to have shifted from my family to seizing authority over Gartannia. We can fight their armies, but so far we have no working defense against the Khaalzin themselves."

"I wouldn't be too hasty to think they've lost interest in your family, and especially Cameron," Caelder said. "It was only this last spring that they concocted their plan to entrap Larimeyre, Kenyth, and Cameron. With Turk's complicity, they nearly succeeded."

"Caelder's right," Erral agreed. "We've been watching the Khaalzin for years, and I do agree with you that their search for the heirs of Genwyhn has been less earnest in recent years. But their encounter with Cameron last summer changed that. Their focus on planning this war was more committed than we appreciated, and regrettably, we failed to see it and warn you."

Caelder added, "Their war plans have been long in the making, and like Erral, I believe Cameron's appearance has complicated their strategy, perhaps to your militia's benefit. Their focus has returned to your family. Superstitions are deeply ingrained in these men. Arrogance and a lust for power are their primary qualities, but the superstitious warnings that derive from prophecies, to them, are a true threat to their power. And based on my recent discussions with Erral, maybe with good reason—"

"Look," Erral interrupted, "there isn't any point in having that conversation again. The literal interpretation of the Prophecy renders it moot since Gwen's death. And even if the Prophecy were true, it doesn't serve as a guide to destroying the Khaalzin."

Cameron remained silent regarding his own interpretation of the Prophecy. Erral was, after all, right about its value under the current circumstances.

"And you know my position on this Prophecy as well," Joseph said. "You can keep your superstitions for Arnoria."

"But to your point, Joseph, the Khaalzin aren't immortal," Erral continued. "They can be killed. We took one by surprise seven years ago, but there was more luck than skill involved in that encounter. The others won't be so easily caught off guard in a midnight slumber, and they've become far more powerful since then. They continue to build upon the powers of ehrvit-daen. And yet, they *can* still be killed." He looked at Cameron.

Joseph sternly replied, "What are you getting at, Erral? We don't have time to guess at your meaning."

The memory of his encounter with Scar-neck was still raw, and Cameron struggled to think about it, let alone talk about it with others. He had confided in Erral out of necessity, to try to better understand his emerging abilities, but he hadn't confided the story yet to any others, including his father. But now the group was silent, and their eyes followed Erral's gaze toward him.

"Cameron?" Joseph said with a concerned look. "Is there something you haven't told me?"

Cameron avoided eye contact with the others, but relented to his father. "Look, I don't know how to tell you what happened, because I still don't know myself. But it was mostly a combination of luck and whatever's in that shield that Gram gave me. There's no recipe that I know of for how to kill the Khaalzin. Yes, it happened, but I don't know if I could ever pull it off again."

He felt no compelling reason to mention Alanna's role in the incident, seeing no way to translate her quick wits to some grand plan. But after reflecting for a moment, he added, "The only advice I *can* offer—keep your friends close."

"Yer still full of surprises, ain't ya? And I'll second that advice," Jaeblon said.

Joseph stared at Cameron while trying to unravel his comments. "Are you telling us that you fought one of the Khaalzin . . . and defeated him?"

Cameron took in a deep breath and sighed, unsure what more to say.

"Cameron, I can understand how it may be difficult for you to talk about this, but we're all facing this same enemy. We're in it together, and we need any insight you may have."

"I know. It's just complicated. It happened after Turk led them to the cabin. Two Khaalzin followed me and caught us off guard."

"*Us?*" Joseph interrupted.

"Alanna and me. It turns out, the shield can repel their attacks. The one with the scar on his neck, he wasn't expecting me to protect myself with it. His attacks, somehow, reflected back on him. But I can't really control these things when they happen."

"What about the other one?" Joseph asked.

"Alanna was able to get away from him, and then he ran off after the first one died."

Cameron could tell by Joseph's expression that the story didn't completely add up, but he wasn't prepared to explain Alanna's involvement. "Look, like I said, I can't explain everything. And for Alanna's part, it's just not my place . . ."

Erral and Caelder sat silently, reading between the lines and filling the gaps in the larger picture. But they didn't press him for any more.

Joseph was temporarily speechless but finally sighed and said, "Alright, so where does that leave us?"

After a silence, Jaeblon spoke his opinion. "If we was only able to git 'em cornered, we could stomp right on over 'em with enough men and horses."

"They could be overpowered with enough men, but it would be difficult," Caelder said. "It would be almost impossible to get them cornered. They always seem to have an escape route."

"Well," said Joseph, "we need to come up with something. I don't think the Gartannian people will have the stomach for a long war. An unexpected offensive may be our best alternative. They aren't the kind of enemy that we're used to dealing with. These devils have been a step ahead of us, and we need to turn that around. You understand them better than I, so any suggestions you have are welcome." He cast a sympathetic look toward Cameron before leaving them.

Joseph was occupied with military briefings and planning operations through the remainder of the morning, and Erral accompanied Caelder into the city both to talk and to acquire any additional information they could find. They had accumulated a far-reaching network of friends and informants across the land and took the opportunity to connect with the local sources.

Jared and Alanna spent the morning in privacy, and when they finally emerged from the tent, Alanna's eyes were reddened. Jared gave her one last hug and a kiss on the forehead, then walked away to the north, into the city. He didn't look back but wiped his eyes repeatedly while he walked.

Alanna spotted Cameron and Garrett and came over to them. Cameron sensed her sorrow and immediately gave her a consoling hug. At her touch, the sorrow and anguish filling her mind spilled into him, and she didn't try to conceal it. He squeezed her tighter.

"Your father seems like a good man," she said after the long embrace. "He stopped by our tent early this morning to see if we needed anything. He didn't have to do that. He's obviously a busy man with a lot of responsibility."

"Yeah, he seems a little different since I left home. Closer, I guess. I wouldn't have expected it, being in the middle of a war and all. With my being gone, I think it's made him realize even more that all we have is each other."

"No, you have more than that. You have us too." And she reached out to hold Garrett's hand, which, unsuspecting, he awkwardly accepted.

"Yeah," Cameron replied, "I guess we do."

Across the field, under the canopy within the officers' circle, Joseph watched his son and his companions. He thought about the day he proposed to Gwen, her heritage, and the prophetic words that she used to sing as a lullaby to console their infant son. Worry and helplessness filled his heart, but there was no consolation for what he knew lay ahead.

"Captain . . . *Captain!*" his lieutenant repeated. "Do you agree or not?"

Joseph refocused on the officers' meeting. There would be time to worry later.

DESTINY'S FIRST ACT

It was late the same morning when messengers began to arrive with ominous reports. Joseph was urgently summoned to the Eastmoorland camp, and a pervasive disquiet enveloped the Southmoorland militia. All were kept in the dark, however, until early afternoon, after Joseph returned and called a meeting with the other Southmoorland officers. When they finally disbanded, the lieutenants fanned out to their respective companies, and a tumult arose across the encampment while the soldiers quickly broke down the tents and readied their gear.

Joseph found Cameron and filled him in. "The Khaalzin are leading their armies directly toward Candora from the south. Half of the Eastmoorland militia is still deployed to the east, well out of striking distance. We're preparing to take the brunt of a large-scale attack just south of the city." He looked to Alanna and Garrett. "I suggest anyone not prepared to fight should take refuge in the city."

"We understand," Cameron reassured him. "I'm staying here with you."

Joseph gave Cameron a grim smile and two heavy pats on the shoulder. "I'd be proud to have you with me."

The three companions, and especially Garrett, were stunned at the speed with which the militia broke down camp and moved to their defensive positions several miles south. Cameron searched the passing lines, but he was unable to find Rylak. Alanna came up behind him while he watched and held fast to his arm, letting him know she felt his concern.

The officers' circle was broken down as well and moved to form a combined command center with the Eastmoorland officers closer to the river at the city's south end. In light of the imminent attack, the militia commandeered a large building where wagons and ferries were built to use as the command post. A ferry crossing sat within sight and could be used in the event a sudden retreat was required of the command officers.

A large agricultural depot at the river's edge could also be secured by the companies of militia assigned to protect the command post.

By evening, the building's main production area was filled with officers. But behind the building was a large, enclosed lumber shed with a locked door leading to the interior. Garrett secretly picked the lock and explored the space. The door accessed three offices normally used by the owner and staff. When Cameron discreetly asked his father if he and his cohorts could use the space, Joseph furrowed his brow in a disapproving look, saying, "This is no place for—"

"I know what you're gonna say," Cameron interrupted, "but you don't know Alanna. You have to trust me . . . and her. Besides, if you want to be the one to tell her she can't stay here, well, may the gods be on your side."

Joseph stared briefly at Cameron, then turned to walk away. He hadn't the time to argue. Cameron took his silence as implicit permission, then hesitantly added, "And Father . . . we have a wyvern."

Joseph took one more step, then stopped to process what Cameron just said. "You have a *what?*"

Cameron simply stared back at his father.

"I don't wanna know," Joseph said and walked away.

So, in the darkness of night, Garrett borrowed a lumber cart and brought Aiya surreptitiously to the lumber storage shed covered in a tarp. She accepted her confines, but only after inspecting the shed to find every possible path of egress.

The night was unusually quiet for such a large city. Word of the impending attack spread rapidly, and the residents had already hunkered down, anticipating a long siege. Alanna sat silently by herself in an office while ruminating over her troublesome visions and wishing the dark hours away. The visions remained unyielding, and her contempt and determination against the Khaalzin further solidified.

The next morning brought early reports about the enemy's onslaught against the defending forces. Messengers cycled back and forth between the battle and the command post throughout the morning. At least one gray-cloak was casting his fiery assaults against any soldier who appeared to be giving orders, but removing the red bands and plumes conferred at least some protection to the officers.

Joseph longed to be at the front with his soldiers but knew his leg would be a liability. So he poured his knowledge and experience into planning and reacting from afar, hoping the inherent delay in communication would not cost lives. He reminded himself that the field captains were well-trained and experienced, and he trusted them to handle the urgent decisions.

So the chess game continued through the daylight hours. The enemy had adopted a strategy of attacking and retreating, attacking and retreating. The defenses held, and the attackers were unable to gain any meaningful ground except for one major roadway where the mercenary forces attacked relentlessly. The field captain requested reinforcements, so the Eastmoorland captain in command sent one of the two companies protecting the command post to his aid. Joseph argued against the decision, but being subordinate, he had no authority to overrule.

"That road's vital, and we're well behind the front," the Eastmoorland captain had argued. Casualties were mounting, and he feared a breach in the defensive line. Ultimately, the fighting ceased at sunset, an unwritten rule in gentlemen's warfare, so the dead and injured could be taken from the fields and attended humanely.

After the evening meal, Cameron became restless just sitting and waiting and wandered over to the river. Alanna joined him, also looking for a diversion. The clear sky forecasted a splendid sunset over the Southmoorland prairies just across the massive river flowing before them. It was an ironic contrast to the carnage of war not far away.

They were situated on the east bank of a long, sweeping river meander. To the north, the city sprawled over a vast area, but the confluence of the Alurien and Candora Rivers was well beyond their sight. South, the meander sharpened, then gently curved back in the other direction into the distance. A small harbor had been dredged to the left of where they stood, taking advantage of the river's complex currents to allow for easy entry and docking of ferries and barges.

Cameron was enthralled when he first looked to their right, toward the city, and spotted a massive paddle wheel suspended over the water on a wooden frame and platform. It was connected to a driveshaft extending into the adjacent building, which itself was built partially over the water onto pilings. The granary was attached to the same building, although the bins were empty this time of year, and he assumed the wheel powered a grain mill inside. They wandered to the mill, but the doors were closed and locked. So they continued toward the city, past a warehouse also connected to the mill, where an older man was loading bags of wheat flour onto a wagon. He noticed Cameron's curiosity and said, "It's quite a contraption, eh? They won't run it again till after harvest, but you should hear it asingin' and agrumblin' when it's agoin', he-he-he!" Cameron smiled and waved at the friendly character, and

Alanna actually giggled after the man waved back and disappeared into the warehouse.

The silly interaction seemed to raise her spirits a smidge. She was more talkative than she had been recently, but still reserved by her usual standards. They walked further north into the city, but the streets were nearly empty. The citizens were hunkered down, and the few they did pass were far less jovial than the man at the warehouse. Cameron tried to be friendly by offering simple greetings as they passed, but most were withdrawn and unsociable. It had become an entertaining game by the end of the walk and actually elicited a few more giggles from Alanna. They almost forgot about the war outside the city for a time. One man they passed as they neared the command post stared briefly at Cameron, then turned his head and walked briskly away. Cameron was about to offer a greeting when something familiar in the man's face interrupted him. He couldn't place it and brushed it off when Alanna started giggling again. He was just happy to see her laughing.

They slept in the back offices again. The night was calm, but an uneasiness crept insidiously into Cameron's dreams. He tossed and turned through the first half of the night until the nightmarish scene that began his flight from the Khaalzin replayed in his dreams. He was next to Erral and spurred his horse forward toward the Khaalzin while his grandparents made their escape. The Khaalzin's leader dodged Erral's advance while the second sprang out of Cameron's path. It was dark, but the features of the man's face were highlighted in this dream unlike the previous times the scene had replayed in his mind. *It was the familiar face of the man on the road!*

Cameron surged out of his restless slumber and sat straight up. "They're here," he exclaimed, jumping to his feet and stumbling over a chair in the darkness. He crashed out of the office and down the hallway to the back door before his senses caught up, and he stopped. Alanna came into the hallway first, then Garrett appeared from the other doorway, defensively poised and ready for a fight. Their hearts were pounding.

Garrett scanned the hallway and Alanna asked, "Who's here? What's going on, Cameron?"

"I need my sword. The Khaalzin. We passed him on the street!"

Alanna gasped, then Cameron rushed back down the hall to put on his shoes. He grabbed his sword before running out the door, half expecting to be ambushed in the darkness. A warmth spontaneously filled his chest, further unsettling him while he ran around the building to the main entrance. A startled guard stepped in front and yelled, "Halt!"

before recognizing Cameron. But Cameron mindlessly plowed into the man, knocking him several steps back. His momentum unchecked, Cameron crashed through the door and into the officers' quarters.

"Wake up!" Cameron yelled. "They're here! The Khaalzin, they're here!"

Several officers staggered away from their cots, and several swords were drawn out of sheer surprise.

"Get out of bed! Everyone! Where's the captain?" He moved through the open room in search of his father.

Finally, Joseph bellowed, "What in the name of Gartannia is going on? Cameron, is that you?"

Cameron followed the voice until shuttered oil lamps were reopened, and a swarm of armed officers descended on him.

"Wait! The gray-cloaks are here, in the city. He was just across the road last night. I didn't recognize him then, but it was him. I've seen his face before. They're setting an ambush. I know it!"

"Slow down, son," one of the lieutenants said, trying to calm Cameron. "Wait for the captain."

They heard bustling, stomping, and cussing coming from behind a wall, and shortly, the Eastmoorland captain in command stormed angrily out of his private quarters. "There better be a damn good reason for this!"

Joseph came to stand next to Cameron. "What exactly did you see, son, and when?"

"It was around sunset, and we were walking back from the city. I saw a man's face just before he turned and walked away, right across the road." He pointed toward the spot. "I didn't place it until just now—it was one of the gray riders from that night, you remember, when they almost killed Gram and we fled."

"Are you absolutely sure?"

"Yeah! He wasn't wearing the gray cloak, but it was him."

Joseph looked toward the Eastmoorland captain and said, "We could have a big problem if our enemy's been wandering around our backyard."

"Those fire-bleeding gray-cloaks were at the front yesterday!" the captain bellowed.

"Not all of them," Cameron retorted. "There's five!"

"Calm down, everyone," Joseph begged. "I trust my son's eyes, and we need to consider this seriously. There's no logical reason for the gray-cloaks to be in the city if they weren't planning something. At a minimum, we should increase our vigilance around the city, and then consider bringing one or two companies back from the front until we can muster reinforcements from Southmoorland."

"We can't spare the troops from the front, Joseph. We've already been through this," the Eastmoorland captain said. "Wake twenty soldiers and put them on patrol in the city and around our perimeter, and not another word about this. We've got another long day ahead of us."

Joseph grabbed Cameron's arm and escorted him outside, where Garrett and Alanna were anxiously waiting. "What's going on, Cameron?" Alanna asked.

"The Khaalzin are scouting the city, and now they know we're here."

Garrett surmised, "The only reason they'd be scouting here is if they were gonna invade."

"That's my fear," Joseph agreed. "They'd have to break through our defensive line or somehow skirt around it. But we have scouts watching the flanks."

"What about the river?" Garrett asked.

Joseph scratched his chin in thought. "Maybe. We drove them south out of the city when we retook it. But they could still mount a small-scale invasion from the north if they had enough mercenaries in place."

"They'd come at night," Garrett added. "They'd have to come in the dark."

The consideration clearly bothered Joseph, but his hands were tied regarding troop deployment. He could defy the Eastmoorland captain and recall a company of Southmoorland militia, but that would leave a weak point in the front lines. The captain in command was truly a master of battlefield strategy, but an unexpected ambush would be another matter altogether. Joseph would spend the remaining dark hours of night deliberating the situation, his mental energy ultimately wasted over a solution too late in materializing.

To the dismay of the Eastmoorland captain, their fears were realized early that morning under the first glow of light on the eastern horizon. Mercenary soldiers had commandeered ferries and barges from Clearwater Lake and the northern run of the Candora River, then concealed them deep in the channels permeating the Moraien Fens north of the city and just a few hours travel with the river current. They arrived silently in the darkness of early morning. The mercenaries disembarked at multiple locations along the river and snaked through the streets toward the command post. The sentries were either slain or, if lucky, retreated back to the small encampment by the command post, but they found their comrades already engaged with mercenaries who had landed nearby.

Cameron, Alanna, and Garrett had been sitting in the lumber shed with Aiya for the remainder of the night. They spoke very little and waited with trepidation for the dark hours to pass. Aiya sensed their anxiety and intermittently paced the floor. Then, in the early morning, she suddenly raised her head and twisted her neck to the north. She emitted a low, rumbling growl and got to her feet, posturing her torso low to the ground. Several moments later, they heard the first alarms rise out of the eerie silence. Soldiers yelled, and the clanking of sword against sword began in the distance. Aiya scurried about in an instinctive panic, having already been bitten once by the sharp metal. Garrett tried to calm her, but with little effect, while Cameron and Alanna rushed outside.

Joseph and several lieutenants emerged from the building, and Joseph began barking orders. Two lieutenants ran forward to pull the company back, and when Jaeblon arrived, he joined them to help instill order out of the initial chaos. Together, they succeeded in organizing the befuddled soldiers to form a defensive half circle against the attack. Mayhem ensued, but the swarm of gray-banded mercenaries intensified, and after a short time, the defense began to collapse.

Jaeblon continued to battle alongside the enlisted men. Erral and Caelder emerged from their tent not far away and ran forward to stand with Joseph. Seeing them, Cameron motioned for Alanna to stay back near the building where she might find safety. He dropped his bow and quiver next to the building, knowing it would be of no use in the chaotic fray, and moved out to stand next to his father.

Joseph looked over at his son and soon recognized the courage and conviction in his eyes. They were no longer the eyes of a boy consumed by indecision. Then the mercenaries began to break through the defense and zigzagged through the melee toward the officers. The four men drew their swords simultaneously, and Cameron raised his shield.

After leaving the lumber shed, Garrett found himself in the midst of a chaotic scramble. He was weaponless and tried his best to avoid careening bodies and flailing weapons. There seemed nowhere to escape the frantic melee until his evasive movements landed him in front of the command post building. The door stood open, and he glanced over to see the captain in command confidently march out, stern-faced and resolute, to join the fray. Several of his lieutenants had been dancing around behind the fighting with their swords drawn but were clearly uninterested in engaging the enemy. Garrett watched them with disdain as they ducked, one by one, into the building after the captain left, and he followed.

Several moments later, the cowardly lieutenants, except for one, reemerged through the door with Garrett close behind, wielding the sword of the one who lay bleeding from his shattered nose. He followed each one, prodding and shaming them into action. But he soon realized the sword attracted attention from the enemies, and his impulse to intervene may have gotten him in over his head. His dirty and worn civilian clothing was probably the only thing that spared him from the mercenaries' immediate attention.

Alanna backed up against the building and tucked her body next to a stack of scrap lumber. She watched the bloody hand-to-hand combat in the distance and recoiled at the barbarity. But the violence moved ever closer. She squinted and turned her head away, then wished she had never stayed. The scene became unbearable when Cameron and the others finally engaged in the madness. Three different times, mercenaries glimpsed her in hiding and advanced, only to turn away when they saw that she was but a young woman.

After Garrett left the lumber shed, Aiya frantically climbed the stacks and squeezed through a ventilation gap onto the building's main roof. She watched the chaos from above and kept her eye keenly on Garrett. The young wyvern was not adapted to defend herself from swords and arrows, and she knew it well, but still she watched and would have sacrificed herself for Garrett if the need arose.

Erral stayed close to Cameron out of his sense of duty while they engaged the sword-wielding mercenaries. He attempted several times to interpose himself in Cameron's engagements but found himself to be more of a hindrance to the young man. He felt the chill air when he moved too close and even sensed his own energy drawn away at times. Cameron moved with astounding agility, and no opponent seemed able to overpower him. The powers of ehrvit-daen had unquestionably emerged within him, and he drew upon them instinctively.

Garrett ran back toward the building and noticed Cameron's bow lying on the ground. He looked at the sword in his hand and realized its uselessness. He'd never been trained to use one, so he dropped it and picked up the bow and quiver. He ran around to the lumber shed and hid inside, hoping for a clear shot at the enemy through gaps in the weathered planking. He pulled a piece of rotted board away to create a larger opening and peered through. To his dismay, framed in the opening were two gray-cloaked figures walking arrogantly through the fray toward the building. Wanting no interaction with the deadly villains, the fighting mercenaries and soldiers actually paused their duels to move from the Khaalzin's paths as they advanced.

Still tucked against the building, Alanna helplessly watched the frenetic battle for what seemed an eternity before it began to lose momentum. Neither side appeared to have an advantage, and many combatants now lay dead or injured. She saw Erral and Cameron still on their feet, but they had drifted some distance away from Joseph and Caelder in the chaos. Joseph, bleeding, dropped to one knee in exhaustion, while Caelder breathed heavily at his side. And not far away, the Eastmoorland captain lay motionless on the ground surrounded by three slain lieutenants.

Then, at the river's edge by the harbor, two more Khaalzin stepped off a small ferry boat and marched toward the building. Alanna's heart seemed to stop, then began again with a palpable throb. Her anger seethed while she stood and stepped out of hiding, subconsciously reaching into her pockets to remove the wyvern-skin gloves.

Cameron sensed the emerging lull in the battle and scanned the area to see the four Khaalzin approaching. They moved forward with purposeful intent, their eyes never deviating from their targets. He watched as three converged toward him and Erral and the fourth strutted toward Caelder and Joseph. Caelder helped Joseph to his feet, and the two prepared themselves against the contemptuous villain. None of the Khaalzin spoke as they approached with deadly determination. Their swords were drawn, and they made no attempt to cast their fiery attacks. Without hesitation, they raised swords against the fatigued cadre.

Joseph and Caelder struggled against the single attacker in front of Alanna, and they soon began to falter. Alanna recognized the Khaalzin as the man who had held the knife to her throat. In desperation, she stepped forward and tried to enter the man's mind, as she had before, but found it willfully closed to her. At a distance, she simply wasn't strong enough. Her attempt only inflamed his wrath. He glanced toward her and sneered before unleashing a whirlwind of attacks, disarming Caelder and knocking Joseph to the ground. She became enraged, and with no regard for herself, rushed at the man, trying to get her hands on him. But he was too strong, and he pushed her back, knocking her to the ground by the building. He growled but withheld his blade for the moment.

"Not today, sweet girl," he taunted. "I'll deal with you shortly." He was going to savor her death.

Meanwhile, Caelder grabbed a wooden pole and reengaged the tireless Khaalzin, who dodged and parried the attacks with an arrogant expression. Catching the pole with his free hand, the Khaalzin wrenched it away from Caelder and dropped his own sword. He retaliated in a pompous display, sweeping Caelder's legs from under him and striking him unconscious with a forceful blow to the head. The man walked over to Joseph, who lay bleeding from several wounds, and struck him in the temple, knocking him unconscious as well. Satisfied, he turned back to Alanna with a hateful sneer.

Cameron parried blows from two attackers. His body felt energy-starved, and he realized the Khaalzin were drawing upon the same energies that he was. The cold air around them bit at his exposed skin and lungs. Their attacks were coordinated, one repeatedly striking at his shield while the other aimed at his head and legs. He blocked the blows, but the assault was too much, and before long, a well-placed blow knocked the shield from his hand. It rolled away toward the building while his opponents intentionally impeded him from retrieving it. The Khaalzin advanced, forcing him to retreat backward and away from the others.

Erral was outmatched by the fourth Khaalzin and fatigued quickly. Like Joseph, he had suffered several wounds and was knocked to the ground under his opponent's blade. The Khaalzin was preparing to finish him when an arrow plunged into his thigh from behind. He staggered and turned, then released a fireball at the lumber shed where Garrett hid. The dry, weathered planks burst into flames, driving Garrett back. The Khaalzin paused to pull the arrow shaft from his flesh while letting out a painful groan. Erral collapsed, unconscious and bleeding, but the Khaalzin wasn't satisfied. He limped over to finish him while Garrett ran from the shed and poised himself for another shot.

Garrett already had the arrow nocked and let it loose. The Khaalzin ducked and shifted, and the arrow missed its mark. But the villain was distracted and sent another fiery missile at Garrett. The young acrobat deftly rolled out of its path and sprang back to his feet, then ran toward the grain mill for cover.

Meanwhile, the cocky, gray-cloaked savage stepped toward Alanna and tossed the wooden pole to the ground. She crawled backward away from him until her back pushed against the building, and she dug her hands into the ground while focusing her mind into his. Again, he successfully kept it walled off and said, "You won't do that again." But he was wary enough of her strength that he stopped short and prepared a fiery attack from where he stood.

Alanna was terrified and helpless. She instinctively reached her hands out to the sides, grasping for anything to throw or use to block his attack. Her right hand fell onto the rim of Cameron's shield, and she pulled it in, holding it up just as the fireball came. The heat burned her fingers where she held the shield's rim and caused her to lose her grip. But before letting go, a wave of intense warmth entered through her arms and spread into her chest. She gasped in shock. Her breath was taken, and she rolled over, panicked, onto her hands and knees, unable to exhale. When she looked up, her eyes met the rage-filled glare of the Khaalzin, and he thrust a second fiery attack directly at her. Still breathless, she raised her hands reflexively and forced the heat from the depth of her chest, expelling it forward as she thrust out her hands. Her breath finally released, and she screamed. A blinding flash of light burst before her face as the fireball annihilated against her unexpected defense. The force propelled her back against the building, where she slumped, unmoving against the wall.

From where he stood, Cameron saw his father lying on the ground and the flash from the first fiery attack against Alanna. His anger swelled, and he struggled to get to her. But it was all he could do to ward off the attacks from the two Khaalzin, who now seemed to be toying with him.

Moments later, the second fiery attack struck Alanna. The flash generated by the merging forces was blinding even to Cameron, and once his vision cleared, he saw her limp body slumped against the wall. He became enraged, but his stamina was all but spent. He fought back with all the strength he could muster while Garrett streaked across the open ground away toward the river, calling for Cameron to follow.

He thought about making his final stand there and then, but something deep within him wasn't ready to give up just yet. The Khaalzin who had engaged Erral now limped toward him, and he knew there was no chance against all three in the open. He turned and ran after Garrett to search for a defensive position while dodging the few remaining soldiers and mercenaries still on their feet. He glanced back but saw no movement from his father, Alanna, or his other companions.

The three Khaalzin followed, walking arrogantly toward the mill, while the fourth remained temporarily stunned from the blinding flash. Cameron remembered the locked doors and veered toward the warehouse while beckoning Garrett to follow. After running inside, they pulled the large doors closed behind them and secured the flimsy bar to lock it shut. Garrett ran up the stairs to the upper storage loft while Cameron hurriedly looked for a suitable defensive position on the main level. Garrett looked for an escape, knowing they would likely need it, and found only a window at the back of the building. He smashed open the shutter and looked out, but it was a straight drop to the river below. He yelled to Cameron, "There's no way out from up here! Just a long drop to the river."

The Khaalzin were now pulling and shaking at the doors, and Garrett, hoping to find a clear vantage from which to shoot, ran back to the edge of the loft where it overlooked the main floor. He pushed over two large bags of wheat flour to gain a better view, and they crashed to the floor below, tearing open to create a billowing cloud in the air near Cameron.

Cameron coughed and choked, then saw the bar holding the doors shimmy out of its channel. He felt trapped knowing the Khaalzin would soon unleash their fiery attacks. Then it struck him, and he yelled to Garrett, "More. More bags! Dump them all!"

He ran up the stairs before the Khaalzin opened the first door, and he sliced open two bags of flour, dumping them over the railing. He whispered something to Garrett and then moved into the open. The first of the Khaalzin strutted through the doorway and growled to his comrade, "It's dark. Open the other door!"

The second door creaked open, further illuminating the warehouse. Cameron cried, "Now!" Garrett fired the arrow above the first Khaalzin's head, and the incensed villain looked up to the loft and spotted them.

The Khaalzin formed a fireball between his hands and prepared to launch it. The two young men turned to run from the coming attack as the second Khaalzin screamed, "No! You fool!" And the fireball flew into the cloud.

Back at the command center, Alanna had been severely stunned, as was the Khaalzin who had attacked her. When she finally regained her senses, she forced open her eyes against searing pain but found only darkness. She forced her eyelids up with her throbbing fingers, but darkness still obscured her sight. She twisted up to her hands and knees and felt for the dragon-shine headband. It was gone, knocked off by the powerful blast. Regardless, she reached her mind out, searching for anyone . . . Cameron . . . Garrett . . . Erral. But they were gone. She sensed only the distant nebulous veil obscuring Aiya's mind. She was alone, blind, and separated from everyone who was a source of strength to her. Despair descends rapidly under isolation, and she quickly felt its bitter emptiness.

Then she heard a shuffling sound not far away, and desperation overtook her thoughts. She crawled away from the sound, knowing in her heart it was the Khaalzin, but then came a different sound—that of a sword scraped over the ground and lifted. She crawled faster until her arms struck a body, causing her to recoil. Escape was futile, and her body shook in spasms as she sobbed.

The Khaalzin's soft steps were getting closer, and she prepared to accept her fate when an unexpected presence emerged in her mind. The veil that shrouded Aiya's mind had lifted. Thoughts drifted out, but they were strange and unintelligible. Aiya probed unimpeded through Alanna's mind, and vision began to fill the darkness left by the Khaalzin's attack.

Aiya had been watching the scene unfold from her perch on the roof when she sensed Alanna reaching out in distress. She jumped from the roof and glided clumsily down on her immature wings, then crept silently behind the Khaalzin, as closely as she dared.

Through Aiya's steady eyes, Alanna watched the Khaalzin slip past Joseph's limp body toward her own kneeling image. The scene was surreal, like a vivid dream, and Alanna trembled in terror. Then, she felt Aiya's intense instinctive urge to strike at the Khaalzin building. The protective rage was overwhelming. But just before she released, Aiya's eyes darted over to follow Joseph's now-moving arm. She hesitated while Joseph pulled a knife from his belt, then struck out, slicing across the backs of the Khaalzin's legs.

The man howled in pain and surprise, then stumbled back while raising the sword to strike at Joseph. Alanna sprang up, guided through Aiya's vision, and lunged at him. Once her hands found the villain's cloak, Aiya released her mental connection and sprang to clamp her jaws around the man's arm before it struck down.

Alanna clawed her way up his back and gripped her hands around his head while he struggled against Aiya's tearing grip. Her fury exploded through her hands and burst the Khaalzin's defenses. He collapsed to his knees and bellowed in agony at the pain filling his head, his face red and eyes bulging.

Joseph pushed up and found himself face to face with the wretched scene. Alanna was perched above the agonized Khaalzin clutching at his head, her face severely burned around inflamed and bleeding eyes. Her facial features were further distorted by a vengeful madness, and a fearsome beast, pulled straight from a nightmare, tore at the tormented man's arm.

Joseph cringed at the scene, then plunged his knife under the Khaalzin's breast and twisted upward, quickly and finally releasing the villain from a well-justified torment. Joseph looked back at Alanna with both pity and awe, and he began to understand her connection with his son. Undoubtedly, she shared similar Arnorian heritage.

Alanna felt the life drain from the contemptible Khaalzin, and she released her grip from his head, allowing his limp body to collapse to the ground. She stumbled back and fell to her knees. The rage in her expression melted away, exposing once again the fragile countenance beneath. She put her shaking hands slowly to her face, terrified of what her tender fingers would find, but the sensitive skin felt intact. Her eyebrows and hair were singed. But darkness still held her sight.

It was then that the explosion rocked the warehouse. The few remaining skirmishes around the command post drew still while the combatants gawked at the billowing flames spreading out through the windows and doors. Moments later, a massive secondary explosion shook the ground and ejected splintered planks outward as the walls disintegrated. The explosive concussion impacted every soldier in the vicinity, knocking them to the ground. Flaming wooden planks and fragments rained down upon them, and a massive billowing cloud of smoke rose skyward.

Jaeblon picked himself up from the ground and shook off disorientation following the blast. He had seen Cameron and Garrett run toward the warehouse followed by the Khaalzin and feared the worst. The mercenaries began to retreat, so he ran toward the warehouse's leveled remains. Two still-burning bodies lay on the ground in front of where the building had stood, and he went to them. The tattered remnants of gray cloaks still clung to them while their charred lungs gasped for air.

"May you devils burn for eternity," he muttered and moved further into the debris. Another Khaalzin lay dead some distance to the north, his body impaled with a large, splintered plank. Jaeblon searched everywhere in the debris for the young men but found no remains. Then he spied movement along the riverbank just downstream. First Garrett, then Cameron crawled up the bank and stood, briefly eyeing the devastation before Cameron ran back toward the command post.

Back in the warehouse, the young men had sprinted for the open window. Garrett dove through at the instant the fireball ignited the dust cloud. The resulting billowing flame escorted Cameron through the window behind Garrett, singeing his hair and igniting his pant legs. They both plummeted to the river below and plunged deep underwater where they were spared the concussion from the more massive secondary explosion.

The initial explosive flames engulfed the two Khaalzin who had entered the warehouse, hurtling them back and inflicting fatal burns. They would suffer intensely before death finally arrived. And the third, who walked around the building to cut off any escape, ran from the initial explosion. The second, however, pummeled him with a barrage of splintered planking, killing him instantly.

Cameron approached with elation to see Joseph, though covered in blood, pushing himself up to sit, and Alanna, surpassing his deepest hopes, was upright and kneeling not far from Joseph. He rushed toward her. She shook and wept uncontrollably where she knelt. But when he crouched in front of her, the full extent of the burns around her eyes became apparent. Her eyelids briefly rose enough for Cameron to see the redness obscuring the whites, and the beautiful blue irises were now hazy and dull. Her eyes looked past him, and he reached out to touch her arms. She flinched at the touch, fearfully retracting her arms, and he knew then that she was blind.

"Alanna, it's me," he said softly.

She gasped in elated relief, then reached up and grabbed his arms, pulled herself forward and collapsed onto him, weeping and clutching the back of his shirt. She sobbed over Cameron's shoulder, still shaking, then relaxed back and clutched his arms.

"I can't see you. I can't see anything."

"I know . . . I know."

With renewed panic, she tightened her grip on his arms and screeched, "Are they gone?"

"Yeah, I think so. They're all dead."

"What about Garrett?"

"He's fine. He's right behind me."

Garrett stepped forward, stunned and aggrieved to see her injuries, and awkwardly said, "I'm here."

"Garrett's going to sit with you," Cameron said. "I need to check on the others." He squeezed her arms, then wiped the tears from his eyes before getting up to check on his father.

Jaeblon went to Joseph and restrained him from trying to stand. He had several deep wounds that required attention. Jaeblon flagged a medic while Cameron held pressure to slow the bleeding.

"What about Erral?" Cameron said, looking over to where he had fallen.

Jaeblon lumbered over, picked Erral up, and carried him back to the medic. "He's tore up pretty bad. It's a right big pool o' blood he was layin' in." The medic quickly and tightly bound his wounds to stem the bleeding before returning to Joseph.

Caelder regained consciousness but remained befuddled most of the morning. The Eastmoorland captain in command perished from his wounds, along with three loyal lieutenants who had fought at his side.

After Cameron had done what he could to help his father and friends, he wandered to the warehouse ruins. He found the bodies of the three Khaalzin ravaged by the explosions. By now, they had all succumbed to their injuries, and he fought against the nausea elicited by the horrific scene. He had expected to feel prideful elation in overcoming his foes, but in the reality of the moment there was none. He felt nothing of the kind, and the hatred that he had harbored for so long felt impotent.

BLIND RESOLVE

After the few remaining mercenaries fled, healers and good Samaritans descended out of the city to care for the wounded. Jaeblon and two surviving lieutenants formed three separate posses with the surviving soldiers and led them through the city to root out the enemy. Many fled in such panic after the Khaalzin were killed that they forgot to remove the gray armbands and still carried their weapons openly. They were easy to identify, but many others escaped by blending into the city or paddling small boats out into the river. The handful that floated south would surely carry word to the last surviving Khaalzin and his mercenary army.

Messengers began to arrive from the front with reports of aggressive advances by the Caraduan and mercenary forces. They were stunned to find the command post ravaged and their captain in command slain. Caraduan reinforcements continued to arrive from the southeast, and the brutal attacks by the one remaining Khaalzin were being deployed with deadly efficiency against the Eastmoorland leadership. The leader of the Khaalzin was not among those who perished that morning, so it was he who still led the invading army, as yet unaware of his comrades' fate. But it would not be long before the news reached him.

Alanna's facial burns were severe. They extended across her nose and around her eyes, then up to a line running across her forehead just above her singed eyebrows where the wyvern-skin band had been. Cameron begged a healer for an ointment to treat her injuries but had to go into the city to acquire it. Garrett, in the meantime, searched for and found her headband near the building. The outer layers of tan cloth were burned away, so he removed the remaining shreds and returned the circlet to her, still bound securely to the undamaged wyvern-skin leather. She held it and twisted it in her fingers while agonizing over her blindness. Garrett had no words to soothe her, so he sat silently beside her.

"Aiya opened her mind to me," she said. "She saved my life. I couldn't see, and then she was there. She knew I was blind, somehow, and then she gave me her sight." Alanna's damaged eyes welled up with tears. "Her mind was so powerful. I felt completely vulnerable to it, not that I would have tried to stop her."

Garrett still sat silently.

"I don't think my sight's ever coming back. I think I'm going to be like this forever. I don't know if I can go through life like this. The only visions I have left are the ones that torment me every night."

Tears were streaming down her reddened cheeks, and Garrett was still at a loss for comforting words. So he gently reached over and took her hand, carefully interlocking his fingers with hers. His gesture was unexpected but comforted her. Garrett closed his eyes and concentrated for several moments, then slowly opened them again.

Alanna felt something probing her mind, just briefly, before a vision opened before her. It was almost as clear as if she were looking through her own eyes, like it had been when Aiya's mind had connected with hers. She gasped and held her breath before exhaling in astonishment, then she squeezed Garrett's hand while she both laughed and cried.

"How? How?" her shaking voice echoed.

He turned to look at her, and she reflexively closed her eyes, obviously with no effect.

"Don't! Please don't look at me." And she quickly pulled her hand away from his, terrified of seeing herself through his eyes.

Garrett took her hand again, now looking over the river, and shared his vision with her. "I'm not as strong as Aiya, but it's something we share."

"What else do you share with her . . . No! I don't need to know. I mean, I don't mean to be nosey. But thank you . . . for *this*," and she waved her hand in front of her and then in front of Garrett with a giggle. She let go of his hand and reached over to find his face, then gave him a gentle kiss on the cheek. She didn't see the intense flush suffuse his skin.

By the time Cameron returned with the ointment for Alanna, Joseph's numerous wounds had been sewn closed by a healer. But he refused bedrest and wandered out to check on his men. His shredded uniform was a patchwork of blood, so Cameron took him into the command post, where he helped his father change into a clean uniform.

"Your mother would be proud of you, Cameron. Even before all this mess with the gray-cloaks, she would have been proud to see the man you've grown into. I wish she could have had the chance. She didn't have much of a stomach for fighting and war, but I guess she understood its place in our world."

"She never talked about it when you were gone. I guess I never thought about it back then, but she probably worried a lot when you were away fighting the nomads."

"I know she did. But she managed to keep her fears hidden from you, for the most part anyway. And all that time I was away, I thought I was helping to keep her safe, both of you."

"You were. You were keeping all of us safe. Even if you *had* been home that day, it wouldn't have changed anything."

"I know. But it sure left a hole in our lives." Joseph pulled clean trousers on while struggling against the painful wounds. "She would have had an easier time understanding what's going on with you and your new friends. I saw things today that I'll never be able to explain. How is she? Is Alanna going to be alright?"

"She's blind. Her eyes look really bad. I don't think it's gonna get better, but otherwise, she's doing alright."

"She's quite a girl. If our enlisted men had half her courage, our militia would be practically invincible."

Cameron chuckled. "Courage or impulsiveness—it's not so easy to tell with her. But yeah, I know what you mean. It might surprise you, but I owe my life to her. When we talked yesterday, I didn't tell you everything about that encounter with the two gray riders back in Eastwillow. She's the kindest, gentlest, and smartest person I've ever known, but she's capable of things that I'm not sure *she* even comprehends yet."

"It doesn't surprise me at all. I saw it firsthand today. She and I owe one another the same debt, I suppose. Keep her close, Cameron, and keep her safe. Now, I need to move this painful body before it freezes up. I can't take another day of bedrest, not after nearly three months in leg traction."

Despite a splitting headache, Caelder was functioning normally later that day. Erral, however, had deep wounds that required sutures and bedrest in the infirmary. He was pale and weak from blood loss and wouldn't be on his feet for at least several days, according to the healer. And with the Eastmoorland captain's death, Joseph took charge of the local militia's remnants while deferring command at the front to a subordinate Eastmoorland captain.

The following day, reports began to arrive from the front detailing confusion and disorder in the attacking force's ranks. The Caraduan nomads were the first to retreat, and by day's end, the few who remained were routed by the regional militia. The mercenaries, likewise, saw little chance of their next payday arriving after hearing rumors of the gray-cloaks' demise in the city, and the Khaalzin's leader quietly disappeared amidst the turmoil. Without their leader, many of the mercenaries simply surrendered themselves to the militia, while others ran in hopes of evading capture.

While the militia mopped up after the retreating forces, the population of Candora breathed a collective sigh of relief. Citizens emerged with a rekindled civic spirit, bringing food and other supplies to the militia still lingering at the city's outskirts. Cameron, Alanna, and Garrett remained for the time being, still occupying the back rooms of the commandeered production facility.

Alanna struggled with her blindness, though Garrett hardly left her company and offered help when he could. In her darkness, she toyed with the dragon-shine headband and was able to wear it over the less-affected part of her forehead. The burns were painful and ugly, but the ointment helped to soothe the discomfort.

Outwardly, she accepted and dealt with her loss of sight better than Garrett or Cameron had expected. But inside, she agonized over the disability, and it only compounded the issues already plaguing her. Sleep still tormented her. So, in the darkness of night when the others slept, she crept outside and sat against the building to meditate and practice acumma.

Cameron remained somewhat detached for the better part of two days. He had disappeared into the manufacturing building's work area but remained secretive about his activity. Finally, he emerged with a newly made bow and handed it to Garrett while he sat holding hands with Alanna. It was nearly identical to Cameron's bow with a slightly lighter pull and no dragon-shine adornments, of course.

Garrett's face lit up as he took it from Cameron, and he said simply, "Thank you."

Alanna smiled and excitedly asked, "Did you make it yourself?"

Cameron glanced over to see Alanna's blank stare and replied, "Make *what?*"

"The bow. Did you make it yourself?"

"How did you know . . . are you getting your sight back?"

She giggled. "Not exactly."

Garrett clasped her hand again, and after a moment she added, "It's really beautiful, Cameron."

Cameron stood bemused while glancing back and forth between them.

Alanna saw his expression through Garrett's eyes and gave Garrett's hand a quick squeeze before saying, "You should go try it out. I need to talk to Cameron." Garrett was happy to oblige and ran off to the armory to hustle a few arrows and a quiver.

"Sit down with me."

Cameron sat and leaned back against the building, nudging his arm against her.

"I miss those days," she said, "you and me just wandering by ourselves. I didn't worry about so much back then."

"I worried enough for both of us."

"And I talked enough for both of us." She giggled. "That was really nice of you to make the bow for him. It made him really happy, way more than he showed."

"Yeah, I know. I think I'm starting to understand him a little better."

"He's a lot more like us than he ever let on, and he has a really deep connection with Aiya, more than he's admitted. She opened her mind to me that day, to help me. And she trusted me, because she completely dropped her defenses. And what I saw in her mind, even though I couldn't understand it, was intelligence way beyond what I ever guessed."

"So, seriously, how did you know I was holding a bow?"

"That's for me to know and you to find out." She jabbed him with her elbow.

"You're killing me."

"But seriously, there's something I want to show you. At night, when I can't sleep, I've been going out and meditating like Jaletta showed me. I'm starting to see things when I do it."

"More of those visions, you mean?"

"No, not like that. You know how we imagine ghosts would look if they were real?"

"Yeah, I guess."

"Well, it's like that. And I want to show you, if that's alright?"

Cameron didn't object, so she took the headband out of her pocket and slipped it on. She spun around in front of him, took both of his hands in hers, and said, "Give me a moment and then close your eyes, and don't try to fight it. Let me have your mind."

Her eyelids fluttered closed while he stared sympathetically at her scarred face, then her breathing gradually slowed and became shallower. After a short time, her grip on his hands involuntarily tightened, and he closed his eyes, allowing her to enter his mind. Before long, shimmering shapes and images appeared. They were ethereal and evanescent at first, but then persisted. He felt her mind processing as the images shifted and reordered, finally forming a three-dimensional scene. Then the scintillating silvery-white apparitions took more defined shapes. He opened his eyes to the realization that she had reconstructed the physical scenery around them, but he also felt the chill sensations from the air around her. Crude though the imagery was, she was using ehrvit-daen to actually *see*. She sensed his mind's departure and released her concentration, then removed the headband.

"I can't believe it! That's amazing," Cameron said.

"It's getting easier. It makes my brain really tired, and I actually slept a little the last two nights after doing it. I don't want to get too excited about it, but maybe I won't have to be led around on a leash for the rest of my life."

"That's not a bad idea, actually. Your father should've had you on one a long time ago. He'd be way less stressed-out."

"You're so funny!" she said sarcastically, then pushed him over and pinned him to the ground while he laughed.

After letting him back up, she said, "So what now? If I heard the rumors right, the last Khaalzin just disappeared. Are you going to see your grandparents? I hope I'm not being too pushy, but I'd love to meet them."

"I don't know. I haven't really thought about it. Maybe." He reflected quietly for a time, then confessed, "I still feel uneasy about all this. Something tells me it's not over yet. He's still out there."

Alanna scooted back against the wall. "He's alone now, and his army deserted him. Maybe he'll just disappear and leave your family alone."

"I hope you're right. But one thing's for sure—I'm not running anymore."

They sat silently for a time, thinking about all they had been through together. Alanna felt around the ground beside her until her hand fell upon the journal that she had laid there. She handed it to Cameron. "Will you read Baron's Prophecy to me?"

He pulled the loose parchment out and unfolded it, then read it aloud.

"Hope may yet come where none is known
The winds of despair may bear a seed and carry forth
Over raging waters fate unknown
Through lives of men dark seasons shall pass
New hope be found in impure blood
An heir of Genwyhn to return at last
Three are foreseen to return again
To span the hopeless divide
The path of a second is veiled in fog

Pure of heart though world awash in treachery
Allegiance uncertain a choice to be made
And worth unseen by eyes of men
But clearly discerned through those more keen
A gem in the rough shall complete the three
Born anew under astral sign
And in darkness leads them in unity
Uncertainty veils our destiny
Until their souls converge."

"Every part of it has come true, Cameron. It was seven generations ago, but every part of it's true. It can't just be coincidence."

"I don't know, Alanna. But it's made me think twice about destiny. I used to think we were completely in control of our own lives, but now I'm not so sure."

Later that night, Alanna immersed herself in the lonely darkness again, meditating deep into the night. The tranquility was broken, however, by shuffling movement in the distance. She reached her mind out in the same direction, but whatever made the sound was beyond her reach. The shuffling was soon followed by a brief, muffled voice, then silence, and finally something heavy being dropped to the ground. Trepidation turned to fear, and she pushed herself up to find the door. But before the apparitions dissolved, a new one appeared, though shapeless, and moved directly toward her. With her hand on the door handle, she started to scream but was silenced with the impact, and pain exploded through her head before unconsciousness took her.

Aiya was on the roof when the brief scream woke her. She clawed her way down the charred remnants of the partially burned lumber shed, then scurried into the darkness to follow the unknown sounds. After sniffing the air, she watched a dark horse gallop away with a rider and a limp human form draped over the saddle. She knew Alanna's scent, but the familiar presence of her strong mind was no longer there.

DESTINY'S SECOND ACT

Garrett woke to Aiya's frantic clawing at the outer door, then felt the familiar tug of her mind. Her vision of the fleeing horseman pushed in and stole away the remnants of his slumber. After waking Cameron, Garrett darted outside and sent Aiya to trail them. Her message had been clear. And when the two young men emerged from the building, they were primed for a fight.

"We need horses," Garrett said.

"No. I don't think so. He's not taking her far. It's not her that he wants, it's me. He's using her as bait."

"Fine, let's go before I lose Aiya. It's this way."

Garrett led the way south, away from the city and the militia. They ran nearly two miles before catching up with Aiya, who was lying in deep grass not far from the riverbank. The militia had abandoned the area days before, so they were quite alone.

Cameron scanned the darkness but saw only the outlines of several large willow trees along the river's edge. The quarter moon shone overhead, casting deep shadows beneath them. Then he made out the horse's shadowy form near the largest of the trees before them.

"Aiya's showing me that big willow over there," Garrett said.

"Yeah, I see the horse there too. Maybe you two should take the flank. And Garrett . . . be careful. I'm guessing he's more powerful than the others, and desperate."

Garrett and Aiya crept around, away from the river. Aiya moved furtively, but Garrett felt conspicuous under the moon's reflected light. He stayed low and moved slowly while keeping to the shadows—a thief in his domain.

Cameron knelt in the grass waiting for Garrett to get in position and peered out over the expansive river. The moonlight reflected from the ripples created by its unremitting currents, painting a delicate coruscating backdrop to the sagging willow branches before him. The dancing reflections conjured memories of the conversation he had with Alanna concerning destiny. In contrast to that day, his path forward now seemed so clear. His place in the world *was* determined, though rooted by no action of his own, and he was finally ready to embrace it, to whatever end. Destiny wasn't just a series of choices, but rather a river of opportunities with a beginning and an end. By his new reckoning, it did have an unalterable end, but navigating the snags and turns was what truly defined one's life. The part that he was meant to play in destiny's grand scheme *did* matter. But whether this moment was the end, or just a snag, was beyond his control. The river's course, after all, was already laid out by forces beyond him, and he had no alternative but to navigate it the best he could. He looked back out to the currents flowing into the distant landscape as the remnants of his fears and indecision drifted away with the waters, and he resolved to complete the journey. He stood and stepped forward into the moonlight.

A light emerged near the tree's trunk, first illuminating the leader of the Khaalzin, then Alanna's limp form propped against the tree. The Khaalzin's face was now fully illuminated in the light kindled between his hands, and he spoke with an arrogant flair. "Hope may yet come where none is known. I think that's how it goes, if my memory doesn't betray me. So the great heir comes forth out of a prophecy to bring *hope*—an empty sentiment if ever there was one. Such a noble calling, though. But still a useless notion, devoid of substance or power, like the ancestors of your failed family. So here you hide, mingled with the flock of sheep, unable to provide what they really need—a *shepherd*. Why don't you come forward, little lamb? It's time to meet *your* shepherd."

Cameron continued to walk toward the cocky Khaalzin and played along with his verbal contrivance. "So, you call yourself a shepherd? I thought a shepherd looked after his flock to keep them safe. Yet you'd slaughter them all without a second thought. Unfortunately for you, a shepherd bearing wolf's teeth won't keep his flock for long. They know what hides behind the mask."

"You're an insolent little lamb, aren't you? Your Arnorian blood runs thin, boy. You're no match for me, and it's time you learned your place!" He raised his hands with the shimmering light, and it grew into a blinding orb. He released it toward Cameron in a violent assault. The shield bore the scorching insult, but the force was unexpected and knocked Cameron back.

During the exchange, Cameron's voice had stirred something in Alanna's unconscious mind. She fought to regain her senses and finally woke. Her body was leaning back against the trunk of a massive tree, and her gloved hands rested over the splaying roots where they entered the ground. With its deep, living connections into the soil, the energies emanating from it were almost overpowering in her mind's exploration of the surroundings. Its fluorescence obscured the Khaalzin, who stood very near, but she sensed his powerful mind nonetheless.

Cameron straightened and regained his breath. He raised the shield again, his gloved hand now tolerating the heat and energy flow. The energy from the attack pulsed within him, and his mind's focus sharpened. "Who are you to lecture me? Your cult brings nothing to the world but pain and suffering and death. Your greed is a blight." He fought to tame his temper while he waited patiently for an opportunity.

Alanna gradually pieced together her surroundings. She pulled her hands away from the tree, and the quivering apparitions remained. The Khaalzin was standing right next to her.

The Khaalzin was irate—this *boy*, this inexperienced boy, born to a common man, stood resolute against him. And as his anger seethed, he marshaled his strength to summon another attack against Cameron. Alanna felt the energies disrupted around her, and his apparition grew and brightened with ferocious violence. The energy bolt that unleashed toward Cameron was comparable to the attack he had suffered from the wyvern, and he was suddenly lying on the ground, reeling in a disoriented stupor. But the shield had saved him.

Garrett stood at a safe distance with Aiya and watched the powerful exchange. He felt helpless against the Khaalzin. But the powerful attack had drained the villain's reserves, and it became apparent as he stooped briefly with his hands upon his knees. Garrett nocked an arrow and carefully aimed while the Khaalzin staggered. Cameron struggled on his hands and knees, trying to shake off the assault.

Garrett was forced to lower the bow when Alanna unexpectedly lunged at the recovering enemy. He brushed off her initial grasp and knocked her to the ground. She grappled for his leg and clamped her hands around his ankle, struggling for a pathway to enter his mind. But his mind repelled her assault, and he kicked her violently in the stomach, launching her insubstantial body back against the tree. The kick knocked the wind from her lungs, and she struggled to breathe under the suffocating clutch.

Cameron had forced himself to his feet while Alanna struggled with the Khaalzin, but he was still stunned and vulnerable. Garrett aimed again and released the arrow, but the Khaalzin sensed the fear and hate in Garrett's mind and reacted too quickly. He shattered the arrow in its approach with a swift defense, then countered with another attack while

Garrett dove to safety. The force exploded into the ground dangerously close to Garrett's head. The concussion stunned him and blasted sand into his eyes. He rolled away and struggled to overcome the disorientation. But the distraction had been enough.

Cameron recovered his bearings and fought to retain the surge of energy that had entered his body with the last attack. The shield had protected him, barely, but he knew well he couldn't stand long against the powerful attacks. The shield lay on the ground beside him, and he held his bow with an arrow trained on the Khaalzin. With a self-assured resolve, he released the string, and the arrow blazed with a fiery trail toward the Khaalzin's chest.

The powerful villain's stamina was severely tested, but he managed a defense against the oncoming projectile that nearly vaporized the arrow's shaft. The metal arrowhead continued forward and scored the left side of his chest, challenging his sense of invincibility.

Cameron could no longer restrain the bursting flood, nor did he try. As he had anticipated, the arrow left a shimmering path in the air toward the Khaalzin, and he focused along it, willfully unleashing the surge. The dragon-shine strip flashed and focused an energy bolt forward, splitting the night air in a thunderous crack.

The Khaalzin's skin tingled like a barrage of penetrating needles, and he lunged to the side. The stream followed the shimmering path to its termination where the Khaalzin had stood, then forked outward into the undisturbed air behind him. It had missed, but the concussion briefly stunned the Khaalzin and knocked him onto the ground.

Cameron pulled another arrow from the quiver and put it to the bowstring, and the Khaalzin, for the first time in his adult life, was afraid. He stumbled to his feet and ran to Alanna, grabbed the back of her shirt and lifted her like a sack of potatoes. He pulled her in front of him as a shield, then drew his knife and raised it to her neck.

Recognizing the standoff, Cameron held his aim, and in a psychological gamble, continued to antagonize his enemy. His mind had never before felt so focused and sharp, and he spoke now with a purposeful calmness. "Your mind retains nothing resembling human compassion, just corruption and hate. Your convictions grow out of paranoia. Before your meddling, I knew nothing of Arnoria, or prophecies, or the House of Genwyhn. And in your ignorance, you've shaped the path to your own destruction, the path that bore the Prophecy to fulfillment, like a rat carrying poison back to its nest."

Alanna felt the panic building within the Khaalzin, and she struggled in his powerful grip. Then, in a desperate move, he reached around and pulled her forehead back to better expose her neck. She seized the opportunity and thrust her hands up to clamp his hand firmly against the headband. The knife sliced through the tender skin on her arm, and she shrieked at the burning pain. But she held fast and used the now intimate connection to burrow into his thoughts. The full force of her powerful mind was more than his defenses could repel.

Alanna uprooted the tormenting visions that had for so long afflicted her and forced them into his mind in a torrent. The onslaught of anguish and despair that accompanied them inflicted unbearable agony within his mind, and his pitiful groan filled the night. He was immobilized in his agony for several moments, but finally wrenched his hand free from her grip and broke the connection. Aiya appeared from the darkness, and her jaws clamped down on his arm, tearing into sinew. The knife dropped from his hand, and Aiya released her grip. The Khaalzin stumbled back into the darkness and cast a final attack, a blazing fireball that struck the tree and left a blinding shower of sparks to temporarily stun them all.

Receding hoofbeats announced the Khaalzin's escape to the south while Cameron and Garrett rushed over to Alanna. They bound the stinging wound on her arm. She was still doubled over from being kicked and had a large lump on the back of her head but appeared otherwise intact.

"We can't let him get away," Garrett said.

Cameron agreed. "But we'll have to go back for horses. I'm sure Caelder can help us track him."

Alanna, still breathless, said, "No, let him go. I sensed his intent. He's going to Kantal, the port city at the end of this river. I think he's leaving Gartannia."

EPILOGUE

Several days later, Caelder returned to Candora from a scouting trip to Kantal. He had returned in time for the memorial service to be held the following morning to honor men slain in the battles. Erral was finally on his feet and gaining strength but was still confined to the infirmary. So Caelder and the young friends paid a visit to pass along Caelder's news.

"Well?" said Erral, even before they sat down.

"Just as Alanna thought, he boarded a ship in Kantal," Caelder replied. "The dock hands said it was a large schooner loaded with supplies and spare mast sections and sails. It was prepped for a *long* voyage."

"The odds of making that crossing aren't in his favor. Either way, he's not Gartannia's problem any longer."

"So, how are you healing?" Alanna asked.

"Just fine. They're letting me out of here tomorrow, in time for the memorial. How about those eyes of yours?"

"They're the same. But I'm getting around better on my own." She actually sounded enthusiastic. Her bubbly nature was resurfacing.

"So, where will you go from here, Cameron?" Caelder asked.

"I'm taking Alanna and Garrett to meet my grandparents. We're leaving tomorrow morning with Rylak and Jaeblon after the memorial service."

Caelder smiled and nodded.

"After that, we'll just have to see where the river carries us."

Alanna smiled.

That night, Cameron tossed and turned, unable to sleep. He submitted to the insomnia and crept outside for some air. Alanna was sitting in her usual place, on the ground and leaning back against the building. Her movement startled him as he stepped through the doorway. She sniffled and subconsciously wiped her shirt sleeves over her tear-covered cheeks. His heart bled for her lonely misery, and he plopped down beside her.

"Since when do you have trouble sleeping?" she asked.

"I'm just anxious about going home, I guess."

She dabbed her eyes.

"I really thought you'd start sleeping better since the Khaalzin are gone," he said.

"Me too . . . at least I hoped I would."

They sat quietly for a time listening to the insects chirping and buzzing in the night.

"So, will you tell me what's got you crying?"

"No," she replied playfully.

"I'll fill your bed with crickets if you don't."

"Go ahead. I never use it anyway."

"Seriously, Alanna, what's going on?"

She paused briefly, then said, "I feel like I'm abandoning them."

"What do you mean?"

"It's not just the same old visions anymore. There's new ones. They used to feel like memories, the old ones I mean, but the new ones are different. It's like someone knows I'm there, when I meditate, and they're reaching out to me." She wiped her eyes again.

"Reaching out from where?"

"I don't know."

"There must be something in the visions, a clue to tell you where they are. And what if you did know? What if you found out w—"

"I'd *find* them! And I'd help them."

Cameron put his arm around her shoulders and pulled her close. "*We'd* find them."

She laid her head on his shoulder, letting the tears spill onto his shirt, and soon drifted into sleep.

The next morning, Jaeblon and Rylak, who, with good fortune, avoided any major injuries in the battles, joined Cameron, Alanna, and Garrett before the memorial service. They waited outside the infirmary while Caelder collected Erral. The men finally emerged and walked toward the group.

"Here they come," Garrett said to Alanna.

She reached out and found Garrett's hand, interlocked her fingers with his and gently squeezed, her hint that she wanted to see Erral coming. He concentrated and shared his vision with her. Alanna smiled broadly at the sight of Erral recovered well enough to be up and walking. But as they came closer, her smile vanished. She took in a gasping breath and held it before Garrett noticed and released his concentration.

"What's wrong?" he whispered.

"Those armbands . . ."

The two men wore dark green armbands below their left shoulders. They were frayed and worn and bore identical emblems, an emerging seedling in the foreground of the setting sun. The emblems were yellowed from age. The men would later explain that they had carried them since leaving Arnoria and that the armbands were traditionally worn there by people in mourning. They had become a symbol of hope in Arnoria for those who still struggled against the Khaalzin, and a remembrance for those who had sacrificed.

". . . I've seen them before."

Now available:

Baron's Prophecy

Book Two

The River's End

A river's currents sweep ever forward over a landscape of opportunity, through gentle meanders and turbulent falls, but always toward an inevitable end.

Turn the page for a sneak peek at *The River's End*, the gripping sequel to *The River's Course*.

When destiny lies an ocean away . . .

PROLOGUE

The prophetic words had been uttered seven generations ago by Baron, a trusted advisor to the Arnorian stewards. And to the present day, the descendants of those who had lived at the time still clung with fading hope for their salvation to come. For the boots of their oppressors still trod ruthlessly upon the Arnorian people's resolve, trampling freedom's emergence and choking what breath of hope remained. The land was poisoned by humanity's lust for power, rendering it infertile to prosperity.

And yet, inviolate, a seedling grew, spared from tyranny's tread to one day bear the fruit that might feed the unabated hunger of the downtrodden. For even under gloomy light in the most obscure of places, a dormant seed may germinate and grow from forgotten, fallow soil. For that is nature's indomitable way. Her proclivity for balance, her patience, her hatred of that which is dark and empty, and her love and reclamation of that which is light and pure—these are the forces that guide all things, invisible as they may be until a light beyond the visible realm reveals them.

SEED OF HOPE

The wagon was brimming with baskets of vegetables and sacks of early wheat. Flynn secured a knife to his belt, though he prayed nothing arose where he would need to use it. Doing so would land him in the labor camp, or worse. The other men were similarly armed and stood nervously in twilight's deepening darkness. Anxious to depart, they gathered outside Flynn's rural farm, the same starting point as before.

The donated goods were cautiously smuggled to places of need, often small villages punished by confiscation of food, grain stores, or livestock for minor rebellious behaviors, late tax payment, or transgressions by individual community members. The unfair administration of justice by a corrupt government left entire communities in extreme poverty and facing starvation.

Such was the situation throughout Arnoria. Flynn happened to live in a rural area within the province of Haeth, where oppression of the people was generally less severe than in population centers, though nonconforming individuals were still routinely taken to labor camps as punishment.

The destination this particular night was a small village fifteen miles away, and the group needed to deliver the goods and return home before light of day. The marshals rarely patrolled at night, offering the only reasonable chance to succeed. It was a dangerous business, and the punishment expectedly harsh if caught.

The girl, who had pleaded with Flynn not to go, watched somberly through the window of their home. Flynn had reached his limit and grounded her inside the house. "I don't know what's gotten into her," he told Mary, his wife. "She's never been like this before when we've gone out."

"She's no stranger to the risks of what you're doing, Flynn. Don't forget, she was there. She watched her own parents murdered for standing against them, for doing the same kind of thing you're doing now."

"I'm aware of that, Mary. I can't change what's happened. You know I've tried to involve her in what we're doing so she'll understand better, but all she wants to do is sleep."

"She's not sleeping, Flynn. I've told you that. She's meditating, and if that's what it takes to deal with losing her parents, then so be it."

"Call it what you want, but I won't stand idly by while our communities starve."

"I know, but I'm just asking you to have some empathy. You know she's not like the other girls her age."

Flynn sighed. "I'll talk to her when I get back." He glanced over to the house, but the girl was no longer in the window.

"Be careful, Flynn. This is a long trip, and there are a lot of eyes along the road."

He walked back toward the other men and was suddenly blindsided in the darkness by the small, dark-haired girl. She had slipped out the back door. She grabbed his belt and his shirt and pulled him backward, crying and pleading, "You can't do this! Why won't you believe me? Something's going to happen this time!"

Flynn spun and was about to push her away when Mary's words echoed. He held his temper in check and grabbed her by the wrists, gently restraining her until she stopped fighting.

"They're coming, Flynn. You don't need to do this anymore."

Flynn gathered himself, seeing that his usual firm approach wasn't going to work any longer. He knelt in front of the sixteen-year-old girl, for he towered over her when he stood, and gently gripped her hands. "Terra, for three years you've been clinging to this. Nobody's coming. We have no choice. We have to take care of ourselves and each other."

"But they *are* coming."

"Our people have been clinging to that hope for generations. Where has it gotten us? People sit around waiting for some savior to come and rid the world of evils and do nothing themselves to that end. The Prophecy that you've embraced so strongly has done nothing but instill apathy in them. We need to change that or there's no hope for your children or theirs."

"But you don't understand. I'm not saying you should stop helping, just not *this* time."

Flynn was growing frustrated. "Terra, this is nonsense. Dreams can't foretell the future. When are you going to outgrow this? Look, even if an army came today and defeated all the Khaalzin, those villagers would still starve. They need relief now."

Terra glowered at him in the darkness and pulled her hands away. Flynn rose and turned to walk toward the other men, saying to her, "Go back in the house with Mary. I'll see you in the morning."

The men gathered in front of the wagon to go over the plan once more, then were on their way. One scout rode ahead and one behind while Flynn and a local villager named Stanton drove the horses from the bench in the wagon. Mary watched through the window, worry clouding her mind, but she was fully aware of the risks and supported the decision to take aid to the struggling community. She would hope for the same should their situations be reversed.

As the men had hoped, no marshal or peacekeeper hindered their travel. The cadre of smugglers neared the distant village midway through the night, and their confidence grew accordingly. The wagon rattled over a wooden bridge crossing a deep stream, and Flynn's wagon-mate said, "I recognize this bridge. We're less than a mile from the village."

"Good," Flynn replied. "This took longer than expected. We'll be lucky to get home before dawn."

The canvas covering the goods in the back of the wagon rustled, then flipped up. Flynn was startled and looked back to see a tangle of black hair pop up from under it. "Are we there yet?" Terra asked, defiance coloring her soft voice.

"Terra!" he said in a harsh whisper. "What are you doing?"

Stanton halted the wagon, and Flynn jumped down from the seat. Terra flung herself out and ran to the opposite side, playing cat and mouse with Flynn. He ran around the wagon after her, but she disappeared into the darkness away from the road. He started after her, then stopped and looked back to Stanton. "She's a damn fool! We don't have time for this."

"Maybe so, but you gotta go get her," Stanton said. "It's not far. Just meet us in the village or wait here for us to pick you up on the way back."

"Fine," Flynn agreed, and he ran into the darkness after her.

Terra hadn't run far, but when she heard Flynn following, she stayed just far enough ahead that he wouldn't catch her. She eventually doubled back toward the road and stopped. Flynn followed the sound of her footsteps and caught up. She was breathing heavily and sat at the road's center. Her expression, barely visible in the moonlight, reflected both defiance and fright. Flynn seethed with anger and wanted to strangle her until he recognized her genuine fear. She was shaking, but her defiance and resolve remained.

Flynn stood, hands on hips, catching his breath while he consciously tucked his anger away. He sat next to her and was silent for a long while before saying, "Help me to understand this, Terra. Why would you put yourself in danger like this? You're just not prepared to protect yourself if anything unexpected happens."

"I should ask you the same question."

"We've done this before. There's nothing different about this trip—"

"But that's what I'm trying to tell you, this time *is* different. Why don't you believe me? I'm sixteen, so I can't possibly know anything! Am I getting warm?"

Flynn stood up and said in exasperation, "Terra, you can't expect people to believe everything just based on blind faith, or dreams and feelings."

"Fine," she said, "if it's proof you want . . ."

She stood and started running along the road toward the village. Flynn jogged after her, but once she realized he wasn't trying to catch her, she slowed to a walk. Before long, they approached the village, and Flynn was staggered by the commotion that arose ahead—shouting and hoofbeats, then silence. Flynn grabbed Terra's arm and pulled her forward along the road's edge, avoiding the moonlight by staying within the shadows of bordering trees. The wagon was at the edge of the village, and men were milling around. A light emerged out of the darkness and brightened before being flung into the wagon. It erupted in flames along with the food supplies. The horses were being led away through the flickering light, but the fire also illuminated Flynn's comrades, the forward scout and Stanton, hands tied, following them.

The rear scout arrived behind Flynn and Terra while the fire raged in the distance. He looked with surprise to see Terra, then asked, "Was it an ambush?"

"I don't know. We were behind them," Flynn said.

"They knew you were coming," Terra whispered matter-of-factly.

Flynn looked at her, his face gently contorted in growing disbelief over her premonition. He said, "Either way, we can't just leave them."

"Didn't you see the fire?" Terra said. "It grew out of his hands. He's one of the Khaalzin."

"If that's true, Flynn, it'd be suicide to try to get them out. They knew the risks just like we did. We should be thankful we weren't *all* caught."

Flynn looked at Terra and she back at him. She said softly, "This wasn't to be your end." He looked at her curiously, still trying to understand.

"We need to go before they start searching for others," the scout said. He was right. Flynn hoisted Terra into the saddle, and they turned back on the road. Terra rode while the men walked briskly along in the darkness, eventually reaching Flynn's home well after sunrise.

Mary was distressed to hear the news, but she gathered herself and joined Flynn and Terra on the walk to Detmond, their local village, to pass along the news. Once they arrived, word spread quickly as neighbor gathered neighbor to meet in the village center. Once the majority had arrived, Flynn spoke to them.

"As most of you know, we went to Crandon last night with supplies. The Khaalzin were waiting for us. Whether by chance or some treachery, I don't know, but they have Trey and Stanton. I don't need to tell you, there will be consequences for our village. This was my doing, and I'll take responsibility when they come."

"Flynn!" Mary said.

"It has to be, Mary. They'll punish the entire village otherwise. I just ask that you all help look after Mary and Terra. I knew the risk, and I don't regret what we've done for our fellow Arnorians. Hide what supplies you have. They'll no doubt send their tax collectors soon enough."

The villagers were speechless at first, then spoke softly amongst themselves. Then one voice rose above the others, "I don't accept your offer. Most of us contributed something to the supplies you took. This wasn't your decision alone, and I for one won't let you take responsibility alone. We should stand as a community."

Another spoke, "They'll be far harsher in punishing you alone, and Trey and Stanton. We might never see them again, or you, if you do this."

"Hear! Hear!" yelled the crowd.

Terra grabbed Flynn's arm and looked up to him. "They're right, you know. You've said it a hundred times yourself—together we will prevail, alone we're sure to fail."

Flynn looked down at her imploring eyes, and his hard resolve began to soften.

"It's settled then," the first man said before Flynn could object. "We stand together."

Several villagers descended on Flynn and Mary to hear the details of the night's misadventure while a young man just two years older than Terra came over to her. "Are you alright, Terra?" he asked.

"I'm fine, Jonah. I'm just worried for Trey and Stanton."

"You look really tired."

"Yeah, a little. Would you give us a ride back to the farm in your wagon?"

"Do you think it's safe? I mean, they might be looking for Flynn or something."

"It's no less safe than being here," Terra replied, a bit irritated.

"Yeah, I guess so. Come on, we'll go hook up the wagon." He grabbed her hand and they walked away, stopping only to let Mary know they would be back soon. It was no secret in the village that Jonah was attracted to the beautiful young girl, and they seemed happy together.

Flynn stayed in the village but sent Mary and Terra back to the farm with Jonah. He knew the governor's marshals, if not the Khaalzin themselves, would arrive in the village soon enough. Trey and Stanton would have nothing to gain by trying to conceal where they lived. The Khaalzin would find out sooner or later. Flynn planned to stand with the rest of his community while the punishment was levied.

The village was prepared for just such a situation, as many other villages were also. Unannounced tax collection was not uncommon, so hidden supply stores were the norm. Spaces under floorboards, hollowed trees, even wooden crates buried underground made convenient stashes. The severity of disobedience determined how thoroughly the marshals searched for hiding spaces. In this instance, the village was fortunate to be let off relatively easy. The marshals arrived without the Khaalzin and questioned the villagers. To the last family, they admitted their complicity and accepted the punishment. Throwing their fellow villagers under the wagon, so to speak, would only lead to distrust. Outside of joining the corrupt government, community was the only thing they had to tide them over through hard times.

The senior marshal said to them, "Since you have so much food to spare, we'll be pleased to distribute more to the needy. The governor decides what resources go where. I'm sure you'll not forget that again."

The marshals confiscated a substantial portion of what food stores they found from each family and left the village. The stores would never be distributed to the needy, of course, but would go to the overflowing pantries of the ruling elite.

Two weeks later, Trey and Stanton walked into town, having finally been released from the labor camp. To emphasize the message already conveyed to the village, they had been severely beaten and starved, but their resolve against the tyranny was unbroken. The other villagers stood around them sympathetically but also with admiration for their courage.

Flynn, hearing about their return, went to the village wearing a stern face and greeted the men. It took every measure of strength he had not to break down while speaking with them. But after he returned to the farm, the guilt arising from their suffering overwhelmed him. Alone in the small stable behind the house, he wept freely. His spirit was broken, and the shame of letting the tyrants defeat him only compounded his misery.

Terra sat behind the stable, a place she often went for quietude, listening without emotion to his sobs, her mind simultaneously in a faraway place. His misery would pass. His defeat would be forgotten. For she knew his path into the future.